CHRISTINE FEEHAN

DARK PRINCE

LEISURE BOOKS NEW YORK CITY

*This book is dedicated to my mother, Nancy King,
for encouraging me in my vivid imagination. To my
beloved husband, Richard, who is now and forever,
in this world and the next, my true soulmate. And to
my friend, Kathi Firzlaff, who loves my characters
in all my books and insisted I share.*

A LEISURE BOOK®

April 2005

Published by

Dorchester Publishing Co., Inc.
200 Madison Avenue
New York, NY 10016

ISBN 0-8439-5528-7

The name "Leisure Books" and the stylized "L" with design are
trademarks of Dorchester Publishing Co., Inc.

Printed in the United States of America.

Visit us on the web at www.dorchesterpub.com.

DARK PRINCE

Chapter One

He could no longer fool himself. Slowly, with infinite weariness, Mikhail Dubrinsky closed the leather-bound first edition. This was the end. He could no longer bear it. The books he loved so much could not push away the stark, raw loneliness of his existence. The study was lined with books, floor to ceiling on three of the four walls of the room. He had read every one, committed a great many to memory over the centuries. They no longer provided solace for his mind. The books fed his intellect but broke his heart.

He would not seek sleep at dawn, at least not the healing sleep of renewal; he would seek eternal rest, and God have mercy on his soul. His kind was few, scattered, persecuted—gone. He had tried it all, skills, physical and mental, every new technology. Mikhail had filled his life with art and philosophy, with work and science. He knew every healing herb and every poison root. He knew the weapons of man and had learned to become a weapon himself. He remained alone.

His people were a dying race and he had failed them. As their leader, he had been committed to finding a way to save those he looked after. Too many of the males were turning, giving up their souls to become the undead in desperation. There were no women to continue their species, to bring them back from the darkness in which they dwelled. They had no hope to continue. The males were essentially predators, the darkness growing and spreading in them until they had no emotion, nothing but the dark in a gray, cold world. For each it was necessary to find his missing half, the life mate that would bring him forever into the light.

Grief overwhelmed him, consumed him. He lifted his head and roared out his pain like the wounded animal he was. He could no longer bear to be alone.

The trouble is not really in being alone, it's being lonely. One can be lonely in the midst of a crowd, don't you think?

Mikhail became still, only his soulless eyes moving warily, a dangerous predator scenting danger. He inhaled deeply, closing his mind instantly, while all senses flared out to locate the intruder. He was alone. He couldn't be wrong. He was the oldest, the most powerful, the most cunning. No one could penetrate his safeguards. No one could approach him without his knowledge. Curious, he replayed the words, listened to the voice. Female, young, intelligent. He allowed his mind to open slightly, testing paths, looking for mental footprints. *I have found it to be so,* he agreed. He realized he was holding his breath, needing the contact. A human. Who gave a damn? He was interested.

Sometimes I go into the mountains and stay by myself for days, weeks, and I'm not lonely, yet at a party, surrounded by a hundred people, I am more lonely than ever.

His gut clenched hotly. Her voice, filling his mind, was soft, musical, sexy in its innocence. Mikhail had not felt anything in centuries; his body had not wanted a woman in hundreds of years. Now, hearing this voice, the voice of a human woman, he was astonished at the gathering fire in his veins. *How is it you can talk to me?*

I'm sorry if I offended you. He could clearly hear that she meant it, felt her apology. *Your pain was so sharp, so terrible, I couldn't ignore it. I thought you might like to talk. Death is not an answer to unhappiness. I think you know that. In any case, I'll stop if you wish it.*

No! His protest was a command, an imperious order given by a being used to instant obedience.

He felt her laughter before the sound registered in his mind. Soft, carefree, inviting. *Are you used to obedience from everyone around you?*

Absolutely. He didn't know how to take her laughter. He was intrigued. Feelings. Emotions. They crowded in until he was nearly overwhelmed.

You're European, aren't you? Wealthy, and very, very arrogant.

He found himself smiling at her teasing. He never smiled. Not for six hundred years or more. *All of those things.* He waited for her laughter again, needing it with the same craving an addict felt for a drug.

When it came, it was low and amused, as caressing as the touch of fingers on his skin. *I'm an American. Oil and water, don't you think?*

He had a fix on her now, a direction. She would not get away from him. *American women can be trained with the right methods.* He drawled it deliberately, anticipating her reaction.

You really are arrogant. He loved the sound of her laughter, savored it, took it into his body. He felt her drowsiness, her yawn. So much the better. He sent her a light mental push, very delicate, wanting her to sleep so he could examine her.

Knock it off! Her reaction was quick withdrawal, hurt, suspicion. She retreated, slamming up a mind block so swiftly, he was astonished at how adept she was, how strong for one so young, strong for a human. And she was human. He was certain of it. He knew without looking that he had exactly five hours till sunrise. Not that he couldn't take the early or late sunlight. He tested her block, careful not to alarm her. A faint smile touched his well-cut mouth. She was strong, but not nearly strong enough.

His body, hard-corded muscle and superhuman strength, shimmered, dissolved, became a faint crystal mist seeping beneath the door, streaming into the night air. Droplets beaded, collected, connected, formed a large winged bird. It dipped, circled, and swept across the darkened sky, silent, lethal, beautiful.

Mikhail reveled in the power of flight, the wind rushing against his body, the night air speaking to him, whispering secrets, carrying the scent of game, of man. He followed the faint psychic trail unerringly. So simple. Yet his blood was surging hotly. A human, young, full of life and laughter, a human with a psychic connection to him. A human filled with compassion, intellect, and strength. Death and damnation could wait another day while he satisfied his curiosity.

The inn was small, at the edge of the forest where the mountain met the timberline. The interior was dark, with only a few lights glowing softly in one or two rooms and perhaps a hallway, while the humans took their rest. He settled on the balcony outside her second-story window and became still, a part of the night. Her bedchamber was one of the rooms with a light proclaiming that she was unable to sleep. His dark, burning eyes found her through the clear glass, found her and claimed her.

She was small-boned, curvy, with a tiny waist and a wealth of raven hair tumbling down her back to draw attention to her rounded bottom. His breath caught in his throat. She was exquisite, beautiful, her skin like satin, her eyes incredibly large, intensely blue, fringed with thick, long lashes. Not a detail escaped him. A white lace gown clung to her skin, hugged her high, full breasts, and bared the line of her throat, her creamy shoulders. Her feet were small, like her hands. So much strength in so small a package.

She brushed her hair, standing at the window, looking out with unseeing eyes. Her face held a faraway expression; there were lines of strain around her full, sensuous mouth. He could feel pain in her, and the need for sleep that refused to come. He found himself following every stroke of the brush. Her movements were innocent, erotic. Imprisoned within the bird's form, his body stirred. He reverently turned up his face to the heavens in thanks. The sheer joy of feeling after centuries of enduring no emotion was beyond measure.

Every action with the brush lifted her breasts invitingly, emphasized her narrow rib cage and small waist. The lace clung to her body, revealing the dark vee at the juncture of her legs. Talons dug deeply into the railing, left long scars in the soft wood. Still Mikhail watched. She was graceful, enticing. He found his hot gaze dwelling on her soft throat, the pulse beating steadily in her neck. *His.* Abruptly, he pulled away from the thought, shook his head.

Blue eyes. Blue. She had blue eyes. It was only then that he realized he was seeing in color. Vivid, brilliant colors. He went utterly still. It could not be. Males lost the ability to see anything but drab gray about the same time they lost their emotions. It could not be. Only a life mate could bring emotions and color back into a male's life. Carpathian women were the light to the male's darkness. His other half. Without her, the beast would slowly consume the man until he was complete darkness. There were no Carpathian women left to give birth to life mates. The few remaining women seemed able to produce only males. It was a seemingly hopeless situation. Human women could not be converted without becoming deranged. It had been tried. This human woman could not possibly be his life mate.

Mikhail watched as she snapped off her light, lay on the bed. He felt the stirring in his mind, the searching. *Are you awake?* Her question was tentative.

At first he refused to answer, not liking that he needed this so much. He couldn't afford to be out of control; he didn't dare. No one had power over him. Certainly not some slip of an American, a small woman with more strength than good sense.

I know you can hear me. I'm sorry I intruded. It was thoughtless of me; it won't happen again. But just for the record, don't try flexing your muscle on me again.

He was glad he was in the form of a creature, so he couldn't smile. She didn't know what muscle was. *I was not offended.* He sent the reassurance in gentle tones. He had to answer; it was nearly a compulsion. He needed the sound of her voice, the soft whisper brushing in his head like fingers on his skin.

She turned over, rearranged her pillow, rubbed at her temple as if she ached. One hand curled over the thin sheet. Mikhail wanted to touch that hand, feel her warm, silky skin under his. *Why did you try to control me?* It wasn't purely an intellectual question, as she wanted it to be. He sensed he had hurt her in some way, disappointed her. She moved restlessly, as if waiting for her lover.

The thought of her with another man enraged him. Feelings after hundreds of years. Sharp, clear, in focus. Real feelings. *It is my nature to control.* He was exhilarated, joyous, yet at the same time all too aware that he was more dangerous than he had ever been. Power always needed control. The less emotion, the easier the restraint.

Don't try to control me. There was something in her voice, something he sensed more than named, as if she knew he was a threat to her. And he knew he was.

How does one control one's nature, little one?

He saw her smile even as it filled his emptiness, as it registered in his heart and lungs, sent his blood soaring. *Why would you think I was little? I'm as big as a house.*

I am to believe this?

The laughter faded from her voice, her thoughts, lingered in his blood. *I'm tired, and again, I apologize. I enjoyed talking with you.*

But? He prompted gently.

Good-bye. Finality.

Mikhail took flight, soaring high above the forest. It wasn't good-bye. He wouldn't allow it. He couldn't allow it. His survival depended on her. Something, *someone* had aroused his interest, his will to live. She had reminded him that there was such a thing as laughter, that there was more to life than existence.

He soared above the forest, for the first time in centuries marveling at the sights. The canopy of waving branches, the way the rays of the moon spilled over the trees and bathed the streams in silver. It was all so beautiful. He had been given a priceless gift. A human woman had somehow managed to do this for him. And she *was* human. He would have known instantly had she been of his race. Could her voice alone do the same for the other males on the edge of despair?

In the protection of his home, he paced with a long-forgotten restless energy. He thought of her soft skin, how it would feel beneath his palm, under his body, how it would taste. The thought of her mass of silky hair brushing his heated body, the line of her vulnerable throat exposed to him, excited him. His body tightened unexpectedly. Not the mild physical attraction he had felt as a fledging, but a savage, demanding, relentless ache. Shocked at the erotic twist his thoughts began to pursue, Mikhail imposed rigid discipline. He could not afford real passion. He was shocked to find he was a possessive man, deadly in his rages and protective beyond measure. This kind of passion could not be shared with a human; it was far too dangerous.

This was a woman of freedom, strong for a mortal, and she would fight his nature at every turn. He was not human. His was a race of beings with animal instincts, imprinted before birth. Better to keep his distance and satisfy his curiosity on an intellectual level. He meticulously locked every door and window, safeguarded every point of entry with impassable spells before descending to his sleeping chamber. The room was protected from even greater threats. If he gave up his existence, it would be of his own choosing. He lay down on the bed. There was no need of healing soil deep within the earth; he could enjoy mortal comforts. He closed his eyes, slowed his breathing.

Mikhail's body refused to obey. His mind was filled with pictures of her, with erotic, taunting scenes. A vision of her lying on her bed, her body naked beneath white lace, her arms outstretched to greet her lover. He swore softly. Instead of his body taking hers, he pictured another man. A human. Rage shook him, raw and deadly.

Skin like satin, hair like silk. His hand moved. He built the picture with deadly precision and purpose in his mind. He paid every attention to detail, even to the silly polish on her toenails. His strong fingers circled her small ankle, felt the texture of her skin. His breath caught in his throat, his body tightening in anticipation. He slid his palm up her calf, massaging, tantalizing, moved up farther to her knee, her thigh.

Mikhail knew the precise moment she awakened, her body on fire. Her alarm slammed into him, her fear. Deliberately, to show her what she was dealing with, his palm found the inside of her thigh, stroked, caressed.

Stop! Her body ached for his, for his touch, for his possession. He could hear the frantic pounding of her heart, feel the strength of her mental struggle with him.

Has another man touched you like this? He whispered the words in her mind, dark, deadly sensuality.

Damn you, stop! Tears glittered like jewels in her lashes, in her mind. *All I wanted to do was help you. I said I was sorry.*

His hand moved higher because he had to, found heat and silk, tiny curls guarding treasure. His palm covered the triangle possessively, pushed into the moist heat. *You will answer me, little one. There is still time for me to come to you, to put my mark on you, for me to own you,* he warned silkily. *Answer me.*

Why are you doing this?

Do not defy me. His voice was husky now, raw with need. His fingers moved, probed, found her most sensitive spot. *I am being exceptionally gentle with you.*

You already know the answer is no, she whispered in defeat.

He closed his eyes, was able to calm the raging demons knifing pain through his body. *Sleep, little one; no one will harm you tonight.* He broke contact and found his body hard, heavy, bathed in perspiration. It was far too late to stop the beast in him from breaking free. He was burning with hunger, consumed with it, jackhammers beating at his skull, flames licking along his skin and nerve endings. The beast was unleashed, deadly, hungry. He had been more than gentle. She had inadvertently released the monster. He hoped she was as strong as he believed her to be.

Mikhail closed his eyes against his self-loathing. He had learned centuries ago that there was little point. And this time he didn't want to fight it. This was not simply a strong sexual attraction he felt; it was far more than that. It was something primal. Something deep within him calling to something deep within her. Perhaps she craved the wildness in him as he craved the laughter and compassion in her. Did it matter? There would be no escape for either of them.

He touched her mind gently before closing his eyes and allowing his breath to cease. She was weeping silently, her body still in need from the effects of his mind touch. There was hurt and confusion in her, and her head was aching. Without thought, without reason, he enveloped her in the strength of his arms, stroked her silky hair and sent warmth and comfort to surround her. *I am sorry I frightened you little one; it was wrong of me. Go to sleep now and be safe.* He murmured the words against her temple, his lips brushing her forehead in gentleness, brushing her mind with tenderness.

He could feel the curious fragmentation in her mind, as if she had been using her mental capabilities to follow some sick and twisted path. It was as if she had raw, gaping wounds in her mind that needed to heal. She was too worn out from their previous mental battle to fight him. He breathed with her, for her, slow and even, matching her heartbeats until she relaxed, drowsy and worn. He sent her to sleep, a whispered command, and her lashes drifted down. They fell asleep together, yet apart, she in her room, Mikhail in his sleeping chamber.

The pounding on her door penetrated the deep layers of sleep. Raven Whitney fought the thick fog forcing her eyes closed, making her body heavy. Alarm spread. It was as if she had been drugged. Her gaze found the small alarm clock on the bedside table. Seven o'clock in the evening. She had slept the day away. She sat up slowly, feeling as if she was wading through quicksand. The pounding on her door began again.

The sound echoed in her head, thundered at her temples. "What?" She forced her voice to be calm, although her heart was slamming against her chest. She was in trouble. She needed to pack quickly, run. She knew how futile it could be. Wasn't she the one who had tracked four serial killers following the mental path of their thoughts? And this man was a thousand times more powerful than she. The truth was, she was intrigued that another person had psychic abilities. She had never met anyone like herself before. She wanted to stay and learn from him, but he was far too dangerous in his casual use of power. She would have to put distance, perhaps an ocean, between them to be truly safe.

"Raven, are you all right?" The male voice was filled with concern.

Jacob. She had met Jacob and Shelly Evans, a brother and sister, last night in the dining room when they had first come in off the train. They were traveling with a tour group of about eight people. She had been tired and the conversation was a blur.

Raven had come to the Carpathian Mountains to be alone, to recover from her last ordeal of following the twisted mind of a depraved serial killer. She had not wanted the company of the tour group, yet Jacob and Shelly had sought her out. They had been wiped from her thoughts very efficiently. "I'm fine, Jacob, just a touch of the flu, I think," she assured him, feeling far from fine. She shoved a shaky hand through her hair. "I'm just so tired. I came here to rest."

"Aren't we having dinner?" He sounded plaintive, and that annoyed her. She didn't want any demands on her, and the last thing she needed was to be in a crowded dining room surrounded by a lot of people.

"I'm sorry. Another time, maybe." She didn't have time to be polite. How could she have made such a mistake as she had last night? She was always so cautious, avoiding all contact, never touching another human being, never getting close.

It was just that the stranger had been broadcasting so much pain, so much loneliness. She had known instinctively that he had telepathic powers, that his isolation far exceeded hers, that his pain was so great, he was considering ending his life. She knew what isolation was. How it felt to be different. She had been unable to keep her mouth shut; she had to help him if she could. Raven rubbed her temples in an attempt to relieve the pain pounding in her head. It always hurt after using her telepathic powers.

Pushing herself up, she moved slowly to the bathroom. He was controlling her without contact. The thought terrified her. No one should be that powerful. She turned the shower on full force, wanting the steady stream of water to clear the cobwebs.

She had come here for rest, to clear the stench of evil from her mind, to feel clean and whole again. Her psychic gift was draining to use, and physically she was worn. Raven lifted her chin. This new adversary would not frighten her. She had control and discipline. And this time she could walk away. No innocent lives were at stake.

She pulled on faded jeans and a crocheted sweater in defiance. She had sensed he was Old World and would frown on her American clothes. She packed quickly, haphazardly, tossing clothes and makeup as fast as she could into the battered suitcase.

She read the train schedule in dismay. There was no service for two more days. She could use charm to beg a ride from someone, but that meant being in the small confines of a car for an extended period of time. It probably was the lesser of two evils.

She heard male laughter, low, amused, mocking. *You would try to run from me, little one.*

Raven sank down onto the bed, her heart beginning to pound. His voice was black velvet, a weapon in itself. *Don't flatter yourself, hotshot. I'm a tourist; I tour.* She forced her mind to be calm even as she felt the brush of his fingers on her face. How did he do that? It was the lightest caress, but she felt it down to her toes.

And where were you thinking of touring? He was stretching lazily, his body refreshed from his sleep, his mind once more alive with feeling. He was enjoying sparring with her.

Away from you and your bizarre games. Maybe Hungary. I've always wanted to go to Budapest.

Little liar. You think to run back to your United States. Do you play chess?

She blinked at the strange question. *Chess?* she echoed.

Male amusement could be very annoying. *Chess.*

Yes. Do you?

Of course.

Play with me.

Now? She began to braid her heavy mass of hair. There was something captivating in his voice, mesmerizing. It tugged at her heartstrings, put terror in her mind.

I must feed first. And you are hungry. I can feel your

headache. Go down to dinner and we will meet at eleven tonight.

No way. I won't meet with you.

You are afraid. It was a clear taunt.

She laughed at him, the sound wrapping his body in flames. *I may do foolish things occasionally, but I am never a fool.*

Tell me your name. It was a command, and Raven felt compelled to obey it.

She forced her mind to go blank, to be a slate wiped clean. It hurt, sent darts of pain through her head, made her stomach clench. He was not going to take what she would have given freely.

Why do you fight me when you know I am the stronger? You hurt yourself, wear yourself out, and in the end I will win anyway. I feel the toll that this way of communicating takes on you. And I am capable of commanding your obedience on a much different level.

Why do you force what I would have given, had you simply asked?

She could feel his puzzlement. *I am sorry, little one. I am used to getting my way with the least amount of effort.*

Even at the expense of simple courtesy?

Sometimes it is more expedient.

She punched the pillow. *You need to work on your arrogance. Simply because you possess power does not mean you have to flaunt it.*

You forget, most humans cannot detect a mental push.

That isn't an excuse to take away free will. And you don't use a push anyway; you issue a command and demand compliance. That's worse, because it makes people sheep. Isn't that closer to the truth?

You reprimand me. There was an edge to his thoughts this time, as if all that male mockery was wearing thin.

Don't try to force me.

This time there was menace, a quiet danger lurking in his voice. *I would not try, little one. Be assured I can force your compliance.* His tone was silky and ruthless.

You're like a spoiled child wanting your own way. She

stood up, hugging the pillow to her protesting stomach. *I'm going downstairs to dinner. My head is beginning to pound. You can go soak your head in a bucket and cool off.* She wasn't lying; the effort to fight him on his level was making her sick. She edged cautiously toward the door, afraid he would stop her. She would feel safer if she was among people.

Your name, please, little one. It was asked with grave courtesy.

Raven found herself smiling in spite of everything. *Raven. Raven Whitney.*

So, Raven Whitney, eat, rest. I will return at eleven for our chess match.

The contact was broken abruptly. Raven let out her breath slowly, all too aware that she should be feeling relief, not feeling bereft. There was seduction in his hypnotic voice, his masculine laughter, in their very conversation. She ached with the same loneliness as he did. She didn't allow herself to think of the way her body had come alive at the touch of his fingers. Burned. Wanted. Needed. And he had only touched her with his mind. The seduction was far more than physical; it was some deep, elemental thing she could not precisely put her finger on. He touched her inside her soul. His need. His darkness. His terrible, haunting loneliness. She needed, too. Someone to understand what it was like being so alone, so afraid to touch another being, afraid to be too close. She liked his voice, the Old World elegance, the silly male arrogance. She wanted his knowledge, his abilities.

Her hand trembled as she opened the door, breathed the air in the hallway. Her body was her own again, moving lightly and fluidly, obeying her instructions. She ran down the stairs, entered the dining room.

Several tables were occupied, certainly more than the night before. Ordinarily, Raven avoided public places as much as possible, preferring not to have to worry about shielding herself from unwanted emotions. She took a deep breath and walked in.

Jacob looked up with a welcoming smile, stood, as if waiting for her to join the group at his table. Raven made herself smile back at him, unaware of the way she looked, innocent, sexy, completely unattainable. She crossed the room, greeted Shelly, and was introduced to Margaret and Harry Summers. Fellow Americans. She tried not to let her alarm show on her face. She knew her picture had been plastered all over the newspapers and even on television during the investigation of the last killer. She didn't want to be recognized, didn't want to relive the horrible nightmare of the man's twisted and depraved mind. There would be no discussion of such a hideous thing at dinner.

"Sit here, Raven." Jacob graciously pulled out a high-backed chair for her.

Carefully avoiding skin contact, Raven allowed herself to be seated. It was hell to be so close to so many people. As a child she had been overwhelmed by the bombardment of emotions around her. She had nearly gone insane until she learned to protect herself, to build a shield. It worked unless the pain or distress was too concentrated, or if she physically touched another human being. Or if she was in the presence of a very sick and evil mind.

Right now, with conversation flowing all around her and everyone seemingly having a good time, Raven was experiencing classic signs of overload. Shards of glass pierced her skull, her stomach roiled in protest. She couldn't possibly eat a thing.

Mikhail inhaled the night air, moved slowly through the small town, seeking what he needed. Not a woman. He couldn't bear to touch another woman's flesh. He was aroused, dangerous in his highly sexual state, and far too close to turning. He might lose control. So it had to be a man. He moved among the people easily, returned greetings from those who knew him. He was well respected, looked up to.

He slipped up behind a young man who was physically fit, strong. His scent spoke of health, veins bursting with life. After a brief, easy conversation, Mikhail spoke his command softly, laid a friendly arm across the other's shoulder. Deep within the shadows he bent his dark head and fed well. He was careful to keep his emotions firmly in control. He liked this young man, knew his family. There could be no mistakes.

As he lifted his head, the first wave of her distress hit him. *Raven*. He had unconsciously been seeking contact with her, touching her mind gently to assure himself that she was still with him. Alert now, he finished his task quickly, releasing the young man from his trance, implanting the continuing conversation, laughing amicably, accepting the handshake with ease, steadying the man when he was a bit dizzy.

Mikhail opened his mind, focused on the thread and followed it. It had been years—his skills were rusty—but he could still "see" when he wanted. Raven was seated at a table with two couples. Outwardly she looked beautiful, serene. But he knew better. He could feel her confusion, the unrelenting pain in her head, her desire to leap up and run from everyone. Her eyes, brilliant sapphires, were haunted, shadows in the paleness of her face. Strain. It amazed him how strong she was. There was no telepathic spillage, no way for anyone with telepathic ability other than he to tell she was in distress.

And then the man beside her leaned forward, looked into her eyes, raw longing on his face, desire in his eyes. "Come for a walk with me, Raven," he suggested, and his hand moved from the table to rest just above her knee.

At once the pain in Raven's head increased, crushing at her skull, stabbing at her behind her eyes. She jerked her leg out from under Jacob's hand. Demons leaped, raged, burst free. Never had Mikhail felt such terrible fury. It rushed over him, claimed him, became him. That someone could hurt her like that, so casually, without even knowing or caring. That someone might touch her while she was so vulnerable and unprotected. That a man would presume to put his hands on her. He hurtled through the sky, the cool air fanning his rage.

Raven felt the force of his anger. The air in the room thickened; outside, the wind rose, whirled fiendishly. Branches pelted the outside walls; the wind rattled ominously at the windows. Several waiters crossed themselves, looking with fright out into the black, suddenly starless night. The room was unexpectedly, strangely silent, as if everyone was collectively holding his and her breath.

Jacob gasped, both hands going to his throat, tearing at it as if at strong, strangling fingers. His face was first red, then mottled, his eyes bulging. Shelly screamed. A young waiter ran to assist the choking man. People were standing, craning their necks to see.

Raven forced calmness into her slender body. Emotions were running far too high for her to remain unscathed. *Release him.* Silence answered her. Even with the waiter behind him, desperately working at the Heimlich maneuver, Jacob fell to his knees, his lips blue, his eyes rolling back in his head. *Please, I'm asking you, please. Release him. For me.*

Jacob suddenly inhaled, a terrible gagging sound, labored and harsh. His sister and Margaret Summers were crouched at his side, tears in their eyes. Instinctively, Raven moved toward him.

Do not touch him! The command was stark, without any mental enhancement, more frightening than if he had forced her compliance.

Raven was besieged with emotion, from everyone in the room. Jacob's pain and terror. Shelly's fear, the innkeeper's horror, the other Americans' shocked reaction. They were swamping her, beating at her already fragile state. But it was *his* all-consuming rage that sent needles shooting through her head. Her stomach heaved, cramped, and Raven nearly doubled over and looked desperately for the ladies room. If anyone touched her, tried to come to her aid, she might go mad.

"Raven." The voice was warm, sensual, caressing. Calm in the eye of the storm. Black velvet. Beautiful. Soothing.

A curious hush fell in the dining room as Mikhail strode in. He had a hard arrogance, an air of complete command. He was tall, dark, well muscled, but it was his eyes, burning with energy, with darkness, with a thousand secrets, that drew immediate attention. Those eyes could mesmerize, hypnotize, just like the power in his voice. He moved with purpose, sending waiters scurrying out of the way.

"Mikhail, it is such a pleasure to have you join us," the innkeeper gasped in surprise.

He spared the woman a glance, his eyes sweeping over her buxom figure. "I have come for Raven. We have a date this evening." He said it softly, imperiously, and no one dared argue with him. "She has challenged me to a game of chess."

The innkeeper nodded her head as she broke into a smile. "Enjoy yourselves."

Raven swayed, pressing her hands into her stomach. Her sapphire eyes were enormous, taking up her face at his approach. He was on her before she could move, his hands reaching out for her.

Don't. She closed her eyes, terrified of his touch. She was already on overload; she would not be able to take the overpowering emotions radiating from him.

Mikhail didn't hesitate, gathering her into his arms, imprisoning her against his hard chest. His face was a granite mask as he whirled around and took her from the room. Behind them the buzzing started, the whispers.

Raven tensed, waiting for the battery on her senses, but he had closed his mind and all she knew was the enormous strength of his arms. He took her into the night, moving fluidly, easily, as if her weight was of no consequence.

"Breathe, little one; it will help." There was a trace of amusement in the warmth of his voice.

Raven did as he suggested, too worn out to struggle. She had come here to this wild, lonely place to heal, but instead, she was all the more fragmented. She opened her eyes cautiously, looking up at him through long lashes.

His hair was the color of dark coffee beans, a dark espresso, drawn back and tied at the nape of his neck. His face was that of an angel or a devil, strength and power, with a sensual mouth that hinted at cruelty; his hooded eyes were black obsidian, black ice, pure black magic.

She couldn't read him, couldn't feel his emotions or hear his thoughts. That had never happened to her before. "Put me down. I feel silly with you carrying me off like some pirate." His long strides were taking them into deep forest. Branches swayed, bushes rustled. Her heart was beating out of control. She tensed, pushed against his shoulders, struggled uselessly.

His eyes moved possessively over her face, but his pace didn't slow, and he didn't answer her. It was humiliating that he didn't appear to notice her struggles.

Raven allowed her head to fall back against his shoulder with a slight sigh. "Did you kidnap me or rescue me?"

Strong white teeth gleamed at her, a predator's smile, a man's amusement. "Perhaps a little of both."

"Where are you taking me?" She pressed a hand to her forehead, not wanting a battle, physical or mental.

"To my home. We have a date. I am Mikhail Dubrinsky."

Raven rubbed at her temple. "Tonight might not be so good for me. I'm feeling . . . " She broke off, catching a glimpse of a moving shadow pacing them. Her heart nearly stopped. She looked around, sighted a second, then a third. Her hand clutched his shoulder. "Put me down, Dubrinsky."

"Mikhail," he corrected, not even slowing down. A smile softened the edges of his mouth. "You see the wolves?" She felt the indifferent shrug of his broad shoulders. "Be calm, little one; they will not harm us. This is their home, as it is mine. We have an understanding and are at peace with one another."

Somehow she believed him. "Are you going to hurt me?" She asked the question softly, needing to know.

His dark eyes touched her face again, thoughtful, holding a thousand secrets, unmistakably possessive. "I am not a man who would hurt a woman in the way you are imagining. But I am certain our relationship will not always be a comfortable one. You like to defy me." He answered as honestly as he was able.

His eyes made her feel as if she belonged to him, as if he had a right to her. "You were wrong to hurt Jacob, you know. You could have killed him."

"Do not defend him, little one. I allowed him to live to please you, but it would be no trouble to finish the task." *Pleasurable. No man had the right to put his hand on Mikhail's woman and hurt her as that human had done. The inability of the male to see that he was causing Raven pain did not absolve his sin.*

"You don't mean that. Jacob is harmless. He was attracted to me," she tried to explain gently.

"You will not speak his name to me. He touched you, put his hand on you." He stopped abruptly, there in the heart of the deep forest, as wild and untamed as the pack of wolves surrounding them. He was not even breathing heavily, though he had covered miles carrying her in his arms. His black eyes were merciless as they stared down into hers. "He caused you much pain."

Her breath caught in her throat as he lowered his dark head to hers. His mouth hovered inches from hers, so that she could feel the warmth of his breath on her skin. "Do not disobey me in this, Raven. This man touched you, hurt you, and I see no reason for his existence."

Her eyes searched his hard, implacable features. "You're serious, aren't you?" She did not want to feel the warmth spreading through her at his words. Jacob had hurt her; the pain was so intense, it had stolen her breath and somehow, when no one else knew, Mikhail had known.

"Deadly serious." He began moving again with his long, ground-eating strides.

Raven was silent, trying to work out the puzzle. She knew evil, had chased it, soaked in it, the obscene, depraved mind of a serial killer. This man spoke casually of killing, yet she could not feel evil in him. She sensed that she was in danger, grave danger from Mikhail Dubrinsky. A man with unlimited power, arrogant in his strength, a man who believed he had a right to her.

"Mikhail?" Her slender frame was beginning to tremble. "I want to go back."

The dark eyes drifted over her face again, noting the shadows, the fear lingering in her blue gaze. Her heart was pounding, her slight body trembling in his arms. "Go back to what? Death? Isolation? You have nothing with those people and everything with me. Going back is not your answer. Sooner or later you will not be able to take their demands. They continually take pieces of your soul. You are much safer in my care."

She pushed at the wall of his chest, found her hands trapped against the heat of his skin. He merely tightened his hold, amusement spreading warmth to the coldness of his eyes. "You cannot fight me, little one."

"I want to go back, Mikhail." She worked to keep her voice under control. She wasn't sure she was telling the truth. He knew her. He knew what she felt, the price she paid for her gift. The pull between them was so strong, she could hardly think straight.

The house loomed up, dark, threatening, a rambling hulk of stone. Her fingers twisted in his shirt. Mikhail knew she was unaware of that nervous, telltale gesture. "You are safe with me, Raven. I would not allow anyone or anything to harm you."

She swallowed nervously as he pushed open the heavy iron gates and mounted the steps. "Just you."

He allowed his chin to brush the top of her silky hair, feeling the jolt in the core of his body. "Welcome to my home." He said the words softly, wrapping her up in them as if they were firelight or sunshine. Very slowly, reluctantly, he allowed her feet to touch the threshold.

Mikhail reached past her to open the door, then stepped back. "Do you enter my home of your own free will?" He asked it formally, his eyes burning on her face, over it, dwelling on her soft mouth before returning to her large blue eyes.

She was frightened, he could read it easily, a captive wild thing wanting to trust him yet unable to, run to the ground, cornered, but still willing to fight with her last breath. She needed him almost as much as he needed her. She touched the door frame with a fingertip. "If I say no, will you take me back to the inn?"

Why did she want to be with him when she knew he was so dangerous? He wasn't "pushing" her; she had too much talent of her own not to know. He looked so alone, so proud, yet his eyes burned over her with hungry need. He didn't answer her, didn't try to persuade her, simply stood in silence, waiting.

Raven sighed softly, knowing she was defeated. She had never known another human being she could just sit and talk with, even touch, without the bombardment of thoughts and emotions. That in itself was a type of seduction.

She started across the threshold. Mikhail caught her arm. "Your own free will; say it."

"My own free will." She stepped into his home, her lashes sweeping down. Raven missed the look of savage joy that lit his dark, chiseled features.

Chapter Two

The heavy door swung closed behind Raven with a thud of finality. She shivered, rubbed her arms nervously. Mikhail whirled a cape around her, enveloping her in warmth, in his woodsy, masculine scent. He strode across the marble floor to throw open the doors to the library. Within minutes he had a fire roaring. He indicated a chair near the flames. It was high-backed, deep cushioned, an antique, yet curiously not worn.

Raven studied the room with awe. It was large, with a beautiful hardwood floor, each parquet piece a part of a larger mosaic. On three sides there were floor-to-ceiling shelves, completely filled with books, most leather bound, many very old. The chairs were comfortable, the small table, in between the chairs, an antique in perfect condition. The chessboard was marble, the pieces uniquely carved.

"Drink this."

She nearly jumped out of her skin when he appeared beside her with a crystal glass. "I don't drink alcohol."

He smiled the smile that made her heart beat faster. His acute sense of smell had already processed that particular bit of information about her. "It is not alcohol; it is an herb mixture for your headache."

Alarm slammed into her. She was crazy for being here. It was like trying to relax with a wild tiger in the same room. He could do anything to her and no one would come to help. If he drugged her . . . Decisively, she shook her head. "No, thank you."

"Raven." His voice was low, caressing, hypnotic. "Obey me."

She found her fingers curling around the glass. She fought the order, and pain sliced through her head so that she cried out.

Mikhail was at her side, looming over her, his hand closing over hers around the fragile glass. "Why do you defy me over so trivial a thing?"

There were tears burning in her throat. "Why would you force me?"

His hand found her throat, circled it, lifted her chin. "Because you are in pain and I wish to ease it."

Her eyes widened in astonishment. Could it be so simple? She was in pain and he wanted to ease it? Was he really that protective, or did he enjoy imposing his will? "It's my choice. That's what free will is all about."

"I can see pain in your eyes, feel it in your body. Knowing I can help you, is it logical for me to allow you to continue to hurt yourself just so you can prove something?" There was genuine puzzlement in his voice. "Raven, if I was going to harm you, I would not need to drug you. Allow me to help you." His thumb was moving over her skin, feather-light, sensuous, tracing the pulse in her neck, the delicate line of her jaw, the fullness of her lower lip.

She closed her eyes and let him put the glass to her mouth, tilt the bittersweet contents down her throat. She felt as if she was placing her life in his hands. There was far too much possession in his touch.

"Relax, little one," he said softly. "Tell me about yourself. How is it that you can hear my thoughts?" His strong fingers found her temples, began a soothing rhythm.

"I've always been able to do it. When I was little, I just assumed everybody else could do the same thing. But it was terrible to know other people's innermost thoughts, their secrets. I heard and felt things every minute of the day." Raven never talked about her life, her childhood, to anyone, least of all a complete stranger. Yet Mikhail didn't feel like a stranger. He felt like a part of her. A piece missing from her soul. It seemed important to tell him. "My father thought I was a freak, a demon child, and even my mother was a little afraid of me. I learned never to touch people, not to be in crowds. It was better to be alone, in places of solitude. It was the only way I could stay sane."

Gleaming teeth bared above her head, a predator's menace. He wanted to be alone with her father for a few minutes, to show him what a demon really was. It interested him, yet alarmed him that her words could bring about such rage in him. To know she was alone so long ago, had endured pain and loneliness when he was in the world, angered him. Why hadn't he gone looking for her? Why hadn't her father loved and cherished her as he should have?

His hands were working magic, slipping to the nape of her neck, his fingers strong, hypnotic. "A few years ago a man was murdering families, small children. I was staying with a friend from high school and when I returned after work, I found them all dead. When I went into the house I could feel his evil, knew his thoughts. It made me sick, the terrible things running around in my head, but I was able to track him and finally led the police to him."

His hands moved down the length of her thick braid, found the tie and loosened the heavy mass of silk, tunneling his fingers to release the woven strands, still damp from her shower hours before. "How many times did you do this thing?" She was leaving things out. The details of horror and pain, the faces of those she helped as they watched her work, shocked, fascinated, yet repulsed by her ability. He saw those details, sharing her mind, reading her memories to learn her true nature.

"Four. I went after four killers. The last time I fell apart.

He was so sick, so evil. I felt as if I was unclean, as if I could never get him out of my head. I came here hoping to find peace. I decided I would never do anything like that again."

Mikhail, above her head, closed his eyes for a moment to calm his mind. That she could feel unclean. He could look into her heart and soul, see her every secret, know she was light and compassion, courage and gentleness. The things she had seen in her young life should never have been. He waited until his voice was calm and soothing. "And you get these headaches if you use telepathic communication?" At her solemn nod, he continued, "Yet when you heard me, unguarded, in pain, you reached out to me, knowing the price you would pay."

How could she explain? He was like a wounded animal, radiating so much pain that she had found tears streaming unchecked down her face. His loneliness was hers. His isolation, hers. And she had sensed his resolve to end his pain, his existence. She could not let that happen, no matter what the cost to herself.

Mikhail let out his breath slowly, astonished and shocked by her nature, so giving. She was hesitant to put into words why she had reached out to him, but he knew it was her nature to give. He also knew the call had been so strong because that something in him that reached for her had found whatever it needed. He inhaled her scent, taking her into his body, enjoying the sight and smell of her in his home, the feel of her silky hair in his hands, her soft skin under his fingertips. The flames from the fire put blue lights in her hair. Need slammed into him, hard and urgent and, as painful as the ache was, he reveled in the fact that he could feel it.

Mikhail seated himself across the small table from her, his eyes drifting lazily, possessively over her alluring curves. "Why do you dress in men's clothes?" he asked.

She laughed, soft and melodious, and her eyes lit with mischief. "Because I knew it would annoy you."

He threw back his head and laughed. Real, genuine, incredible laughter. There was happiness in him and the stirrings of affection. He couldn't remember what those feelings were like, but the emotions were sharp and clear and a sweet ache in his body.

"Is it necessary to annoy me?"

She arched an eyebrow at him, realizing that her headache was completely gone. "So easy," Raven teased.

He leaned closer. "Disrespectful woman. So dangerous, you mean."

"Mmm, maybe that, too." She slid her hand through her hair, pushed it away from her face. The action was an innocent habit, incredibly sexy, drawing his gaze to the perfection of her face, the fullness of her breasts, the smooth line of her throat.

"So just how good a chess player are you?" she challenged impudently.

An hour later Mikhail leaned back in his chair to watch her face as she studied the board. She was frowning in concentration, trying to puzzle out his unfamiliar strategy. She could sense that he was leading her into a trap, but she couldn't find it. Raven leaned her chin on the heel of her hand, relaxed, in no hurry. She was patient and thorough and twice had gotten him into trouble simply because he was too sure of himself.

Suddenly her eyes widened, a slow smile curving her soft mouth. "You are a cunning devil, aren't you, Mikhail? But I think your cleverness may have gotten you into a bit of trouble."

He watched her with hooded eyes. His teeth gleamed white in the firelight. "Did I happen to mention, Miss Whitney, that the last person impertinent enough to beat me at chess was thrown in the dungeon and tortured for thirty years?"

"I believe that would have made you about two at the time," she teased, her eyes glued to the chessboard.

He sucked in his breath sharply. He had been comfortable in her presence, felt totally accepted. She obviously believed he was mortal, with superior telepathic powers. Mikhail lazily reached across the board to make his move, saw the dawning comprehension in her eyes. "I believe what we have is checkmate," he said silkily.

Christine Feehan

"I should have known a man who walks in the forest surrounded by wolves would be devious." She smiled up at him. "Great game, Mikhail. I really enjoyed it." Raven sank back into the cushions of the chair. "Can you talk to animals?" she asked curiously.

He liked her in his home, liked the way the fire burned blue in her hair and the way the shadows clung so lovingly to her face. He had memorized every inch of it, knew that if he closed his eyes, the picture would still be there, the high, delicate cheekbones, her small nose and lush mouth. "Yes." He answered truthfully, not wanting lies between them.

"Would you have killed Jacob?"

Her lashes were beautiful and held his attention. "Be careful of what you ask, little one," he cautioned.

She curled her legs beneath under her, regarded him steadily. "You know, Mikhail, you are so used to using your power, you don't even stop to think if it's right or wrong."

"He had no right to touch you. He was causing you pain."

"But he didn't know he was. And you had no right to touch me, but you did anyway," she pointed out reasonably.

His eyes glittered coldly. "I have every right. You belong to me." He said it calmly, his voice soft, with a hint of warning. "More importantly, Raven, I did not cause you pain."

Raven's breath caught in her throat. Her tongue moistened her lips with a small, delicate gesture. "Mikhail"— her voice was hesitant, as she chose her words carefully—"I belong to myself. I'm a person, not something you can own. In any case, I live in the United States. I'm going back there soon and intend to be on the next train to Budapest."

His smile was that of a hunter. Predatory. For a moment the firelight gleamed red, so that his eyes glowed like a wolf's in the night. He said nothing, simply watched her unblinkingly.

Her hand fluttered defensively to her throat. "It's late; I should be going." She could hear the pounding of her own heart. What was it she wanted from him? She didn't know, only that this was the most perfect, frightening night of her life and she wanted to see him again. He was utterly motionless, menacing in his complete stillness. She waited breathlessly. Fear was suffocating her, sending tremors through her slender form. Fear he would let her go; fear he would force her to stay. She drew air into her lungs. "Mikhail, I don't know what you want." She didn't know what she wanted either.

He stood up then, power and grace combined. His shadow reached her before he did. His strength was enormous, but his hands were gentle as they pulled her to her feet. His hands slid up her arms, rested lightly on her shoulders, thumbs stroking the pulse in her neck. His touch sent warmth curling in her abdomen. She was so small beside him, so fragile and vulnerable. "Do not try to leave me, little one. We need one another." His dark head bent lower, his mouth brushing her eyelids, sending little darts of fire licking along her skin. "You make me remember what living is," he whispered in his mesmerizing voice. His mouth found the corner of hers, and a jolt of electricity sizzled through her body.

Raven reached up to touch the shadowed line of his jaw, to place a hand on the heavy muscles of his chest in an attempt to put space between them. "Listen to me, Mikhail." Her voice was husky. "We both know what loneliness is, isolation. It's beyond my imagination that I can be this close to you, physically touch you, and not be swamped with unwanted burdens. But we can't do this."

Amusement crept into the dark fire of his eyes, a hint of tenderness. His fingers curled around the nape of her neck. "Oh, I think we can." His black velvet voice was pure seduction, his smile frankly sensual.

Raven felt his power right down to her toes. Her body was boneless, liquid, aching. She was so close to him that she felt a part of him, surrounded by him, enveloped by him. "I'm not going to sleep with someone I don't know because I'm lonely."

He laughed softly, low and amused. "Is that what you think? That you would be sleeping with me because you are lonely?" His hand was at her throat again, stroking, caressing, heating her blood. "This is why you will make love with me. This!" His mouth fastened on hers.

White heat. Blue lightning. The ground shifted and rolled.

Mikhail dragged her slender form against his male length, his body aggressive, his mouth dominating, sweeping her into a world of pure feeling.

Raven could only cling to him, a safe anchor in a storm of turbulent emotions. A growl rumbled deep in his throat, animal, feral, like that of an aroused wolf. His mouth moved to the soft, vulnerable line of her throat, down to rest on the pulse beating so frantically beneath her satin skin.

Mikhail's arms tightened, pinning her to his body, possessive, certain, his hold unbreakable. Raven was on fire, needing, burning, hot silk in his arms, her body pliant, liquid heat. She was moving against him restlessly, her breasts aching, nipples pushing erotically against the thin yarn of her sweater.

His thumb brushed her nipple through the crocheted lace, sending waves of heat curling through her body, making her knees go weak so that only the hard strength of his arms held her up. His mouth moved again, his tongue like a flame licking over her pulse.

And then there was white-hot heat, searing pain, her body coiling with need, burning for him, craving him. Waves of desire beat at her. His mouth on her neck was producing a combination of pleasure and pain so intense that she didn't know where one started and the other left off. His thumb tipped her head back, exposing her throat, his mouth clamped to her skin, his throat working as if he were devouring her, feeding on her, drinking her in. It burned, yet fed her own craving.

Mikhail whispered something in his native tongue and lifted his head slightly, breaking the contact. Raven felt warm liquid run down her throat to her breast. Mikhail's tongue followed the path, sweeping across the creamy swell of her breast. Mikhail caught at her small waist, aware suddenly of the way his body raged at him for release. He had to claim her for his mate. His body demanded, burned.

Raven caught at his shirt to keep from falling. He swore softly, eloquently, a mixture of two languages, furious with himself as he cradled her in his arms protectively.

"I'm sorry, Mikhail." Raven was appalled, frightened at

her weakness. The room was spinning; it was difficult to focus. Her neck throbbed and burned.

He bent his dark head to kiss her gently. "No, little one, I am moving us too fast." Everything in his nature, beast and centuries-old man raged at him to take, keep her, but he wanted her to come to him willingly.

"I feel funny, dizzy."

He had been that little bit out of control, the beast in him hungry to put his mark on her, hungry for the sweet taste of her. His body was on fire, demanding release. Discipline and control fought with his instinctual predatory nature and won. He breathed deeply, carried her to the chair beside the fire. She deserved a courtship, deserved to know him, to come to feel affection if not love for him before he bound her to him. A human. A mortal. It was wrong. It was dangerous. As he gently placed her on the cushions, he caught the first warning of disturbance.

He swung around, his handsome features dark and menacing. His body lost its protective posture, all at once threatening and powerful. "Stay," he ordered softly. He moved so fast that he blurred, closing the doors to his library, turning to face the front door. Mikhail sent a silent call to his sentries.

Outside, a lone wolf howled, a second answered, a third, until there was a united chorus. When the noise subsided he waited, his face an implacable, granite mask. Mist drifted through the forest, tendrils of fog, collecting, moving, massing outside his home.

Mikhail lifted his arm and his front door opened. The fog and mist seeped in, collected in pools until his foyer was thick with it. Slowly the mists connected; bodies shimmered and became solid. "Why do you disturb me this night?" he challenged softly, his dark eyes glittering dangerously.

A man stepped forward, his fingers clasped solidly in his wife's. She looked pale and drawn, was obviously pregnant. "We seek your council, Mikhail, and bring you news."

Inside the library, Raven felt fear slam into her, the emotion beating in her head, swamping her, driving out the heavy, trancelike cobwebs. Someone was distraught, crying, feeling pain as sharp as a knife. She staggered to her feet, clutched at the back of a chair. Images pushed in. A young woman with pale, white skin, a large stake protruding from her chest, blood running in rivers, her head detached from her body, something sickening placed in her mouth. A ritual killing, symbolic, a warning of others to come. A serial killer, here, in this land of peace.

Raven gagged, both hands going to cover her ears, as if that could somehow stop the images pouring into her mind. For a moment she couldn't breathe, didn't want to breathe; she just wanted it to end. Wildly, she looked around her, saw a door to her right leading in the opposite direction from the over-whelming emotions. Blindly she stumbled to her feet, weak, disoriented, and dizzy. She staggered out of the library, need-ing to get some fresh air. Away from the details of death and horror that were so vivid in the minds of the newcomers.

Their fear and anger was a living thing. They were animals wounded and ready to tear and rend in retaliation. Why were people so ugly? So violent? She had no answer, no longer wanted one. She had taken several steps down a long hall when a figure loomed up. A man a little younger than Mikhail, thinner, with glittering eyes and chestnut, wavy hair. His smile was taunting and held menace as he reached for her.

An unseen force hit the man square in the chest, knocking him backward, and slamming him into the wall. Mikhail loomed up, a dark, malevolent shadow. He towered over Raven, protectively thrust her behind him. This time the throaty growl was a beast's roar of challenge.

Raven could feel the terrible rage in Mikhail, rage mixed with grief, his emotions so intense they beat at the air itself. She touched his arm, her fingers curling halfway around the thickness of his wrist, a tiny deterrent to the violence swirling within him. She felt the tension running through him as if it was alive.

There was a collective, audible gasp. Raven realized she was the center of the group's attention. There was one woman and four men. All eyes were on her fingers circling his wrist as if she had committed some terrible, criminal act. Mikhail's larger body moved to shield her completely from their scrutiny. He made no attempt to shake off her hand. If anything, he moved his body protectively, backing her farther into the wall so that he was pressing against her, obscuring their vision of her.

"She is under my protection." A declaration. A challenge. A promise of quick, savage retribution.

"As we all are, Mikhail," the woman said softly, appeasingly.

Raven swayed; only the walls were holding her up. Vibrations of rage and grief were beating at her until she wanted to scream. She made a sound, a single, threadlike sound of objection. Mikhail turned to her at once, his arms sweeping around her, enveloping her. "Guard your thoughts and emotions," he hissed at the others. "She is very sensitive. I will escort her to the inn and return to discuss this disturbing news."

Raven had no real chance to see the others before he was striding past them, taking her with him to the small car waiting in the garage. She smiled tiredly, her head resting against his shoulder. "You don't seem like you belong in this car, Mikhail. Your views on women are so archaic, in a former life you must have been 'lord of the castle.' "

He glanced at her quickly. His gaze slid over the paleness of her face, dwelt on his mark on her neck, visible through the long mane of her hair. In truth, he hadn't meant to leave a mark, but now it was there, his brand of ownership. "I am going to help you sleep tonight." He made it a statement.

"Who were those people?" She asked because she knew he didn't want her to ask. She was so tired, even dizzy. She rubbed at her head and wished that for once in her life she was normal. He probably thought she was the fainting type.

There was a short silence. He sighed heavily. "My family."

She knew he spoke the truth, yet he didn't. "Why would someone do such a terrible thing?" She turned her face up to his. "Do they expect you to track this killer, to stop him?" There was raw pain in her voice, pain for him. Worry. His grief was sharp, edged with guilt and the need for violence.

He turned her question over in his mind. She knew then, knew one of his people had been killed. She probably had picked the details out of someone's head. The worry and pain was for him. There was no condemnation. Simply worry. Mikhail felt the tension ease from his body, felt warmth curl in his stomach. "I will try to keep you as far from this mess as possible, little one." No one worried about him, about his state of mind or his health. No one thought to feel for him. Something inside him seemed to soften and melt. She was wrapping herself inside him, deep, somewhere he needed her.

"Perhaps we shouldn't see each other for a few days. I've never been so tired in my life." She tried to give him a gracious way out. Raven looked down at her hands. She wanted to give herself an out, too. She had never felt so close to anyone, so comfortable, as if she had known him forever, yet was terrified that he would take her over. "And I don't think your family was thrilled to see an American with you. We're too . . . explosive together," she finished ruefully.

"Do not try to leave me, Raven." The car drew up in front of the inn. "I hold what is mine, and make no mistake, you are mine." It was both a warning and a plea. He had no time for soft words. He wanted to give them to her—God knew she deserved them—but the others were waiting and his responsibilities weighed heavily on him.

She raised her hand to the line of his jaw, rubbing gently. "You're so used to having your own way." There was a smile in her voice. "I can go to sleep all by myself, Mikhail. I've been doing it for years."

"You need to sleep untroubled, undisturbed, deeply. What you 'saw' tonight will haunt you if I do not help you." His thumb stroked across her lower lip. "I could remove the memory if you wished."

Raven could see he wanted to do it, believed that it would be best for her. She could see it was difficult to ask her to make a decision. "No, thank you, Mikhail," she said demurely. "I think I'll keep all my memories, good and bad." She kissed his chin, slid across the seat to the door. "You know, I'm not a porcelain doll. I won't break because I see something I shouldn't. I've chased serial killers before." She smiled at him, her eyes sad.

He shackled her wrist in an unbreakable grip. "And it almost destroyed you. Not this time."

Her lashes swept down, hiding her expression. "That's not your decision." If others persuaded him to use his talents to chase the insane, evil killers in the world, she would not leave him alone. How could she?

"You are not nearly as afraid of me as you should be," he growled.

She flashed him another smile, tugging at her wrist to remind him to release her. "I think you know what's between us would be worth nothing if you forced me to do your will in everything."

He held her captive a heartbeat longer, his dark, dangerous eyes moving possessively over her fragile face. She was so strong-willed. She was afraid, but she looked him in the eyes and stood up to him. It made her ill, brought her to the brink of madness to chase evil, but she did it time and time again. He was still a shadow in her mind. He read her determination to help him, her fear of him and his incredible powers, but she would not leave him to face this horrible killer alone. He wanted to keep her with him safe in his lair. Almost reverently, Mikhail trailed his fingers down her cheek. "Go, before I change my mind," he ordered, abruptly releasing her.

Raven walked away from him slowly, trying to overcome the dizziness that had taken hold of her. She was careful to walk straight, not wanting him to know she felt as if her body was lead, that every movement was difficult. She walked with her head up and kept her mind purposely blank.

Mikhail watched her enter the inn. He saw her hand go up to her head, rub at her temple, the nape of her neck. She was still dizzy from his taking her blood. That had been selfish, beneath him, yet he couldn't stop himself. Now she was paying for it. Her head ached from the bombardment of emotions. His included. All of his people would have to be more careful to shield their minds.

Mikhail unfolded his large frame from the vehicle, moved to the shadows, his senses flaring out to tell him he was alone. He took the form of mist. In the heavy fog it was unnoticeable, and he could easily seep beneath her unsecured window. He watched her as she sank onto the bed. Her face was pale, her eyes haunted. She swept her mane of hair back, touching

39

his mark as if it ached. It took her a few minutes to kick off her shoes, as if the task was too great.

Mikhail waited until she had flung herself face down, fully clothed on the bed. *You will sleep.* He gave the order forcefully, expected her compliance.

Mikhail. His name echoed in his head, soft, drowsy, with a hint of amusement. *Somehow I knew you would just have to have your way.* She didn't fight it, but went under willingly, a smile curving her soft mouth.

Mikhail undressed her, slid her slender body beneath the covers. He safeguarded the door, a powerful spell guaranteed to keep even the strongest of his own people out, let alone pathetic mortal assassins. He secured the windows and provided the same guards at every possible entry point. Very gently he brushed his lips across her forehead, then reached down to touch his brand on her neck before leaving her.

The others fell silent when he entered his home. Celeste smiled tentatively, pressed a protective hand to the child lying in her womb. "Is she all right, Mikhail?"

He nodded abruptly, curiously grateful for her concern. No one would question him, yet his behavior was completely out of character for him. He got right to the point. "How did the assassins find Noelle unprotected?"

The others looked at one another. Mikhail drilled it into them never to forget the smallest details guarding their safety, but over the years it was so easy to forget, to slip up.

"Noelle had her baby only two months ago. She was so tired all the time." Celeste tried to excuse the slip.

"And Rand? Where was he? Why did he leave his exhausted wife unprotected while she slept?" Mikhail asked softly, dangerously.

Byron, the man who had been in such trouble earlier, stirred uncomfortably. "You know how Rand is. Always after the women. He took the child to Celeste and went out hunting."

"And forgot to provide Noelle with the proper safeguards." Mikhail's disgust was all too evident. "Where is he?"

Celeste's life mate, Eric, answered grimly. "He was crazy, Mikhail. It took all of us to subdue him, but he sleeps now.

The child is with him deep in the ground. The healing will do them good."

"We could not afford to lose Noelle." Mikhail pushed grief away; it was not the time to feel it. "Eric, can you keep Rand under control?"

"I think you should talk to him," Eric answered honestly. "The guilt is making him crazy. He nearly turned on us."

"Vlad, where is Eleanor? She is at risk, heavy with child. We must protect her as we will Celeste," Mikhail said. "We cannot afford the loss of any of our women and certainly not their children."

"She is so close to term, I was worried about her traveling." Vlad sighed heavily. "She is safe and well-guarded for the moment, but I think this war is starting again."

Mikhail tapped a finger on the small table near the chessboard. "Perhaps it is significant that we have three of our women giving birth for the first time in a decade. Our children are few and far between. If the assassins somehow have gained knowledge of our women's condition, they will be afraid we are multiplying, growing strong again."

Mikhail shot the most muscular of the men a quick glance. "Jacques, you have no life mate to encumber you." There was the faintest trace of affection in his voice, affection he could never feel or show before and maybe wasn't aware anyone else knew of. Jacques was his brother. "Neither does Byron. You two will get word to all the others. Lie low, feed only in the deepest cover, sleep deep within the ground, and always use the most powerful safeguards. We must watch our women and get them to safety, especially those who are with child. Do not draw attention to yourselves in any way."

"For how long, Mikhail?" Celeste's eyes were shadowed, her face tearstained. "How long must we live like this?"

"Until I find and dispense justice to the assassins." There was a fierce, savage note in his voice. "All of you have become soft, mixing so much with mortals. You are forgetting the gifts that could save your lives," he reprimanded them harshly. "My woman is mortal, yet she knew of your presence before you knew of hers. She felt your unguarded emotions, knows of the assassins through your thoughts. There is no excuse for that."

"How can this be?" Eric dared to ask. "No mortal has such power."

"She is telepathic and very strong in her gift. She will be here often; she will be protected, as will all of our women."

The others exchanged bewildered, confused looks. According to the legend, only their strongest members might be able to convert a mortal. It simply wasn't done, was far too risky. It had been tried centuries earlier, when the ranks of their women had been depleted and the men were without hope. But no one dared try it anymore. Most of them believed it was a myth made up to keep their males from losing their souls. Mikhail was unreadable, implacable, his judgment never questioned throughout the centuries. He settled arguments and protected them. He hunted the males who had chosen to turn vampire, dangerous to mortals and immortals alike.

Now this. A mortal woman. They were shocked and it showed. They were obligated to put the life of Mikhail's woman before their own. If Mikhail said she was under his protection, he meant it. He never said anything he didn't mean. And if she was harmed, the penalty would be death. Mikhail was a savage, merciless, and unrelenting enemy.

Mikhail felt the weight of his responsibility for Noelle's death. He had known of Rand's weakness for women. Mikhail had objected to the union, but he hadn't forbidden it, as he should have. Rand was not Noelle's true life mate. Chemistry would never allow a true mate to cheat on his woman. Noelle, his beautiful sister, so young and vibrant, lost to them forever. She had been headstrong, wanting Rand because he was handsome, not because her soul called to his. They had lied, but he had known they were lying. Ultimately it had been his responsibility that Rand continued to try to find emotion by being with other women, and Noelle had grown into a bitter, dangerous woman. She must have died instantly or Mikhail would have felt it, even deep in his sleep. Rand should never have had the care of one of their women.

Mikhail had thought that, in time, each would find their true life mate, but Nicole only grew more dangerous and Rand worse in his promiscuous behavior. It was impossible for Rand to feel anything with the women he bedded, yet he continued, almost as if it was a punishment for Noelle's tight hold on him.

Mikhail closed his eyes for a moment, allowing the reality of Noelle's senseless murder to sweep over him. The loss was intolerable, his grief wild and intense, mixed with an ice-cold rage and deadly resolve. He bowed his head. Three blood-red tears made their way unchecked down his face. His sister, the youngest of their women. It was his fault.

Mikhail felt the stirring in his head, warmth, comfort, as if arms had stolen around him. *Mikhail? Do you need me?* Raven's voice was drowsy, husky, worried.

He was shocked. His command had been strong, far stronger than anything he had ever used on a human, yet his sorrow had penetrated her sleep. He glanced around him, took in the faces of his companions. None of them had picked up the mental contact. It meant that, as groggy as she was, Raven was able to focus, channel, and send directly to him without any spillage. It was a skill few of his people had bothered to accomplish, so complacent were they that humans could not tune into them.

Mikhail? This time Raven's voice was stronger, alarmed. *I'll come to you.*

Sleep, little one. I am well, he reassured, reinforcing his command with the tone of his voice.

Be well, Mikhail, she whispered softly, succumbing to his power.

Mikhail gave his attention to those awaiting his orders. "Send Rand to me tomorrow. The child cannot stay with him. Dierdre lost another child a couple of decades ago. She still mourns her many losses. The child will be taken to her. Tienn will guard them carefully. No one is to use a mental link until we know whether one of our adversaries possesses the same power my woman does."

The shock on their faces was complete. None of them considered a human capable of that kind of power and discipline. "Mikhail, you are certain this woman is not the one? She could be a threat to us." Eric ventured the suggestion cautiously, even as Celeste's fingers dug warningly into his arm.

Mikhail's dark eyes narrowed slightly. "Do you believe I have grown lazy, bloated with my own power? Do you think so little of me that I could be in her mind and not recognize a threat to us? I warn you, I am willing to step down as your leader, but I am not willing to withdraw my protection of her. If any of you wish to harm her, know that you will deal with me. Do you wish me to pass on the mantle of leadership? I weary of my duties and responsibilities."

"Mikhail!" Byron's voice was a sharp protest.

The others voiced quick, alarmed denials, like frightened children. Jacques was the only one who stood silently, one hip lazily resting against the wall, regarding Mikhail with a secret mocking half-smile. Mikhail ignored him.

"It is nearly sunrise. All of you go to ground. Use every guard possible. When you awaken, check around your dwelling; feel for intruders. Do not overlook the slightest incident. We must stay in close communication and watch each other."

"Mikhail, the first year is so critical, so many of our children do not survive." Celeste's fingers were twisting nervously within her husband's hand. "I am not sure Dierdre could bear another loss."

Mikhail's smile was gentle. "She will guard the child as no other, and Tienn will be twice as watchful as any other. He has been trying to get Dierdre to conceive and she has refused. At least this way, her arms will not be empty."

"And she will long for another child," Celeste said angrily.

"If our race is to continue, we must have children. As much as I would like to provide them, it is only our women who can produce such a miracle."

"It is heartbreaking to lose so many, Mikhail," Celeste pointed out.

"For all of us, Celeste." His tone was final, and no one dared to argue or question. His authority was absolute, his rage and grief beyond boundaries. Not only Rand had failed to protect Noelle, a young, beautiful, vibrant woman, but her life had been lost because of some sadistic game Rand and Noelle had played together. He knew that he was every bit as responsible as Rand for Noelle's fate. His loathing of Rand was directed at himself as well.

Chapter Three

Raven woke slowly, in a dense fog, layers and layers of it. Somehow she knew she wasn't supposed to wake, but never the less it was imperative she do so. She pried her eyes open and turned her head toward the window. Sunlight was streaming in. She pushed herself into a sitting position, the covers sliding away to expose bare skin.

"Mikhail," she whispered aloud, "you take altogether too many liberties." She reached out to him automatically, as if she could not deny herself that need. Sensing he was asleep, she withdrew. The slight touch was enough. He was safe.

Raven felt different, happy even. She could talk to someone, touch someone, never mind that it was a bit like sitting on the back of a hungry tiger. The freedom to relax in another's presence was a joy. Mikhail had heavy responsibilities. She didn't know who he was, only that he was someone important. Obviously he was comfortable with his talents, unlike Raven, who still felt she was some kind of freak of nature. She wanted to be more like he was: confident, not caring what others thought.

She knew very little of Romanian life. The rural populations were poor and superstitious. Yet they were a friendly people and truly artistic. Mikhail was different. She had heard of Carpathians; not Gypsies, but a people who were well educated, had money, and lived deep in the mountains and forests by choice. Was Mikhail their leader? Was that why he was so arrogant and aloof?

The shower felt good on her body, rinsing away the heavy, groggy feeling. She dressed carefully, in jeans, a turtleneck, and a sweater. Even with the sunlight, it was cold in the mountains, and she intended to go exploring. Her neck throbbed for a moment, burned. She peeled back her top to examine the wound. It was a strange mark, like a teenager's love bite, but more intense.

She blushed at the memory of how he'd put it there. Did the man have to be sexy on top of everything else? And she could learn so much from him. She noticed that he was able to shield himself from the ever-present bombardment of emotions all the time. That would be such a miracle—to be able to simply sit in the middle of a crowded room and not feel anything but her own emotions.

Raven pulled on her hiking shoes. A murder in this place! It was a sacrilege. The villagers must be frightened. As she passed through the doorway she felt a curious shifting in the air. It felt as if she had to push through some unseen force. Mikhail again? Trying to lock her in? No. If he was capable of such a thing, the locks would stop her. More likely he was protecting her, locking others out. Torn by grief and rage at the senseless, hideous murder, Mikhail had still helped her go to sleep. The thought of him taking the time to protect and aid her made her feel cherished.

It was three in the afternoon—well past lunch but too soon for dinner—and Raven was hungry. In the kitchen the landlady obligingly fixed her a picnic dinner. Not once did the woman mention a murder. Indeed, she seemed totally oblivious of any such news. Raven found herself reluctant to broach the subject. It was strange; the innkeeper was so friendly and engaging—she even talked of Mikhail, a long-time friend of whom she spoke very highly—yet Raven could not bring herself to say a single word about the murder and what it meant to Mikhail.

Outside, she shrugged into her backpack. She couldn't sense the horror of murder anywhere. No one at the inn, no one in the street seemed unduly upset. She couldn't have been wrong; the images had been strong, the grief wild and very real. The images of the murder itself were very detailed, unlike anything her imagination could conjure up.

"Miss Whitney! It is Whitney, isn't it?" A feminine voice called to her from several feet away.

Margaret Summers hastened toward her, anxiety on her face. She was in her late sixties, frail, with gray hair and a down-to-earth, sensible way of dressing. "My dear, you're so pale this morning. We all were so afraid for your safety. That young man carrying you off the way he did was very intimidating."

Raven laughed softly. "He is rather intimidating, isn't he? He's an old friend and overanxious about my health. Believe me, Mrs. Summers, he watches over me very carefully. He really is a respectable businessman; ask anyone in the village."

"Are you ill, dear?" Margaret asked solicitously, moving closer so that Raven felt threatened.

"Recovering," Raven said firmly, hoping it was true.

"I have seen you before!" Margaret sounded excited. "You're that extraordinary young lady who helped the police catch that murdering fiend in San Diego a month or so ago. What in the world would you be doing here of all places?"

Raven rubbed her forehead with the heel of her palm. "That type of work is very draining, Mrs. Summers. It sometimes makes me ill. It was a long chase, and I needed to get far away. I wanted to go somewhere remote and beautiful, somewhere steeped in history. Somewhere people didn't recognize me and point me out like I was a freak of nature. The Carpathian Mountains are beautiful. I can hike, sit quietly, and let the wind blow all the memories of a sick mind out of my head."

"Oh, my dear." Margaret put out her hand in concern.

Raven sidestepped quickly. "I'm sorry; it bothers me to

touch people after I follow a demented mind. Please understand."

Margaret nodded. "Of course, although I noticed your young man thought nothing of touching you."

Raven smiled. "He's bossy, and he has such a flair for the dramatic, but he's really good to me. We've known each other a while. You see, Mikhail travels quite a bit." The lie seemed to roll easily off her tongue. She hated herself for that. "I don't want anyone to know about me, Mrs. Summers. I dislike publicity and need solitude right now. Please don't tell anyone who I am."

"Of course not, dear, but do you think it's safe to go wandering off by yourself? There are wild animals roaming these parts."

"Mikhail accompanies me on my little jaunts, and I certainly don't go poking around in the wilds at night."

"Oh," Margaret looked mollified. "Mikhail Dubrinsky? Everyone talks of him."

"I told you, he's overprotective. Actually, he likes the landlady's cooking," she confided with a laugh, holding up the picnic basket. "I'd better get going or I'll be late."

Margaret stepped aside. "Do be careful, dear."

Raven gave a friendly wave and sauntered unhurriedly along the path that led through the woods, up the footpath into the mountains. Why had she felt compelled to lie? She liked her solitude, never felt the need to justify herself. For some reason she didn't want to discuss Mikhail's life with anyone, least of all Margaret Summers. The woman seemed too interested in him. It wasn't anything she said; it was in her eyes and voice. She could feel Margaret Summers watching her curiously until the path made an abrupt turn and the trees swallowed her up.

Raven shook her head sadly. She was becoming such a recluse, not wanting to be close to anyone, not even a sweet older woman worried about her safety.

"Raven! Wait up!"

She closed her eyes against the intrusion. By the time Jacob caught up with her, she managed to plaster a smile on her face. "Jacob, I'm glad you recovered from that terrible choking spell last night. It was lucky the waiter knew the Heimlich maneuver."

Jacob scowled. "I didn't choke on a piece of meat," he said defensively, as if she was accusing him of bad table manners. "Everyone thinks so, but it wasn't that."

"Really? The way the waiter grabbed you . . . " Her voice trailed off.

"Well, you didn't stick around long enough to find out," he accused sulkily, his brows drawing together. "You just let that . . . that Neanderthal carry you off."

"Jacob," she said gently, "you don't know me; you know nothing about me or my life. For all you know, that man could be my husband. I was very ill last night. I'm sorry I didn't stay, but once I could see you were fine, I didn't think it would be appropriate to throw up all over the dining room."

"How do you know that man?" Jacob demanded jealously. "The locals say he's the most powerful man in this region. He's wealthy, owns all the petroleum rights. Quite the businessman; very high-powered. How would you meet a man like that?"

He was crowding close to her, and Raven was suddenly all too aware of how alone they were, how secluded their surroundings. He had a spoiled, petulant look twisting his boyish good looks. She sensed something else—a kind of sick excitement in his guilty thoughts. She knew she was a big part of his perverse fantasies. Jacob was a rich boy thinking he could have any new toy he wanted.

Raven felt a stirring in her mind. *Raven? You fear for your safety.* Mikhail was heavy with sleep, fighting his way up through the layers to the surface.

Now she was worried. Mikhail was a question mark in her mind. She didn't know what he would do, only that he felt protective toward her. For herself, for Mikhail, for Jacob, she needed to make Jacob understand that she wanted no part of him. *I can handle this,* she sent a sharp reassurance. "Jacob," her voice was patient, "I think you should leave; go back to the inn. I'm not the kind of woman to be bullied by your attitude. This is harassment, and I'll have no compunction about registering a complaint with the local police, or whatever they're called." She held her breath, feeling Mikhail waiting.

"Fine, Raven, sell yourself to the highest bidder! Try to find yourself a rich husband! He'll use you and dump you; that's what men like Dubrinsky do!" Jacob shouted. He spat out a few additional ugly words and stomped away.

Raven let out her breath slowly, thankfully. *See,* she forced laughter into her thoughts. *I took care of the problem all by my little feminine self. Amazing, isn't it?*

From the other side of a grove of trees, out of her sight, Jacob suddenly screamed in terror, the sound fading to a thin wail. The roar of an enraged bear mingled with Jacob's second scream. Something heavy crashed through the underbrush in the opposite direction of Raven.

She felt Mikhail's laughter, low, amused, very male. *Very funny, Mikhail.* Jacob was broadcasting fear, but not pain. *You have a questionable sense of humor.*

I need sleep. Quit getting into trouble, woman.

If you wouldn't stay up all night, you might not need to sleep the day away, she reprimanded. *How do you get work done?*

Computers.

She found herself laughing at the thought of him with a computer. He didn't belong with cars or computers. *Go back to sleep, you big baby. I can handle things just fine, thank you very much, without any great big he-man to protect me.*

I would much prefer that you return to the safety of the inn until I rise. There was the merest hint of command in his voice. He was trying to soften his manner with her and she found herself smiling at his efforts.

It isn't going to happen, so learn to live with it.

American women are very difficult.

She continued on her way up the mountain, his laughter still playing softly in her head. She allowed the stillness of nature to seep into her mind. The birds sang to one another softly; the wind whispered through the trees. There were flowers of all colors carpeting the meadow, lifting their petals to the sky.

Raven climbed higher finding peace in her solitude. She perched on a craggy boulder up above a meadow surrounded by forests of thick trees. She ate her lunch and lay back, reveling in her surroundings.

Mikhail stirred, allowing his senses to read his environment. He lay in shallow earth, undisturbed. No human had come near his lair. It was less than an hour to sunset. He burst from the earth into the cold, damp cellar. Even as he showered, adopting the human way to cleanliness, although it wasn't necessary, his mind reached out to touch Raven's. She was dozing in the mountains, unprotected, with the darkness gathering. He frowned. The woman had no idea of safety measures. He had an urge to shake her, yet more than that, he wanted to gather her up and hold her forever safe in his arms.

He made his way out into the setting sun, climbing the mountain trails with the speed of his kind. The sun touched his skin, warmed his coolness, made him alive. The specially constructed dark glasses protected his ultrasensitive eyes, yet he still felt a pinprick of unease, as if a thousand needles were waiting to stab at his eyes. As he approached the rock where Raven slept, he caught the scent of another male.

Rand. Mikhail bared his teeth. The sun dipped low beneath the edge of the mountain, cast a dark shadow across the rolling hills, and bathed the forest in murky secrets. Mikhail moved out into the open, his arms held out from his sides, his body a fluid combination of power and coordination. He was pure menace, a stalking demon, silent and lethal.

Rand had his back to him, approaching the woman on the rock. Sensing the power in the air, he spun around, his handsome features grief-stricken and ravaged. "Mikhail—" His voice cracked, his eyes dropped. "I know you can never forgive me. You knew I was not a true life mate to Noelle. She would not let me go. She threatened to kill herself if I left her, if I attempted to find another. Like a coward, I remained with her."

"Why do I find you crouched over my woman?" Mikhail snarled, fury rising until the bloodlust coiled in him like a living thing. Rand's excuses sickened him, true though they might be. If Noelle had threatened to walk into the sun, the matter should have been brought before him. Mikhail had power enough to stop Noelle from her destructive behavior. Rand well knew that Mikhail was their prince, their leader, and, although he had not shared blood with Rand, he still could read the male's perverse pleasure in his sick relationship with Noelle, his dominance over her and her obsession.

Behind them, Raven stirred, sat up, shoved at her hair from long habit. She looked drowsy, sexy, a siren waiting for her lover. Rand had turned his head to look at her, and there was something sly and crafty in his expression. She felt Mikhail's instant warning to be silent, Rand's unrestrained grief, his jealousy and dislike of Mikhail, the thick tension between the two men.

"Byron and Jacques told me she was under your protection. I could not sleep and knew she was alone without safeguards. I had to do something or I would have chosen to join Noelle." There was a plea for understanding, if not for forgiveness, yet Raven was unconvinced that Rand meant anything he said. She didn't know why because his sorrow was real. Perhaps he was desperate for Mikhail's respect and knew he would not get it.

"Then I am in your debt," Mikhail said formally, working at controlling his loathing of a man who would leave unprotected a woman who had just given birth to his child to deliberately torment her with another woman's scent on him.

Raven slid from her perch, a small, fragile woman with compassion in her enormous blue eyes. "I'm truly sorry for your loss," she murmured softly, careful to keep her distance. This man was the murder victim's husband. His guilt and grief crawled through her body with torturous intent, yet she worried for Mikhail. Something was not right with Rand. He was twisted inside; not evil, yet not completely right.

"Thank you," Rand said tersely. "I need my child, Mikhail."

"You need the healing earth," Mikhail disagreed calmly, implacable in his decision, merciless in his resolve. He would not turn over a precious, helpless baby to this male in his present state of mind.

Raven's stomach knotted, twisted, and pain went through her heart at the cruelty in those words. She only partially understood what Mikhail's decree meant. This man, grieving for his murdered wife, was being deprived of his child, accepting Mikhail's word as absolute law. She felt his deep pain as if it were her own, yet on some level she couldn't help agreeing with Mikhail's decision.

"Please, Mikhail. I loved Noelle." Instinctively, Raven knew Rand was not pleading for his child.

Fury lent darkness to Mikhail's features, cruelty to his mouth, a red glint to his eyes. "Do not speak of love to me, Rand. Go to the earth; heal. I will find this assassin and avenge my sister. No longer will I be swayed by sentiment. If I had not listened to her pleading, she would be alive today."

"I cannot sleep. It is my right to hunt." Rand sounded defiant, sulky, like a child who wanted respect and equality, yet knew it would never come.

A flicker of impatience, of menace, crossed Mikhail's brooding features. "Then I will command you and give you the healing rest your body and mind require." His voice was as soft and neutral as ever. If it hadn't been for the fury burning in his black eyes, Raven would have thought him gentle and caring toward the man. "We cannot afford to lose you, Rand." His voice softened to velvet, enticed, commanded. *You will sleep, Rand. You will go to Eric and have him prepare you, guard you. You will remain until you are no longer a threat to yourself or others.*

Raven was shocked and alarmed at the absolute power in his voice, the power he wielded as if it was his due. Mikhail's voice alone could produce a hypnotic trance. No one questioned his authority, even over so grave a decision as keeping a child. She bit at her lip, confused over her feelings. He was right about the baby. She sensed something wrong in Rand, yet that a grown man would obey his order—*had* to obey his orders—frightened her. No one should have such a voice, such a gift. Something so strong could be misused, could easily corrupt the one who wielded it.

They stood, regarding each other in the gathering darkness once Rand left them. Raven could feel the weight of

Mikhail's displeasure pressing down on her. She lifted her chin defiantly. He moved closer, gliding unbelievably fast, his fingers finding her throat as if he might strangle her. "You will never repeat this foolhardy act again."

She blinked up at him. "Don't try to intimidate me, Mikhail; it won't work. No one tells me what to do or where I can go."

His fingers slipped to her wrists, tightened, threatened to crush her fragile bones. "I will not tolerate any foolishness that might put your life in jeopardy. We have lost one of our women already. I will not lose you."

His sister, he had said. Compassion warred with self-preservation. Most of this confrontation was because he was so afraid for her. "Mikhail, you can't put me in a box and keep me on a shelf." She spoke as gently as she could.

"I will not argue over your safety. Earlier, you were alone with a man who thought of forcibly taking you. Any wild animal could have attacked you, and if you had not been under my protection, in his present state, Rand might have harmed you."

"None of those things happened, Mikhail." She touched his jaw with gentle, placating fingers, a tender caress. "You have enough to worry about, enough responsibilities, without adding me to them. I can help you. You know I'm capable."

He tugged at her wrist so that she lost her balance and fell against his hard strength. "You are going to make me crazy, Raven." His arms came up, pinning her soft slenderness against him. His voice dropped to a drawling caress, mesmerizing, pure black magic. "You are the one person I long to protect, yet you will not obey. You insist on independence. All others lean on my strength, yet you seek to help me, to shoulder my duties." He lowered his mouth to hers.

There was that curious shifting of the ground beneath her feet, the crackle of electricity in the air around them. Flames licked over her skin, heated her blood. Colors whirled and danced in her head. His mouth claimed hers, aggressive, male, totally dominating, sweeping all thoughts of resistance aside. She opened her mouth to him, allowed his probing exploration, his sweet, hot assault.

Her hands found the broadness of his shoulders, crept up to circle his neck. Her body felt pliant, boneless, like hot silk. Mikhail wanted to press her to the soft ground, tear the offending clothes from her body, and make her irrevocably his. There was far too much innocence in the taste of her. No one had asked to share the weight of his countless burdens. No one, until this little slender slip of a mortal, had even thought of the price he continually paid. A human. She had the courage to stand up to him and he could do no other than respect her for it.

His eyes were closed, savoring the feel of her body against his, the fact that he could want her with such intensity. He held her, wanting her, needing her, burning for her, not even understanding how such a firestorm could consume him. Reluctantly he lifted his head, his body raging at him. "Let us go home, Raven." His voice was pure seduction.

A slow smile curved her soft mouth. "I don't think it's safe. You're the kind of man my mother warned me about."

He kept his arm possessively around her shoulders, shackling her to him. Mikhail had no intention of allowing her to leave his side again. His body urged her in the direction he wanted. They walked together in companionable silence.

"Jacob wasn't going to hurt me," she denied suddenly. "I would have known."

"You were not touching him, little one, and it was lucky for him."

"He's certainly capable of violence. It's always hard to miss violence." She flashed him her mischievous smile. "It clings to you like a second skin."

He tugged at her thick braid in retaliation for her teasing. "I want you to come stay in my home. At least until we find and dispose of the assassins."

Raven walked several steps in silence. He had said *we,* as if they were a team. That pleased her. "You know, Mikhail, it was the strangest thing today. Not one person at the inn or in the village seemed to know of the murder."

His finger flicked along her delicate cheekbone. "And you said nothing."

She flashed him a quelling glance from under long lashes. "Of course. Gossiping is not my form of entertainment."

"Noelle died cruelly, senselessly. She was Rand's life mate . . ."

"You used that term before. What does it mean?"

"It is like a wife or husband," he explained. "Noelle had given birth to a child only two months ago. She was my responsibility. Noelle is not food for gossip. We will find her killers ourselves."

"Don't you think if there's a serial killer loose in so small a village, the people have a right to know?"

Mikhail chose his words carefully. "The Romanians are not in any danger. And this is not the work of one individual. The assassins wish to stamp out our race. True Carpathians are almost extinct. We have bitter enemies who would see us all dead."

"Why?"

Mikhail shrugged. "We are different; we have certain gifts, talents. People are afraid of what is different. You should know that."

"Maybe I have Carpathian blood in me, a diluted version," Raven said with a trace of wistfulness. It was nice to think she had an ancestor with the same gift.

His heart went out to her. Her life must have been terribly lonely. Mikhail wanted to wrap her up, safe in his arms, sheltered from life's unpleasantness. His was a self-imposed isolation; Raven had no choice.

"Our petroleum and mineral rights in a country where most have very little is cause for concern and jealousy. I am the law to my people. I deal with the threats to our position and our lives. It was my poor judgment that placed Noelle in danger; it is my duty to hunt her killers and bring our justice to them."

"Why haven't you called the local authorities?" She was struggling to understand, feeling her way carefully.

"I am the sole authority to my people. I am the law."

"Alone?"

"I have others who hunt, many in fact, but it is at my command. I hold the sole responsibility in all decisions."

"Judge, jury, and executioner?" she guessed, holding her breath for the answer. Her senses couldn't lie. She would have felt the taint of evil in him, no matter how good a shield he constructed. No one could be so good that they never once slipped up. She didn't realize she had stopped walking until his hands ran up and down her arms, warming her shivering body.

"Now you fear me." He said it softly, wearily, as if she had hurt him. And it did hurt. He had wanted her to be afraid of him, had deliberately provoked her fear, yet now, his goal achieved, it wasn't at all what he wanted.

His voice tugged at her heartstrings. "I don't fear you, Mikhail," she denied gently, tipping her face up to study his in the moonlight. "I fear for you. So much power leads to corruption. So much responsibility leads to destruction. You make life-and-death decisions that only God should make."

His hand caressed her silken skin, moved to trace the fullness of her lower lip. Her large eyes were enormous in her small face, her feelings naked to his mesmerizing gaze. There was concern, compassion, the beginnings of love, and a sweet, sweet innocence that shook him to his very core. She worried for him. *Worried.*

Mikhail groaned aloud, turned from her. She had no idea what she was offering to one such as he. He knew he wasn't strong enough to resist it, and he loathed himself for his selfishness.

"Mikhail." She touched his arm, sending flames licking along his skin, heating his blood. He hadn't fed, and the combination of love, lust, and hunger was explosive, heady, but very, very dangerous. How could he not love her when he was in her mind, reading her thoughts, knowing her intimately? She was light to his darkness, his other half. Forbidden though it might be, mistake of nature probably, he could not help loving her.

"Let me help you. Share this terrible thing with me. Don't cut yourself off from me." Just the touch of her hand, the concern in her eyes, the purity and truth in her voice, brought out an unfamiliar softness in him.

He dragged her to him, all too aware of the urgent demands of his body. With a low, animal growl he lifted her, whispered a soft command to her, and moved with all the speed of which he was capable.

Raven blinked and found herself in the warmth of Mikhail's library, with the fire throwing shadows on the wall, unsure how she had gotten there. She didn't remember walking there, yet they were within the walls of his home. Mikhail's shirt was open, exposing the heavy muscles of his chest. His black eyes were steady on her face, watching her with a stillness, a watchfulness reminiscent of a predator. He made no attempt to hide his desire for her.

"I will give you one last chance, little one." He spoke the words in a harsh, hoarse voice, as if they tore painfully at his throat. "I will find the strength to let you go if you say it. Now. Right now."

The length of the room separated them. The air stilled. If she lived to be a hundred, that moment would be etched forever in her mind. He stood waiting for her decision to share herself with him or damn him to eternal isolation. His head was held up proudly, his body fiercely hard, aggressively male, his eyes burning with hunger.

He drove every sane thought from her head. If she condemned him, wasn't she condemning herself to the same fate? Someone needed to love this man, care for him just a little. How could he continue so alone? He waited. No compulsion, no seduction, just his eyes, his need, his total isolation from the rest of the world. Others relied on his strengths, demanded his skills, yet they didn't show him affection, didn't thank him for his unceasing vigilance. She could sate his hunger where no other could. She knew it instinctively. There would be no other woman for him. He wanted her. He needed her. She could not walk away from him.

"Take off your sweater." He said it softly. There was no other path for him now. He had read the decision in her eyes, in the soft trembling of her mouth.

She stepped back, her blue eyes widening. Very slowly, almost reluctantly, she pulled off the sweater, as if somewhere deep inside she knew she was giving him more than her innocence. She knew she was giving him her life.

"The shirt."

Her tongue touched her lips, moistened the satin finish. The answering jolt in his body was savage, primitive. As she drew off the turtleneck, his hands went to the buttons of his pants. The fabric was stretched taut and confining, hurting him. He was careful to use the human form of disrobing, not wanting to frighten her any further.

Her bare skin gleamed in the firelight. The shadows brushed the contours of her body. Her rib cage was narrow, her waist small, emphasizing the generous fullness of her breasts. The man in him inhaled sharply, raged with need; the beast in him roared for release.

Mikhail dropped his shirt on the floor, no longer able to stand the feel of the material against his ultrasensitive skin. A sound started deep in his throat, animal, feral, a fierce savage claim. Outside the wind began to rise, and dark, ominous clouds roiled across the moon. He kicked aside human garments, exposing his body, chiseled muscle and burning need.

Her throat worked convulsively as she slid the lacy straps of her bra loose, let the material slide to the floor. Her breasts thrust invitingly, nipples hard and erotic.

He took the length of the room in a single fluid leap, uncaring of later explanations. Age-old instinct was taking over. He ripped the offensive jeans from her body with a single slash and tossed them aside.

Raven cried out, blue eyes going smoky with fear at his intensity. Mikhail calmed her with a touch, stroking his hands over her body, committing every line to memory. "Do not fear my hunger, little one," he whispered softly. "I would never hurt you. It would be an impossibility for me to do such a thing." Her bones were small, delicate, her skin hot silk. The mass of hair came loose with his marauding fingers, brushing the hard length of him, sending fiery arrows piercing his groin. His body tightened, raged. God, he needed her so much. So much.

His hand closed over the nape of her neck in an unbreakable grip, his thumb tipping back her head to expose her throat and lift her breasts to him. His hand moved slowly, tracing the swell of her breasts, resting for a moment on his mark on her neck so that it burned and throbbed, returned to cup velvet softness. He traced every line of her ribs, feeding his hunger, soothing her fears. Mikhail trailed his fingers over her flat stomach and the ridge of her hipbones, to rest in the triangle of silky curls at the juncture of her legs.

She had felt his touch before, but this was a thousand times more potent. His hand created desperate need, a sensation of drowning in a world of pure feeling. Mikhail snarled something low in his own language and took her to the floor in front of the fire. His body was so aggressive, trapping hers against the wood floor, that for a moment she had the impression of a wild animal forcing its mate into submission. Mikhail had not realized until that moment just how close to turning he really was. The emotions, the passion and lust, were swirling together until he feared for both of them.

The light from the flames cast a demonic shadow over him. He looked huge, invincible, a dangerous animal as he crouched over her. "Mikhail." She said his name softly, reaching out to ease the lines in his contorted features, needing him to go slower.

He caught and pinned both her wrists in one hand, stretched her arms above her head and held her there. "I need your trust, little one." His voice was a combination of hoarse demand and black velvet magic. "Give it to me. Please give it to me."

She was afraid, so vulnerable, stretched out like a pagan sacrifice, like an offering to a long-dead god. His eyes moved over her, hot, glowing, burning her skin everywhere his gaze touched. Raven lay quiet beneath his merciless strength, sensing his implacable resolve, aware of some terrible inner struggle within him. Her blue gaze drifted over the lines etched in his face; his mouth, so sensual, capable of such cruelty; his eyes, burning with such fierce need. Raven moved her body, testing his strength, knowing it would be impossible to stop him. She feared their joining because she was unsure of herself, of what to expect, but she believed in him.

The feel of her soft, exposed body writhing beneath his only inflamed him more. Mikhail groaned her name, his hand sliding up her thigh, finding her heated core. "Trust me,

Raven. I need your trust." His fingers sought velvet, probed, claimed, produced a rush of hot liquid. He bent his head to taste her skin, the texture, the scent of her.

She cried out softly when his hot mouth found her breast, when his fingers probed deeper in her center. Her body rippled with pleasure. He moved lower, tracing the earlier path of his hands with his tongue. With every stroke his body tightened, his heart opened, and the caged beast became stronger. A mate. His. He inhaled her scent deeply, drawing her into the very essence of his body; his tongue slid across her slowly, a long caress.

She moved again, still uncertain, but subsided when he raised his head and looked at her with stark possession burning in his eyes. Deliberately he pushed her knees apart, exposing her vulnerability to him. His eyes holding hers in warning, he lowered his head and drank.

Somewhere deep inside, Mikhail recognized that she was too innocent for this particular brand of wild lovemaking, but he was determined that she would know pleasure from their union, pleasure he gave her, not some hypnotic suggestion. He had waited too long for a mate, endless centuries of hunger and darkness and total desolation. He could not be gentle and considerate when his entire being was demanding that she belong to him totally for all time. He knew her trust was everything. Her faith in him would be her safeguard.

Her body convulsed; she cried out. Mikhail dragged himself over her, savoring the feel of her skin, her softness, how small she was. Every detail, no matter how small, was imprinted on his mind, became part of the savage pleasure in which he was indulging.

He released her wrists, bent to kiss her mouth, her eyes. "You are so beautiful, Raven. Belong to me. Belong only to me." He was pressing against her, his body still, corded muscle, unbelievably strong, trembling with his need for her.

"There could be no one else, Mikhail," she answered softly, her fingers soothing on his burning skin. She smoothed the lines of deep despair from his face, reveled in the feel of his hair in her palms. "I do trust you, only you."

Mikhail caught her small hips in his hands. "I will be as

gentle as I can, little one. Do not close your eyes; stay with me."

She was hot liquid, ready for him, but as he eased his hard length into her, he felt her protective barrier. She gasped, stiffened. "Mikhail." There was real alarm in her voice.

"Just for a moment, little one, and then I will take you to the heavens." He waited for her consent, waited and burned in agony.

Her blue eyes shimmered, looked up at him with wondrous trust. No one, his kind or hers, down through the centuries, had ever looked at him the way she was looking at him now. Mikhail surged forward, buried himself in her tight, fiery sheath. She moaned softly, and he bent his head to find her mouth, to erase the pain with his tongue. He held himself still, felt their combined heartbeats, the blood singing in their veins, her body adjusting to accommodate his.

He kissed her gently, tenderly, opening his mind as much as he dared, wanting to share himself with her. His love was wild, obsessive, protective, certainly not given easily, but given completely to her. He moved then, slowly and carefully at first, judging her reaction by her expressive face.

Mikhail's body's demands began to assert themselves. Fire licked along his skin, roared in his belly. His muscles contracted, flexed, little drops of perspiration beading on his skin. He dragged her closer, claiming her for his own, his body burying itself in hers over and over, intent on sating an insatiable hunger.

Raven's hands moved to his chest, fluttered there as if in protest. He growled a warning, bent his dark head to the spot over her left breast. Soft velvet skin, a fiery hot sheath. He burned, drove harder, seeking relief in the only way he could. They were one; she was his other half. She moved again, shifted away from him, a breathless, inarticulate cry voicing her fear of the rippling pleasure consuming her. He growled again, the animal protesting, sinking his strong teeth into the hollow of her shoulder, pinning her to the library floor.

The fire built into a conflagration, turbulent, out of control. Thunder cracked, shaking the house as bolt after bolt of lightning struck the ground. He roared, a cry to the heavens, as he took her with him beyond the earth. It went on and on, pain edging pleasure, needing more and more. His body's seed spilling triggered a ravenous, sensual hunger, the beast in him totally aroused.

Mikhail's mouth slid from her shoulder, traced a path along her throat to find the steady beat of her heart beneath her full, inviting breast. His tongue stroked her hardened nipple, returned to trace the swell of her breast, once, twice. His teeth sank deep and he fed, his body taking hers again, hot and fast, insatiable in its sexual frenzy. The taste of her was sweet and clean and very addicting. He craved more and more, his body building power and strength, driving harder and harder, burying himself deeply in her, pushing her toward another shattering release.

Raven struggled with herself, not recognizing Mikhail in the beast whose emotions were pure sensual hunger and ravenous appetite. Her body responded to him, seemingly endless in its need for his. His mouth burned and tortured her skin, fed an endless, spiraling climax. She could feel herself weakening, a curious euphoria stealing over her, languid and sexy. She cradled his head to her, giving herself up to his terrible hunger as his body convulsed over and over.

It was her acceptance that brought him back to sanity. This woman was not in a trance; she was offering herself freely because she felt his raging need, because she trusted him to stop before he hurt her, before he killed her.

Mikhail's tongue lapped across her breast, closed the wound. He lifted his head, his dark eyes still glowing with the beast, the taste of her in his mouth, on his lips. He swore softly, bitterly, his self-loathing total. She was under his protection. He had never hated himself or his kind more. She had freely given of herself; he had taken selfishly, the beast in him so strong he had given in to the ecstasy of uniting with one's life mate.

He gathered her limp body to him, cradled her in his arms. "You will not die, Raven." He was furious with himself. Had he done this on purpose? In some dark corner of his mind, had he wanted this to happen? He would try to find the answer to the question at a later date. Right now she needed blood, and she needed it fast.

"Stay with me, little one. I remained in this world because of you. You will have to be strong for both of us. Can you hear me, Raven? Do not leave me. I can make you happy. I know I can."

He slashed a burning wound across his chest. He pressed her mouth to the dark crimson stain pouring freely from the slash. *You will drink; obey me in this.* He knew better than to have her drink directly from his flesh, but he needed to hold her, needed the feel of her soft mouth against his skin taking his very essence, his life's blood, into her starving body.

Her obedience was reluctant, her body threatening to reject his life-giving fluid. She gagged, tried to turn her head away. Ruthlessly he clamped her to him. "You will live, little one." *Drink deeply.*

Her will was incredibly strong. Even his own people did not require so much effort to force obedience. Of course, his people trusted in him, wanted to obey. Although Raven was unaware of what he was forcing on her, some deep sense of self-preservation fought his commands. It didn't matter. His will would prevail. It always prevailed.

Mikhail carried her to his sleeping chamber. He crushed sweet, healing herbs around the bed, covered her small, still form. He placed her in a deep sleep. In an hour he would make her drink again. He stood for a moment staring down at her, feeling the need to cry. She looked so beautiful, a rare, precious treasure he had treated cruelly, when he should have guarded her against the beast in him. Carpathians were not human. Their lovemaking was intensely wild. Raven was young, inexperienced, a human. He had not been able to keep his newly acquired emotions under control in the heat of passion.

With trembling fingers he touched her face, a light caress, then bent to kiss her soft mouth. With an oath, he spun around and left the room. The safeguards were the strongest he knew, locking her in, everyone and everything out.

The storm raged outside, as furious and turbulent as his

soul. He took three running steps and launched himself into the sky, hurtling toward the village. The winds whirled and screamed around him. The house he sought was no more than a small shack. He stood at the door, his face a mask of torment.

Edgar Hummer opened the door silently, stood aside to allow him entrance. "Mikhail." The voice was gentle. Edgar Hummer was eighty-three years old. Most of his years had been spent in the service of the Lord. He considered himself deeply privileged to be counted among Mikhail Dubrinsky's few real friends.

Mikhail filled the small room with his presence, his power. He was agitated, deeply disturbed. He paced restlessly, the storm outside increasing in fury, in strength.

Edgar settled himself in his chair, lit his pipe, and waited. He had never seen Mikhail anything but completely calm, without emotion. This was a dangerous man, a man Edgar had never even glimpsed.

Mikhail slammed a fist against the rock fireplace, creating a fine network of lines across the stones. "I nearly killed a woman tonight." He confessed it harshly, his dark eyes wounded. "You told me God made us for a purpose, that we were created by him. I am more beast than man, Edgar, and I cannot continue to delude myself. I would seek eternal rest, but even that is denied to me. Assassins stalk my people. I have no right to leave them until I know they are protected. Now my woman is in danger, not only from me but from my enemies."

Edgar puffed at his pipe calmly. "You said 'my woman.' You love this woman?"

Mikhail waved a dismissing hand. "She is mine." It was a statement, a decree. How could he say love? It was an insipid word for what he felt. She was purity. Goodness. Compassion. Everything that he was not.

Edgar nodded. "You're in love with her."

Mikhail scowled darkly. "I need. I hunger. I want. That is my life." He said it in torment, as if he could make it true.

"Then why do you feel such pain, Mikhail? You wanted her; maybe you needed her. I presume you took her. You hungered; I presume you fed. Why should you feel pain?"

"You know it is wrong to take the blood of women for whom we feel other appetites."

"You have said you have not felt sexual need in centuries. That you cannot feel at all," Edgar reminded him softly.

"I feel for her," Mikhail confessed, his dark eyes alive with pain. "I want her every moment of the day. I need her. God, I have to have her. Not only her body, but also her blood. I am addicted to the taste. I crave her, all of her, yet it is forbidden."

"But you did it anyway?"

"I almost killed her."

"But you didn't. She still lives. She cannot be the first time you fed too deeply. Did the others cause you pain?"

Mikhail turned away. "You do not understand. It was the way it happened, what I did afterward. I feared it from the moment I first heard her voice."

"If it never happened before, why did you fear it?"

Mikhail hung his head, his fingers curling into fists. "Because I wanted her, I could not bear to give her up. I wanted her to know me, know the worst. See all of me. I wanted to bind her to me so she could never leave my side."

"She is human."

"Yes. She has abilities, a mental link to me. Compassion. She walks in beauty. I told myself I would not do this thing, that it was wrong, but I knew I would."

"And knowing you would do something you believe is wrong, you still did it. You must have had a good reason."

"Selfishness. Did you not hear me? I, I, I. Everything for myself. I found a reason to continue my existence and I took what did not belong to me and still, even now, talking to you, I know I will not give her up."

"Accept your nature, Mikhail. Accept yourself as you are."

Mikhail's laughter was bitter. "Everything is so clear to you. You say I am one of God's children. I have purpose; I should accept my nature. My nature is to take what I believe is mine, hold it, protect it. Chain it to my side if necessary. I cannot let her go. I cannot. She is like the wind, open and free. If I caged the wind, would it die?"

"Then don't cage it, Mikhail. Trust it to stay beside you."

"How can I protect the wind, Edgar?"

"You said *cannot,* Mikhail. You cannot let her go. Not would not, will not. You said cannot; there is a difference."

"For me. What of her? What choice am I giving her?"

"I have always believed in you, in your goodness and your strength. It is very possible that the young lady needs you as well. You have heard the legends and lies associated with your kind for so long, you are beginning to believe the nonsense. To a true vegetarian, a meat-eater can be repulsive. The tiger needs deer to survive. A plant needs water. We all need something. You take only what you need. Kneel, receive God's blessing, and go back to your woman. You will find a way to protect your wind."

Mikhail knelt obediently, his head bent, allowing the peace of the old man and his words to comfort him. Outside, the fury of the storm abated abruptly, as if it had spent its anger and now could rest in the aftermath.

"Thank you, Father," Mikhail whispered.

"Do what you must to protect your race, Mikhail. In the eyes of God, they are His children."

Chapter Four

Mikhail wrapped his arms around Raven's slender form, pulled her tight against his hard frame. His body curved protectively around hers. She was heavily asleep, her body light, her face pale. There were deep shadows beneath her eyes. He whispered to her softly. "I am sorry for this, little one, sorry I have placed you in this position. Beast that I am, I know I would do it again. You will not die; I cannot allow it."

He traced a line over the vein in his wrist, filled the glass beside his bed with the dark red liquid. *Hear me, Raven. You need this drink. Obey me at once.* He pressed the glass to her pale lips, tilted some of the contents down her throat. His blood was very healing, would ensure her life.

Raven choked, gagged, tried to turn her head away as she had before. *Obey me at once. You will drink all of it.* His command was stronger this time. She detested the contents, her body striving to reject it, but the force of his will won, as it always did.

Mikhail! He heard the forlorn cry in his head.

You must drink, Raven. Continue your trust in me.

She relaxed and sank back into the layers of sleep, obeying him reluctantly.

Mikhail had caught a brief glimpse of her confused thoughts, the swirl of alarmed emotions. She believed she was fighting a nightmare. Her color was better. Satisfied, he lay down beside her. She would remember the blood exchange as only a part of her nightmare. He propped himself up on one elbow, taking the time to study her face, her long thick lashes, her flawless skin and high cheekbones. It wasn't just her beauty, he knew that; it was what was inside her, the compassion and light that allowed her to accept his wild, untamed nature.

It was beyond his imagination that such a miracle could occur. Just when he knew he would walk into the sun without hesitation, he had been sent an angel. A slow smile softened his mouth. His angel refused to do anything he told her. She responded far better when he thought to ask. He had been too long accustomed to obedience from all those under his protection. He had to remember that she was mortal, raised in a different time, with different values. It was imprinted on male Carpathians before their births that it was their duty to protect the women and children. With few women and no female children born in the last centuries, it was essential to safeguard every woman they had.

Raven was mortal, not Carpathian. She did not belong in his world. When she left, she would take his color and emotions with her. She would take the very air he breathed. He closed his eyes against the thought. Where would he find the strength to let her walk away? He had so much to do before sunrise. He wanted to stay with her, hold her, persuade her not to leave him, tell her what was in his heart, tell her what she meant to him, tell her she couldn't leave him, that he might not survive. He wouldn't survive.

He sighed heavily, rose once more. He needed to replenish himself, get to work. Again he crushed healing herbs, then thrust her more deeply into sleep. He was meticulous about the safeguards in his home and added a command to the creatures in the forest. If anyone came near his lair, threatened her in any way, he would know immediately.

At Mikhail's call, Jacques and Byron met him in the trees above Noelle and Rand's home. Once the body had been discovered, it had been properly burned, as was their way. "You touched nothing else?" Mikhail asked.

"Only the body. All of their clothes and personal items were left as we found them," Byron assured him. "Rand did not go back in the house. You know they must have some sort of trap set for you. The body was left deliberately as bait."

"Oh, I am certain of that. They will use all the modern technology they can come up with—cameras, videos." Mikhail's dark features were brooding. "They believe all the legends. Stakes, garlic, beheading. They are so predictable and primitive." There was a snarl in his voice, contempt for the murderers. "They take so much trouble to learn about our kind before they condemn us to death."

Byron and Jacques exchanged an uneasy glance. Mikhail in this mood could be lethal. His hooded eyes, burning with fury, slid over them. "You stay and observe. If I get into trouble, you get out. Do not show yourselves." He hesitated. "If something goes wrong, I ask a favor."

Mikhail had slipped into old-word formality. Byron and Jacques would lay down their lives for him. It was a rare privilege to be asked a favor by the prince of their people. "My woman is sleeping deeply. She rests in my home. The safeguards are many and perilous. You must be careful and take great care to unravel them meticulously. She is to be healed, taught how to shield herself, and if she chooses, to stay in your protection. Through our bloodline, Jacques, you will inherit the mantle of leadership. I believe it should be offered to Gregori at this time, to give you the time you will need to educate yourself to lead. If Gregori should refuse to accept— and most likely he will—my mantle *must* pass to you, Jacques. You will find it not to your liking, as I suspect you are already aware. If such becomes the case, you will have to ensure Gregori's loyalty to you and to our people. You will do these things for me. Byron, you will aid Jacques as Gregori has aided me. Both of you will give your sworn allegiance to Gregori should he accept."

Both answered formally, speaking the words that bound

them to their vow. Byron cleared his throat. "Have you . . . that is, is she one of us?" He ventured the question with great caution. They all knew vampires had attempted the conversion of human women. They had even discussed the possibility that they try, because they were in such a desperate situation. The risk far outweighed the advantages. The women that had been converted had gone mad, had murdered small children, and had been impossible to save. Carpathians were born with their abilities and taught rigid discipline. The few who broke their laws were dealt with instantly and harshly. The race respected all forms of life. Because of their tremendous power, it had to be that way.

Mikhail shook his head. "I know that she is my true mate. The ritual was hard on her. I had no choice but to replenish her." His words were terse, surly, daring them to continue the inquisition, warning them that it would be at their peril. "I did not bind her to me. She is mortal and it would be wrong."

"We will do as you wish," Byron reiterated with an uneasy glance at Jacques, who looked more amused than worried.

Mikhail dissolved effortlessly, streamed down through the heavy branches of the fir tree. Once on the ground he took the form of a wolf. Mist couldn't scent, and he needed the unique capabilities of his furred brethren. He would find spoor and follow it. After all, first and foremost, above all else, he was a predator. His shrewd intellect only served to enhance his hunting abilities.

The wolf circled the clearing warily, nose close to the ground, examining each tree in the vicinity near the house. The wolf smelled death. It filled his nostrils with its sour, pungent odor. He began to crisscross the ground, covering every inch in his search pattern, identifying Rand's odor, Eric, and Jacques. He found where the assassins had approached the house. Four men. He lingered over each scent until they were imprinted deeply in his mind. He took his time unraveling the macabre, gruesome story.

The men had approached stealthily, even crawling from cover to cover at times. The wolf followed their path, straying here and there to cover ground, looking for hidden traps. At the door he paused, circled warily, backed off. Suddenly his hind legs dug into the dirt, and he launched himself straight through a window, shattering glass and landing a good six feet into the room. Deep within the wolf's body, Mikhail's laughter was grim and without humor. The four assassins had returned to the scene of their grisly murder to set up cameras to capture images of his kind. If the assassins had had guts, they would have stayed and waited for the body to be discovered. They had done their brutal business and had run like the cowards they were.

Bile rose in his throat. The wolf shook its head, growled low. Three of the scents were unknown to him, the fourth very familiar. *A traitor.* How much had he received to betray Noelle? The wolf leapt again, crashing through a second window. The camera would record a huge wolf, a blurred movement of shattered glass and mist and the wolf again. Only Mikhail, and a few other hunters, Jacques and Gregori, Aidan and Julian were capable of such speed in shape-shifting.

He began backtracking the assassins. One scent split off from the rest, wound into deep forest, came out near the timberline very close to Edgar Hummer's cabin and Dr. Westhemer's office. The wolf stayed in the trees, staring at the small house behind the office with cruel, red, unblinking eyes. Abruptly the wolf spun around, trotted back to where the assassins had split paths, and picked up the trail of the other three. It led straight to the inn where Raven was staying.

Mikhail joined Byron and Jacques in the treetop. "Three of them stay at the inn. I will recognize them when I am close to them. Tomorrow I will escort my woman back to collect her things. While I am there, I will be able to pick out their scents. There is no way of knowing if others are involved. Until we find out, we will have to be very careful. They have a video camera set up in the house; the trigger is on the door. Everyone needs to stay out of there." Mikhail was silent for a long moment.

"Does Celeste go to Dr. Westhemer?" he finally asked softly.

"I think she sees Hans Romanov's wife. She works with the doctor and delivers most of the babies," Jacques replied.

"And Eleanor?" Mikhail asked.

Jacques stirred uncomfortably. "I believe so."

"This woman assisted Noelle's birth?"

Byron cleared his throat. "Noelle delivered the child at home with Heidi Romanov helping her. Rand was there; I came at his call. After the midwife left, Noelle hemorrhaged. Rand had to give her blood. I stayed with Noelle while Rand hunted. And no, Mrs. Romanov did not see any of it. There was no one close; I would have known."

"It was Hans Romanov who led the others to Noelle. I do not know if his wife was involved, but someone informed the assassins that the Carpathians were reproducing." Mikhail gave the information in a soft monotone. His eyes burned, glowed, his body trembled with fury; his hands opened and closed, but his voice was perfectly controlled. "It is necessary to know if the woman is involved."

"She must be," Byron snapped. "Why are we waiting?"

"Because we are not the barbaric animals these evil ones have named us. We have to know if the midwife is a traitor. And it is not your duty to dispense justice, Byron. It is not an easy thing to live with, the taking of life." Mikhail had felt the weight of each of those lives down through the centuries, but as his power and responsibilities grew, so did the ease with which he killed. As his emotions had faded, it was only his strong will and sense of right and wrong that prevented him from losing his soul to the insidious whispers of the darkness struggling for supremacy.

"What do you want us to do?" Jacques asked.

"It is not safe for Eleanor or Celeste to be in their homes. No more trips to the midwife. Take Celeste to my home above the lake. Eric will be able to study the ancient arts, which he has neglected. It is an easy place to defend. Eleanor cannot travel as far."

"They can use my home," Byron offered. "They will be close if they need help." Eleanor was his sister, and he had always loved her dearly. Despite the fact that his emotions were long gone, he remembered what it felt like.

"It is risky. If your relationship is known and she is under suspicion, or if you were seen assisting Rand . . . " Mikhail shook his head, not liking the idea. "Maybe they should take over my home."

"No!" The simultaneous protests were instant and sharp.

"No, Mikhail, we cannot afford the risk to you." Jacques sounded alarmed.

"Our women come first before any of us, Jacques," Mikhail reminded him gently. "Without them, our race will die. We can have sex with humans, but we cannot procreate with them. Our women are our greatest treasures. Each of you must eventually mate and father children. But be certain the one you choose is your true life mate. All of you know the signs: colors, emotions, the burning for her. The bond is strong. When one dies, the other usually chooses to die also. It is death or vampire. We all know that."

"But Rand . . . " Byron trailed off.

"Rand became impatient with the waiting. Noelle was obsessed with him, but they were not true life mates. I think they ended up hating each other, trapped in the sickness of their relationship. He will survive her passing." Mikhail worked to keep the disgust from his voice. True life mates could not survive long without each other. That fact and the high mortality rate of their children, had taken a huge toll on their dwindling race. Mikhail was not certain his people would survive into the next century. No matter how hard he tried, he could not find the hope necessary to keep the males from turning vampire.

"Mikhail—" Jacques chose his words carefully—"only you and Gregori know the secrets of our race. You know Gregori will choose his solitary existence. Only you can teach the rest of us, lead us, help us to grow. If we are to survive, grow strong again, it cannot be done without you. Your blood is the life of our people."

"Why do you say this to me?" Mikhail snapped, not wanting to hear the truth.

Jacques and Byron exchanged a long, uneasy glance. "We have been concerned for some time about your continued withdrawal."

"My withdrawal was inevitable and is hardly your business."

"You have chosen to remain completely alone, even among those of us you call blood kin," Jacques went on.

"What is it you are trying to say?" Mikhail snapped impatiently. He had been away from Raven for too long. He needed to see her, hold her, touch her mind with his.

"We cannot afford to lose you. And if you do not wish to continue your life, you will begin to take greater risks, become careless," Jacques drawled slowly.

Mikhail's dark, brooding eyes slowly warmed, and a smile tugged at the hard corners of his mouth, softening the lines in his beautifully chiseled features. "You young devils. How have you managed to watch me without my knowledge?"

"The alpha pair fear for you also," Jacques admitted. "As I am of your blood and under your protection, they accept and speak with me. They watch over you when you take your solitary walks and when you run with the pack. They say there is no joy in you."

Mikhail laughed softly. "I need a good wolf hide for this winter. Whatever my feelings, Noelle was our sister, one of my people. I will not rest until her murderers are brought to justice."

Jacques cleared his throat, a cocky grin dispelling the ruthless set of his dark features. "I do not suppose this woman you are hiding has anything to do with your sudden desire to rise with the night."

The toe of Mikhail's boot nearly pushed Jacques from his perch in retaliation for his audacity.

Byron caught at the branch with a tight grip. "Eleanor and Vlad can stay with me. It will be double protection for her and her unborn child."

Mikhail nodded. Though he was uncomfortable with the decision, he could see that they would continue their protests if he insisted on taking the personal risk. "For a couple of days, until we find a safer solution."

"Take great care, Mikhail," Jacques warned.

"Sleep deep tomorrow," he responded. "They hunt us."

Byron paused, suddenly alarmed. "How can you go to ground if the human woman is with you?"

"I will not leave her." Mikhail's voice was implacable.

"The deeper we are in the earth, the harder to hear your call if you are in trouble," Jacques reminded quietly.

Mikhail sighed. "You two are as relentless as two old maiden aunts. I am certainly capable of protecting my lair." His body shimmered, bent, and became that of an owl. He spread giant wings and soared into the sky, making his way back to Raven.

He inhaled deeply, filling himself with the pure, clean scent of her, wiping out the ugliness of the night's discoveries. Her scent was in the library, mingled with his own. He took their combined scents deep within his lungs, bent to pick up their scattered clothing. He wanted to be inside her, to touch her, to fasten his mouth to hers, their blood one, to recite the ritual words so that they would be tied for eternity the way they were meant to be. The thought of her offering him that gift, accepting his offering, was so arousing that Mikhail had to stand still until the urgent demands of his body eased somewhat.

He took a long shower, washing away the wolf from his body, the dust and dirt, the odor of a traitor. All Carpathians took great care to acquire the habits of mortals. Food in the cupboards and clothes in the closets. Lamps throughout the house. All of them took showers when there was no real need, and most of them found they enjoyed it. He left his coffee-colored hair hanging free and went to Raven. For the first time he took pride in his body, the way he hardened, thrusting aggressively at the sight of her.

She was asleep, her hair spilling like a curtain of silk across the pillow. The blanket had slipped and her long hair was the only covering across her breast. The picture was erotic. She lay waiting for him, needing him even in her sleep. He gently murmured the command to release her from her trance-induced sleep.

She lay gleaming in the moonlight, her skin soft, the color of peaches. Mikhail slid his hand over the contour of her leg. The feel of her jolted his insides. He stroked her hips, traced her small, tucked-in waist. Raven stirred, shifted restlessly. Mikhail stretched out beside her, pulled her into the shelter of his arms, his chin resting on the top of her head.

He wanted her, any way he could get her, but he owed her some semblance of honesty. At least as much as he dared give her. She emerged from the layers of sleep slowly, burrowing against his hard strength as if for comfort from a bad dream. How could a human possibly understand the needs of a Carpathian male in the sexual frenzy of a true mating ritual? Down through the long ages, he had feared few things, yet more than anything he feared to see himself through her innocent eyes.

He knew by her breathing the moment she was fully awake, and by her sudden tension that she realized where she was and with whom. He had taken her innocence brutally, had nearly taken her life. How could she forgive such a thing?

Raven closed her eyes, trying desperately to separate fact from fiction, reality from fantasy. Her body was sore, hurting in places she didn't know she had. She felt different, more sensitive. Mikhail's body against hers was like hot marble, immovable and aggressive, unbearably sexy. She could hear the creaks and rustles of the house acutely, the sway of branches outside the window. She pushed at the wall of Mikhail's chest to try to put space between their bodies.

Mikhail tightened his arms, buried his face in her hair. "If you can touch my mind, Raven, you know what I feel for you." His voice was husky, vulnerable.

In spite of herself, Raven felt her heart turn over.

"I do not want you to leave me, little one. Have the courage to stay with me. Perhaps I am a monster. I do not know anymore, I truly do not, only that I need you to stay with me."

"You could have made me forget," she pointed out, more for herself than for him, more of a question than a statement. He had been wild, but she couldn't say he'd hurt her. Rather, he had taken her to the very stars.

"I thought about it," he admitted reluctantly, "but I do not want that between us. I am sorry I was not more careful with your innocence."

She heard the ache in his voice, felt an answering one in her body. "You know you made sure I felt pleasure." Ecstasy was more like it. A baptism by fire, an exchange of souls. He was wild, and he had swept her up with him in the firestorm. And she wanted him again, craved his touch, the driving strength of his body. But he was dangerous, really, really, dangerous. She knew that now. She knew he was different, that something lived in him, more animal than man.

"Mikhail." Raven pushed against the solid wall of his chest. She needed to breathe, to think without feeling the heat of his skin and the urgent demands of his body.

"Do not do this!" His voice was a sharp command. "Do not shut me out."

"You're talking about a commitment to something so beyond anything I can imagine . . . " Raven bit at her lip. "My home is so far from here."

"You have nothing but sorrow there, Raven." He refused the simple out for both of them. "You know you will not survive on your own, and although it is in your mind to deny them your talents when they come to you with another hideous crime, you know in your heart you will be unable to say no. It is not in you to allow a killer to go free when you might save his next victim." His hand bunched in the silken length of her hair, as if that could hold her to him. "They cannot care for you as I can."

"What of our differences? You have this attitude toward women, as if we're second-class citizens and not too bright. Unfortunately, you have the capability to force your will on anyone who might oppose you. And I would. All the time. I have to be myself, Mikhail."

He lifted the weight of her hair from the nape of her neck and brushed a kiss, feather light, on her exposed skin. "You know my attitude toward women reflects my need to protect them, not that I think them less than myself. Oppose me all you wish, little one. I love everything about you."

His thumb was stroking the soft swell of her breast, heating her blood, sending a shiver of excitement down her spine. Raven wanted him wild and untamed, wanted him needing her. He was so in control; it was a powerful aphrodisiac to realize she could make him lose that control.

Mikhail bent his head to the hardened nipple beckoning him. His tongue touched her gently; he kissed the velvet peak, drew her into the moist, hot cavern of his mouth. Raven made a sound, a soft sigh, closed her eyes. Her body was coming alive, every nerve ending screaming for his touch. She felt boneless, pliant, her body melting into the heat of his.

She didn't want this. Tears burned in her throat, behind her eyes. She didn't want this, but she needed it. "Don't hurt me, Mikhail." She whispered the words against the heavy muscles of his chest. It was a plea for their future. Raven knew he would never hurt her physically, but their life could be very stormy together.

He lifted his head, shifted so that his weight pinned her beneath him. His dark eyes moved possessively over her small, fragile face. His hand cupped her face, his thumb stroking across her chin, her full lower lip. "Do not fear me, Raven. Can you not feel the strength of my emotions, my tie to you? I would give my life for you." Because he wanted truth between them, he admitted the inevitable. "It will not be easy, but we will work things out between us." His hand stroked her flat stomach, moved lower to nestle in her midnight-black curls.

Her hand stilled his. "What happened to me?" She was confused. Had she fainted? Everything was so jumbled. She knew for certain Mikhail had forced her to drink some disgusting medicinal concoction. She had slept. Later there had been nightmares. She was used to nightmares, but this one had been horrible. She had been forced to a naked chest, her mouth clamped to a terrible wound. Blood, running like a river, forced down her throat. She choked, gagged, fought, but somehow, in that nightmare world, she could not pull away. She had tried to call for Mikhail. And then she had looked up and there he was, looking down at her with his dark, mysterious eyes, his hand forcing her head against the wound in his chest. Was it because she was in the heart of Dracula country and Mikhail reminded her of a dark, mysterious prince?

Raven couldn't help herself; she smoothed gentle fingertips over his unblemished chest. Something had happened to her and she knew she was changed for all time, that she was somehow a part of Mikhail and he was a part of her.

Mikhail's knee gently pushed her legs apart. He shifted once more above her, blocking out everything with his broad shoulders. He took her breath away with his size and power, his strength and beauty. Very gently, the way he should have the first time, he eased into her.

Raven gasped. She would never get over the way he filled her, stretched her, the way he could turn her body to liquid fire. If he had been wild the first time, he was tender and gentle this time. Every deep stroke built a heavy craving for more, an urgency that had her hands caressing the chiseled muscles of his back, her mouth moving over his neck, his chest.

Mikhail worked at control, called on his extraordinary discipline. Her mouth was driving him mad, the feel of her fingers on his skin. Raven was so tight; hot velvet gripped him, fed the fires. He could feel the beast in him fighting to break free, his hunger raging, his body moving harder, faster, burying itself in her, merging their bodies, their hearts. He opened his mind, sought hers. The need in her drove him on. Her fingernails dug into his back as wave after wave rippled through her body. Mikhail gave in to the fire before the beast could break free. He surged into her, felt her body, tight and hot, grip his. He allowed himself a low growl of total satisfaction.

Mikhail lay over her slender body, still joined to her, momentarily sated. He felt her tears on his chest. Lifting his head slowly, he bent to taste her tears. "Why do you cry?"

"How will I ever find the strength to leave you?" she murmured softly, painfully.

His eyes darkened dangerously. Mikhail rolled over, felt how uncomfortable she was with her nudity, and dragged a blanket around her. Raven sat up, pushed the heavy fall of hair from her face with that curiously innocent, sexy gesture of hers that he loved. Her blue eyes were frankly wary.

"You will not leave me, Raven." His voice was much harsher than he intended. With great effort, he forced himself to gentle it. She was young and vulnerable; he had to remember that above all else. She had no idea what the cost of separation would be to either of them. "How can you share what we have and just walk away?"

"You know why. Don't pretend you don't. I feel things, sense them. This is all too bizarre for me. I don't know the laws in this country, but when someone is murdered, the law and the press are notified. That's just one thing, Mikhail; we won't even get into the things you're capable of doing— nearly strangling Jacob, for heaven's sake. You're way out of my league and we both know it." She pulled the blanket closer around her shoulders. "I want you, I can't even think about being without you, but I'm not certain what is going on here."

His hand stroked down the length of her hair in a disturbing caress, his fingers moving through silken strands to wisp down her back to the base of her bare spine. His touch melted her insides, curled her toes. Raven closed her eyes, laid her head on her knees. She was no match for him in any way.

Mikhail shifted his hand to her nape, his fingers soothing. "We are already committed to one another. Can you not feel it, Raven?" He whispered the words, a husky blend of warmth and sensuality. He knew he was fighting her instincts, her innate sense of self-preservation. He chose his words carefully. "You know who I am, what is inside me. If distance separated us, you would still need to feel my hands on you, my mouth on yours, my body in yours, a part of yours."

Just his words alone warmed her blood, fed the ache deep inside. Raven covered her face, ashamed that she had such need of what amounted to a total stranger. "I'm going home, Mikhail. I'm so wrapped up in you, I'm doing things I never thought possible." It wasn't only physical: She wished it were. She didn't want to feel his loneliness, his greatness, his incredible will and drive to keep those he led safe from harm. But she did feel it. She could feel his heart, his soul, his mind. She had talked to him without speaking aloud, she had shared his mind. She knew he was in her.

His arm curved around her shoulders, drew her huddled form beside him. To comfort or to restrain? Raven swallowed the burning tears. There were sounds pouring into her head, rustlings, creaks. She put her hands over her ears to shut them out. "What's happening to me, Mikhail? What did we do that's changed me like this?"

"You are my life, my mate, the half of myself that was missing." His hand returned to stroking her hair with infinite gentleness. "My people mate for life. I am a true Carpathian; I am of the earth. We have special gifts."

She turned her head, regarding him with enormous blue eyes. "Telepathic ability. Yours is very strong, much stronger than mine. And so developed. It amazes me, the things you can do."

"The price for these gifts is high, little one. We are cursed with the need for one mate, a sharing of souls. Once this occurs—and the ritual can be brutal to an innocent woman—we cannot live apart from our mates. Our children are few; we lose many in the first year and most of those born are male. We are both blessed and cursed with longevity. For those of us who are happy, a long life is a blessing; for someone alone and tormented, it is a curse. It is one long eternity of darkness, a barren, stark existence."

Mikhail cupped her chin in the palm of his hand, tipped her chin up so that she could not escape his dark, hungry eyes. He took a deep breath, let it out. "We did not have sex, little one; we did not make love. Ours was as close to a true Carpathian mating ritual as is possible without your being of our blood. If you leave me . . . " His voice trailed off, and he shook his head. He needed to bind her to him irrevocably. The words were in his mind, his heart. The beast raged to say them. She would never escape, yet he could not do that to her, say the words to a mortal. He had no idea what would happen to her.

The spot over her left breast ached, throbbed, even burned. Raven looked down, saw the dark evidence of his brand, touched it with her fingertips. She remembered the feel of his teeth pinning her to the floor, his strength, the warning growl rumbling in his throat like that of an animal. He had taken her body as if it belonged to him, wildly, a little brutally, yet something in her had responded to the ferocious hunger and need in him. At the same time, he had been tender, insuring her pleasure before his own, so careful of her size and the frailty of her small bones. The mixture of his tenderness and wild nature was so impossible to resist, Raven knew no other man could ever touch her as he had. There would only be Mikhail for her.

"Are you telling me you're of another race, Mikhail?" She was striving to put it all together.

"We believe that we are of another species. We are different. We hide it well—we have to—but we can hear things humans cannot. We speak to the animals, share our minds as well as our bodies and hearts. Understand, this information in the wrong hands would doom us all. My life is literally in your hands." *In more ways than one.*

She caught the echo of his thought before he could censor it. "Would you have stopped if I had panicked?"

He closed his eyes, ashamed. "I would like to lie to you, but I will not. I would have soothed you, made certain you could accept me."

"Commanded me?"

"No!" He denied that vehemently. He would not have gone that far. He was certain of that. He believed absolutely that he could have persuaded her to accept him.

"These gifts." She rubbed her chin across her knees. "You are stronger physically than any human I've ever met. And that leap in the library—you reminded me of a great jungle cat—is that part of your heritage, too?"

"Yes." His hand tangled in her hair again, brought a fistful up to bury his face in it, breathing her in. His scent lingered on her, would remain in her. A trace of satisfaction touched his fathomless eyes.

"You bit me." She touched first her neck, then her breast. A sweet, hot ache filled her at the memory of him wild in her arms, his body frenzied with need, his mind a turbulent, red desire, his mouth working eagerly, hungrily at her.

What was wrong with her that she wanted more? She had heard of women so enthralled by sex that they were virtual slaves. Was that what was happening to her? She flung up a hand as if to ward him off. "Mikhail, this is so fast. I can't fall in love in a couple of days, decide my life in a few minutes. I don't know you; I'm even a little bit afraid of you, of what you are, the power you wield."

"You said you trusted me."

"I do. That's what makes me so crazy. Can't you see that? We're so different. You do crazy things, yet I want to be with you, hear your laughter, argue with you. I want to see your smile, the way your eyes light up, the hunger and need in you when you look at me. I want to take that coldness from your eyes, the distant, faraway stare when your mouth hardens and you look cruel and ruthless. Yes, I trust you, but I have no reason to."

"You are very pale. How do you feel?" He wanted to tell her it was too late, that they had gone too far, but he knew it would only build her resistance and alarm her needlessly.

"Funny, sort of sick to my stomach, like I should eat something, but the thought of food makes me ill. You gave me one of your herb concoctions, didn't you?"

"Drink water and juices for a few days, a little fruit. No meat."

"I'm a vegetarian." She looked around. "Where are my clothes?"

He grinned unexpectedly, a perfect male smirk. "I got carried away and ripped your jeans. Just stay with me tonight and I will get you new clothes tomorrow."

"It's nearly morning now," she pointed out, unwilling to lie down with him again. She couldn't lie beside him and not burn for him. "Besides, I want a shower." Before he had a chance to protest, she slid off the bed, wrapped safely in the old-fashioned quilt.

Mikhail kept his smile to himself. Let her feel safe; it cost him nothing. No way was she leaving his house, not with the assassins residing at her inn. To keep his mind off the image of her naked beneath the spray of water, he concentrated on the details of her emotions before he had taken her by force from the inn's dining room.

What had caused her frantic distress that night? She had been literally sick, her head pounding. She thought her reaction was caused by his rage, but he had been enraged at her distress. He had felt it before that oaf of a human had laid an unholy hand on her.

Mikhail touched her mind because he had to. He found what he expected, tears and confusion. Her body was changing, had changed with his blood running in her veins. Legend required a human and Carpathian to exchange blood three times for conversion. The blood he had given her from the cup would not count, because she had not taken it directly from his body. He had no intention of converting her, of taking a chance that she might become a deranged vampiress. As it was, he had gone dangerously over the line. He would once more. It would have to last an eternity.

Raven had heard his words, all of which held truth, but he knew she had no idea of the reality. She would hear the whispers from every room in the inn, know when a bee entered the downstairs dining room. The sun would bother her eyes and she would burn easily. Animals would reveal their secrets to her.

Most foods would make her sick. But most of all, she would need him close, need to touch his mind, feel his body, burn with him. She already felt it, and she was fighting it in the only way she knew how—fighting to free herself from him, fighting to understand what was happening to her.

Raven leaned her body against the glass shower stall. She knew she couldn't hide in the bathroom like a runaway child, but he was so potent, so compelling. She wanted to ease those lines of strain around his mouth, wanted to tease him, argue with him, hear his laughter. She was curiously weak still, a bit dizzy.

"Come on, little one." Mikhail's voice wrapped her in a black-velvet caress. His arm reached into the glass shower, turned off the water. He shackled her wrist and pulled her from the safety of the large stall, enveloped her slender body in a towel.

Raven wrung out her long hair, a blush stealing over her entire body. Mikhail was so comfortable, uncaring of his nudity. There was something untamed and magnificent about his raw strength, the casual way he accepted it. He rubbed her body with a large bath towel, buffing her skin until she was warm and rosy. The towel brushed her sensitive nipples, lingered along her rounded bottom, delved in the crease of her hip.

Despite her resolve, her body came alive under his ministrations. Mikhail cupped her face, bent to brush his mouth against hers, feather light, enticing. "Come back to bed," he whispered, leading her there.

"Mikhail," she protested softly, breathlessly.

He tugged on her wrist, unbalanced her so that her body came up against him. Her body melted into his, soft breasts pushing against heavy muscle, the evidence of his desire pressing against her stomach. His thighs were two strong columns welded with hers. "I could love you all night, Raven," he murmured enticingly against her throat. His hands moved over her body, leaving fire in their wake. "I want to love you all night."

"Isn't that the point? It's dawn." Her hands had a mind of their own, finding every defined muscle with her fingertips.

"Then I will spend the day making love to you." He whispered the words against her mouth, bent closer to nibble at the corners of her lower lip. "I need you with me. You chase away the shadows and lighten the terrible load that threatens to drown me."

She skimmed her fingertips across the hard edges of his mouth. "Is this possession, or is it love?" She dipped her head to press her mouth to the hollow of his sternum, to slide her tongue over the ultrasensitive skin above his heart. There was no mark, no scar, but the sweep of her tongue followed the exact line of his earlier wound, where he had forced her to accept his life's blood. She was merged with him, reading his mind, his erotic fantasies, wanting to bring them to life.

His gut clenched hotly, his body responding with fierce aggression. Raven smiled at the feel of his hard length burning against her skin. She had no inhibitions when she lay with him, only a fierce desire to burn with him. "Answer me, Mikhail, the truth." Her fingertips brushed his velvet tip, fingers curled around the heavy thickness of him sending hunger raging through his body. She was playing with fire, but he didn't have the strength to stop her; he didn't want to stop her.

His hands curled in her damp hair, two tight fists. "Both," he managed to gasp.

He closed his eyes when her mouth moved over his flat

belly, leaving behind a trail of fire. Wherever she touched him, her mouth, hot and moist, followed. He dragged her closer, urging her onto him. Her mouth was tight and hot and driving him mad. A low, ominous growl escaped, the beast shuddering with pleasure, needing primitive satisfaction.

Her fingernails raked the hard column of his thighs, light, erotic, sending fire leaping, coiling in his gut. His mind blurred, merged more deeply with hers, a red haze of lust and need, love and hunger. He craved her touch, her hands, her silky mouth turning him into a living, breathing flame.

Mikhail dragged her up, his hands like bands, although he made every effort to be conscious of his strength. His mouth took hers, mating, dancing, so much hunger beating in him she caught it, pressing closer, her body sliding against his, rubbing, heating.

"Say you want me." His mouth moved over her throat, closed over her aching breast. Every strong pull sent an answering rush of liquid heat.

"You know I do." She pressed him to her, wound a leg around his.

She could barely breathe with her need, clawing at him to get closer, to crawl inside the shelter of his body, his mind, to feel his body in hers, taking possession as he was meant to, to feel his mouth at her breast, dragging her further into his world.

"All of it," he said hoarsely, his fingers probing the nest of tiny curls, stroking, caressing. "Mate with me my way."

She moved in a kind of anguish against his hand. "Yes, Mikhail." She was frantic for release, frantic to relieve him. She was consumed with the same red haze, not separating love from lust or hunger from need. She was on fire, hurting, aching, body and mind, even her soul in torment, not knowing where his wild, uninhibited emotions left off and hers began.

Mikhail lifted her easily with his enormous strength, slid her slowly, erotically down his clenching belly until she was pressed against his raging velvet tip. Her heat seared him, beckoned. Raven's arms slid around his neck, her legs around his hips, opening for him. Slowly he lowered her body over his, impaled her on the thick length of fire so that she surrounded him with such a moist, tight sheath he shuddered, somewhere beyond mere pleasure, a kind of erotic heaven and hell.

Her nails dug into his shoulders. "Stop! You're too big this way." Alarm was spreading across her face.

"Relax, little one. We belong together; our bodies were made for one another." He slid in farther, began to move in a long, slow rhythm, his hands caressing, soothing.

He shifted his shoulders so that he could see her face, his body claiming hers with deep, sure, possessive strokes. Without conscious thought, the words poured out of his soul. "I claim you as my life mate. I belong to you. I offer my life for you. I give to you my protection, my allegiance, my heart, my soul, and my body. I take into my keeping the same that is yours. Your life, happiness, and welfare will be cherished and placed above my own for all time. You are my life mate, bound to me for all eternity and always in my care." With those words, a male Carpathian bound his true life mate to him for all eternity. Once said, she could never escape him. Mikhail had no intention of binding her to him, but every instinct in him, everything he was, forced the words out of his soul so that their hearts were one as they were meant to be. Their souls were finally united, their minds one.

Raven allowed his words and the hot strength of his possession to calm her. Her body seemed to melt around his. He took them higher, bending his head to lap at her nipple, his hands cupping her small bottom possessively. She threw back her head, her hair flowing around them, over them, brushing their bare skin so that their flesh burned. She felt as if she truly was where she belonged. She felt wild and free. She felt a part of him, his other half. There could be no other than this man who was so hungry for her. Who needed her so desperately, who knew her own kind of lonely existence.

He moved harder, deeper, turning so that he could lay her half across the end of the bed, so he could drive them closer and closer to the edge. He felt her body ripple, tighten, drag at his, once, twice. She cried out with pleasure, felt as if her body was dissolving into his. There was so much pleasure, wave after wave until Raven thought she couldn't possibly stand any more.

He bent his dark head to her slowly, giving her every opportunity to stop him. His body continued to bury itself in hers, his dark eyes holding her blue ones captive. Mesmerizing, pleading, so in need. Raven arched her body toward him, thrusting her breasts invitingly, offering to assuage his burning hunger.

Mikhail's soft growl of satisfaction rumbled in his throat, sent a thrill of excitement leaping in her blood. His body was aggressive now, his hands lifting her small hips for better access. She felt the brush of his lips so gently over her breast, her heart. His tongue slid over her skin, over his mark on her, erotic and warm. He surged into her powerfully, filling her, stretching her. He sank his teeth into soft flesh.

Raven cried out as white-hot heat seared her breast. She cradled Mikhail's head to her, feeling the whirlwind of emotions storming through him as the fire in him built and built, higher and higher, until she thought they would both go up in flames. His mouth moved over her skin, devouring her as he took her, consuming them both. The feeling was like nothing she had ever experienced, erotic and burning.

She could hear herself screaming his name in joy, in wild abandon, her nails digging into his back. She had a primitive desire to find the heavy muscle over his breast with her mouth. They were exploding together, disintegrating, flying to the sun. Mikhail lifted his head to give a throaty growl, dipped his head to feed more.

He was careful this time, just taking enough for an exchange. His body was still locked with hers. He gave one last flick of his tongue to close the wound, heal even the smallest of pinpricks. Mikhail studied her face. Pale. Drowsy. He uttered his command, his body hard and eager at the idea of what he was doing.

Her body was still rippling with life, accepting his long, possessive strokes. He made the slash across his chest, pressed her soft mouth to his burning skin. It was ecstasy, his body convulsing almost painfully. The beast in him threw back its head and roared with pleasure, contentment, the terrible hunger temporarily assuaged.

He cupped the back of her head in his large hand, held her to him, stroking her throat, savoring the feel of her feeding. It was pure eroticism, pure beauty. He spoke softly, reluctantly, when he was certain she had taken enough for an exchange, enough to replenish what he had taken. He caressed the length of her hair, allowed her to surface.

She blinked up at him, a frown creasing her forehead. "You did it again." She rested her head tiredly against the quilt. "Either that, or every time we get carried away I'm going to faint." She tasted a faint coppery taste in her mouth.

Before she had a chance to identify what it was, Mikhail kissed her, his tongue licking along her teeth, the roof of her mouth, probing, exploring, dancing with hers. Very slowly he eased from her body, his hands caressing her soft skin.

"I can't move," Raven admitted with a smile.

"We will catch a nap and face the world later," he suggested, his voice pure black magic. Very gently he cradled her in his arms, placed her properly in the bed, and pulled up the blanket. Her long lashes caught and held his fascinated gaze. His fingertip stroked her throat, traced the valley between her breasts. She was still so sensitive, he could feel her shiver beneath his touch, and it flooded him with warmth.

"If I really wanted you to love me, I should have presented more of a challenge." She burrowed deeper into a pillow. "My hair is a mess."

Mikhail sat on the edge of the bed, took the mass of silk in his hands, and gently began to weave the thick strands into a long, loose braid. "If you presented much more of a challenge, little one, my heart would never be able to take it." He sounded amused.

Her fingertips brushed the bare skin of his thigh, but she didn't lift her long lashes. Mikhail sat for a long time on the edge of the bed, just watching her drift off to sleep. She was so small, a human, yet she had changed his life overnight. And he had taken hers. Taken her life. He had not wanted to say the ritual words; he had been as much under compulsion as his own prey when they exposed their throats to him.

She might say he was a stranger, but they had been in one another's minds, shared the same body and offered their lives for each other. The exchange of blood as they made love was the ultimate in confirmation of their commitment. Each literally offered his life, vowed to give up his own life to safeguard the other. It was a beautiful, erotic ritual. It was a oneness of mind, heart, soul, body . . . blood.

Carpathians safeguarded their sleeping quarters from one another. They were vulnerable in sleep and while they were in the throes of sexual passion. The decision to take a life mate was not a conscious act; it was instinct, a hunger and need. They knew. They recognized their other half. Mikhail recognized Raven as his. He had fought the binding ritual, yet his animal instinct had overcome his civilized trappings. He had dragged her halfway into his world and he was totally responsible for the consequences.

Light was beginning to filter in from upstairs. Mikhail completed the task of making his home safe against intruders. The next night would be long. Work had piled up, and he needed to go hunting. But he had this moment for peace and contentment.

Mikhail slid into bed beside Raven, dragged her hard against his body, wanting to feel every inch of her. She murmured his name sleepily, snuggled into him with the innocent trust of a small child. Instantly his heart somersaulted, and a curious warmth and contentment spread through him. Peace. He touched her because he could. His hand cupped the fullness of her breast, his mouth brushed her nipple, feather light, just once. After pressing a kiss to the vulnerable line of her throat, he sent the command for deep sleep, regulating his breathing to join her.

Chapter Five

Raven surfaced through layer after layer of sleep, felt as though she were wading through quicksand. *You did it again!* It was sheer outrage that brought her awake, had her sitting up quickly. She was alone in the bedroom. His bedroom.

His mocking, masculine laughter echoed in her mind. Raven threw the pillow against the wall, wishing she could hit him with it. She had lost another day. What was she becoming? His sex slave?

The idea has possibilities, he mused.

Get out of my head! she snapped indignantly, then stretched languidly, a lazy, feline quality to her movements. Her body was deliciously sore, aching everywhere, an intimate reminder of his possession. She couldn't be angry with him; he made her laugh at his outrageous behavior. How could she mind when her body felt the way it did?

When she rose to take her shower, she saw clothes laid out for her at the end of the bed. Mikhail had already been out shopping. Raven found herself smiling, absurdly pleased that he had remembered. She fingered the skirt, the soft, full midnight-blue material, the matching blouse. *You didn't buy me jeans*. She couldn't resist teasing him.

Women do not belong in men's clothing. He was unruffled.

Raven stepped into the shower, released the thick braid so she could shampoo her hair. *You don't like the way I look in a pair of jeans?*

His laughter held deep, genuine amusement. *That is a loaded question.*

Where are you? Without realizing it, Raven was communicating a sultry invitation. She touched his mark over her breast with light fingertips. The contact caused her blood to heat, the mark to throb.

Your body needs rest, little one. I have not exactly been the gentlest of lovers, have I? There was self-mockery in his tone, guilt in his mind.

She laughed softly. *I don't have very much to judge you by, do I? There hasn't been a parade of men in my life.* Her soft laughter wrapped him in loving arms. *If you like, I could always find someone to compare you with.* She offered it sweetly.

She felt the brush of strong fingers on her throat, curling around the fragile column. How did he do that? *I'm so scared, macho man. Someone needs to drag you kicking and screaming into this century.*

The fingers brushed her face, caressed her lower lip. *You love me the way I am.*

Love. The smile faded from her soft mouth at the word. She didn't want to love him. He already had far too much power over her. *You can't hold me here, Mikhail.* Obsession might be the right word, not love.

Little rabbit. There are no chains on the doors, and the telephone is in working order. And you do love me; you cannot help yourself. I am perfect for you. Hurry up; you need to eat.

You're a pain in the neck. As she brushed out her hair, she realized how much easier their telepathic communication was. Practice? Her temples didn't ache from the effort. She tilted her head for a moment, listened to the sounds of the house. Mikhail was pouring liquid into a glass; she could hear it clearly.

Raven dressed slowly, thoughtfully. Her telepathic abilities were increasing; her senses were more acute. Was it simply Mikhail's company, or was it something in the herb concoctions he was always pouring down her throat? There was so much she wanted to learn from him. He had great psychic talent.

The skirt swung around her ankles with a sexy little swish, and the blouse clung to her curves. She had to admit that the outfit made her feel feminine, as did his choice of sheer lace panties and matching bra.

Are you going to sit there and moon about me all night?

Night! It had better not be night again, Mikhail. I'm turning into some kind of a mole. And don't flatter yourself; I was not mooning over you. It took great effort to lie blatantly; she was proud of herself.

And you think I believe your nonsense? He was laughing again, and Raven found she couldn't help giving in to her own sense of humor.

She found her way though the house, marveling at the artwork, the sculpture. Outside, the sun had already disappeared behind the mountains. Raven gave a little resigned sigh. Mikhail had set a small antique, beautifully carved table on the porch outside the kitchen. He turned his head as she approached, a smile warming his eyes, chasing away the shadows. Heat pooled in her abdomen, ran liquid through her body.

Mikhail bent his dark head to hers, his mouth brushing hers tenderly. "Good evening." He touched her hair, skimmed his fingers down the side of her face in a long caress. She allowed him to seat her at the table, marveling at his gallant, old-world courtesy. He placed a glass of juice in front of her. "Before I go to work, I thought we could collect your things from the inn." His long fingers selected a blueberry muffin and transferred it to the antique plate. It was exquisite, but Raven was so shocked at his words, she could only stare at him for a moment, her blue eyes enormous.

"What do you mean, collect my things?" It hadn't occurred to her that he might expect them to live in the same house together. His house.

His smile was slow, wicked, sexy. "I could keep providing you with new things."

Raven's hand trembled. She put it in her lap, out of sight. "I'm not moving in with you, Mikhail." The idea was scary. She was a very private person, needing large amounts of time alone. He was the most overwhelming being she had ever encountered. How would she ever be able to sort things out with him so near all the time?

His eyebrow shot up. "No? You accepted our ways; we went through the required ritual. In my eyes, the eyes of my people, you are my life mate, my woman. My wife. Is it the way of the American women to live apart from their husbands?"

There was that infuriating trace of mocking male amusement in his voice, the note that always made her want to throw something at him. She had an idea he was laughing at her secretly, amused by her caution.

"We aren't married," she said decisively. It was difficult to ignore the way her heart leapt with joy at his words.

Tendrils of fog were drifting into the forest, winding around thick tree trunks, spreading out to hover a few feet from the ground. The effect was eerie, but beautiful.

"In the eyes of my people, in the eyes of God, we are." There was an implacable resolve, a my-word-is-law in his voice that set her teeth on edge.

"What about in my eyes, Mikhail? My beliefs? Do they count for nothing?" she demanded belligerently.

"I see the answer in your eyes, feel it in your body. You struggle needlessly, Raven. You know you are mine. . . . "

She stood up quickly, pushed the chair out of her way. "I don't belong to anyone, least of all you, Mikhail! You can't just decree what will be in my life and expect me to fall in with your plans." Raven ran down the three steps to the path winding into the forest. "I need some air. You're driving me crazy."

Mikhail laughed softly. "Are you so afraid of yourself?"

"Go to the devil, Mikhail!" Raven set her foot on the path and began walking quickly before he could charm his way around her. And he could; she knew it. It was his eyes, the shape of his mouth, the little grin he gave her when he was deliberately provoking her.

The fog was very dense, the air wet and heavy with it. With her acute sense of hearing, she could hear every rustling in the bushes, every swaying of the branches, the beat of wings in the sky.

Mikhail paced himself behind her. "Perhaps I am the devil, little one. I am certain that has crossed your mind."

She glared at him over her shoulder. "Stop following me!"

"Am I not a gentleman, obligated to see his lady home?"

"Stop laughing! If you laugh at me one more time I swear I won't be responsible for what I do." Raven became aware of the slinking figures then, the burning eyes following her. Her heart nearly stopped, then began to pound. "Fine!" She whirled around and glared at him. "This is great! Just great, Mikhail. Call in the wolves to eat me alive. I find the idea so *you*. So logical."

He bared his white gleaming teeth at her like a hungry predator and laughed softly, teasingly. "It is not the wolves that would find you delicious."

Raven picked up a broken branch and flung it at him. "Stop laughing, you hyena! This is not funny. Your arrogance is enough to make me want to throw up." It took every ounce of self-control she had not to laugh. The beast; he was far too charming for his own good.

"Your American colloquialisms are very colorful, little one."

She threw another branch, then followed it up with a small rock. "Someone needs to teach you the lesson of a lifetime."

She looked like a beautiful little spitfire, all sparks and flame. Mikhail drew in his breath slowly, carefully. She was his, all fire and fury, all independence and courage, all heated passion. She melted his heart with it, entered his soul with her soft laughter. He felt it in her mind, although she was being extremely careful not to allow him to see it. "And you think you are the one to do this thing?" he teased.

Another rock came flying at his chest. He caught it easily. "Do you think I'm afraid of your wolves?" she demanded. "The only big bad wolf around here is you. Call all your wolves. Go ahead!" She pretended to glare into the secret, dark interior of the forest. "Come and get me. What did he tell you?"

Mikhail pried her fingers loose from the branch she held like a club, allowed it to fall. He curved an arm around her slender waist, brought her small, soft body up against his much larger, rock-hard frame. "I told them you tasted like warm honey." He whispered the words with his black velvet sorcerer's voice. Turning her in his arms, he cupped her small, beautiful face in his hands. "Where is all that marvelous respect a man as powerful as myself deserves?"

His thumb stroked across her full lower lip, a sensuous caress. Raven closed her eyes against the inevitable. She wanted to cry. Her feelings for him were so strong, her throat was aching and burning. Mikhail brushed her eyes with his lips, tasted a tear, sought refuge in the sweetness of her mouth. "Why would you cry for me, Raven?" He murmured the words against her throat. "Is it that you still want to run from me? Am I really so terrible? I would never allow any living creature, man or beast, to harm you, not if it was in my power to prevent it. I thought our hearts and minds were in the same place. Am I wrong? Is it that you no longer want me?"

His words tore at her heart. "It isn't that, Mikhail, never that," she denied quickly, afraid she had hurt him. "You defeat my every good intention." She caressed his face with her fingertips, reverence in her touch. "You are the most fascinating man I've ever known. I feel as if I belong here with you, as though I know you completely. It's impossible in the short time we've been together. I know if I could put some distance between us, I could think more clearly. Everything happened so fast. It's as though I'm obsessed with you. I don't want to make a mistake that will cause both of us pain."

His hand cupped her cheek. "It would cause me great pain if you were to desert me, to leave me alone again after I have found you."

"I just want some time, Mikhail, to think things through. It's frightening, the way I am about you. I think about you every minute; I want to touch you, just to know I can, to feel you beneath my fingers. It's as if you crawled into my head and my heart, even my body, and I can't get you out." She said it like a confession, her head bent, ashamed.

Mikhail took her hand, tugged at her to get her walking with him. "This is the way of my people, the way we feel about a mate. It is not always comfortable, is it? We are passionate by nature, highly sexual, and very possessive. The things that you are feeling, I feel, too."

Her fingers tightened around his, and she sent him a small, tentative smile. "Am I right in thinking you're deliberately keeping me here?"

Mikhail shrugged his broad shoulders. "Yes and no. I do not want to force you against your will, but as to my wanting you to stay, I believe us to be life mates, bound more irrevocably than by your marriage ceremony. I would be extremely uncomfortable without you here, both in body and mind. I do not know how I would react to your contact with another man and, quite frankly, I fear it."

"We really are from two different worlds, aren't we?" she asked sadly.

He brought her hand to the warmth of his mouth. "There is such a thing as compromise, little one. We can move between the two worlds or create our own."

Her blue eyes slid over him, a faint smile touching her mouth. "That sounds so good, Mikhail, so twentieth century, but somehow I think it's more likely I would be the one compromising."

With his strange old-world courtesy, Mikhail held up a branch for her to pass beneath. The path was a large oval leading back to his home. "Perhaps you are right"—male amusement again—"but then, it has always been my nature to control and protect. I have no doubt you are more than a match for me."

"Then why are we back at your house instead of at the inn?" she asked, one hand on her hip and a smile dancing in her blue eyes.

"What would you do there so late at night anyway?" His voice was pure velvet, more enticing than ever. "Stay with me tonight. You can read while I work, and I will teach you how to build better shields to protect yourself from the unwanted emotions of those around you."

"How about for my hearing? Your little medicinal concoctions have increased my hearing to the point of absurdity." She arched an eyebrow at him. "Do you have any idea what else is going to happen to me?"

His teeth grazed the back of her neck, his fingers brushed across her breast possessively. "I have all kinds of ideas, little one."

"I'll just bet you do. I think you're a sex maniac, Mikhail." Raven slipped out of his grasp. "I think you put something in that concoction to make me a sex maniac, too." She seated herself at the table, calmly picked up her glass of juice, and looked up at him steadily. "Did you?"

"Drink that slowly," he ordered absently. "Where do you come up with your ideas? I have been so careful with you. Have you felt me giving you suggestions?"

She found herself reluctant to drink. "You're always making me sleep." Raven took a cautious sniff of the juice. Pure apple, nothing else. She hadn't had a thing to eat or drink in nearly twenty-four hours, so why was she reluctant?

"You needed to sleep," he said without remorse. Mikhail watched her with his brooding, hawklike eyes. "Is something wrong with your juice?"

"No, no, of course not." Raven put the glass to her lips, felt her stomach clench in protest. She replaced the glass on the table, the contents untouched.

Mikhail sighed softly. "You know you must take nourishment." He leaned close. "How simple it would be if you allowed me to help you, but you have said I should not. Does this make sense?"

Her gaze slid from his; her fingers nervously fiddled with the glass. "Maybe I'm just coming down with the flu. I've been feeling funny for a few days, dizzy and weak." She pushed the glass away.

Mikhail pushed it back. "You need it, little one." He touched her slender arm. "You already are too small. I do not think losing weight is a good idea. Take a sip."

She speared a hand through her hair, wanting to please him, knowing he was right. Her stomach insisted on rebelling. "I don't think I can, Mikhail." She raised a troubled gaze to his. "I'm really not trying to be difficult; I think I'm sick."

His face, dark and sensual, had a slightly ruthless set to it. He loomed over her, his fingers curling around the glass of juice. *You will drink.* His voice was pitched low and intense, brooking no argument, making it impossible to disobey. "The juice will stay down; your body will accept it." He spoke gently aloud, his arms protective as he circled her shoulders.

Raven blinked up at him, then looked at the empty glass on the table. She shook her head slowly. "I can't believe you're capable of doing that. I don't remember drinking it and I'm not sick now." She turned her face from him, staring out into the dark mystery of the forest. The fog caught the light from the moon, glistened and gleamed.

"Raven." His hand caressed the nape of her neck.

She leaned into him. "You don't even know how really special you are, do you? The things you can do are beyond anything I've ever seen. You scare me, you really do."

Mikhail leaned his weight against the post, genuine puzzlement on his face. "It is my duty and my right to take care of you. If you need the healing of sleep, then I must provide it. If your body needs to drink, then why should I not aid you? Why should this frighten you?"

"You really don't understand, do you?" Raven fixed her gaze on a particularly intriguing wisp of fog. "You are a leader here. Obviously your skills are far superior to mine. I don't think I could ever fit into your life. I'm a loner, not the first lady."

"I have great responsibilities, yes. My people count on me to keep our businesses running smoothly, to hunt down the assassins murdering our people. They even think I should single-handedly find out why we lose so many of our children in their first year of life. There is nothing special about me, Raven, except that I have a will of iron and I am willing to shoulder these burdens. But I have nothing for myself; I never have had. You give me a reason to go on. You are my heart, my soul, the very air I breathe. Without you, I have nothing but darkness, emptiness. Just because I have power, because I am strong, that does not mean I cannot feel utterly alone. It is cold and ugly to exist alone."

Raven pressed a hand to her stomach. Mikhail looked so remote, so alone. She hated the way he stood silent, straight and proud, waiting for her to rip his heart out. She had to comfort him and he knew it. He read her mind; he knew she couldn't bear that loneliness in his eyes. She crossed the distance separating them. Raven didn't say anything. What could she say? She simply laid her head over his heart and slipped her arms around his waist.

Mikhail closed his arms around her. He had taken her life away from her, without her knowledge. She was comforting him, declaring him to be a special man, great in her eyes, yet she didn't know of his crime. She was bound to him, could not be away from him for long. He had no words to explain it to her without giving away more about their race than he could safely do. She thought she couldn't live up to his greatness. She made him feel humble and ashamed of himself.

His hand cupped her face, his thumb caressing the delicate line of her jaw. "Listen to me, Raven." He brushed a kiss on the top of her silky head. "I know I do not deserve you. You think you are somehow less than what I am, but in truth, you are so far above me, I have no right even to reach for you."

When she stirred as if to protest, Mikhail held her tighter. "No, little one, I know this is true. I see you clearly, whereas you do not have access to my thoughts and memories. I cannot give you up. I wish I was a stronger, better man so that I could do so, but I cannot. I can only promise you that I will do everything in my power to make you happy, to provide for you everything I can possibly give you. I ask for time to learn your ways, for room to make mistakes. If you need to hear words of love"—his mouth skimmed down the side of her face to find the corner of her mouth—"then I can say them to you in all honesty. I have never wanted a woman for my own. I have never wanted anyone to have that kind of power over me. I have never shared with any woman what I have shared with you."

His kiss was infinitely tender, a searing, smoky flame tasting of love and longing. "You are in my heart to stay, Raven. I know better than you the differences between us. I ask only for a chance."

She turned herself in his arms, pressed her body lovingly against his. "You really think we can make this work? We can find a middle ground?"

She really had no idea of the risk he would be taking. Once she lived with him, he could never seek the safety and sanctuary of the earth. He could not leave her without his protection even for a day. From the moment she moved in with him, the danger to him would increase tenfold, as it would to her. The assassins would not differentiate between them. She would be condemned in their eyes. On top of all his other crimes, he was dragging her into a dangerous world.

His hand moved to the nape of her neck. So fragile, so small. "We will never know unless we try." His arms closed around her, holding her to him as if he would never let her go.

Raven felt the sudden tensing of his body. He lifted his head alertly, as if scenting the wind, as if listening to the night. She found herself doing the same, inhaling deeply, striving to hear deep into the forest. Far away, the faint, distant howls of the wolf pack floated on the breeze as they called to one another, called to Mikhail.

Shocked, Raven flung back her head. "They're talking to you! How do I know that, Mikhail? How could I possibly know such a thing?"

He ruffled her hair lightly, affectionately. "You hang out with the wrong crowd."

He was rewarded with a bubble of laughter. It tugged at his heart, left him open and vulnerable. "What is this?" she teased. "Lord of the manor picks up nineties slang?"

He grinned at her boyishly, mischievously. "Maybe I am the one hanging out with the wrong crowd."

"And maybe there's hope for you yet." She kissed his throat, his chin, the stubborn line of his blue-shadowed jaw.

"Did I tell you how beautiful you look in that outfit?" His arm curved around her shoulders, turned her toward the table. "We are about to have company." With unhurried movements he poured half a glass of juice into the goblet on his side of the table, crumbled a small piece of pastry to dust between his fingers, and sprinkled it over both of their plates.

"Mikhail?" Raven's voice was wary. "Be careful if you use mental contact. I think there is another person besides me who has telepathic abilities."

"All of my people have this ability," he answered carefully.

"Not like you, Mikhail." She was frowning, rubbing her forehead. "Like me."

"Why did you not mention this to me?" he asked softly, his voice a whip of demand. "You know my people are being stalked, our women murdered. I tracked three of the assassins to the very inn where you are staying."

"Because I don't know for certain, Mikhail. I try never to touch people. Over the years I've taught myself not to have contact, not to allow anyone to touch me." She speared her hand through her hair, a little frown creasing her forehead. "I'm sorry. I should have said something about my suspicions, but I wasn't certain."

Mikhail smoothed the line on her forehead with a gentle fingertip, touched her mouth tenderly. "I did not mean to jump down your throat, little one. We need to discuss this at our first opportunity. Can you hear it?"

She reached out into the night. "A car."

"A mile or so away." He dragged the night air into his lungs. "Father Hummer and two strangers. Women. They wear perfume. One is older."

"There are only eight guests besides myself staying at the inn." Raven was finding it hard to breathe. "They came in on a tour together. An older couple from the States, Harry and Margaret Summers. Jacob and Shelly Evans are a brother and sister from Belgium. There were four men from different places, somewhere on the Continent. I really haven't spoken much to them."

"Any of them could be with the assassins," he said grimly. He was secretly pleased that she hadn't paid much attention to the other men. He didn't want her looking at other men, not ever.

"I think I would have known, don't you?" she asked. "I

deal with killers more than I would like to admit. Only one of these people has telepathic abilities, and certainly no stronger than mine."

She could hear the car easily now, but the dense fog prevented them from seeing it. Mikhail tipped up her chin with two fingers. "We are already bound together in the way of my people. Will you speak vows in the way of yours?"

Her blue eyes widened with shock, eyes a man could drown in. Eyes a man could spend eternity staring into. A small, very male smile tugged at his mouth. He had succeeded in shocking her.

"Mikhail, are you asking me to marry you?"

"I am not really certain I know how it is done. Should I be on my knee?" He was grinning openly at her.

"You're proposing to me with a carload of assassins approaching?"

"Wanna-be assassins." He displayed knowledge of Stateside slang with a small, heart-wrenching smile. "Say yes. You know you cannot possibly resist me. Say yes."

"After you made me drink that disgusting apple juice? You set your wolves on me, Mikhail. I know there's a long list of sins I should be reciting." Her eyes were sparkling with mischief.

He pulled her into his arms, against the heavy muscles of his chest, fitting her neatly into the cradle of his hips. "I can see this is going to take some heavy persuasion." His lips moved over her face like a brand, fastened on her mouth and rocked the very earth.

"No one should be able to kiss like this," Raven whispered.

He kissed her again, tantalizingly sweet, his tongue sliding over hers sensuously, pure magic, pure promise. "Say yes, Raven. Feel how much I need you."

Mikhail dragged her closer so the hard evidence of his desire was clearly imprinted against her flat stomach. Taking her hand in his, he brought it down to cover the aching bulge, rubbed her palm slowly back and forth across him, tormenting both of them. He opened his mind so she could feel the sharpness of his hunger, the edge to his passion, the flood of warmth and love enveloping her, them. *Say yes, Raven;* he whispered it in her head, needing her to want him back, to accept him, good or bad.

You take such unfair advantage. Her reply held a trace of amusement, was warm honey spilling over with love.

The car nosed out of the mist, came to a halt under a canopy of trees. Mikhail turned to face the outsiders, instinctively placing his body protectively between Raven and the three visitors. "Father Hummer, what a pleasant surprise." Mikhail extended a welcoming hand to the priest, but there was a hard bite to his voice.

"Raven!" Shelly Evans pushed rudely past the priest and rushed toward Raven, although her eyes were devouring Mikhail.

Mikhail saw the ripple of dismay in Raven's eyes before Shelly reached her, flinging her arms around Raven and hugging her tightly. Shelly had no idea Raven could read her envy and her sexual interest in Mikhail. He could feel Raven's natural revulsion to physical touch, to the woman's concern, to her fantasies about Mikhail, but Raven managed a smile and returned the hug.

"What's this all about? Is something wrong?" Raven asked softly, gently disentangling herself from the taller woman.

"Well, my dear," Margaret Summers said firmly, glaring at Mikhail and reaching for Raven. "We insisted Father Hummer bring us to check on you."

The moment the thin, wrinkled hand touched her arm, Raven recognized the push at her mind. At the same time her stomach heaved, rolled, and shards of glass pierced her skull, fragmenting her mind. For a moment she couldn't breathe. She had touched death. She drew away instantly, wiping her palm on her thigh.

Mikhail! She focused on him entirely. *I'm sick.*

"Mrs. Galvenstein did not assure you Raven was safe in my care?" Mikhail gently but firmly inserted his body between Raven and the older woman. He had felt the older woman's clumsy attempt at a probe when she brushed by him. His teeth gleamed whitely. "Please enter my home and make yourselves comfortable. I believe it is growing rather cold out."

Margaret Summers was twisting this way and that, observing the table with two glasses and plates, the crumbs of pastry on two plates. Her eyes pinned Raven, as if trying to see through the material of her dress to her neck.

Mikhail's arm curved around Raven's shoulder, swept her into the healing shelter of his body. He hid his smile as he watched Mrs. Summers hold Shelly back until Father Hummer preceded them into Mikhail's house. They were so predictable. He bent his head. *Are you all right?*

I'm going to throw up. The apple juice. She looked up at him accusingly.

Let me help you. They will not know. He turned, blocking her smaller frame with his large one. He spoke a soft command, kissed her gently. *Better?*

She touched his jaw, her fingers conveying what she felt. *Thanks.* They turned together to face their visitors.

Margaret and Shelly were staring in awe at Mikhail's home. He had money, and the interior of his home reeked of it: marble and hardwood; soft, warm colors; artwork and antiques. It was obvious Margaret was both surprised and impressed.

Father Hummer seated himself comfortably in his favorite armchair. "I believe we interrupted something important." He looked pleased with himself and secretly amused, his faded eyes twinkling every time they met the blackness of Mikhail's fathomless gaze.

"Raven has consented to become my wife." Mikhail brought her fingers to the warmth of his mouth. "I did not have enough time to give her the ring. You drove up before I could put it on her finger."

Margaret touched the well-worn Bible sitting on the table. "How very romantic, Raven. Do you plan on being married in the Church?"

"Of course the child must be married in the Church. Mikhail is strong in his beliefs and would consider nothing less," Father Hummer said in a mild rebuke.

Raven kept her hand in Mikhail's as they curled up together on the sofa. Margaret's faded eyes were as sharp as talons. "Why have you been hiding out, my dear?" Her gaze was darting everywhere, trying to ferret out secrets.

Mikhail stirred, leaned back lazily. "You could hardly call it hiding out. We phoned Mrs. Galvenstein, your landlady, and let her know Raven was staying with me. Surely she told you."

"The last I heard of Raven, she had gone into the wilds to meet you for a picnic," Margaret declared. "I knew she was ill and I was worried, so I found out your name and asked the priest to escort us here." Her sharp gaze rested on a silver antique mirror.

"I'm sorry I caused you distress, Mrs. Summers," Raven said sweetly. "I've had a terrible case of the flu. If I had known anyone would be worried, I would have called." She said it pointedly.

"I wanted to see you for myself." Margaret pursed her lips together stubbornly. "We're both Americans, and I feel responsible for you."

"I am grateful for your concern. Raven is the light of my life." Mikhail leaned forward with his predator's smile. "I am Mikhail Dubrinsky. I do not believe we have been formally introduced."

Margaret hesitated; then, with a lift of her chin, she placed her hand in his and muttered her name. Mikhail oozed goodwill and love spiced mischievously with a healthy dose of lust for Raven.

Shelly eagerly introduced herself. "Mr. Dubrinsky?"

"Mikhail, please." His charm was so intense, Shelly nearly fell off her chair.

She wiggled a lot and crossed her legs to give him a better view. "Mikhail, then." Shelly flashed a coquettish smile. "Father Hummer tells us you are somewhat of a historian and would know all the folklore in and around the country. I'm doing a paper on folklore. Specifically, if there is any truth to the local legends. Would you know anything about vampires?"

Raven blinked, tried not to burst out laughing. Shelly was definitely in earnest, and she had fallen for Mikhail's magnetism. She would be very embarrassed if Raven laughed. She concentrated on Mikhail's thumb stroking the inside of her wrist. It helped her feel stronger.

"Vampires." Mikhail repeated the term matter-of-factly. "Of course the most popular area for vampires is in Transylvania, but we have our own stories. All through the Carpathian Mountains there are extraordinary tales. There is a tour, following Jonathan Harker's route to Transylvania. I am sure you would find it most enjoyable."

Margaret leaned forward. "Do you believe there is truth to the stories?"

"Mrs. Summers!" Raven showed her shock. "You don't, do you?"

Margaret's face closed down, her lips pursed again belligerently.

"I always have believed there is a grain of truth in nearly every story handed down through the ages. Perhaps that is what Mrs. Summers believes," Mikhail said gently.

Margaret nodded her head, relaxed visibly, and bestowed a benevolent smile on Mikhail. "I'm so glad we agree, Mr. Dubrinsky. A man in your position should certainly be a man with an open mind. How could so many people over hundreds of years tell such similar stories without some truth to the legend?"

"A living corpse?" Raven's eyebrows shot up. "I don't know about the Middle Ages, but I'd notice if dead people started walking around dragging off children."

"There is that," Mikhail agreed. "We haven't had a large number of unexplained deaths that I'm aware of in the last few years."

"But some of the locals tell stories of some pretty strange things." Shelly was loath to give up her ideas.

"Of course they do." Mikhail grinned engagingly. "It is so much better for business. A few years ago . . . when was it, Father? You remember when Swaney wanted to drum up the tourist trade and he poked himself in the neck with a couple of knitting needles and had the newspaper take pictures. He hung a wreath of garlic around his neck and walked about town, claiming the garlic made him sick."

"How do you know it wasn't real?" Margaret demanded.

"The pinpricks became infected. It turned out he was allergic to the garlic and he had no option but to confess." Mikhail grinned mischievously at the two women. "Father Hummer made him do penance. Swaney said the rosary thirty-seven times in a row."

Father Hummer threw back his head and laughed heartily. "He certainly had everyone's attention for a while there. Newspaper people were flying in from all directions. It was quite an entertaining show."

Mikhail grimaced. "As I recall, I had to spend so much time out of my office, I worked day and night for a week to catch up."

"Even you had enough of a sense of humor to appreciate his little venture, Mikhail," Father Hummer said. "I've been around a long time, ladies, and I've never once encountered a walking corpse."

Raven swept a hand through her hair, rubbed at her pounding head. The slivers of glass were relentless. She always associated such pain with prolonged exposure to a sick mind. Mikhail's hand came up, brushed her temple tenderly, trailed his fingers down her soft skin. "It is getting late, and Raven is still feeling the effects of the flu. Perhaps we could continue this discussion another evening?"

Father Hummer instantly rose. "Of course, Mikhail, and I do apologize for barging in at such an inopportune moment. The ladies were very agitated and it seemed the most expedient way to alleviate their fears."

"Raven can come back with us," Margaret offered solicitously.

Raven knew she would never survive a car ride with the woman. Shelly was nodding her head eagerly, giving Mikhail her best smile. "Thank you so much, Mikhail. I would love to discuss this further with you, maybe take some notes?"

"Of course, Miss Evans." Mikhail handed her his business card. "I am swamped with work right now, and Raven and I want to be married as soon as possible, but I will do my best to find some time." He was ushering his guests to the door, using his large, muscular frame and his beguiling smile to prevent anyone from touching Raven. "Thank you, Mrs. Summers, for offering to look after Raven for me, but we were interrupted, and I intend to make certain she does not leave me without the all-important ring."

When Raven moved to step around him, he cut her off, his body so graceful and subtle, that his movement was not noticed. His hand slid down her arm, shackled her fragile wrist. "Thank you for coming," she called softly from behind him, afraid that if she spoke too loud her head would shatter into a thousand fragments.

When their visitors had left, Mikhail dragged her protectively into his arms, his face a mask of dark menace. "I am sorry, little one, that you had to endure such a thing." He carried her into his house and made for the library.

Raven could hear soft words in his own language muttered under his breath. He was swearing and it made her smile. "She isn't evil, Mikhail; she's twisted, fanatical. It was like touching the mind of a burning crusader. She believes what she's doing is right." She rubbed the top of her head against the rigid set of his jaw.

"She is beneath contempt." He spat the words. "She is obscene." Very gently Mikhail deposited her in the comfort of his armchair. "She came to test me, to bring a priest into my home and try to outwit me. Her brush in my mind was clumsy and inept. She uses her gift to mark others for murder. She read only what I allowed."

"Mikhail! She believes in vampires. How could she possibly think you're a walking corpse? You have unusual gifts, but I can't see you murdering a child to keep yourself alive. You go to church; you're wearing a cross. The woman is nuts." She rubbed at her pounding temples in an effort to relieve the pain.

Chapter Six

Mikhail loomed over her, a dark shadow holding one of his herb concoctions in his hand. "And what if I was a mythical vampire, little one, holding you captive in my lair?"

She smiled up at his serious face, the pain in his brooding eyes. "I would trust you with my life, Mikhail, vampire or no. And I would trust you with the life of my children. You're arrogant and sometimes overbearing, but you could never be evil. If you are a vampire, then a vampire is not the creature of the legends."

He moved away from her, not wanting her to see how much her words meant to him. Such total, unconditional acceptance. It didn't matter to him that she didn't know what she was saying. He felt the truth of her words. "Most people have a dark side, Raven, I more than others. I am capable of extreme violence, cruelty even, but I am not a vampire. I am a predator, first and foremost, but I am not a vampire." His voice was husky, strangled.

Raven moved to close the distance between them, to touch the edge of his mouth, smooth a deep line. "I never thought such a thing. You sound like you believe such a terrible being exists. Mikhail, if such a thing was true, I would know you could not be one of them. You always judge yourself so harshly. I can feel the good in you."

"Can you?" he asked grimly. "Drink this."

"It better not put me to sleep. I'm going back to the inn to my own bed sometime this night," she told him firmly as she took the glass from him. Her voice teased him, but her eyes were anxious. "I do feel the good in you, Mikhail. I see it in everything you do. You put everyone else first in your life."

He closed his eyes in pain. "Is that what you think, Raven?"

She studied the contents of the glass, wondering why her words were hurting him. "I know it. I have done what is being asked of you, yet I did not have to follow through and bring the killer to justice. That must eat away at you all the time."

"You give me far too much credit, little one, but I thank you for your faith in me." His hand curled around the nape of her neck. "You are not drinking. It will help with your headache." His fingers found her temples with their soothing magic. "How can you go back to that inn when we both know the assassins are staying there? It is the old woman who leads them to our people. She is curious about you already."

"She can't possibly believe I'm a vampire, Mikhail. Why would I be in danger? I might even be of some help to you." A mischievous smile curved her soft mouth. "I can hear so much better these days." She toasted him with the glass and drank the mixture.

"There is no argument when your safety is involved. I will not have you in the middle of this battle." His black gaze was clearly troubled.

"We agreed to compromise. Your world and mine. I have to be my own person, Mikhail. I have to make my own decisions. I know you would never let me go through the torment of tracking a killer by myself. I want to help you, be there for you. That's what a partnership is."

"Being apart from you even under normal circumstances would torment me. How can I tolerate such a thing as you being in the same house with those who murdered my sister?"

She attempted to tease him, wanting the darkness to recede

from his eyes. "Do one of your sleeping numbers on yourself, or teach me how to do it. I'll be more than happy to put you out."

His hand slipped around her throat experimentally. "I bet you would. How does your head feel, little one? Better?"

"Much, thank you. So, tell me what you know so far." Raven watched him pace across the hardwood floor, all restless energy. "I have done this Mikhail. I'm not an amateur, and I'm not stupid. Mrs. Summers may look like a sweet old lady, but she's very sick. If she's targeting people as vampires and has a fanatical following, a lot more people could be hurt. And these people must believe Mrs. Summers. They killed the woman . . ."

"Noelle," he supplied softly. "Her name was Noelle."

Her eyes touched his face, her mind flooding his with warmth and comfort. "Noelle," she echoed gently, "was killed in a textbook style for vampires. Stake, beheading, garlic. This is a sick group. We at least have a place to start. I think it would be safe to assume Mr. Summers is involved. So that's two of them."

"That silly girl Shelly is a blind. They are using her to help them by asking her ridiculous questions. She is not directly involved; they do not trust her to keep her mouth shut. Her brother planted the idea of studying folklore in her head and this tour is supposedly a research trip for her. She is easily led by him." He raked a hand through his thick hair. He needed to feed soon. There was a dark, cold anger in him. It crawled through his body, dangerous and deadly. Jacob was unscrupulous, even with his sister, it seemed. And he had looked upon Raven with lust.

Raven looked up and found unblinking eyes on her. They were dark, fathomless, the eyes of a hunter. A prickle of unease ran down her spine. She felt her hand tremble as she smoothed out her skirt. "What is it?" Sometimes Mikhail looked like a stranger, not the warm man she knew with laughter and tenderness in his heated gaze, but someone calculating and cold, someone more lethal and cunning than any she could imagine. Automatically her mind reached out to his.

Do not! He slammed a block down hard.

Raven's lashes fluttered against a sudden spurt of tears. Rejection was painful, and coming from Mikhail it hurt like hell. "Why, Mikhail? Why are you shutting me out? You need me. I know you do. You're so willing to help everybody, be everything for everybody. I'm supposed to be your partner, be all things, everything to you. Let me help you." She approached him slowly, cautiously.

"You do not know what could happen, Raven." He stepped backwards away from temptation, away from her pain.

She smiled. "You always help me, Mikhail. You look after me. I'm asking you to trust me enough to let me be what you need." He was allowing his mind block to fragment, bit by bit. She sensed grief mixed with rage at Noelle's senseless murder and fear for Raven's safety. Love, strong and growing, a hunger, sexual and physical. Raw need. Someone definitely needed to love and comfort this man.

"I need you to do as I ask you," he said in desperation, fighting the beast lifting its head hungrily.

Her laughter was soft, enticing. "No, you don't. Too many people think your word is law. You need someone to defy you a little bit. I know you won't hurt me, Mikhail. I can feel your fear of yourself. You think there's something in you I can't love, some kind of monster you're afraid for me to see. I know you better than you know yourself."

"You are so reckless, Raven, so heedless of danger." He gripped the back of a chair so hard the wood threatened to disintegrate into dust. As it was, it would hold the imprint of his fingers for all time.

"Danger, Mikhail?" She tipped her head to one side, her hair falling in a slide over one shoulder. Her hands went to the top button of her blouse. "I would never be in danger from you, even if you were furious with me. The only danger right now is to my clothes." She took a step back, laughing again, letting the sound warm him, ignite the fuse deep inside him.

Heat coiled, spread; need slammed into him, hard and urgent. Hunger tore at him, a blind red haze. "You, little one, are playing with fire, and I am totally out of control." He made one last attempt to save her. Why couldn't she see how selfish he really was? How he had taken over her life and would never release her? He was the monster she couldn't see. Perhaps with the rest of the world cold logic and justice ruled him, but not with her. With Raven he was taken over by emotions with which he was so unfamiliar that he could not control them. He did things he felt were unconscionable. He let her see the violence in his mind, tearing her clothes, taking her body without thought or control.

She answered him in her mind, warmth, love, her body eager for his, receptive, accepting of his violent side. She had total trust and faith in his feelings for her, in his commitment to her.

He swore softly, ripping the clothes from his fettered body, leaping upon her like an attacking jungle cat. "Mikhail, I love this dress," she whispered against his throat, laughter still spilling into his mind. Laughter. Joy. No fear.

"Get out of the damned thing," he said hoarsely, not realizing he was confirming her belief in him.

She took her time, teasing him by fumbling at buttons, making him find the hook in her skirt. "You do not know what you are doing," he objected raggedly, but his hands were gentle on her body, carefully stripping away her clothes until she was all bare satin skin and long silky hair.

Mikhail curled strong fingers around the nape of her neck. She felt so small and fragile, her skin warm. She had a woman's haunting scent, like wild honey, a breath of fresh air. He backed her into the bookcase, his hands shaping her body, stroking the soft swell of her breast, absorbing the feel of her into his skin, his tissues, his very insides. He lowered his head, found the dark tip of her nipple with his tongue. The demon in him receded at the feel of her soft skin, her acceptance of his nature. He didn't deserve her.

Raven's body went weak at the first touch of his mouth, so hot and demanding, fastened on her breast. The shelf behind her held her up, pushing against the bare skin of her bottom. Excitement surged through her, anticipation. His eyes drifted over her with so much hunger, so much possession. With so much tenderness. That melted her heart, made her want to cry that he could have so much feeling for her. Everywhere his gaze traveled, her skin burned for him, her body ached for his touch.

She reached up to loosen his hair, to fill her hands with it, to revel in her ability to smooth her fingertips over his heavy muscles. She could feel him tremble under her caressing hands, feel the wildness in him striving to break free. It touched something wild in her. She wanted to feel him in her arms, trembling for her, his hard muscles against her soft skin, his body surging into hers. She sent him the erotic pictures dancing in her head as she tasted his skin with her soft mouth.

His hands were everywhere, and so were hers. His mouth blazed fire, and so did hers. His heart pounded, and hers matched it. Their blood surged like molten lava. His fingers found her moist and open to him. Mikhail dragged her to the floor, lifting her hips so he could join them. Blood roared in his ears, his every emotion swirling together in a violent storm of need. The harder and deeper he thrust, the more soft and welcoming she became. Her body was hot and tight, taking his, accepting his storm.

Hunger raged dangerously. He craved the sweet taste of her, wanted the ecstasy of the ritual exchange. If he fed . . . He groaned at the temptation. He would never be able to stop without needing to replenish her. He could not do that. She had to consciously make the decision to become fully a part of his world. It was too big a risk. If she did not survive, he would follow her into the unknown. He knew exactly what the ancients meant when they said one life mate could not survive the passing of the other. He would not want to live in the world without her. There would be no Mikhail without Raven.

His body, his needs, his battered emotions were taking over again, pushing him to the very edge of control. He had never known such a depth of feeling, such a total, encompassing love for another. She was everything. His air. His breath. His heart. Mikhail's mouth found hers in long, drugging kisses, moved to her throat, her breast, found his mark. One taste. Only one.

Raven moved in his arms, turned her head to give him better access, her hands entwined in his hair. "I'd better marry you, Mikhail. You need me desperately." He lifted his head, looked at her face, so beautiful with his lovemaking, so accepting of him and his needs. Her heart wrapped his in love, her mind soothed his, fed his, teased his, matched the wildness in him. His hands framed her face, his black eyes staring into her blue-violet ones, drowning in his feelings for her. Then he was smiling.

"Mikhail," she protested as he very gently eased out of her.

He turned her over, dragging her hips back toward his. When he entered her, his hands pinning her small waist, he felt exultant. She was safe! Joy surged through him and he gave himself up to the sheer pleasure of her body. He moved; she moved. She was incredibly tight, fiery hot, velvet soft. The combination was explosive.

The wolves had said he no longer knew joy, but Raven had brought it back to him. His body sang with it, shone with it. Twice he felt her body ripple, pulse, and still he went on wanting their bodies to be one for all eternity. The dark shadow across his soul was lifting. This small, beautiful woman had given him that. He built the pace of their rhythm, reveling in the way her body followed the lead of his. He felt her body clench, grip, heard her cry out over and over, soft little mewling sounds in her throat that sent him over the edge. His own body burst into flames, carried them both into the sky so that Raven called his name as her anchor.

Mikhail's hands were gentle as he helped her to lie down. He caressed her silky hair, bent to kiss her tenderly. "You have no idea what you did for me tonight. Thank you, Raven."

Her eyes were closed, lashes lying like two dark crescents against her soft skin. She smiled. "Someone has to show you what love is, Mikhail. Not possession or ownership, but real unconditional love." Her hand rose and, even with her eyes closed, her fingertips unerringly found the lines around his mouth. "You need to remember how to play, to laugh. You need to learn to like yourself more."

The hard edges of his mouth softened, curved. "You sound like the priest."

"I hope you confessed that you took advantage of me," she teased.

Mikhail's breath caught in his throat. Guilt washed over him. He *had* taken advantage. Maybe not the first time, when he was so out of control after such isolation. It had been necessary to make the exchange to save her life. But the second time had been pure selfishness. He had wanted the sexual rush, the total completion of the ritual. And he had uttered the ritual words. They were bound. He knew it, felt the rightness of it, felt the healing in his soul only a true life mate could effect.

"Mikhail? I was teasing you." The long lashes fluttered, lifted so her eyes could confirm what her fingertips tracing his frown told her.

His teeth caught her finger, his tongue stroking over her skin. His mouth was hot, erotic, his eyes burning down at her. Answering heat leapt into her eyes. Raven laughed softly. "You have it all, don't you? Charm, you're so sexy you should be locked up, and you have a smile men would kill for. Or women, however you want to look at it."

He bent to kiss her, one hand closing over her breast possessively. "You need to mention what a great lover I am. Men need to hear these things."

"Really?" She arched an eyebrow at him. "I don't dare. You're already as arrogant as I can stand."

"You are crazy about me. I know. I read minds." He suddenly grinned mischievously, like a little boy.

"Next time you make love to me, do you think we might go for convention and find a bed?" She sat up gingerly.

Mikhail's arm curved around her in support. "Did I hurt you?"

She laughed softly. "Are you kidding? Though I wouldn't mind a long soak in a hot tub."

He rubbed the top of her head with his chin. "I think we can arrange that, little one." He should have realized the wood floor would not be the most comfortable of spots. "You

119

tend to drive every sane thought from my head." It was an apology as he lifted her into his arms. His long strides took them through the house to the master bathroom.

Raven's eyes warmed, melted, her smile so loving his breath caught in his throat. "You do tend to get a little primitive, Mikhail."

He growled at her, lowered his head to hers slowly, fastened his mouth to hers. There was such a mixture of tenderness and hunger, she ached for him. Very gently he set her on her feet, her small face framed in his hand. "I will never get enough of you, Raven, never. But you need to soak in the tub and I need to feed."

"Eat." She bent to fill the tub with hot, steamy water. "In English you use the word *eat*. I'm not the greatest cook, but I could put something together for you."

His white teeth gleamed like a predator's as he lit candles for her. "You are not here as my slave, little one. At least not in the domestic sense." His eyes watched without blinking as she knotted her hair on top of her head. It was unnerving, yet Raven's body tingled under the heat of his gaze. He held out a hand to help her into the large tub. The moment his strong fingers closed around hers, Raven had the peculiar sensation of being captured.

Raven cleared her throat, then lowered her body gingerly into the steaming water. "So, do you believe in being faithful?" She tried to sound casual.

A dark shadow crossed his craggy features. "A true Carpathian of my race does not feel the shallow, childish, pale version of human love. If you were to be with another man, I would know, feel you, your thoughts, your emotions." He traced his fingertip along her delicate cheekbone. "You would not want to face the demon in me, little one. I am capable of tremendous violence. I will not share you."

"You would never hurt me, Mikhail, no matter what the cause of your anger," Raven said softly, with complete conviction.

"You will always be safe with me," he agreed, "but I cannot say the same for anyone who would threaten to take you from me. All of my people are telepathic. A strong emotion such as sexual passion is impossible to conceal."

"Do you mean to say those of you who marry . . . "

"Take a life mate," he corrected.

"They never are unfaithful to one another?" she asked incredulously.

"Not a true life mate. There have been instances—" Mikhail's fist clenched tightly. Poor sweet Noelle, so obsessed with wanting Rand. "The few that do betray their chosen mate do not feel as they should; otherwise it would be impossible. That is why it is so important to know absolutely in one's mind, heart, soul, and body. As I know it is so with you." The ritual words could not bind two who were not already one. Life mating united two halves of the same whole, but he could not find a way to express such a thing in terms she would understand.

"But, Mikhail, I'm not one of your people." She was beginning to realize there were differences besides customs that she needed to be aware of, to take into consideration.

He crushed herbs into a bowl, dumped the mixture into her bathwater. It would help with her soreness. "You would know if I touched another woman."

"But you could make me forget," she mused aloud, a small frown pulling at the corners of her mouth. He could feel her heart begin to race, the sudden doubt in her mind.

He crouched beside the tub, cupping her face with gentle fingers. "I am incapable of betraying you, Raven. I might force your compliance for the sake of your safety or your protection, for your life and health, but not to get away with betrayal."

She touched the tip of her tongue to her full lower lip. "Don't force me to do anything unless you ask the way you did when I was feeling sick."

Mikhail hid a smile. She always tried to sound so tough, his small package of dynamite, with more courage than good sense. "Little one, I live only for your happiness Now, I have to go out for a little while."

"You can't go looking for the murderers by yourself. I

mean it, Mikhail; it's too dangerous. If that's what you're doing . . . "

He kissed her, his laughter genuine. "Business, Raven. Take a long soak, look over the house, my books, anything you want." He grinned at her boyishly. "I have a stack of work beside the computer if you want to try your hand at looking at bids for me."

"Exactly how I planned to spend my evening."

"One last thing." Mikhail was gone almost before she could blink, and returned nearly as fast. He took her left hand in his. "Your people will recognize this as a clear sign that you are taken."

She hid her smile. He was so territorial, like a wild animal staking his claim. Like the wolves roaming so freely in his forest. She touched the ring with a reverent finger. It was antique, gold, a fiery ruby surrounded by diamonds. "Mikhail, this is beautiful. Where did you find such a thing?"

"It has been in my family for generations. If you prefer something else . . . something more modern—" It looked as if it belonged on her finger.

"It's perfect and you know it." She touched it reverently. "I love it. Go, but hurry back. I'll find out all your secrets while you're gone."

Mikhail was hungry, needed to feed. He bent to brush her forehead with his mouth, his heart aching. "Just for one day, little one, I would like to have a normal, happy conversation with you. Court you as I should."

She tilted her head to look at him, her blue eyes dark with emotion. "You court me just fine. Go eat now and leave me be."

Mikhail touched her hair just once before he left.

He moved among the townspeople, breathing in the night. The stars seemed brighter, the moon a gleaming silver light. Colors were sharp and clear, smells drifting on the breeze. Wisps of fog trailed here and there in the street. He felt like singing. He had found her after so long and she made the earth move and his blood heat. She brought laughter back into his life and taught him what love was.

The hour was growing late, the couples drifting toward

their homes. Mikhail chose a trio of young men. He was hungry and needed strength. The night would be long. He had every intention of confirming or eliminating Mrs. Romanov as one of the assassins. The women needed a midwife and a sorrowing, bereaved one was better than one who might betray them at the first opportunity.

He drew the trio to him with a single silent command, marveling, as he had so many times, at how easy it was to control his prey. He joined their conversation, laughing with them, confiding a couple of hot business opportunities. In their early twenties, they were thinking more about women than making money. It always amazed him how disrespectful human men were toward their women. Perhaps they could not understand what their lives would be like without them.

He led them to the safety of the darkened trees and drank his fill, making certain not to take too much from any of them. He finished as he did everything, carefully, completely. That was why he was the oldest and the most formidable. He paid attention to the smallest of details. He walked with them for a few more minutes, ensuring that they were all fine before leaving them with a casual wave and a feeling of friendship.

Mikhail turned away from them, the smile fading from his lips. The night concealed the hunter in him, the dark, terrible purpose in his eyes, the cruel edge to his sensuous mouth. His muscles rippled with raw power, flexed and contracted with his enormous strength. He moved around the corner and simply disappeared. His speed was incredible, without compare.

His mind reached out for Raven's, craving the contact. *What are you doing all alone in that spooky old house?*

Her soft laughter filled his utter coldness with warmth. *Waiting for my big bad wolf to come home.*

Do you have your clothes on?

This time her response sent fingers playing over his skin, touching him intimately, heating his body. Warmth, laughter, purity. He hated being away from her, hated the distance separating them. *Of course I have my clothes on! What if more unexpected visitors arrive? I can't very well greet them naked, can I?*

She was teasing, but the thought of anyone approaching

his home with her alone and unprotected made a sliver of fear slice through him. It was an unfamiliar emotion and he almost couldn't identify it.

Mikhail? Are you all right? Do you need me? I'll come to you.

Stay there. Listen for the wolves. If they sing to you, call me right away.

There was that brief hesitation that meant she was annoyed with his tone. *I don't want you to worry about me, Mikhail. You have enough people who make demands on you.*

Perhaps that is so, little one, but you are the only one I truly give a damn about. And drink another glass of juice. You will find some in the refrigerator. He broke the contact, found he was smiling at their brief exchange. She would have argued over the order for nourishment if he had waited long enough. He rather liked to irritate her sometimes. He liked the way her blue eyes deepened into sapphire, and how she got that little edge in her carefully controlled voice.

Mikhail? Her voice startled him, low and warm and filled with feminine amusement. *Try making suggestions next time, or just plain asking. You go do whatever it is you're doing, and I'll go search your extensive library for a book on manners.*

He nearly forgot he was crouched at the base of a tree only a few hundred feet from the shack belonging to Hans and Heidi Romanov. Mikhail managed to suppress his urge to laugh. *You will not find one.*

Why am I not surprised? This time Raven broke contact.

For a brief moment he allowed himself the luxury of wrapping himself in her warmth, her laughter, her love. Why God had chosen this time, when Mikhail was in his darkest hour, to send him such a gift, he had no idea. What he had to do was inevitable; the continuation of his race demanded it. The brutal ugliness of it filled him with revulsion. He would have to return to her with death on his hands, the deaths of more than one human. He could not walk away from it, could not hand the job over to someone else. His regret was not in taking the life of Noelle's murderers, so much as in having to ask Raven to live with his deed. It would not be the first time he'd taken a life.

With a sigh, he shape-shifted. The small rodent scurried easily through the leaves on the ground to cross the open space to the shack. The beat of wings came to his ears and the rodent froze. Mikhail hissed a warning, and the owl gliding in for the attack veered off. The rodent gained the safety of the wooden stairs, flicked its tail, and began to search for a crack or hole in the wall to gain entry.

Mikhail had already picked up two familiar scents. Hans was entertaining. The rodent squeezed through a chink between two rotting boards and found its way into a bedroom. Silently the creature raced across the floor to the doorway. Mikhail allowed the odors of the household to be processed by the rodent's body. He moved carefully in little stops and starts until he managed to gain a position in a darkened corner of the room.

Heidi Ramanov sat in a wooden chair directly across from him, weeping softly, a rosary clutched in her hand.

Hans faced three men, a map spread between them on a table.

"You're wrong, Hans. You were wrong about Noelle," Mrs. Romanov sobbed. "You've gone crazy and you've brought in these killers. My God, you have murdered an innocent girl, a new mother. Your soul is lost."

"Shut up, old woman," Hans shouted rudely, his face a mask of fanaticism. He blazed with it, a crusader fighting a holy war. "I know what I saw." He crossed himself, his eyes darting left and right as a curious shadow like that of a winged creature seemed to pass over the shack.

For a moment everyone in the room went quiet. Mikhail could taste their fear, hear the sudden frantic pounding of their hearts. Inside the house, Hans had hung wreaths of garlic at every window and over the doors. He stood up slowly, licking suddenly dry lips, grabbing at the cross hanging around his neck and moving to a window to assure himself the wreath was in place. "What about that? That shadow just now? You all still think I made a mistake because we found her in a bed and not sleeping in the ground?"

"There was nothing, no dirt, no protections," a dark-haired foreigner said reluctantly. Mikhail recognized the man's spoor. Assassin. One from the inn. Inside the rodent, the beast unsheathed its claws and flexed. They had murdered Noelle without even being certain she was what they sought.

"I know what I saw, Eugene," Hans declared. "After Heidi left, the woman began to lose blood. I had arrived to walk Heidi home because the woods are dangerous. I was going to tell the husband I would bring Heidi back to help. He was very agitated and did not see me as I looked in. I saw it with my own eyes. She drank so much, he was weak and pale. I got out of there and contacted you immediately."

Eugene nodded his head. "You did the right thing. I came as soon as I could and brought the others. If they've learned a way to whelp, we'll be overrun with the devils."

The largest man in the room stirred uncomfortably. "I've never heard of a vampire breeding. They kill the living to enlarge their ranks. They sleep in the ground and guard their lairs. You acted before we could investigate this thoroughly."

"Kurt," Eugene protested, "we saw the opportunity and we took it. And how come her body just disappeared? After we did it, we ran. The husband and child have not been seen since. We know the woman is dead—we killed her—yet there is no hue and cry over her death."

"We must find the husband and child," Hans decreed. "And any others; we must stamp them out." He peered nervously out the warped glass into the night. He let out a low exclamation of alarm. "Look, Eugene—a wolf. That damn Dubrinsky protects them on his land. Someday they're going to overrun our village and make off with the children." He reached down for the old rifle propped against the wall.

Eugene jumped up. "Wait, Hans! Are you certain it's a wolf? A real wolf? Why would a wolf be out of the woods and staring at your house?"

"Who is this Dubrinsky who keeps wolves?" Kurt demanded.

"He is of the Church!" Heidi hissed, shocked at the implication. "He is a good man, in church every Sunday. Father Hummer is one of his dearest friends. They often eat supper together and play chess. I have seen this with my own eyes."

Hans waved her testimony aside. "Dubrinsky is the devil

himself. See it out there, the wolf slinking in the bushes, watching the house?"

"I tell you, that's not natural." Eugene lowered his voice. "It's one of them."

"They couldn't know it was us," Hans denied, but he betrayed his fear with his trembling hands. He lifted the rifle to his shoulder.

"You'll have to get it with the first shot, Hans," Eugene warned.

The rodent raced across the floor into the bedroom and squeezed through the small crack. Mikhail burst from the rodent's body, his mind reaching out into the night with a warning, shape-shifting as he ran, becoming a huge black wolf with burning eyes of vengeance.

He covered the ground in a rush, leaping at the smaller wolf's body. As his heavier frame crashed into the smaller one, Mikhail felt fire exploding in his flesh. The smaller wolf slunk into the heavy woods. Although blood gushed from its hindquarters, the huge black wolf didn't utter a cry, didn't run away. Instead, the wolf turned its large head and stared at the house with two burning coals for eyes, staring with a promise. Vengeance. Retribution. The dark promise of death itself.

Mikhail! Raven's sharp cry rang in his head.

The black wolf stared a moment longer, holding Hans Romanov in his power; then it turned and simply vanished into the night. There was no way that any of the men would dare attempt to track it. The huge wolf had come out of nowhere, leaping to protect the smaller wolf. The black wolf was no ordinary wolf, and not one of them wanted to follow it into the timber.

Mikhail trotted to the safety of the deep forest before pain and loss of blood drove him to take his human form. He staggered, caught at a thick tree branch, and sat down abruptly.

Mikhail! Please! I know you're hurt. Where are you? I can feel your pain. Let me come to you. Let me help you.

Behind Mikhail the bushes rustled. He didn't bother to turn, knowing Byron was there, ashamed, embarrassed, filled with remorse. "Mikhail. God, I am sorry. Is it bad?"

"Bad enough." Mikhail clamped his hand over the wound to stop the blood flowing so freely. "What were you doing there, Byron? It was madness, foolhardy."

Mikhail. Raven's fear and tears were filling his mind.

Be calm, little one. A scratch, no more.

Let me come to you. She was pleading with him, and it broke his heart.

Byron tore a strip from his shirt and bound Mikhail's thigh. "I am sorry. I should have listened to you, should have known you would be hunting. I thought . . ." He trailed off, looking uncomfortable.

"Thought what?" Mikhail prompted wearily. The wound hurt like hell. He felt sick and dizzy, and somehow he had to reassure Raven. She was striving to comfort him, to find him; she was even trying to "see" through his eyes. *Stop it, Raven. Do as I say. I am not alone. One of my people is with me. I will be with you soon.*

"I thought you would be so involved with that woman, you might not have time for the hunt." Byron ducked his head. "I feel like such a fool, Mikhail. I was so worried about Eleanor."

"I have never shirked my duties. The protection of our people has always come first." Mikhail could not attempt to heal the wound with Raven dwelling in his mind.

"I know, I know." Byron raked a hand through his chestnut hair. "After what happened to Noelle, I could not bear for the same thing to happen to Eleanor. And this was the first time you ever warned one of us off a woman."

Mikhail managed a wry smile. "The experience is new to me. Until it is not quite so new and raw, it is best I keep her as close to me as possible. Right now she is arguing with me."

Byron looked shocked. "She argues with you?"

"She has her own mind." He allowed Byron to help him up.

"You are far too weak to shape-shift. And you will need blood and healing sleep." Byron sent a call for Jacques.

"I dare not go deep. It would leave her unprotected. She wears my ring and bears my mark. One wrong move and they would murder her."

"We need you at full strength, Mikhail." Whirling leaves like miniature tornadoes heralded Jacques's arrival.

Jacques swore under his breath as he knelt beside Mikhail. "You need blood, Mikhail," he said softly, immediately beginning to unbutton his shirt.

Mikhail stopped him with a slight gesture. His eyes, world-weary, pain-filled, made a slow study of their surroundings. Byron and Jacques went still, senses flaring out, scanning the forest. "There is no one," Jacques whispered softly.

"There is someone," Mikhail corrected.

A low warning growl escaped Jacques's throat as he instinctively placed his body in front of his prince. Byron was frowning, confusion on his handsome features. "I can detect nothing, Mikhail."

"Nor can I, but we are being watched." It was a statement so certain, neither Carpathian chose to dispute it. Mikhail never made a mistake.

"Summon Eric with a car," Mikhail ordered and laid his head back to rest. Jacques was on the alert, and Mikhail trusted his judgment. He closed his eyes weakly, wondering where Raven had gone. She was no longer nagging at him. In order to maintain the contact, he would have had to use up precious energy, energy he couldn't spare right now. Yet it worried him, her silence, so unlike her.

Chapter Seven

The ride home in the car was excruciatingly painful. Mikhail's body craved blood to replace what he had lost. His weakness was growing by the moment, the lines in his face deepening, etched with pain. He was an ancient, and all ancients felt emotions and physical wounds intensely. Normally he would simply have stopped his heart and lungs so that his blood would cease to flow. Then the healer would take over and the others would supply him with what he needed.

Raven changed all that. Raven and whatever—or whoever—was watching them. He could still feel the uneasiness washing over him. He knew another studied them from a distance, even as they traveled the miles to his home.

"Mikhail," Eric hissed as they aided him into the sanctuary of his house, "let me help you."

Raven was at the door, taking in Mikhail's pale features. He looked suddenly older than the thirty years she thought him. There were white lines around his mouth, but his mind was serene, his breathing even and relaxed. She stepped back silently to allow them entry.

She was hurt by Mikhail's refusal to allow her to help him. If he preferred the company of his people, she was not going to be so undignified as to let them see that it bothered her. Small teeth bit at her lower lip; her fingers twisted together and her eyes were anxious. She just had to see for herself that he was going to be well.

They carried Mikhail down to his sleeping chamber, Raven trailing after them. "Shall I call a doctor?" she inquired, already knowing the answer. She sensed they wanted her gone, that she was in the way somehow. Instinctively she knew that Mikhail would not receive the treatment he needed until she was gone.

"No, little one." Mikhail held out his hand to her.

She went to him, lacing her fingers through his. He was always so strong, so physically fit, yet now he was pale and drawn. Raven felt close to tears. "You need help, Mikhail. Tell me what to do."

His eyes, so black and cold, warmed instantly when his gaze settled on her face. "They know what to do. This is not my first wound, nor the worst I have received."

A small, humorless smile touched her soft mouth. "This was the business you needed to do this evening?"

"You know I hunt those that murdered my sister." He sounded tired and drained.

Raven hated arguing with him, but some things had to be said. "You told me you were just going out, nothing dangerous. It wasn't necessary to lie to me about what you were doing. I know you're the big hotshot around here, but this is what I do. I track killers. We were supposed to be partners, Mikhail."

Byron, Eric, and Jacques exchanged raised eyebrows. Byron mouthed the word *hotshot*. No one dared smile, not even Jacques.

Mikhail frowned, knew he had hurt her. "I did not deliberately speak an untruth. I merely went out to do a little investigating. Unfortunately, it turned into something altogether different. Believe me, I had no intention of getting hurt. A careless accident."

"You have this penchant for getting yourself into trouble when I'm not with you." Raven's smile did not quite reach her eyes. "How bad is your leg?"

"A scratch, no more; nothing for you to worry about."

She was silent again, her blue eyes moving over his face with a faraway, pensive look, as if she had turned inward.

Mikhail felt something twisting deep in his gut. She had that look, the one that meant she was thinking too much again. It was the last thing he wanted when he lay wounded, forced to go to ground at the first opportunity. He did not want her pulling away from him, and there was something in her stillness that worried him. She couldn't leave him. He knew that intellectually, but he didn't want her to *want* to leave him, to even be able to think about it. "You are angry with me." He made it a statement.

Raven shook her head. "No, I'm honestly not. Maybe disappointed in you." She looked sad. "You said there could be no lies between us, yet at the first opportunity, you did lie to me." For a moment her small teeth bit down hard on her lower lip. There was a sheen of tears in her eyes, but she blinked them away impatiently. "When you're asking for so much trust, Mikhail, it seems to me you need to trust me as well. You should have had more respect for me, at least for my abilities. I hunt using a psychic link. I trail using someone else's eyes. Some of you people are very sloppy and complacent. A few of you don't even bother with mind blocks. All of you are so arrogant, it doesn't occur to you that a human, not one of your superior race, can crawl inside your minds. You've got someone out there just like me, fingering your people for death. If I can get inside your minds, she can do it. My advice, for what it's worth, is to take far more precautions."

Raven stepped away from Mikhail's placating outstretched hand. "I'm just trying to save your lives, not be vindictive." It was only pride that was keeping her from falling apart. Already she felt the loss of him, of their unique closeness. Somehow she knew there would never be another man, another time in her life when she laughed and talked the way they had and was totally accepted and comfortable. "You don't need to say anything else, Mikhail. I 'saw' your 'little scratch' firsthand. You were right; you weren't alone out there—I was watching. Honesty in my language means truth."

Raven took a deep breath, tugged off the ring, and laid it carefully, regretfully, on the small table beside the bed. "I'm sorry, Mikhail, I really am. I know I'm letting you down, but I don't fit into this world of yours. I don't understand it, or the rules. Please do me the courtesy of staying away, of not trying to contact me. We both know I'm no real match for you. I'm leaving on the first available train."

She turned and started toward the door. It flew shut with a loud crash. She stared at it, not turning around. The air was thick with tension, with some dark feeling, one she couldn't put a name to. "I don't think it's going to do any good to prolong this. You need help right now. Obviously whatever they intend is some secret thing not to be shown to outsiders. I am just that. Let me go home where I belong, Mikhail, and let them help you now."

"Leave us," Mikhail ordered the others. They obeyed reluctantly.

"Raven, come here to me, please. I am weak and it would take most of my strength to come to you." There was a gentleness in his voice, an honesty she found heartbreaking.

She closed her eyes against the power in his voice, the soft caressing tone that rubbed sensuously like black velvet over her skin and crawled into her body, wrapping itself around her heart. "Not this time, Mikhail. We not only live in two different worlds, we have two separate value systems. We tried—I know you wanted to—but I can't do this. Maybe I never could have. It happened too fast and we don't really know one another."

"Raven." Heat curled in her very name. "Come here to me."

She pressed her fingers to her forehead. "I can't, Mikhail. If I let you get around me again, I'll lose respect for myself."

"Then I have no choice but to come to you." He shifted his weight, using his hands to move his injured leg.

"No!" Alarmed, she whirled around. "Stop it, Mikhail. I'm calling the others back inside." She pressed him back among the pillows.

His hand caught the nape of her neck with unexpected strength. "You are the only reason I am living right now. I told you I would make mistakes. You cannot give up on me, on *us*. You do know me, everything important. You can look into my mind and know I need you. I would never hurt you."

"You have hurt me. This hurts. Those people out there are your family, your people. I'm from another country, a different race. This isn't my home and it never will be. Let me call them to you and just let me go."

"You are right, Raven. I told you there would be no lies between us, yet I have this need to protect you from anything violent or frightening, anything that can hurt you." His thumb moved over her delicate cheekbone, slid lower to caress her silken mouth. "Do not leave me, Raven. Do not destroy me. It would kill me if you left me." His eyes were eloquent, persuasive, meeting hers unflinchingly, not attempting to hide the raw truth of his words from her, his total vulnerability.

"Mikhail," she said softly in despair. "I look at you and something deep within me says we belong together, you do need me, and I will never be complete without you. But I know it's nonsense. I've lived most of my life on my own, and I was quite happy."

"You were isolated, in pain. No one saw you, knew who you were. No one else could appreciate you or care for your needs as I can. Do not do this thing, Raven. Do not."

His hand on her arm drew her inevitably closer. How could she resist Mikhail at his most tempting? It was too late, far too late. His mouth was already finding hers. His lips were cool, tender, so gentle it brought tears to her eyes. She rested her forehead against his. "You hurt me, Mikhail, really hurt me."

"I know, little one, I am sorry. Please forgive me."

A small smile tugged at the corner of her mouth. "Is it really that easy?"

His thumb erased a tear trickling down her face. "No, but it is all I have to give you at this moment."

"You need help and I know I can't be the one to help you. I'll go. You can contact me when you feel up to it. I promise not to go anywhere until you're better."

"Put my ring back on your finger, Raven," he said softly.

She shook her head, drew away from him. "I don't think so, Mikhail. Let's let things be for a while. Let me think things through."

His hand caressed her nape, slid over her shoulder, down her arm until his fingers circled her wrist. "I need to sleep tomorrow, really sleep. I want you protected from these people." He knew she would assume he meant that they would drug him.

Raven smoothed back the tangle of coffee-colored hair from his forehead. "I'll be fine on my own, as I have been for years. You're so busy looking after the world, you think there's no one who is capable of looking after themselves. I promise you I won't leave, and I promise I will be careful. I won't go hiding in their closets or under their beds."

Mikhail caught her chin firmly. "These people are dangerous, Raven, fanatical. I found that out tonight."

"Can they identify you?" All at once she couldn't breathe. She was becoming desperate to have his friends take care of his wounds.

"No way. And there is no way they will know. I found out two more names. Eugene, very dark, a Hungarian accent."

"That would be Eugene Slovensky. He came in on the train with the tour group."

"Someone named Kurt?" He lay back against the pillow, no longer able to block out the pain in his thigh. It was cutting at his nerve endings like a rusty saw blade going through his skin.

"Kurt Von Halen. He was on the tour also."

"There was a third man. No one spoke his name." His voice revealed his weakness. "He was about seventy, gray hair, a thin gray mustache."

"That must be Harry Summers, Margaret's husband."

"The inn harbors a nest of assassins. The worst of it was, the midwife told her husband, told all of them that Noelle was not of the undead. How could they believe such nonsense when she gave life to a child? God! What a terrible waste of life." Grief washed over him anew, added to his burden of pain.

Raven could feel it hammering at her insides cruelly. "I'm

135

going to go now so they can help you, Mikhail. You're getting weaker by the minute." She bent to kiss his forehead. "I can feel their anxiety."

He caught her hand. "Put my ring back on your finger." His thumb caressed the inside of her wrist. "I want you to wear it. It is important to me."

"All right, Mikhail, but only so you'll rest. We'll sort it out when you're feeling better. Call your friends now. I'll drive your car back to the inn." She touched his skin.

He was cold, very cold. Raven pushed the ring back on her finger. He caught at her again. "Do not go near those people. Stay in your room. I will sleep through the day. You rest, and I will come for you in the evening."

"Very ambitious of you." Gently she pushed a stray lock of hair from his forehead. "I think you'll be in bed for a while."

"Carpathians heal quickly. Jacques will see you home safely."

"That really isn't necessary," she declined, uneasy in the presence of strangers.

"It is necessary for my peace of mind," Mikhail said softly, his black eyes imploring her to give in to him. At Raven's small nod he pushed his luck. "Before you go, please try another glass of juice. It will go a long way to alleviate my worry for you." He knew by reading her mind that she had tried some juice earlier. Her stomach had rebelled, before the first sip had even passed her lips. He cursed himself for that. He was directly responsible for her body's rejection of human nutrients. Raven was already far too thin. She couldn't afford weight loss.

"The smell of it makes me sick," she admitted, wanting to humor him but knowing it was impossible. "I think I really do have the flu. I'll try later, Mikhail."

"I will help you." He murmured the words softly, his dark eyes clouded with worry. "I need to do this for you. Please, little one, allow me to do this simple thing."

Behind her, the door opened and his three friends entered. One stood to the side of the door expectantly. He looked like a gentler version of Mikhail. "You must be Jacques." Raven touched Mikhail's cold hand once before leaving the room.

"And you are Raven." He was looking at the ring on her finger, not even trying to hide his smirk.

She lifted an eyebrow. "I didn't want him upset. It seemed the quickest way to get out of here so you people can help him." She had been unable to use Jacques to "see" Mikhail. His mind shield had been too strong to penetrate. Byron had been an easy target.

When she headed for the front door Jacques shook his head and crooked his finger at her. "He wants you to drink some juice."

"Oh, give it a rest. I didn't say I would."

"We can stay here all night." He shrugged broad shoulders and flashed a quick, lopsided grin. "I would not mind. Mikhail's house is comfortable."

She scowled at him, tried to look fierce when something in her was beginning to find the entire lot of them comical. Males thought they were so logical. "You're just like him. And don't take it as a compliment either," she added, when he looked pleased.

He grinned again, that lopsided, heart-stopping grin that must break hearts everywhere he went.

"You're related to him, aren't you?" Raven guessed, certain she was right. How could he not be? He had that same charm, the same eyes, the same good looks.

"When he claims me." He poured a glass of fresh apple juice and handed it to her.

"He wouldn't know." It was going to kill her to drink it.

"He would know. He knows everything. And where you are concerned, he can get a mite testy. So drink."

She sighed in resignation, and tried to force herself to swallow the juice without disturbing Mikhail. She knew Jacques was right about Mikhail. He would know if she didn't drink it, and it seemed so desperately important to him. Her stomach rolled, heaved in protest. Raven gagged, coughed.

"Call to him," Jacques instructed. "Let him help you."

"He's so weak, he doesn't need this."

"He will not go to sleep until you are taken care of," Jacques persisted. "Call him or we will never get out of here."

"You even sound like him," she murmured. *Mikhail, I'm sorry. I need your help with this.*

He sent her warmth, love. The soft command allowed her to drain the glass, keep the juice in her stomach. She rinsed the glass in the sink and turned it upside down. "You were right. He wouldn't let them treat him until I drank it. He's so stubborn."

"Our women come first always. Do not worry about him; we would never allow anything to happen to Mikhail." He led the way out of the house to the car hidden under the canopy of trees.

Raven paused. "Listen to them. The wolves. They're singing to him, for him. They know he's hurt."

Jacques opened the car door for her. His dark eyes, so like Mikhail's, slid over her. "You are very unusual."

"So Mikhail says. I think that's beautiful, that the wolves are calling encouragement to him."

Jacques started the engine. "You know you cannot say a word to anyone of Mikhail's injury. It would put him in danger." He made it a statement, but she could sense his deep need to protect Mikhail.

Raven liked him all the more for that, felt a bond with him, but she sent Jacques a little frown of reprimand all the same. "You people are so arrogant. You insist on believing that because the human race does not have great telepathic abilities, we're somehow lacking in intellect. I assure you, I have a brain, and I'm perfectly capable of figuring that out all by myself."

He grinned at her again. "You must make him completely crazy. The hotshot thing was great. I would be willing to bet it was the first time he was ever called that."

"It's good for him. If more people gave him a little trouble, he would be more—" She hesitated, searching for the right word. She laughed softly. "He'd be more something. Amenable."

"Amenable? There's a description that we can never use in the same sentence with Mikhail. None of us have ever seen him happy like this. Thank you," Jacques said softly.

Deliberately he drew the car into the shadows. "Be very

careful tonight and tomorrow. Do not leave your room until Mikhail contacts you."

Raven rolled her eyes, made a face at him. "I'll be fine."

"You do not understand. If anything happened to you, we would lose him."

She paused, her hand on the doorknob. "They will take care of him, won't they?" She didn't want to say it, but she felt as though part of her was missing, a chunk wrenched from her soul. Her mind cried out for contact with Mikhail, just a touch. Anything to reassure her that he was perfectly fine and they were still united.

"They know what to do. He will heal fast. I must get back to him. Without Gregori, I am the strongest, the closest to him. He needs me right now."

Mikhail was weak, consumed with pain, hunger clawing at him along with guilt. He had hurt her, come close to losing her. How could he make so many mistakes when she was all that mattered to him? He should never have told her an untruth over something so unimportant. *Raven.* He needed to reach out to her, touch her mind with his, feel her, know she was there. Despite pain and weakness and hunger, the worst of it was the terrible aching hole in his very soul. Intellectually, he knew the ritual binding them together had caused this overwhelming need, but the knowledge didn't alleviate his need to touch her mind.

"Mikhail, drink!" Jacques materialized beside the bed, caught his older brother to him, his face a mask of fury. "Why did you allow him to go without aid, Eric?"

"He thought only of the woman," Eric said in self-defense.

Jacques swore softly. "She is safe in her room, Mikhail. You must drink for both of you. One cannot exist without the other. If you do not survive, you doom her to death, or at best a half life."

Jacques swallowed his anger, took a deep calming breath. "Take my blood. I give it to you freely, without reservation. My life is your life; together we are strong." He used the formal words, meaning every one of them. He would have given his life for their leader. The others began the ritual healing chant. They spoke in a hypnotic rhythm, and the ancient tongue was beautiful.

Behind him, Jacques heard the murmur of voices, smelled the sweet aroma of soothing, healing herbs. Carpathian soil, so rich in healing properties, was mixed with herbs and saliva from their mouths and placed over the wounds. Jacques held his brother in his arms, felt his strength, his life flow into Mikhail, and he thanked God for his ability to help him. Mikhail was a good man, a great man, and his people could not lose him.

Mikhail felt strength pouring into him, into his depleted muscles, into his brain and heart. Jacques's strong body trembled, and he sat abruptly on the edge of the bed, still cradling Mikhail in his arms, still holding his brother's head to make it easier for him to replenish what he had lost.

Mikhail resisted, surprised at how strong Jacques still was, how weak he remained despite the transfer. *No! I endanger you!* He said the words sharply in his mind because Jacques refused to release him.

"It is not enough, my brother. Take what is freely offered with no thought but to heal." Jacques continued the chant as long as he was able, signaling Eric when he was growing too weak to continue.

Eric slashed his wrist without thought, without wincing at the gaping, painful wound, offering his wrist to Jacques, who continued to supply Mikhail with his life's blood. Eric and Byron provided the soft rhythmic words of ritual while Jacques replenished himself and Mikhail.

The room itself seemed filled with warmth and love, smelled clean and fresh. The ritual healing signaled a new beginning. It was Eric who called a halt when he could see Mikhail's color had returned, when he could hear the steady beat of his heart and feel the blood flowing freely, safely, in his veins.

Byron put a supporting arm around Jacques, helped him to a chair. Without a word he took Eric's place, supplying life-giving fluid to Jacques.

Mikhail stirred, accepted the pain of his injury as part of

the healing process, as part of the mechanics of living. He turned his head. His dark gaze sought and found Jacques, rested on him like a touch.

"Is he all right?" His voice was very soft, but commanding all the same. Mikhail was authoritative no matter what the circumstances.

Jacques looked up, pale and wan, flashed a grin, and winked. "I spend a lot of time pulling your butt out of trouble, big brother. You would think a man a good two hundred years older than me would have the sense to watch his own backside."

Mikhail smiled tiredly. "You get pretty cocky when I am lying on my backside."

"We have four hours till sunrise, Mikhail," Eric said gravely. "Byron and I must feed. You need to go underground. Soon the separation between you and your woman will begin to eat at you. You cannot afford to expend the energy for mind touch. You need to go to ground now before you cannot stand it."

"I will set the safeguards and sleep a few feet above you to ensure your protection," Jacques said softly. He had lost his sister to the assassins; he was not about to lose his brother. He needed the soil himself. Even with Eric and Byron to replenish him, he knew he was still weak and needed the healing sleep.

Mikhail lifted an eyebrow. "Five minutes in her company and you are ready to mutiny." A small, weary smile softened the hard line of his mouth.

He closed his eyes tiredly, guilt washing over him. It would be Raven who bore the brunt of this night. He would be deep in the ground, far beyond pain, beyond knowledge of separation, beyond grief and the hatred for his species. Raven would be surrounded by the assassins, in danger every moment. More than that, she would have to endure the loss of their mind touch. *Little one.* He put a wealth of love in his summons.

You are better? Relief.

I am getting there quickly. Are you in bed?

141

Always the bed thing. I heard you earlier, your fear for Jacques. I know it was Jacques. You have affection in your thoughts of him. Is he okay too?

He is tired. He gave me blood. It was draining to make the contact, to cover the distance, but he needed it desperately for both their sakes.

I can hear your weariness. Sleep now. You're not to worry about me, she instructed softly. She ached for the touch of his fingers, the sight of him.

"Mikhail, you are speaking with her," Eric thundered. "You cannot."

Jacques waved a dismissing hand at Eric. "You should have known he would do so. Mikhail, if you wish it, one of us can send her to sleep."

It will be uncomfortable for you. You will find it difficult to sleep, to eat. You will need to be with me. Your mind will seek mine, yet you will be unable to reach me. I do not have the strength to aid you this night in sleeping. Will you allow Eric or Byron to command you?

Mikhail didn't like the idea. Raven found herself smiling. He had no idea how much she could read of him. He wanted her safe, wanted her asleep while he was, but he didn't like the idea of another man doing something so intimate as commanding her to sleep. *I'll be fine, Mikhail. The truth is, it's hard enough for me to accept that kind of thing from you. I could never accept it from one of them. I'll be fine, I promise.*

I love you, little one. Those are the words of your people and they come from my heart. Mikhail used a last burst of strength to send a plea to the only human he could trust to ensure Raven's safety.

Raven closed her eyes, knowing she had to let him go before his strength was gone. *Sleep, Mikhail. In the words of your people, you are my life mate.*

She stared up at the ceiling for a long time after he was gone. She had never felt so alone, so completely barren and cold. She wrapped her arms around herself, sat in the middle of the quilts, and rocked herself in an effort to relax. She had spent a lifetime alone, had learned to enjoy her own company as a young child.

Raven sighed. It was so silly. Mikhail was going to be perfectly fine. She would take the opportunity to read a book, continue her study of the language. Mikhail's language. She walked barefoot around the room. Paced. She felt cold and rubbed her arms to warm herself.

Snapping on the lamp, Raven dragged the latest in paperback fiction from her suitcase, determined to get into the tangled web of deceit and murder spiced with romance. She stuck to it for an hour, reading the same paragraph two and three times. It happened repeatedly, but Raven was determined until she realized she had not comprehended a single word. She threw the book across the room in frustration.

What was she going to do about Mikhail? She had no family left in the States, no one who would care if she never returned. After everything that had happened, she still wanted to be with Mikhail, needed to be with him. Common sense dictated that she should leave before it went on much longer. She had no room in her mind or heart for common sense. Raven swept a hand tiredly through her hair. She had no wish to return to the work of chasing serial killers.

So what to do about Mikhail? She hadn't learned to say no to him. She knew what love was. She had met a few couples who shared the genuine article. But what she felt toward Mikhail was so far beyond that emotion. It was more than passion and warmth; it bordered on obsession. Mikhail was in her somehow, flowing in her blood, wrapped in her insides, around her heart. He had somehow entered her mind, stolen some secret part of her soul.

It wasn't simply that her body craved his, burned for his, that her skin crawled with need for him. She was like a drug addict desperate for a drug. Was that love or some sick obsession? And then there was what Mikhail felt for her. His emotions were so sharp, so intense. The way he felt around her made what she felt seem a pale imitation. Their relationship frightened her. He was so territorial, so possessive, so wild and untamed. He was dangerous, a man who ruled others and was used to having complete authority. Judge, jury, and executioner. So many people depended on him.

Raven put her hands over her face. He needed her. There

was no one else for him. He truly needed her. Only her. She wasn't sure how she knew that, but she did. There was no doubt in her mind. She saw it in his eyes. They were cold and emotionless when he looked at others. Those same eyes smoldered with molten heat when they looked at her. His mouth could be hard, edged with cruelty until it softened when he laughed with her, talked to her, kissed her. He needed her.

She went back to pacing. His customs, his way of living, were so different from hers. *You're scared, Raven,* she chastised herself. She pressed her forehead against the windowpane. *You're really afraid you won't ever be able to leave him.* He wielded so much power, used it without thought. It was more than that, if she was to be strictly fair. She needed him. His laughter, the way he touched her so gently, so tenderly. The way he burned for her, his gaze hungry and possessive, scorching, his need so urgent that he was wild for her. His conversation, his intellect, his sense of humor so close to her own. They belonged to each other. Two halves of the same whole.

Raven stood in the center of her room, shocked at her thinking. Why did she believe that they were meant to be together? Her mind seemed terribly distracted, chaotic even. Usually Raven was cool at all times, thinking things through rationally, yet it seemed she was almost incapable of that now. Everything in her cried out for Mikhail, just to feel his presence, to know he was near. Without conscious thought she reached out to him and found—space. He was either too far away or too deep in a drug-induced sleep for her to reach him. It left her shaky and feeling more alone than ever. Bereft even. She bit at her knuckles anxiously.

Her body moved because it had to. Back and forth across the room, over and over until she was totally exhausted. The weight in her heart seemed to have increased with every step. She was losing her ability to think straight, to breathe. Desperately she reached out again just to touch Mikhail's mind once, to know he was somewhere safe. She found—emptiness.

Raven drew her knees up, dragged the pillow to her. There

in the darkness, rocking back and forth, grief overwhelmed her. It consumed her so that all she could think was of Mikhail. He was gone. He had left her and she was completely alone, half a person, a mere shadow. Tears burned, ran down her face, and emptiness clawed at her insides. She could not possibly exist without him.

All her thoughts of leaving, all her careful calculations didn't matter, couldn't matter. The sane part of her whispered that it was impossible to feel this way. Mikhail couldn't be her other half; she had survived for years without him. She couldn't want to throw herself off the balcony simply because she couldn't reach him with a mind touch.

Raven found herself walking across the room, step by slow step, as if someone other than herself compelled her to do so. She flung open the doors to the wraparound balcony. Cold air rushed in, with a hint of dampness. Fog completely veiled the mountains and forest. It was so beautiful, yet Raven was unable to see it. There could be no life without Mikhail. Her hands found the wooden railing, her fingers digging absently into two deep scars she found in the wood. She ran her fingertip back and forth in the depressions, a small caress, the only real thing in a barren world of emptiness.

"Miss Whitney?"

Wrapped up in her own grief, she had noticed no one. She whirled around, her hand going defensively to her throat.

"Forgive me for startling you." Father Hummer's voice was gentle. He rose from a chair positioned in the corner of her balcony. A blanket was wrapped around his shoulders, but she could see he was shivering from long exposure to the night air. "It isn't safe out here for you, my dear." He took her arm, led her like a child back to her room, and carefully locked the balcony doors.

Raven found her voice. "What in the world were you doing out there? How did you get out there?"

The priest smiled smugly. "It wasn't hard. Mrs. Galvenstein is a member of the Church. She knows Mikhail and I are close friends. I simply told her Mikhail was engaged to you and that I needed to deliver a message. As I am old enough to be your grandfather, she thought it safe enough to allow me to wait on the balcony until you returned. And, of course, she would never pass up an opportunity to do something for Mikhail. He is very generous and asks very little in return. I believe he made the original purchase of the inn and allowed Mrs. Galvenstein to make much smaller, more reasonable and manageable payments to him."

Raven kept her back to him, unable to stem the flood of tears. "I'm sorry, Father. I can't talk right now. I don't know what's wrong with me."

He reached his hand over her shoulder to wave a handkerchief at her. "Mikhail was worried this night would be . . . difficult on you. And tomorrow. He hoped you would spend it with me."

"I'm so afraid . . . " Raven confessed, "and it's silly. There's no reason to be afraid of anything. I don't know why I'm behaving so badly."

"Mikhail is fine. He's indestructible, my dear, a great jungle cat with nine lives. I have known him for years. Nothing will keep Mikhail down."

Sorrow. It invaded every inch of her body, crawled in her mind, lay heavy on her soul. Mikhail was lost to her. Somehow, some way, during those few hours he was apart from her, he had slipped away. Raven shook her head, her grief so deep and wild she was strangling on it, unable to get enough air to breathe.

"Raven, stop this!" Father Hummer caught her small, bent figure and guided her to the edge of the bed. "Mikhail asked me to be here. He said he would come for you early this evening."

"You don't know . . . "

"Why would he have gotten me out of bed at such an hour? I'm an old man, child. I need my rest. You need to think, use your intellect."

"But it feels so real, as if he's dead and I've lost him forever."

"But you know it isn't so," he argued reasonably. "Mikhail chose you for his own. What you share with him is what his people share with their mates. They take the physical and mental bond for granted. They cherish it, and from what I have learned over the years it is so strong, one rarely survives the loss of the other. Mikhail's people are more of the earth, wild and free like the animals, but with phenomenal abilities and a conscience."

He surveyed her tear-ravaged face, the grief in her eyes. She was still laboring to breathe, but he felt her tears lessen. "Are you listening to me, Raven?"

She nodded, striving desperately to latch onto his words, to regain her sanity. This man knew Mikhail, had known him for years. She could read his affection for Mikhail, and he was certain of Mikhail's strength.

"For some reason God has given you the ability to form a mental as well as physical link to Mikhail. With that comes awesome responsibility. You literally hold his life in your hands. You must get beyond this feeling and use your brain. You know he isn't dead. He told you he would return. He sent me to you, afraid you might harm yourself. Think; reason. You are human, not an animal crying out for its mate."

Raven tried to grasp what he was saying. She felt as if she was in a deep hole and couldn't claw her way out. She concentrated on each of his words, forcing them into her mind. Deep breathing forced air into her burning lungs. Was it possible? *Damn him for putting her through this, for knowing it would happen. Was she really that far gone?*

Raven brushed the tears from her face, determined to pull herself together. She was determined to push the grief aside enough to let in rational thought. She could feel it eating at her, waiting on the outer edges of her consciousness to consume her. "And why can't I eat or drink anything but water?" She rubbed at her temples, missing the alarm that spread across the priest's weathered features.

Father Hummer cleared his throat. "How long has that been going on, Miss Whitney?"

The terrible emptiness crouched in her gut, in her mind, waiting to leap, to sink its teeth into her again. Raven struggled for control. She lifted her chin. "Raven; please call me

Raven. You seem to know all about me anyway." She was trying to control the trembling. Holding out her hands, she stared at them as they shook. "Isn't this silly?"

"Come to my house, child. It will be dawn soon. You can spend the day with me. I would consider it a great honor."

"He knew this would happen to me, didn't he?" Raven asked softly, beginning to understand. "That's why he sent you. He was afraid I might actually harm myself."

Edgar Hummer let out his breath slowly. "I'm afraid so, child. They are not as we are."

"So he tried to tell me. But I'm not like them. Why would this happen to me?" Raven asked. "It doesn't make any sense. Why did he think this would happen?"

"You completed the ritual with him. You are his other half. The light to his darkness. One can't be without the other. Come with me, Raven, back to my house. We'll sit together and talk of Mikhail until he comes for you."

Chapter Eight

Raven hesitated. The idea of learning more about Mikhail was tempting. Very tempting. "I think now that I know what is happening to me, I might be able to handle it on my own. It's very late, Father, and I already feel ashamed that you've had to sit in the cold and watch over me."

Father Hummer patted her wrist. "That's nonsense, girl. I enjoy these little errands. At my age, one looks forward to the unusual. At least come downstairs and spend some time with me. Mrs. Galvenstein keeps a fire going in the parlor."

Raven shook her head vigorously, an instinctive act of protection for Mikhail. The inn held many of his enemies within its walls. She would never place him in danger no matter how difficult a time she might be experiencing.

Edgar Hummer sighed softly. "I can't leave you, Raven. I gave my word to Mikhail. He has done so much for my congregation, the people in this village, and asks little in return." The priest rubbed his jaw thoughtfully. "I must stay, child, in case it grows worse."

Raven swallowed hard. Margaret Summers was asleep somewhere in the building. Raven could guard herself, even

Christine Feehan

her most intense grief, but she could easily read Father Hummer's natural worry. If she could do it, Margaret could. Making up her mind, Raven caught up her jacket, brushed at the tears on her face, and led the way down the stairs before she changed her mind. The most important thing for her at that moment was to protect Mikhail. The need was elemental, part of her soul.

Once outside, Raven zipped her jacket to her chin. She had changed to her faded jeans and a college sweatshirt the moment she had returned to her room. Fog was everywhere, thick, only a foot or so from the ground. It was very cold. She glanced at the priest. His English might be a bit halting, but intelligence and integrity shone on his weathered features and in the faded blue of his eyes. He was cold from the time spent on the balcony. The priest was too old to be dragged from the warmth of his cottage to do such a task in the middle of the night.

She pushed back stray tendrils of hair as she forced herself to walk calmly through the village. It should have been peaceful, but she carried the knowledge that a group of fanatical people was murdering those they believed to be vampires. Inside her heart was aching and heavy. Her mind needed the reassurance of a mind touch with Mikhail. She glanced at the older man beside her. His walk was brisk, his manner restful, soothing. This was a man long ago at peace with himself and those around him.

"You're certain he's alive?" The question slipped out before she could stop it, just when she was so proud of herself for appearing normal.

"Absolutely, child. He gave me the impression that he would be gone this day until nightfall without the usual means of contacting him." He grinned at her, a conspirator's grin. "Personally, I use his pager. Gadgets fascinate me. When I visit him, I play on his computer as often as I can. Once I locked the thing up and it took him a while to figure out what I did to it." He was absurdly pleased with that. "Of course, you understand, I could have told him, but it would have taken all the fun out of it."

Raven laughed; she couldn't help herself. "At last, a man

150

after my own heart. I'm glad someone besides myself gives him a hard time. He needs it, you know. All those people bowing and scraping. It's not good for him." Her hands were freezing so she shoved them into her pockets.

"I do my best, Raven," the priest admitted, "but we don't need to be telling him. Some things are best kept between us."

She smiled at him, relaxing just a little. "I agree with you on that. How long have you known Mikhail?" If she couldn't reach out to him, touch him, maybe she could soothe the gaping raw wound of emptiness by talking about him. She found she was beginning to feel angry at Mikhail. He should have prepared her for this.

The priest looked toward the forest, toward Mikhail's home, then raised his eyes heavenward. He had known Mikhail since his own youth, when he'd been a green priest, sent straight from his homeland to a tiny village in the middle of nowhere. Of course, he had been moved around since, but he was semiretired now, and they let him go where he wanted, the place he had grown to love.

Her blue eyes were sharp as they studied him. "I don't want to put you in the position of having to lie, Father. I find myself doing enough of that for Mikhail, and I'm not even certain why. Lord knows, he doesn't ask me to." There was sorrow in her voice, regret, confusion.

"I wouldn't lie," he said.

"Is omission the same thing as a lie, Father?" Tears made her eyes luminous, sparkling on her long lashes. "Something is happening to me, something I don't understand, and it terrifies me."

"Do you love him?"

She could hear the sound of their footsteps loud in the silence of the predawn hours. Their hearts beat steadily, their blood pumping in their veins. As she passed houses, she could hear snoring, creaks, rustles, the sound of a couple making love. Her fingers sought and found Mikhail's ring as if it was a talisman. She covered it carefully with her palm, as if she could hold Mikhail there.

Did she love him? Everything in her was fascinated, exhilarated by Mikhail. Certainly the physical chemistry between them was powerful, explosive even. But Mikhail was a mystery, a dangerous man who lived in a world of shadows she could not possibly comprehend. "How do you love what you don't understand, what you don't know?" Even as she asked the question, she could see his smile, the tenderness in his eyes. She could hear his laughter, their conversations that went on for hours, their silences that stretched companionably between them.

"You know Mikhail. You are an extraodinary woman. You can sense his goodness, his compassion."

"He has a streak of jealousy, and he's more than possessive," Raven pointed out. She knew him, yes, good and bad, and she had accepted him the way he was. But now she realized that although he had opened his mind to her, she had only glimpsed parts of him.

"Don't forget his protective streak, his deep sense of duty," Father Hummer countered with a small smile.

Raven shrugged, finding she was near tears again. It was humiliating to her to be so out of control when she knew the priest was right. Mikhail was not dead; he was somewhere in a drug-induced sleep and would get in touch with her the moment he was able. "The intensity of what I feel for him scares me, Father. It isn't normal."

"He would give his life for you. Mikhail would be incapable of harming you. If I know anything of him, I know that you can enter a relationship with him knowing he would never be unfaithful, never raise his hand to you, and always put you first in all things." Edgar Hummer said the words with complete conviction. He knew the truth of it as surely as he knew there was a God in heaven.

She swiped at the tears with the back of her hand. "I believe he wouldn't hurt me; I know he wouldn't. But what of others? He has so many special gifts, so much power. The opportunity to misuse such a talent is tremendous."

Father Hummer pushed open the door to his cottage and waved her inside. "Do you actually believe that is what he did? He is their leader by blood. The lineage goes back far in time. He is called their prince, although he would never admit it to you. They look to him for leadership and guidance, just as my congregation often comes to me."

Raven needed something to do, so she built a fire in the stone fireplace while the priest brewed a cup of herbal tea. "He's really a prince?" For some reason that dismayed her. On top of everything else, she was contemplating a commitment to royalty. Those things never worked out.

"I'm afraid so, child," Father Hummer admitted ruefully. "He is considered the last word on everything. Perhaps that is why he tends to look and act as though he might be an important person. He has many responsibilities, and as long as I've known him, he has never failed to meet any of them."

She sat back on the floor, pushing the heavy fall of hair away from her tearstained face. "Sometimes when Mikhail and I are together, it feels as if we're two halves of the same whole. He can be so serious and brooding and so alone. I love to make him laugh, to bring life into his eyes. But then he does things . . . " Her voice trailed off.

Father Hummer set a cup of tea beside her, taking his familiar place in the armchair. "What kinds of things?" he prompted gently.

She let her breath out slowly, raggedly. "I've been alone most of my life. I've always done whatever I wanted to do. When I want, I pick up and move. I travel quite a bit and I value my freedom. I've never had to answer to anyone."

"And you prefer that way of life to what you could have with Mikhail?"

Her hands shook as they circled the teacup, absorbing its warmth. "You ask tough questions, Father. I thought Mikhail and I could come to some sort of compromise. But it all happened so fast, and now I don't know if the things I'm feeling are entirely my own. He's always with me. Now, all of a sudden, he isn't, and I can't stand it. Look at me; I'm a mess. You didn't know me before, but I'm used to being alone; I'm completely independent. Could he have done something to make this happen?"

"Mikhail would never force you to love him. I'm not certain he could do such a thing."

She swallowed a steadying sip of tea. "I know that. But what about now—why can't I be away from him? I like being alone, I value my privacy, yet without his touch, I'm falling apart. Do you have any idea how humiliating it is for someone like me?"

Father Hummer lowered his cup to the saucer and regarded her with troubled eyes. "There is no need to feel that way, Raven. I do know that Mikhail said when the male of his race meets his true life mate, he can say ritual words to her and bind them together as they were meant to be. If she is not the one, neither is affected in any way, but if she is, one can't be without the other."

Raven put a defensive hand to her throat. "What words? Did he tell you the actual words?"

Father Hummer shook his head regretfully. "Only that once said to the right woman, she is bound to him and can't escape. The words are like our marriage vows. Carpathians have a different standard of values, of right and wrong. There is no such thing as divorce to them; it isn't in their vocabulary. The two people are virtually two halves of the same whole."

"What if one was unhappy?" Her fingers were twisting together in agitation. She remembered hearing Mikhail say something unusual. The memory was hazy, like a dream.

"A Carpathian male will do anything necessary to ensure the happiness of his life mate. I don't know or understand how it works, but Mikhail told me the bond is so strong, a male can't do anything else but know how to make his woman happy."

Raven touched her neck, her palm lingering over her pulse. "Whatever he did must work, Father, because I'm not the type to throw myself off a balcony because I've been away from a man a couple of hours."

"I guess we should both be hoping Mikhail is getting a taste of his own medicine," Father Hummer said with a small smile.

Raven's heart slammed hard in her chest, her body shrieking in instant protest. The thought of Mikhail suffering in any way was terribly upsetting. She tried to conjure up an answering smile. "Somehow I think he's safe from feeling anything."

The priest studied her shadowed, grief-stricken face over his teacup. "I think Mikhail is very lucky to have found you. You're strong yourself, just as he is."

"I'm putting up a great front, then"—Raven wiped at her eyes with her knuckles—"because I feel like I'm breaking apart inside. And I'm not very happy with Mikhail."

"Nor do I think you should be, yet your first instinct is to protect him. You were horrified by the idea that he might be suffering as you are."

"I don't like to see anyone in pain. There's something sad about Mikhail, as if he's borne the weight of the world on his shoulders for far too long. Sometimes I look at his face and there's such sorrow there—not in his eyes exactly but etched into his face." Raven sighed. "I guess I'm not making any sense, but he needs someone to take the shadows away."

"That's an interesting assessment, child, and I must say, I know what you mean. I've seen the very same thing in him. Taking his shadows away." He repeated the words aloud, musing over them. "That's it exactly."

Raven nodded. "Like he's seen too much violence, too many terrible things, and it's pulled him deeper and deeper into darkness. When I'm close to him I can feel that. He stands like a guardian in front of some evil, malevolent gate and holds monsters at bay so the rest of us can go about our lives and never know we were even threatened."

Father Hummer's breath caught in his throat. "Is that how you see him? A guardian of the gate?"

Raven nodded. "It's an image very vivid in my mind. I know it probably sounds melodramatic to you."

"I wish I could have said those very words to him myself," the priest said softly. "Many times he has come here seeking comfort, yet I never knew exactly what to say. I prayed God would send help to him to find his answer, Raven, and perhaps he sent you."

She was trembling, constantly fighting the torment in her head, the need to touch Mikhail, the idea that he might be gone from Earth. Raven took a deep, calming breath, grateful for the priest. "I don't think I'm God's answer to anything, Father. Right now I want to curl up into a little ball and cry."

"You can do this, Raven. You know he lives."

Raven sipped at the tea. It was hot and delicious. It put some warmth back into her insides, but it could never hope to heat the terrible emptiness, ice cold and grasping, that was devouring her soul. Slowly, inch by inch, that black hole was growing.

She tried to concentrate on other things, to enjoy her conversation with this man who knew and respected, even had great affection for, Mikhail. Raven took another drink of tea, struggling desperately to hang on to her sanity.

"Mikhail is an extraordinary man," Father Hummer said, hoping to distract her. "He is one of the most gentle men I have ever met. His sense of right and wrong is tremendous. He has a will of iron."

"I've seen that," Raven acknowledged.

"I'll bet you have. Mikhail is a man few would want to have as an enemy. But he is also loyal and caring. I saw him restore this very village nearly single-handedly after a disaster once. Every person in it is important to him. There is a greatness in Mikhail."

She had drawn up her knees and was rocking back and forth. Breathing was so difficult, each separate breath was agony to draw into her lungs. *Mikhail! Where are you?* The cry was wrenched from her heart. She needed him, just once, to answer, to touch her. Just once.

Black emptiness yawned back at her. Deliberately she bit down hard on her lower lip, welcoming the pain, concentrating on it. She was strong! She had a brain. Whatever was consuming her, convincing her that she could not bear to go on without Mikhail, would not defeat her. It was not real.

Abruptly Father Hummer got to his feet, then drew her up beside him. "Enough, Raven. Let's go outside, tend my garden. Once you feel the dirt on your hands, breathe in the fresh air, you will feel so much better." If that didn't work, he would have no choice but to fall to his knees and pray.

Raven managed laughter through her tears. "When you touch me, Father, I know what you're thinking. Is a priest supposed to hate getting down on his knees?"

He released her as if she had burned him, then began to laugh himself. "At my age, my dear, with my arthritis, I feel much more like swearing than praying when I kneel. And you have uncovered one of my greatest secrets."

In spite of everything, they both laughed softly as they went out into the morning sunlight. Raven's eyes watered, protesting the glare. She had to close her eyes against the pain slicing right through her head. She clapped her hand over her eyes. "The sun is so bright! I can hardly see and it hurts to open my eyes. Doesn't it bother you?"

"Mikhail may have left a pair of sunglasses here. He tends to do that sort of thing when he loses a chess match."

The priest rummaged through a drawer, returning with a pair of dark glasses, specially crafted for Mikhail. The frames were too large for her face, but Father Hummer fastened them with a band. Slowly Raven opened her eyes. The frames were surprisingly light considering just how dark the lenses were. The relief to her eyes was instantaneous.

"These are great. I don't recognize the name."

"One of Mikhail's friends makes them."

The garden was beautiful. Raven sank down and buried her hands in the rich, dark soil. Her fingers curled around its richness. Something heavy eased in her heart, allowed a little more air into her laboring lungs. She had an urge to lie down full length in the fertile bed, to close her eyes and absorb the earth into her skin.

It was Father Hummer's garden that got her through the long hours of the morning. The noonday sun sent her seeking the sanctuary of his cottage. Even with the protection of glasses, Raven's eyes burned, watered, ached in the power of the sun. Her skin seemed ultrasensitive, burning and reddening fast, although she had never sunburned before.

They retreated together and managed two chess games, one interrupted while Raven concentrated on fighting her private demons. She was grateful for Father Hummer's presence, uncertain she could have survived her separation from Mikhail. Without him. She drank herbal tea to counteract the terrible weakness in her body from lack of food.

The afternoon hours seemed endless. Raven managed to stave off the yawning emptiness with only a few bouts of weeping. By five o'clock she was exhausted and determined that for her own pride she had to manage the last couple of hours on her own. Mikhail would call for her in two hours, three at the most, if he had spoken the truth. If Raven was to live with herself, recover any of her independence and dignity, she had to face those last hours alone.

Even with the sun so much lower in the sky and clouds beginning to move across the horizon, sunlight still hurt her eyes despite the dark glasses. Without them, she would never have made it through the village streets back to the inn.

Fortunately the inn was relatively quiet. Mrs. Galvenstein and her people were in the midst of preparing dinner and setting up the dining room. None of the other guests were present, so Raven was able to escape unnoticed to her room.

She took a long shower, allowing the hot water to beat on her body, hoping it would drive out her terrible need for Mikhail. She braided her damp, blue-black hair into a long, thick tail and lay down on her bed without a stitch on. The cool air fanned her skin, hot from the shower, traveled over her, soothing her. Raven closed her eyes.

She became aware of the sound of pottery chinking together as the tables were set. Without conscious thought she latched onto that. It seemed a good way to keep misery and grief at bay, to explore this new capability. Raven found that with a little concentration she could turn the volume down low, even off, or she could hear insects beating their wings in the pantry. There was the sound of mice scurrying around in the walls, a few in the attic.

The cook and the maid argued briefly over the maid's duties. Mrs. Galvenstein hummed off key in the kitchen as she worked. Whispers drew Raven's attention, the whispers of conspirators.

"There is no way Mikhail Dubrinsky or Raven Whitney

are undead," Margaret Summers was saying hotly. "He may know these people, but he isn't a vampire."

"We have to go now." That was Hans. "We won't get another chance like this again. We can't wait for the others. I have no intention of waiting until dark."

"It's already too late." Jacob's voice was whiny. "Only a couple of hours until the sun goes down. It will take an hour just to get there."

"Not if we hurry. It's trapped in the ground," Hans insisted. "By tomorrow it will be gone."

"I still think we should wait for Eugene and the others," Jacob complained. "They have experience."

"We can't wait," Harry Summers decided. "Hans is right. The vampires know we're after them and are probably moving their coffins every day. We can't miss this opportunity. Gather the tools quickly."

"I still think that Dubrinsky guy is one of them. Raven is completely under his spell. Shelly told me they were engaged," Jacob protested.

"I am certain of it, as was my father before me. I am convinced he was a young man when my father was born," Hans said grimly.

"I tell you, it is not so." Margaret was adamant.

"It is strange, the effect he has on women, and the lengths they go to protect him," Hans said suspiciously, effectively silencing the older woman.

Raven could hear the sounds as the assassins gathered their deadly equipment. Had Hans and Jacob convinced Harry Summers to kill Mikhail? Or another of Mikhail's people? She rolled off the bed and dragged on clean, faded jeans. As she dressed in thick socks and hiking boots, she sent a call to Mikhail. Again she found a black void.

Muttering a few choice swear words, Raven jerked a soft powder-blue chambray shirt over her head. She didn't know the local police or where to find them. And who would believe there were vampire hunters anyway? It was ludicrous. Father Hummer? He certainly couldn't chase around the mountains at his age.

"I'll put this stuff in the car," Jacob was saying.

"No! It will be faster on foot. We can cut through the forest. Put it in the knapsacks," Hans insisted. "Hurry, hurry, we don't have much time. We must go before they waken and are at full strength."

Raven looked around the room hastily for a weapon. Nothing. When she helped the FBI with a case, the agents accompanying her carried firearms. She took a deep calming breath, kept tuned to the group as they left the inn.

There were four of them for sure: Margaret, Harry, Jacob, and Hans. She should have suspected Jacob. The night she had attempted to eat dinner with them she had been so sick; she should have realized it was her body's natural reaction to the demented minds of killers. But she had put it down to an overload of emotion from everything that had happened to her.

Yet Jacob had touched her. He couldn't have taken part in Noelle's murder or Raven would have known. Harry and Margaret might have convinced him there were vampires around; they were fanatical, dangerous people. Raven knew Shelly wasn't involved. She was sitting on her bed, writing her papers for school. There might be a chance to appeal to Jacob, make him realize just how insane a vampire hunt was.

Catching up the dark glasses, Raven slipped out of her room and moved noiselessly down the hall. It was necessary to guard her thoughts and emotions with Margaret Summers close by. Since knowing Mikhail and using telepathic communication with him, Raven was finding it easier and easier to focus her talent.

She waited until the group had disappeared onto the path leading into the forest. Her heart jumped, nearly stopped for a moment, then began to pound. Her mouth went dry. The path led to Mikhail's home; she was certain it was the same footpath he had used the first time he had taken her to his house. He was helpless, wounded, in a drug-induced sleep.

Raven began to jog, careful not to catch up with the assassins, or get too close. She would defend Mikhail with her life if need be, but she wasn't overanxious for a confrontation if she could avoid it.

Darker, more ominous clouds floated across the blue sky.

The wind began to pick up, just enough to signal a slow-approaching storm. Leaves blew across the footpath in a steady stream, lighter branches swayed and dipped as she passed.

Raven shivered in the cooler air, fear clutching at her. *Mikhail! Hear me!* She sent the imperious demand in desperation, praying as she got closer that she might penetrate whatever barriers the drugs had erected.

She heard the sound of ragged breathing and stopped, shrinking back against a broad tree trunk. Harry Summers had fallen behind the rapidly moving group, stopping to catch his breath. Raven watched as he huffed and puffed, dragging air into his lungs.

They were climbing higher into the mountains. With a sigh of relief, Raven realized they had taken a fork in the footpath and were now moving away from Mikhail. She sent up a silent prayer of thanks and began to pace behind Harry. She moved with the stealth of one of Mikhail's wolves, astonished that she could do so. Not a twig snapped beneath her feet, not a single rock rolled. If only she had their strength. She was so weak from lack of food, exhausted from lack of sleep.

Raven lifted her chin. These people would not commit another senseless murder. It didn't matter that the intended victim was not Mikhail—she had to try to prevent whatever they were going to do. Harry was slowing her down, resting every few minutes. She considered slipping through the trees and getting ahead of him, but that would put enemies both at her front and her back.

Half an hour later Raven glanced anxiously up at the sky. There were thick stands of trees in places, long stretches of meadow in others. That forced her to slow down even more. She didn't dare get caught out in the open. And now the wind was increasing enough to send splinters of cold blasting through her. In her haste to follow the group she had forgotten her jacket. The sun was still a good hour from sinking, but the gathering clouds had dimmed its light. Storms often gathered quickly in these mountains and raged for hours. Over the next ridge, Raven halted abruptly.

A meadow spread out before her covered in green grass,

beds of herbs, and fields of wildflowers. A house was tucked into the trees surrounded by lush bushes. Harry had joined the others a yard or so away from the house, circling an area of ground. Harry held a wooden stake in his hand, Hans, a heavy hammer. They were chanting, sprinkling the ground with water from an urn. Jacob was clutching a shovel and a pick ax.

The first wave of nausea hit Raven, then a peculiar sensation, a wave of pain starting in her lower back, spreading around to her abdomen, tightening every muscle. Not her own pain. It belonged to another. She tasted fear in her mind, her mouth. Desperation. Raven was locked mind to mind with another. *She needed to get to the surface so her baby could be born.*

"It's the devil's harlot, she gives birth," Margaret screamed, her face a mask of revulsion and hatred. "I feel her fear. She knows we're here and she's helpless."

Jacob sank the pick ax deep into the soft earth. Hans began a frenzied digging. The terrible clinking of metal on rock sickened Raven. It provided background music for the depravity of their fanatical minds.

Raven imagined she could hear the very earth scream in pain and outrage. She fought for a calming breath. She needed a plan. The woman must be caught in one of the many mineshaft criss-crossing the area, or an underground cellar of some kind. She was in pain, in labor, afraid for her life and the life of her unborn child.

Raven caught the mental footprints, followed them, blocking out everything else and concentrating on bringing the woman into focus. She waited until the contraction subsided and very gently sent a probe. *The woman with the assassins can hear your thoughts, feel your pain and fear. Guard yourself and any communication with me carefully or we're both in danger.*

Shock—then nothing. Tentatively the woman responded. *Are you one of them?*

No. Are you trapped? They're digging up the earth.

Panic, fear, then the emptiness while the woman struggled for control. *I do not want my baby to die. Can you help me?*

Us? Please help us! Another contraction seized her, took her into its grip.

"She's trying to contact someone!" Margaret shrieked. "Hurry!"

Mikhail! We need you! Raven sent the call hopelessly. What was she going to do? She was too far away to get help, the authorities, a rescue team. She needed someone, anyone, to help her figure a way to save the woman and her unborn child.

I must surface, the woman said in despair. *I cannot allow my baby to die. My life mate will attempt to fight them off while I give birth.*

They will kill all of you. Try to hang on. Can you hold out for a half-hour, an hour? We'll have help after that.

They will get to us first. I feel them above me, disturbing the earth. They have death in their minds.

I'll try to buy you some more time.

Who are you? The woman was calmer now, determined to stay in control now that an outside source was working with her.

Raven took a breath, let it out. What was the most reassuring way to answer? Raven Whitney would hardly inspire confidence. *I am Mikhail's woman.*

The woman's relief spilled over and Margaret shrieked again, whipping the men into a digging frenzy. Raven stepped out of the timberline, began a slow saunter boldly across the meadow, humming to herself as she walked. Harry spotted her first. She heard his curse, his whispered orders to the others. Jacob and Hans stopped work, Hans looking uneasily up at the sky.

Raven waved to the group, flashing an innocent smile. "Hi, everybody. What are you doing? Isn't it beautiful up here?" She turned around in a circle, arms outstretched. "The flowers are brilliant, aren't they?" she continued gushing. She was very careful to keep a good distance between them. "I'm so mad I forgot my camera."

The four assassins exchanged nervous, guilty looks. Margaret was the first to recover, sending Raven a serene, welcoming smile. "How lovely to see you, dear. You're a long way from the inn."

"I thought a hike and some fresh air would be good for me. Are you hiking, too?" Raven didn't have to pretend to shiver as she ran her hands up and down her arms to warm herself. "It looks like we're in for another storm. I was just thinking of turning around when I spotted all of you." She turned her head toward the rambling stone house. "I would love to live this far out in the mountains, surrounded by nature." She looked directly at Hans, smiling guilelessly. "Your place is wonderful. You must love it up here."

They all looked confused and guilty, as if they had no idea what to do. Jacob was the first to recover. He dropped his pick ax and started purposefully toward her. Raven's breath caught in her throat. She was as indecisive as they were. She didn't dare run and give herself away, but she didn't want Jacob to get his hands on her either.

Raven stepped back, allowing the smile to fade from her face. "Have I interrupted something?"

At that moment the woman trapped beneath the earth had another swelling contraction. It rippled through her body like a strong wave, and the woman's pain radiated out from her. Instantly Margaret locked eyes with Raven.

There was only one thing to do and Raven did it. Gasping in horror, she ran forward toward the group. "Oh, my God! There's someone trapped in a mineshaft and she's in labor! Margaret! Is that what's happening? Has someone gone for help?"

In her headlong flight she deliberately chose a path away from Jacob and toward the left, to the timberline side of the others. She stumbled to a halt on the edge of the digging site. The air was heavy, sluggish, almost difficult to breathe. She recognized a pale version of Mikhail's safeguards. The pregnant woman's life mate must have thrown up a barrier hastily in an attempt to slow the progress of the fanatics.

"It will be all right," Margaret said calmly, as if she were talking to a child. "That thing down there is not human."

Raven's head came up, blue eyes wide with shock. "Can't you feel her? Margaret, I told you I have certain abilities. I wouldn't make up something like this. There's a woman trapped down there and she's having a baby. There are mines all through this area. She must have gotten trapped in one of them. I can feel her fear."

"She's not human." Margaret walked carefully around the site toward her. "I'm like you, Raven. We are sisters. I know how painful it was for you to hunt the serial killers you brought to justice, because I have done the same thing."

Raven swallowed a lump of fear. Margaret sounded so sweet and refined. But she reeked of the sour smell of fanaticism. The faded eyes blazed diabolically with it. Raven's stomach heaved. Maybe she could reach Jacques. "Margaret, you must feel her pain, her fear." Raven's mouth was dry, her heart pounding. "You know who I am, what I'm capable of. I would never make a mistake in something like this."

Hans went back to work with the shovel, muttering a warning to the others. The wind tugged at their clothing, raked at their bodies. The clouds darkened to an ominous charcoal, began to roil as the wind shrieked through them. Lightning arced from cloud to cloud and thunder rumbled in warning.

"This is undead. A vampiress. She feeds off the blood of our children." Margaret crept closer to Raven.

Raven shook her head, pressed her hands into her stomach. "You can't believe that, Margaret. Vampires are pure fiction. This woman trapped down there is very real. Vampires don't have babies. Come on, Jacob! You can't believe this nonsense."

"She's a vampire, Raven, and we're going to kill her." Jacob indicated the knapsack lying open with the sharpened stakes. His eyes were overbright with anticipation. He looked eager to do the task.

She backpedaled. "You're all crazy."

Please! Help me! Call him! The desperate cry was edged with terror and pain.

Raven reacted immediately. *Mikhail! Jacques! Help us.*

"The she devil is calling to her," Margaret reported.

Please, call Mikhail. He will come for you, the woman wailed.

"Stop her," Margaret screamed. "The vampiress speaks to her, begs her to call for help. Don't do it, Raven. She tricks you. Don't call Dubrinsky."

Raven spun away from them, took off running, sending out a frantic call into the stormy air for Mikhail, for anyone. She made it into the trees before Jacob caught her, locking onto her legs just below the knees and slamming her hard into the ground.

The fall knocked the wind out of her, her head spun, and for a moment she lay still, facedown on the forest floor wondering what had happened. Jacob flipped her over roughly, straddling her, his boyish good looks twisted with lust and the urge for domination. She caught the sickening chemical odor of cocaine emanating from his pores.

Mikhail! She sent the call like a prayer, knowing what Jacob had in mind, knowing she wasn't strong enough to stop him.

The wind increased. Far off, a wolf howled, and another answered. Farther away, a bear growled irritably.

"You think you're so damned smart, selling yourself to the highest bidder, so innocent and untouchable." Jacob gripped the front of her chambray shirt, jerked hard, and ripped the material right down to her small waist. Her full breasts spilled out, instantly drawing his attention. Roughly he grabbed her, bruising soft flesh.

I'm sorry. The trapped woman's cry was edged with guilt. She had failed to guard her mental cries, had allowed Margaret Summers to hear her calls to Raven.

Mikhail! Please! Raven's hopeless plea went out again. *You must hear me. I need you. God, please help me. Help that poor woman.*

Jacob roared, slapped her once, twice. "He's marked you. My God, you're one of them." His hand closed over her throat, threatening to cut off her air. "He's impregnated you like the others. I knew it was him."

He raised his hand above her and Raven caught the glint of shiny metal. Jacob stabbed down, his face a mask of fury and hate. Pain sliced low and wicked through her abdomen; blood gushed warm. Jacob pulled the dripping knife from her flesh and raised it again.

Chapter Nine

The earth rumbled, shook, rolled. Jacob's knife buried deep a second time. The wind unleashed its deadly power, sent leaves, twigs, and small branches flying through the air like missiles. The knife bit a third time. Lightning sizzled once, twice, three times, slammed into the earth as thunder cracked, shaking the land with the unholy sound. The knife found her a fourth time. The heavens opened up and rain poured down hard and fast, as if floodgates had burst.

Jacob was covered in blood. He pushed away from her, turning his head as the sky grew darker. He could hear the others screaming in fear. "Damn you." He sliced down a fifth time in fury and defiance.

An unseen hand caught his wrist before the blade could find her, fingers curling hard in an unbreakable grip. The knife turned inward toward Jacob's throat, and for one long, eternal moment, he stared in horror at the bloodied blade as it inched toward his flesh. It struck suddenly, burying itself to the hilt.

Wolves boiled out of the forest, circled the meadow, glowing eyes fixed on the three people dodging branches that were hurtling through the air. Margaret screamed and ran. Harry took off blindly and Hans lost his footing and dropped to his knees as the earth heaved and shook again.

"Raven." Mikhail materialized beside her, fear for her clawing at his guts. He ripped the jeans away so he could see the extent of her injuries.

The earth rolled again, split the meadow open. Mikhail clamped his hands over the pumping holes in an attempt to stem the terrible flow of blood. Jacques shimmered into view, then Eric, Byron. Tienn arrived, and Vlad.

Gregori blasted out of the sky toward the three human assassins surrounded by the wolf pack. There on the meadow, with the world coming to an end, he took the shape of a huge, black wolf, a wolf with the hungry, mad eyes of retribution.

"My God." Jacques was on his knees beside Mikhail, gathering handfuls of rich soil. "Go, Byron, for the herbs. Hurry!"

Within minutes they had packed Raven's wounds with their poultices. Mikhail ignored them, cradling Raven in his arms, his large body bent protectively to shield her from the onslaught of the pounding rain.

Mikhail's entire being was concentrated, focused on only one thing. *You will not leave me,* he commanded. *I will not release you.* Lightning sizzled, whipped across the sky, slammed into the earth. On its heels thunder boomed, shook the mountains.

"Jacques! Eleanor is going to give birth." Vlad was desperate.

"Get her into the house. Call Celeste and Dierdre." Jacques toed Jacob's body contemptuously as he added his large frame as a shelter over Raven.

"She is not dead," Mikhail hissed, seeing the compassion in his brother's eyes.

"She is dying, Mikhail." Jacques's chest hurt with the knowledge.

Mikhail dragged her to him, bent his head until his cheek lay against hers. *I know you can hear me; you must drink, Raven. Drink deeply.*

He felt the faint stirring in his mind. Warmth, regret. So much pain. *Let me go.*

No! Never! Do not talk. Just drink. For me, if you love me, for me, for my life, drink what I offer. Before Jacques could guess his intent and try to stop him, Mikhail jabbed deeply into his own jugular.

Dark blood spurted. Mikhail forced her to him, used every power he possessed to force compliance. Her will obeyed; her body was almost too weak to follow. She swallowed what poured into her but could not draw deeply on her own.

Bolt after bolt of lightning slammed to earth. A tree exploded, rained fiery sparks. The earth heaved again, rolled, came apart at the seams. Gregori loomed over them, the darkest of the Carpathians, his pale eyes ice cold and holding the stark promise of death.

"The wolves did their job," Eric reported grimly. "The lightning and earthquakes will do the rest."

Jacques ignored him, gripping Mikhail's shoulder. "Enough, Mikhail. You grow too weak. She has lost too much blood. She has internal injuries."

Black rage filled Mikhail. He threw back his head and roared his denial, the sound exploding through the forest and mountains like the booming of the thunder. Trees burst into flames around them, exploding like sticks of dynamite.

"Mikhail." Jacques refused to relinquish his hold. "Stop her now."

"She has my blood; it will heal her. If we can keep blood in her, get her into the soil and perform the healing ritual, then she will live."

"Enough, damn it!" Jacques voice held very real fear.

Gregori touched Mikhail gently. "If you die, my old friend, we have no chance of saving her. We must work together if we are to do this thing."

Raven's head lolled back, her body limp like a rag doll. Mikhail's blood ran unchecked down his chest. Jacques leaned into his brother, but Gregori was there before him, closing the gaping wound with a single stroke of his tongue.

Mikhail was nearly oblivious to his surroundings, he was directing his entire being, his entire disciplined focus on Raven. She was slipping away from him, fading slowly but surely. Her heart beat erratically, one beat, a miss, a single beat. There was an ominous, eerie silence.

Swearing, Mikhail laid her flat, physically breathed for

her, manually stimulated her heart. His mind sought the trail of hers, found a small, huddled light, dim and fading. She floated on a sea of pain. She was weak beyond his imaginings. Breathe, massage. Call her back, reinforce it with an order. Repeat the process.

A torrent of water raced down the rocky canyon behind them, a solid wall gathering speed and force. The ground shook again. Two trees exploded into fiery conflagrations despite the heavy rains.

"Let us help," Gregori ordered softly.

Jacques moved his brother gently aside, took over CPR while Gregori breathed for Raven. In and out, Gregori filled her lungs with precious air. Jacques forced her heart to continue. It left Mikhail free to concentrate on his mental quest. A stirring in his mind, the lightest of touches, but he knew it was her and he locked onto that trace and followed it ruthlessly. *You will not leave me.*

She tried to move away from him, up and away. There was too much pain in the direction in which he called her.

Panicked, Mikhail screamed her name. *You cannot leave me, Raven. I cannot survive without you. Come back to me, come back to me, or I follow you where you lead.*

"I have a pulse," Jacques said. "It is weak, but it is there. We need transport."

There was a shimmering in the gathering darkness. Tienn appeared beside them. "Eleanor has given birth, and the child lives," he announced. "It is a male."

Mikhail let out his breath in a long, slow hiss. "She betrayed Raven."

Jacques shook his head in warning when Eric would have spoken, would have tried to defend the woman. Mikhail was in a killing rage. The slightest mistake might provoke him. Mikhail's fury was triggering the turbulent weather, the raging storm and heaving earth.

Mikhail sank back into his mind, holding Raven to him, taking as much of her pain as he could. The trip home was a blur to him, the rain pelting the windshield, lightning sizzling and snapping. The village was deserted and dark, the electricity out in the terrible ferocity of the storm. Inside their houses, people were huddled and praying, hoping to live through the ferocious storm, not understanding their very lives could depend on one small human woman's courage and tenacity.

Raven's body, so limp and lifeless, was stripped of her bloodstained clothing and placed on Mikhail's bed. Healing herbs were crushed, some lit. The poultices were replaced with newer, stronger ones to try to stem further blood loss. Mikhail touched the dark bruises on her face with trembling fingers, the dark marks that stood out starkly against her full white breasts where Jacob had deliberately hurt her in his jealous, drugged rage. Fury seized Mikhail and he longed to crush Jacob's throat beneath his hands. "She needs blood," he said abruptly.

"So do you." Jacques waited for Mikhail to draw the sheet over Raven before he offered his wrist. "Drink while you can."

Gregori touched his shoulder. "Forgive me, Jacques, but my blood is stronger. It holds immense power. Allow me to do this small thing for my friend." At Jacques's nod, Gregori drew a single mark over his vein.

There was silence as Mikhail availed himself of Gregori's rich blood. Jacques sighed softly. "She has exchanged blood on three occasions with you?" He forced his voice to be neutral, not wanting to appear to reprimand his leader and brother.

Mikhail's dark eyes flickered warningly. "Yes. If she lives, she will most likely be one of us." It was left unsaid that she might live to be destroyed by the very one who had converted her.

"We cannot seek human medical aid for her. If our way does not work, Mikhail, her doctors will be useless anyway," Jacques cautioned.

"Damn it, do you think I do not realize what I have done? You think I do not know I failed her, that I failed to protect her? That by my selfish actions I put her life in jeopardy?" Mikhail stripped off his bloody shirt, balled it in one hand, and threw it to the farthermost corner of the room.

"This is senseless, looking back," Gregori said calmly.

Mikhail's boots hit the floor, his socks. He dragged himself onto the bed beside Raven. "She cannot take blood our way; she is too weak. We have no choice but to use their primitive transfusion methods."

"Mikhail . . . " Jacques said warningly.

"We have no choice. She did not take all that she needed, not even close. We cannot afford the delay of argument. I ask you, my brother, and you, Gregori, as my friend, to do this for us." Mikhail cradled Raven's head in his lap, sat back among the pillows and closed his eyes tiredly while they began the primitive process.

If he lived another thousand years, Mikhail would never forget that first stirring of unease in his mind while he lay as dead beneath the earth. Knowledge had exploded in his brain, spread terror in his heart and fury in his soul. He had felt Raven's rippling fear. Jacob's hand on her precious body, the brutal blows, the tearing sensation of the knife as it sliced through skin and into her soft insides. So much pain and fear. So much guilt that she had failed to protect Eleanor and her unborn child.

Raven's weak touch had slipped inside his mind, so whispery, edged with pain and regret. *I'm sorry, Mikhail. I've failed you.* Her last coherent thought had been for him. He loathed himself, loathed Eleanor for not having the discipline to learn mental communication, focused and pure.

In that one second of understanding, as he lay helpless, locked in the soil, the very foundations of his life, his beliefs, had been rocked. As he burst free, Jacques rising with him, he had mentally reached for Jacob, had buried the bloodstained knife to the hilt in the murderer's throat.

The storm enabled Vlad to break Eleanor and him free without the fear of blindness or that one moment of complete disorientation that would have given the assassins the time to kill his laboring wife.

Mikhail sought Raven's mind, crawled to her with warmth and love, his arms a shelter. The needle jabbed the inside of his arm, pierced hers. He had no doubt that his brother would monitor the transfusion closely. Jacques held Mikhail's life along with Raven's in his hands. If she died, Mikhail followed her. He knew in his heart, the black fury that remained would endanger anyone near him, Carpathian and human alike. He could only hope that Gregori was up to the job of dispatching Carpathian justice to him swiftly and accurately if Raven should die.

No. Even in an unconscious state, she was trying to save him.

He stroked her hair in long caresses. *Sleep, little one. You are in need of healing sleep.* Using his mind, he breathed for both of them, in and out, forcing oxygen into his lungs, her lungs. He kept the rhythm of their hearts together. He took on as much of the mechanics of her body as he could to enable her to heal.

Jacques knew Mikhail's mind was made up. If this woman failed to live, they would lose Mikhail. Right now Mikhail was using his power to keep her blood flowing, her heart pumping, and her lungs working. It was a draining process.

Gregori met Jacques's eyes over Mikhail's head. He was not going to allow the couple to die. It was up to them to heal her. "I will do it, Jacques." It wasn't a request.

The air stirred beside them and Celeste materialized with Eric. "He chooses to follow her," she said softly. "He loves her that much."

"It is already known?" Jacques asked.

"He is withdrawing," Eric answered. "All Carpathians can feel it. Is there a chance to save them?"

Jacques looked up, his handsome face haggard, his dark eyes, so like Mikhail's, grief-stricken. "She fights for him. She knows he will choose to follow her."

"Enough!" Gregori hissed, bringing them all to attention. "We have no choice but to save them. That is all that can be in our minds."

Celeste reached toward Raven. "Let me do this for her, Jacques. I am a woman; I carry a child. I will make no mistakes."

"Gregori is a healer, Celeste. You are with child and it is difficult," Jacques denied softly.

"Both of you are supplying blood for them. You could make a mistake." Celeste pushed the sheet from Raven's stomach. Her gasp was audible, her horror very real. Involuntarily she stepped back. "My God, Jacques. There is no chance."

Furious, Jacques elbowed her out of the way. Gregori stepped between them, his pale eyes flowing over Celeste like mercury, glittering with a calm, cold menace, with a terrible rebuke. "There is no question that I will be the one to heal her. And she will be healed. While I perform this task I want only those who believe completely to attend. Go now if you cannot give me this aid. I must have only complete conviction in my mind and the minds of those around us. She will live because there is no other alternative."

Gregori placed his hands over the wounds, closed his eyes, and went seeking out of his own body and into the one lying so hideously wounded, as still as death.

Mikhail felt Raven's stirring of pain. She flinched, tried to move away, tried to fade so that this new, painful sensation could not touch her. Mikhail surrounded her effortlessly, held her still for Gregori to do the intricate work of repairing damaged organs. *Relax into it, little one. I am here in this place with you.*

I can't do this. It was more a feeling than words. So much pain.

Choose for us, then, Raven. You will not go alone.

"No!" Jacques's protest was sharp. "I know what you do, Mikhail. Drink now or I will not continue the transfusion."

Fury welled up, shook Mikhail out of his semistupor. Jacques met the rage in his dark eyes with deliberate calm. "You are too weak from loss of blood to oppose me."

"Then let me feed." There was cold fury, black as night in those words. Pure menace, the threat of death.

Jacques exposed his throat without hesitating, managing to prevent a groan of pain as Mikhail bit deep, fed hungrily, ferociously, like a savage animal. Jacques did not struggle or make a sound, offering up his life for his brother and Raven. Eric moved toward them as Jacques's knees buckled and he sat down hard, but Jacques motioned him away.

Mikhail lifted his head abruptly, his shadowed features so haunted and grief-stricken, Jacques ached for him. "Forgive me, Jacques. There is no excuse for my treatment of you."

"There is nothing to forgive when I offer freely," Jacques whispered raggedly. Eric moved immediately to his side, supplying Jacques with blood.

"How could anyone do such a thing to her? She is so good,

so courageous. She risked her life to help a stranger. How could someone want to harm her?" Mikhail asked, raising his eyes toward the heavens. Silence was his only answer.

Mikhail's gaze found Gregori. He watched his friend work with the intense concentration of the healing ritual. The low chant was soothing to him, brought a measure of relief to his tormented soul. He could feel Gregori with them, inside her body, working, weaving the magic of body repair, a painstakingly slow process.

"Enough blood," Jacques whispered hoarsely as he lit the scented candles and began another low chant.

Gregori stirred, his eyes remaining closed, but he nodded. "Her body is attempting the conversion. Our blood is soaking into her organs and working to change and repair tissue. She needs time for the process." He moved back inside to the deep penetrating wounds he was aligning. Her womb was damaged, and it was far too important to take any chances. She must be made perfect.

"Her heart is too slow," Jacques said weakly as he slid from the bed to the floor. He looked startled to find himself there.

"Her body needs more time to make the change and heal," Celeste added, watching Gregori work. She knew she was witnessing a miracle. She had never been this close to the legendary Carpathian everyone whispered about. Few of their people actually saw Gregori up close. Power emanated from his every pore.

"She is right," Mikhail agreed weakly. "I will continue to breathe for her, continue to ensure her heartbeats. Eric, you must care for Jacques."

"Rest, Mikhail, see to your woman. Jacques will be fine. Tienn is here if there is a problem. Gregori has many hours of work ahead of him," Eric replied. "If it is necessary, we can call others in to help."

Jacques reached up his hand to his brother. Mikhail took it. "You must calm your anger, Mikhail. The storm is too strong. The very mountains rage with you." He closed his eyes and laid his head against the bedframe, his hand still clasped in Mikhail's.

Raven felt almost detached from what was happening to

her body. Her awareness of others in the room and their movements came through Mikhail. He was with her somehow, in her body, breathing for her. And there was another, one she didn't recognize, but he was also in her, working like a surgeon would, repairing the extensive damage to her body, to her internal organs, paying special attention to her female organs. She wanted to just stop, allow the pain to swamp her, to carry her someplace far beyond feelings. She could just let go. She was tired, so tired. It would be so very easy. It was what she wanted, longed for.

She rejected the beckoning peace, fought to hang on to life. Mikhail's life. She wanted to brush her fingertips over the lines of strain she knew would be around his mouth. She wanted to ease his guilt and rage, assure him that everything had been her own choice. His love, total, uncompromising, unconditional, endless, was almost more than she could cope with. Most of all she was aware of the strange changes taking place in her body.

None of it touched her, wrapped tightly, protectively in the cocoon of Mikhail's love. He breathed, she breathed. His heart beat, her heart beat. *Sleep, little one. I will watch for both of us.*

After several long, backbreaking hours, Gregori straightened up, his hair damp with perspiration, his face weary and lined, his body aching with fatigue. "I have done my best. If she lives, she will be able to have a child. Mikhail's blood and the soil should complete the healing process. The change is taking place rapidly. She does not understand and does not fight it." He pushed a hand stained with her precious blood through his hair. "She fights only for Mikhail's life, thinks only of his life and how her death would affect him. I think it is better if she does not understand what is actually happening to her. She does not know the extent of her wounds. There is much pain. She suffers greatly, but she is not a quitter, this one."

Jacques was already preparing new poultices to replace the blood-soaked ones. "Can we give her more blood? She is still losing more than I like and is so weak, I fear she will not live through the night."

"Yes," Gregori replied tiredly, thoughtfully, "but no more

than a pint or two. We must do this slowly or we will alarm her. What she would accept unconditionally in Mikhail, she will not accept in herself. Give her my blood. It is potent, like Mikhail's, and he grows weak trying to breathe for her and keep her heart going."

"You are tired, Gregori," Jacques protested. "There are others."

"Not with my blood. Do as I say." Gregori seated himself calmly and watched as a needle was inserted into his vein. No one argued with Gregori; he was a law unto himself. Only Mikhail could truly call him friend.

Celeste drew in a deep breath, wanting to say something to Gregori that would indicate her admiration, but there was a look in his eyes that stopped her. Gregori was calm in the eye of the storm; he was lethal in his coolness.

Jacques allowed Gregori's precious life fluid to flow directly into Raven's veins. It wasn't the best or fastest way for healing, but Gregori's observations alleviated Jacques's concerns. Only after he had assured himself that the blood was flowing easily did Jacques sit down again. They had to organize themselves, make certain every detail was taken care of. Mikhail believed details saved lives. "We need to assess the damage to our people. All of the assassins died; not one escaped?"

"Hans, the American couple, and the man who attacked Raven." Eric counted them off. "They were the only ones present. No mortal could have survived the intensity of the storm, the killing rage in the animals. If there had been an unseen observer, Mikhail or the beasts would have known."

Gregori stirred tiredly, his enormous strength beginning to fade with his continuing efforts. "There was no other." He said it imperiously, as if no one would think to question him, and of course they wouldn't.

Jacques found a small grin touching his mouth for the first time all evening. "But you made a clean sweep of the area, Eric?"

"Absolutely. The bodies are burned, caught together under a tree as if for shelter and hit by lightning. There is no evidence of wounds," Eric reported.

"Tomorrow a search will be launched for the missing tourists and Hans. Byron, your house is close; the other assassins will suspect you. Do not go near your home. Vlad must take Eleanor and the child away from this area completely."

"Are they able to travel?" Gregori asked.

"By car."

"We have the night. I have a house I use in the winter months sometimes, not often. It is well protected, difficult to access." Gregori's smile did nothing to warm his silver eyes. "I like my privacy. At the moment it is unoccupied. I offer it freely for the protection of the woman and child for as long as there is need. The house is well over a hundred miles from this place, and I roam the world, so you will not be disturbed."

Before Vlad could protest, Jacques preempted him. "Excellent idea. That solves one of our problems. Byron has his own bolt-holes. Start now, Vlad. Guard Eleanor well. She is precious to us, as is the child."

"I must speak to Mikhail. Eleanor is very distraught that she put Raven's life in jeopardy."

"Mikhail is not himself." Jacques removed the needle from Raven's limp body and Gregori's arm. Her breath was so light, so shallow, he didn't see how Mikhail could keep her going. "You will have to discuss things at another time. He is forced to use all his energies for Raven's survival. His woman is not breathing on her own."

Vlad frowned, but complied when Gregori waved him out. He might have stayed to argue with Jacques to ease the conscience of his life mate, but all obeyed Gregori. He was Mikhail's right hand, the most relentless of their hunters, the true healer of their people, and he guarded Mikhail as a treasure.

"None of our people have fed this night," Eric pointed out, studying his wife's pale features. "No human will be out."

"The risk is great when we are forced to enter a dwelling." Jacques sighed, wishing he could consult Mikhail.

"Do not disturb him," Gregori said. "She needs him more than we do. If she dies, we lose him and any real chance at a future for our race. Noelle was the last female to survive, and that was more than five hundred years ago. We need this woman to continue our species. We must be at full strength. It is not finished."

Mikhail stirred, opened his dark, haunted eyes. "It is not finished. There are at least two others, possibly four. Eugene Slovensky, Kurt Von Halen. I do not know the identity of the other two travelers, or if they are even involved. Their names should be at the inn; Mrs. Galvenstein can provide them." Long lashes drooped. Mikhail's fingers tunneled deeply into Raven's hair, as if he could drag her back from the brink of death.

Jacques watched those long fingers stroke her hair lovingly. "Can we put her in soil for a few hours, Gregori?"

"It should speed the healing process."

Eric and Jacques went down to prepare the cellar, opening the earth with a single command, creating enough space to lay two bodies side by side. They moved Raven carefully, and Mikhail stayed close to her side, never speaking, focusing his entire concentration on her heart, her lungs, on preserving the dim light that contained her will to live.

He lowered himself deep in the bowels of the earth, felt the healing properties of the rich soil as it settled around him like a welcoming bed. He accepted her slight weight, fit her body into the shelter of his.

Mikhail moved his hands, formed a slight tunnel over their heads and ordered the earth to blanket them. The soil filled in closely around and over his legs, her legs, covered their bodies, pressing them deeper into the earth.

Raven's heart leapt, nearly missing a beat, became erratic in spite of the firm beating of his own heart. *I'm alive! They're burying us alive!*

Be still, little one. We are of the earth. It is offering to heal us. You are not alone, I am here with you.

I can't breathe.

I am breathing for us.

I can't stand it. Make them stop.

The earth has recuperative powers. Let them work. I am Carpathian, of the earth. There is nothing to fear. Not the wind or the soil or the waters. We are one.

I am not Carpathian. There was sheer terror in her mind.

179

We are one. Nothing can hurt you.

She closed herself off from him, began a frantic struggle that could only end her life. Mikhail realized it was futile to argue. She could not accept the earth closing around her, over her head. He released them from the ground immediately, forced her heart to slow to normal, floating upward with her in his arms.

"I feared this," he said to Jacques, who was still in the cellar. "Carpathian blood runs strong in her veins, but her mind sets human limits. Burial represents death. She cannot tolerate the deep earth."

"Then we must bring the soil to her," Jacques said.

"She is so weak, Jacques." Mikhail held Raven to him, his face etched with grief. "It makes no sense that this was done to her."

"No, it does not, Mikhail," Jacques answered.

"I have been so selfish with her. I am still being selfish. I should have allowed her to find peace, but I could not. I would have followed her, Jacques, but I do not know if I would have gone quietly from this world as I should have."

"And then what of the rest of us? She represents our chance, our hope. We have to have hope, Mikhail. Without it none of us can continue for much longer. We believe in you; we believe you will find the answer for the rest of us." Jacques paused at the door out of the cellar. "I will get a mattress. Byron, Eric, and I will cover it in the richest soil we can find."

"Have they fed?"

"The night is on us; we have many hours."

In the cellar they set up a healing bed, used herbs and incense, covered the mattress in three inches of earth. Once again Raven and Mikhail settled together, her head on his chest, his arms holding her close. Jacques packed the soil beneath her so that it contoured to the curves of her body. They formed a thin blanket of it to lay over them, added a sheet so she would be able to feel the reassuring comfort of cotton against her neck, her face.

"Keep her still, Mikhail," Jacques encouraged. "The wounds are closing, but she is still losing blood. Not much, and we can give her more blood in a couple of hours."

Mikhail rested his cheek against her silky head, allowed his eyes to close. "Go feed, Jacques, before you drop," he murmured wearily.

"I will go when the others return. We will not leave you and your woman unprotected."

Mikhail stirred as if he might protest, but then a grin tugged at the hard edges of his mouth. "Remind me to take you out back and teach you a lesson or two when I am feeling more myself." He fell asleep with the sound of Jacques's laughter in his ears and Raven wrapped tightly in his arms.

Outside, the rain eased to a fine drizzle, and the winds died down, taking the thunderclouds with them. The earth was silent after the series of quakes. Cats and dogs and livestock settled down to their normal behavior. Wild animals sought shelter finally from the storm.

Raven awoke slowly, painfully. Before she opened her eyes, she assessed the situation. She was hurt; she should be dead. She was in Mikhail's arms, their mental bond stronger than ever. He had dragged her back from death, then offered to let her go—if he went with her. She could hear the sounds of the house creaking over her head, the soothing sound of rain beating a tattoo on the roof, at the windows. Someone moved in the house. If she worked at it, she would be able to figure out exactly who it was and where in the house he was, but it seemed far too much trouble.

Slowly she allowed the horror of what had happened to replay in her head. The trapped woman about to give birth, the ugly fanaticism that led to such brutal murder and insanity. Jacob's face as he slapped her, ripped her clothing.

Raven's low cry of alarm brought Mikhail's arms tighter around her, his chin nuzzling her head. "Do not think of such things. Let me send you back to sleep."

She curled her fingers against his throat, needing the reassurance of his steady pulse. "No. I want to remember, to get it over."

His uneasiness was instantaneous. It disturbed her as nothing else could. "You are weak, Raven. You will need more blood, more sleep. Your wounds were very serious."

She moved then, just shifted her weight slightly. Pain

clawed at her. "I couldn't reach you. I tried, Mikhail, for that woman."

He brought her fingers to the warmth of his mouth, pressed them there. "Never again, Raven, will I fail you."

There was more pain in his heart and mind than in her body. "I chose to follow them, Mikhail. I chose to involve myself and help the woman. I knew exactly what those people were capable of. I didn't just walk into the situation blindly. I don't blame you; please don't think you failed me." It was such an effort to talk. She wanted to sleep, wanted the blessed oblivion of a numb mind and body.

"Let me send you to sleep," he whispered softly, his voice a caress, his mouth brushing across her fingers an added enticement.

Raven swallowed her assent; she would not be a coward. How could she possibly still be alive? How? She remembered the terrible moment when Jacob's hands had clawed at her breasts. Unclean. Her skin crawled at the memory. She wanted to scrub until she had no skin. His face, so evil, maniacal, malevolent. Every tearing stab a mortal wound.

The storm, the earthquakes, lightning, thunder. Wolves leaping at the Summerses, at Hans. How did she know, see it in her mind so clearly? Jacob's face dissolving into fear, his eyes wide with terror, a knife protruding from his throat. Why wasn't she dead? How did she know everything?

Mikhail's fury. It was beyond imagination, beyond the mere bounds of a physical body. Nothing could contain such turbulent rage. It spilled from him, fed the storm until the very earth heaved and rolled, bolts of lightning slammed into the earth and rain poured down.

Was this all real or some horrendous nightmare? But she knew it was real, and she was close to some terrible truth. There was so much pain; she was so tired and Mikhail was her only comfort. She wanted to crawl back into the shelter he provided and just let him protect her and keep her safe until she was strong again. Mikhail simply waited, allowed her to choose. He was providing warmth, love, closeness, but he was holding something inside himself, away from her.

Raven closed her eyes, concentrated. She remembered

Mikhail suddenly beside her, pain and fear in his dark, mesmerizing eyes, his arms dragging her close, his mind seeking, finding hers, commanding her to stay, holding her anchored to the earth when her body was dying. His brother was there, and more of his people. Something was placed on her abdomen, something that seemed to work its way into her body, something warm and alive. Low, soothing chanting had filled the air all around her.

Shock and alarm emanated from Mikhail's people. Mikhail's blood, hot, sweet, revitalizing, soaking into her body, her organs, reshaping muscle, tissue. Not flowing into veins, but . . .

Raven went rigid, her brain so shocked it was numb. The very breath was driven from her body. *Not the first time.* Other memories surfaced: Mikhail's frenzied feeding, her mouth pressed hungrily over his heart. "Oh, God!" The words escaped as a strangled sob of denial.

It was the truth, not some hallucination. But her human brain refused the truth. It wasn't possible; it couldn't be. She was in the middle of some terrible nightmare and any moment she would wake up. That had to be what was happening. She was mixing everything up—the assassins' fanatical belief in vampires and Mikhail's powers. But her heightened senses told her differently, told her the truth. She was lying in some underground chamber, with soil under her, over her. They had tried to bury her in it. To sleep. To heal.

Mikhail simply waited, allowed her mind to process information, held nothing back from her, even when she drew on his memories. When her reaction came, it took him totally by surprise. He'd expected screams, tears, hysteria.

Raven jackknifed off the mattress, cried out low, an animal sound of pain. She rolled away from him, heedless of the consequences to her mortally wounded body.

He spoke sharply, much more sharply than he intended, his fear for her safety outweighing his compassion. His command paralyzed her body, trapped her helplessly on the floor. Only her eyes were alive with terror as he crouched beside her, ran his hands over her wounds, seeking the extent of the damage.

"Relax, little one. I know this knowledge is shocking to

you," he murmured, frowning as he saw the precious blood seeping from three of the four wounds. He lifted her, cradled her in his arms, close to the shelter of his heart.

Let me go. Her plea sounded in his mind, echoed in his heart.

"Never." Mikhail's harsh features were an implacable stone mask. He looked at the doors over their heads. The doors responded, flying open at the touch of his will.

Raven closed her eyes. *Mikhail, please, I'm begging you. I cannot be as you are.*

"You have no idea what I am," he said gently, floating up to the next level so nothing would jar her body. "Humans mix up the truth about my race with stories of the undead, stealing babies, killing, tormenting victims. I could not have saved you if you were dead. We are a race of people who belong to the earth, the sky, the wind, and the water. Like any other people, we have our talents and our limitations." He did not go into details about where vampires came from. She needed truth, but not everything at once.

Mikhail took her to a guestroom, laid her carefully on the bed. "We are not the vampires in your horror stories, the walking dead, for God's sake. We love, we worship, we work, we give service to our countries. We find it disgusting that the human male can beat his wife or child, that a mother could neglect her child. We are repulsed that the human race can eat the flesh of an animal. To us blood is lifegiving, sacred. We would never dishonor the human by hurting or killing. It is taboo to have sex with a human and then drink of his or her blood. I know I should never have taken your blood—it was wrong—but it was wrong because I did not tell you what could happen. I knew you were my true life mate and my existence could not continue without you. I should have had more control. For that I will pay through all eternity, but it is done. We cannot undo what has already been wrought."

Mikhail finished new poultices, placed them precisely over the wounds to seal them. Her fear, her revulsion, her sense of betrayal beat at his insides, making him want to weep for her, for both of them.

"What I did with you was not the same thing as using a

human woman for sex. We did not have sex; my body recognized you as my life mate. There was no way I could ignore the call. I would have had to choose to end my life. The ritual demands the exchange of blood. It is not feeding hunger; it is purely a sensual exchange, a beautiful, erotic affirmation of love and trust. The first time I took your blood, I inadvertently took too much because I felt such ecstasy. I was out of control. I was wrong to tie you to me without your understanding of exactly what it all meant. But I allowed you to make the choice. You cannot deny it."

Raven stared up at his face, reading the sorrow in his dark eyes, the fear for her. She wanted to touch him, to ease those lines of strain, to reassure him that she could handle what he was asking of her, but her brain could not accept what he was saying.

"I would have chosen death, if you had allowed me to go with you." He pushed the hair from her face with gentle, caressing fingers. "You know that, Raven. The only way I could save you was to make you one of us. You chose life."

I didn't know what I was doing.

"If you had known, would you have chosen death for me?"

Her blue eyes, so bewildered and confused, so haunted, searched his face. *Release me, Mikhail. I do not like to lie here helpless.*

Mikhail covered her body with a thin sheet. "Your wounds are severe; you need blood, healing, and sleep. Do not move around."

Her eyes chastised him. Mikhail touched her chin with gentle fingers. He released her, his eyes watchful. "Answer me, little one. Knowing what we are, would you have sent me to eternal darkness?"

She made a supreme effort to get herself under control. A part of her still could not believe this was happening. A part of her struggled to understand and be fair. "I told you I could accept you, even love you as you are, Mikhail. And I meant that then. The same is true now." She was so weak, she could hardly speak. "I know you're a good man; there is no evil in you. Father Hummer said I couldn't judge you by our standards and I won't. No, I would have chosen life for you. I love you."

There was too much sorrow in her eyes for him to feel relief. "But?" he prompted softly.

"I can accept it in you, Mikhail, but not for me. I could never drink blood. The thought of it sickens me." Her tongue touched her dry lips. "Can you change me back? A transfusion, perhaps?"

He shook his head regretfully.

"Then let me die. Just me. If you love me, let me go."

Mikhail's eyes darkened, burned. "You do not understand. You are my life. My heart. There is no Mikhail without Raven. If you wish to seek eternal darkness, I must go with you. I had never known the pain and ecstasy of our people's love until I found you. You are the very air I breathe, the blood in my veins, my joy, my tears, my very feelings. I would not wish to continue a barren, empty existence. It would be impossible. The torment you felt for those short hours without our mind touch would be nothing compared to the hell to which you wish to condemn me."

"Mikhail"—she whispered his name in anguish—"I am not Carpathian."

"You are, little one. Please give yourself time to heal, to absorb all this and adjust to it." He was pleading with her, his voice soft and persuasive.

She closed her eyes against the tears welling up. "I want to sleep."

Raven needed more blood. The transfer would be easier on her if she had no idea what was happening to her. The healing sleep of the earth might provide her with comfort; in any case, it would speed the healing process of her body. Mercifully, Mikhail obliged her request and sent her into a deep sleep.

Chapter Ten

Raven woke sobbing, her hands curling around Mikhail's neck, clutching him to her, hot tears spilling onto his chest. He dragged her closer protectively, holding her as tight as he dared without crushing her. She seemed so fragile and light, so ready to fly away from him. He let her cry, his hand caressing her hair with soothing strokes.

When she began to quiet, he murmured softly to her, tenderly, in his own language, words of reassurance and hope. Eventually she lay, worn out and exhausted, in the sanctuary of his arms. "It will take time, little one, but give our ways a chance. There are wondrous things we can do. Concentrate on the things you would enjoy. Shape-shifting, flying with birds, running free with the wolves."

Her small fist jammed into her mouth to stop a strangled sound somewhere between fear and hysterical laughter. Mikhail brushed the top of her head with his chin. "I would never leave you to face any of this on your own. Lean on my strength."

She closed her eyes against another wave of hysteria. "You don't even understand the enormity of what you've done.

You've taken away my very identity. Don't, Mikhail! I feel your protest stirring in my mind. What if you woke up no longer Carpathian, but a human. No longer able to run free and fly. No special powers, no healing earth, no more ability to hear and understand animals. Everything that was ever the essence of you would be gone. To survive you had to eat meat." She felt his instant revulsion. "You see, the very thing Carpathians consider disgusting. I'm afraid. I look into the future and I'm so terrified I am unable to think. I hear things, sense things. I . . . " She trailed off before making any admissions. "Don't you see, Mikhail, I can't do this, not even for you."

He stroked her hair with loving fingers, trailed a caress over the soft skin of her face. "You have known for a short time. Your sleep was deep and undisturbed." He did not tell her she had been given blood twice more during her sleep, that her body had gone through the rigorous change, ridding itself of all human toxins. He felt she had to absorb certain aspects of their lifestyle slowly. "Do you wish us to seek eternal rest?"

Her fist thumped his chest. "Not us, Mikhail, me!"

"There is no you or me. There is only us."

She took a deep, calming breath. "I don't even know what or who I am anymore."

"You are Raven, the most beautiful, courageous woman I have ever known." He said it sincerely, stroking back her silken hair.

Her body was tense, almost rigid with wanting to deny his tranquil statements of fact. "Can I exist without blood? With juice and grains?"

His hand found hers, laced their fingers together. "I want it to be so for you, but it is not. You must have blood to live."

She made a sound, a small denial, hunching away from him, withdrawing into herself. It was too far-fetched, too frightening to really comprehend. She wanted to believe it was a nightmare.

Mikhail sat up, let her go so that he could push the sheet from her slender body. Her mind was blocking out every explanation, refusing to deal with the information he was giving her. Wanting to distract her, he bent to examine her abdomen, his fingers splaying possessively over her skin, touching each white scar gently. "Your wounds are nearly healed."

She half sat, astonished. "That's impossible."

He lifted his hands out of the way to show her the long scars. Her eyes widened in disbelief. Mikhail's eyes darkened and burned, brushed her bare breasts with heat. Raven's small teeth tugged at her lower lip and a red flush spread over her entire body. She clutched the sheet, dragged it over her.

His white teeth gleamed at her in a predator's smile, pure taunting male. He leaned close so that his mouth brushed across her ear as he spoke. His warm breath beckoned and enticed. "I have kissed every inch of your body. I have been in every secret corner of your mind." His teeth skimmed her earlobe, sent a shiver along her spine. "I will admit, the blush suits you."

Raven found herself holding her breath, heat coiling deep within her. She pressed her forehead against the heavy muscles of his chest so that he couldn't see the answering flare in her eyes. "Mikhail," she warned, "there is no way you can change what I feel by seducing me. I know I cannot handle this."

"I hear your thoughts, little one. You have closed your mind to all possibilities." He whispered the words like a terrible seduction. "I will give you what you wish. I no longer can bear your unhappiness." His hand moved up to his chest, right below her chin, hovered over his heart.

Her stomach clenched at the sudden knowledge of his intention. The sweet odor of hot blood mingled with his wild, masculine scent. Before she could stop him, before she could voice a protest, his life's blood was streaming freely down his chest. Instinctively she clamped both hands over the wound, applied pressure.

Eyes wild with fear, Raven cried out frantically. "Stop, Mikhail. Don't do this." Tears welled up, spilled over. "Please tell me what to do to save you." There was desperation in her voice.

"You can stop it."

"I can't, Mikhail. Stop this; you're scaring me!" She

pressed as hard as she was capable, but the blood continued to flow between her fingers.

"Your tongue has the power to heal; so does the saliva in your mouth." His voice was dark, hypnotic. He leaned back as if his strength was waning. "But do not counteract my choice unless you live also, because I refuse to go back to a world of darkness."

Frantically she bent her head to his chest, swept her tongue over the edges of the wound, sealing the gap as if it had never been. The revulsion was in her brain, but not in her body. Something wild lifted its head; her eyes went slumberous and sensual. Heat coiled, spread. Her body hungered, craved. The call was so strong within her. She wanted more, needed the erotic ecstasy only he could provide.

Mikhail's hands were in her hair, bunching, dragging her head back, exposing her throat. His mouth moved over her soft skin, her frantic pulse. "Are you sure, Raven?" He whispered it so sensually her body went liquid in answer. "I want you to be completely sure. You must be certain this is your choice."

She circled his neck with her arms, cradled his head. "Yes." The memory of his mouth moving against her, the white-hot pleasure piercing her very soul made heat pool low and wicked in her abdomen. She wanted this, even needed this.

"You give yourself to me freely?" His tongue tasted the texture of her skin, flicked across her pulse, and traced down the valley between her breasts.

"Mikhail." His name was a plea. She feared that he was waiting too long and might not be able to live, to breathe, to merge completely with her.

He lifted her easily, cradled her in his arms. His tongue lapped her nipple, once, twice. Raven gasped, arched closer to him, her body scenting the wildness in him rising to match, to conquer the wildness in her. She seemed to float through the air, every nerve ending raw with hunger and need. The sweet scent of blood called to her.

She smelled fresh air and opened her eyes to discover the

night. It whispered to her with the same sensual power as the ebb and flow of Mikhail's blood. Trees swayed overhead; the wind cooled her body, yet fanned her need.

"This is our world, little one. Feel its beauty, hear its call."

It was all like a dazzling dream, as if they were drifting with the faint mist, a part of the night itself. The stars overhead played hide and seek through the canopy of leaves and branches. The moon was elusive, wandering behind floating clouds. Everywhere Raven heard the sounds of life. It was in the sap of the trees, the rustle of small animals, the beat of wings, the echoing, savage cry of a night hunter as it missed its prey.

Mikhail raised his head and called, a wild sound of joy. It was answered. Raven could feel the rapture in the wolves' rejoinders. It filled her heart and in her, the wildness grew.

He carried her through a maze of paths, deep into the mountains until they were at the entrance of a downward sloping cave. "Hear it," he ordered as he passed into the murky shadows. "Hear the earth sing to you."

Impossibly she could see rich veins of minerals curving on either side of the narrow walls just as if the sunlight were pouring into the tunnel. She could hear the rush of water echoing through the many chambers. Bats called to one another and the earth welcomed it all.

Mikhail was sure-footed, striding through the maze of tunnels without hesitation, every step taking them deeper underground until they were in a huge steam-filled grotto. Water ran in a frothy fall down to pour into a series of pools. Crystals gleamed like jewels all around them.

He took them into the farthest pool from the fall, where the water bubbled up like soda and was warm and fizzy against their skin. He sank into the water, with Raven cradled in his arms and steam rising around them.

The bubbles nibbled at sensitive skin, danced and teased like so many fingers, foamed and caressed like the lapping of tongues. With lazy, languid movements, Mikhail began to wash her slender body, her small feet, her calves, her thighs. Raven moved against his hands, closed her eyes to give herself up to pure sensation. Carpathian blood flowed hotly in her veins. Carpathian needs and desire warred with the human limitations and taboos her brain insisted on.

His hands slid in a tender, loving caress over her flat stomach, his fingertips reverently tracing each scar, wiping away the last traces of the poultices and blood. He paid careful attention to each rib, her back, and finally, her face and hair. Mikhail was so gentle, he made her want to cry. He had not touched her anywhere intimately, yet he had begun a slow fire in her blood, a melting in her body. She ached for him. Needed him.

Raven opened her blue eyes; they were slumberous, sexy, darkened with desire. She tilted her head to look up at him and then moved to rinse his body. She had no intention of being so kind. Her every stroke was designed to tease, to inflame. Fingertips delved into the dark tangled hair veeing toward his flat belly, slid tantalizingly over the heavy muscles of his chest, rinsing every drop of blood from his skin. So much. It worried her, and she wanted him to feed, to replace what was lost.

Some small part of Raven recognized that the thought should be appalling to her, yet with her body needing his so desperately, she craved his mouth on her, felt hunger herself. Her hands wandered lower, moved across his flat belly, dipped over the ridge of his hipbones.

Raven felt his swift intake of breath, the tensing of every muscle. A low growl rumbled deep in his throat, sent darts of fire leaping in her blood. Her fingers sought the hard evidence of his arousal, teased and enticed, her fingertips dancing intriguingly, her palm sliding and gripping, testing the weight of him.

He groaned at the effort it took to control himself. This time she was going to participate in the ritual. There would be no way she could argue that she had not known what she was doing. He spread his legs wider to support his trembling body as she touched his shoulder with her tongue, followed a droplet of water that ran in a bead from his neck to his chest. Raven's body clenched, grew heavy, ached, and burned. Her tongue slid over his heart in a lazy, sensual pattern. Her blood leaped and sang to match his. All the time her hands caressed, teased, promised. Her long hair, masses of silk, brushed his body as she followed little beads of water, lower, lower still. She felt him shudder as she tasted him, his body thrusting to meet her silken mouth. The feeling of power was incredible. His hands bunched in her hair; low, aggressive growls escaped from deep in his throat. She found his thighs with her nails, raking lightly, driving him wild, wanting him crazy for her, wanting him mindless with passion.

Mikhail dragged her up, closer. His hands found the firm muscles of her bottom, cupped, massaged. "I claim you as my life mate." He whispered the words, a black magic incantation, centuries old. His hand moved up her spine, around to the fullness of her breast, down satin skin to find the thatch of midnight black curls.

Raven cried out when his fingers found her beneath the bubbling water, found her and began a slow, torturous exploration. Her mouth was open against his chest, her breath short and coming in little gasps. The craving grew, the fire built; something wild and abandoned in her fought for freedom. She could hear their hearts beating as one, hear his blood, hers. She felt her body pulsing with life, with need, with such hunger that she needed all of him to fill her and make her complete. She needed him in her mind, his erotic, insatiable appetite, the incredible lust he had that made him burn and ache for her. She needed his body possessing hers, taking hers wildly, without reservation. And she needed his . . . *blood*.

His hand cradled the back of her head; he was moving her to the waters' edge. "I belong to you; I offer my life for you. Take what it is you need, what it is you want." His whispered words opened up the door to a terrible craving. His fingers were moving aggressively, his body pressing hers to the earth, half in and half out of the water.

Raven felt the soft dirt beneath her, his hard body imprisoning hers. There was a ruthless stamp to his dark features, a merciless slash to his mouth, and burning hunger in the depths of his eyes. When she touched his mind there was savage, primitive arousal, the animal drive to claim, a Carpathian male's ruthless, implacable resolve to possess his mate. There was also a love so intense, she could barely conceive of it. Tenderness. A male's adoration for the only one he could ever want.

Mikhail tugged her knees apart, saw the sudden admission of commitment to him deep within her eyes. She was hot, pulsating with need, with her body's invitation. He thrust hard, driving deep, burying himself in her hot core. Her spicy feminine scent mixed with his masculine one, drifted up to become part of their desire. His tongue and teeth glided over her throat, down to capture one aching breast. His hands moved over every inch of her, inciting, exploring, claiming. He was rough, his teeth finding her soft skin, his tongue easing every ache. He could not seem to get close enough. Her tight heat coiled around him, clenching and burning, feeding his wildness.

His body moved in hers. Long, deep, filling every part of her, building the friction, then deliberately easing the rhythm. She was making little keening noises, her body begging for release, velvet muscles gripping him hotly.

Frustrated, Raven moved frantically against him, urging him closer, deeper, faster, harder. Her blood was like molten lava and she needed more of him. All of him. She hungered for a deeper mating, hungered for his mouth feeding at her, burning her, branding her, welding them together for all eternity.

"Mikhail," she was pleading.

He lifted his head, dark eyes burning with hunger. "I belong to you, Raven. Take what you need from me as I will take it from you." He pressed her head to his chest, his gut clenching hotly as her tongue slid over his muscles. There was a moment, heart-stopping, intimate, as he felt the tentative scrape of her teeth. White-hot pain, blue lightning erotic pleasure. He swelled even more, huge and hard and inflamed as her teeth sank deep.

Mikhail threw back his head in ecstasy, and a growl of pure pleasure escaped. His body pinned hers to the ground, surging powerfully, building, building while her body spiraled around his, gripping and clenching, climaxing again and again. Mikhail held on to his control. The ritual would be completed and the exchange made voluntarily. Bunching her hair in his hand, he repeated the words that would bind them together. "I give you my protection, my allegiance, my mind, my heart, soul, and body. I take into my keeping the same that is yours. Your life, happiness, and welfare will be cherished and placed above my own for all time. You are my life mate, bound to me for eternity, and always in my care."

He tugged at her hair, forced her head away from him, observed through half-closed eyes, hungry and watchful while she closed the pinpricks, her tongue sending flames dancing over his heated body. Mikhail kissed her with every ounce of male dominance he possessed. His mouth burned over her throat, rested on her frantic pulse. His hands tightened on her small hips. His body rested in the hot feminine mystery of hers. He waited.

She turned her head, offered her throat. "Take what is yours, Mikhail. Take what you require." She murmured the words breathlessly in an agony of anticipation and need. She was trembling with suspense, with the craving of Carpathian erotic hunger.

As his hips thrust powerfully forward, his teeth sank deep. She cried out, wound her arms around him, arching up as he drank his fill, as his body drove wildly into hers, staking his claim, his right, taking them beyond the boundaries of the earth. Her body gripped his tightly, insistently. Mikhail abandoned any pretense of control and took her as he wanted, driving on and on until she was so wild and hot and crying for him, until her little keening whimpers and the sweet spice of her blood took his raging body over the edge. He emptied himself into her, for the first time in his life feeling totally sated, totally content. They lay joined, their hearts pounding, their lungs laboring, little aftershocks rippling and rocking them. Mikhail rolled them over so his hard length was cushioning her slender body. Her breasts were soft and warm nestled in the tangle of hair veeing down to his stomach. Her head was pillowed on his chest.

Mikhail stroked her hair, letting his overwhelming love for

her spill out and surround her. He sensed how fragile the moment was and didn't trust the inadequacy of words. His mind was a warm, safe haven of love and he shared it willingly.

The intense pleasure blocked out reality for a long while. Raven could only revel in her body's powerful reaction. Every tiny cell was alive and shrieking in joy. It didn't seem possible that she could experience such rapture.

She moved a slow hand to push her hair aside. The small movement sent her muscles clenching around him. Mikhail. Who was this man who had so easily taken over her life and her body? Raven lifted her head and studied his face. So handsome. So dark and mysterious. His eyes held so many secrets; his mouth was so sensual, it took her breath away.

"Tell me what I've done, Mikhail."

His eyes were fathomless, watchful. "You have given your life into my care. Rest assured, little one, you are safe in my hands."

She touched the tip of her tongue to her suddenly dry lips. Her heart pounded in alarm at the enormity of her decision. She had the taste of him in her mouth, the smell of him on her body, his seed trickling along her leg, and they were still locked together, her body clenching sensuously, hotly, around his.

"What do I taste like?" His voice was low, compelling. It whispered against her skin like the brush of fingers. The brush of fantasy.

She closed her eyes tightly, like a child wanting to shut him out. "Mikhail." Her body rippled, tightened at the sound of his voice, at the erotic question he whispered.

He eased out of her, retained his hold so he could cradle her close as he slid back into the foaming pool. "Tell me, Raven." He kissed her throat, tiny little kisses, each as potent as wine.

Her arm wound around his neck, her fingers finding his thick mane of hair. "You taste like the forest, wild and untamed and so erotic you make me crazy." The admission broke from her like the confession of a grave sin.

The bubbles fizzed and burst against their sensitized skin, foamed on their most intimate parts. Mikhail leaned back, taking their weight, securing her on his lap. Her rounded bottom brushed against him, sent sweet fire streaking through their blood. "You taste like sweet, hot spice, addictive and so sensual." His teeth grazed the nape of her neck, sent a shiver of excitement down her spine.

Raven lay quietly in his arms, her mind reeling under the impact of what she had done. She would never get enough of Mikhail. There was a wildness between them that could never be sated. Raven was unable to piece it all together; her brain simply refused to acknowledge what she might have become. She had no idea what he meant when he said they "fed." The impressions were there, but she only had knowledge of what Mikhail shared with her. Was sex always involved? He had said no, but she couldn't imagine taking blood deliberately. She closed her eyes tightly. She couldn't do this with anyone else. She couldn't imagine taking blood from a human.

Mikhail pressed her head to him, his fingers soothing in her hair. He murmured softly, his voice pitched low and compelling. She needed time to adjust to her Carpathian blood, the intense emotions and urgent needs. She had willingly participated in the mating ritual. She had made the blood exchange without his silent compulsion. They were irrevocably bound and there was no reason for her to suffer needless human recriminations and fear of the future. Let her mind accept this new reality slowly.

Mikhail was brutally honest with himself. After waiting several lifetimes for this woman, he didn't want her with anyone else. He had never thought of feeding as an intimate thing; it was a simple necessity. But the idea of Raven biting into another man's neck, taking his life force into her body, was abhorrent to him. Every time he gave her his blood, he felt sexual excitement, an overwhelming need to protect and care for her. He had no idea what other Carpathian men felt for their mates, but he knew any man near Raven would be in grave danger. It was just as well her human mind refused to allow her to accept their way of preying on humans.

Raven stirred in his arms, stretched languidly. "I was thinking of something upsetting and you took it away, didn't you?" There was a hint of a smile in her voice.

He allowed her freedom, watched her sink beneath the foaming water, surface a few feet away. Her large eyes were moving over him with definite laughter. "You know, Mikhail, I'm beginning to think my very first assessment of your character was correct. You're arrogant and bossy."

He swam toward her with lazy, easy strokes. "But I am sexy."

She backpedaled, sent a spray of water at him with the flat of her hand. "Stay away from me. Every time you get near me, something crazy happens."

"Now might be a good time to take you to task for placing your life in danger. You should never have followed the assassins from the inn. You knew I was unable to hear if you called for help." He kept swimming toward her, as relentless as a shark.

Raven took the coward's way out and waded out of the pool, flinging herself into the next large one. The water was cold on her heated skin. She pointed a finger at him, her soft mouth curving. "I told you I was going to try to help you. In any case, if you dare to lecture me, I'll have no choice but to go into just how unethical it was to bind me to you without my consent. Tell me—if I hadn't followed the assassins and Jacob hadn't stabbed me, I would have remained human, wouldn't I?"

Mikhail rose out of the pool, water streaming off his body. Raven's breath caught in her throat. He looked magnificent, so masculine and powerful. In one fluid leap, he launched himself into the air, jackknifed, and cut cleanly into the deep pool. She found her heart beating frantically, her blood singing for him. He came up behind her, his hands spanning her waist, dragging her close, his powerful legs keeping them afloat.

"You would still be human," he agreed, his voice a black magic spell that could send heat coiling through her despite the cold water.

"If I had stayed human, how could you have remained with me as a life mate?" She pushed her rounded bottom against the cradle of his hips, enjoying the sudden excitement as his body swelled and hardened in response to the pressure. She laid her head back on his shoulder.

"I would have chosen to grow old with you and die when you died." His reply was husky, and one hand cupped the softness of her breast. Her hair was brushing his body like so much silk, sending darts of pleasure through him.

Raven lifted her head abruptly, swung around to face him, her blue eyes searching the mysterious depths of his eyes. "Do you mean that, Mikhail? You would have stayed with me as I grew older?"

He nodded, trailed his fingers down her cheek in a gentle caress. "I would have aged right along with you. When your breath ceased, so would mine."

She shook her head. "How can I resist you, Mikhail, when you steal my heart?"

His grin turned her heart over, somersaulted her stomach. "You are not supposed to resist me, little one. I am your other half." His hands settled around her neck, urged her close to him until his mouth found hers and they melted together, sinking beneath the cool waters of the natural pool.

Half the night was gone when Mikhail carried her back to their home. Raven hastily wrapped herself in one of his shirts. "Do you realize I don't have any clothes here?" She couldn't quite meet his eyes, blushing every time his dark gaze brushed her body. She could still feel the imprint of his body on hers, the strength of his possession. "I need to get back to the inn. All of my things are there."

His eyebrow shot up. Now was not the time to tell her she really wouldn't need clothes. Her personal things would help ease the transition. He reached a lazy arm for his own clothes. "I'm sure Mrs. Galvenstein will deliver your things for us. I will call and make sure it is done immediately. I will be going out for a short time, Raven. There are a few loose ends that need to be taken care of. You will be safe here."

Her chin lifted in challenge. "I'll throw something together and come with you. I never want to go through another day like the one I had when I couldn't reach you. It was hell. It really was, Mikhail."

At once his dark eyes touched her face with gentleness. "I never wanted that for you. Gregori placed me in a healing sleep, little one, and I could not answer your call. That was not supposed to happen. I sent Father Hummer to you, thinking I would be asleep, but if there was great need, I would surface enough to reassure you."

"But it didn't happen like that."

He shook his head. "No, Raven. Gregori sent me into a healing sleep. One does not surface when Gregori has elected otherwise. He did not know about you, about your need for my touch. It was my failing, not his, and I am sorry."

"I know," she acknowledged. "You can see why I can't be without you now. I'm afraid, Mikhail, afraid of everything, myself, you, what I've done here."

"Not this time, little one," he said very gently, wishing it could be otherwise. "It is essential to find the other assassins. I cannot let any danger come near you. You will be safe here. I am not asleep; I can touch your mind with mine and you can just as easily reach for me if necessary. There is no need for fear."

"I'm not the stay-at-home-and-be-safe type," she objected.

He turned, large, powerful, his face an implacable mask. Mikhail looked menacing, invincible. Raven stepped backwards involuntarily, her blue eyes darkening to a deep sapphire. Instantly Mikhail took her hand and brought it to the warmth of his mouth. "Do not look at me like that. Your life was nearly taken from me. Do you have any idea what it was like for me to awaken to your cry? To feel your fear, know that disgusting excuse for a man hit you? To feel the blade slice into your body again and again? You nearly died in my arms. I breathed for you, kept your heart beating. I made a decision I knew you might never forgive me for making. I am not ready to take a chance with your life. Can you possibly understand that?"

She could feel his body trembling with his intense emotion. His arms wrapped around her, dragged her to him. "Please, Raven, let me just keep you in a cocoon, at least until I get that sight out of my mind." His fingers tunneled into the thick mass of blue-black hair. Mikhail molded her slender form to his larger frame, held her close as if he could shelter her from any further harm.

Raven wound her arms around his neck. "It's all right, Mikhail. Nothing is going to happen to me." She nuzzled his neck, seeking to reassure him, to push his fear away, as well as her own. "I guess both of us are going to have to make some adjustments."

His kiss was tender and very gentle. "You need to take it easy. Six days of sleep and healing were not enough."

"Six days? That's incredible. Has anyone ever analyzed your blood?"

Mikhail released her reluctantly. "None of us can go near a human medical facility. We take care of our own."

Raven picked up a brush, idly began to use long strokes to smooth the tangles from her damp mane of hair. "Who was the woman trapped in the ground?"

His face closed down, all traces of gentleness gone as if they had never been. "Her name is Eleanor. She gave birth to a male." His tone was devoid of emotion.

She sat cross-legged on the bed, tilting her head sideways as she brushed her long hair. "You don't like her?"

"She betrayed you. She allowed that devil woman to over-hear her and I nearly lost you." He was buttoning his shirt, and the sight of his long, lean fingers performing the simple task fascinated her. "You were under my protection. What that means, Raven, is that all Carpathians must put your safety above their own."

Her small teeth tugged at her lower lip. She sensed, be-neath his emotionless mask, a relentless, merciless fury di-rected toward that unknown woman. Mikhail's feelings for her were ferociously intense and unfamiliar to him. Just as Raven was having difficulty adjusting, so was he.

She chose her words carefully. "Have you ever seen a woman give birth, Mikhail? It is painful and frightening. For the woman to be in control, she needs a safe environment. She feared for the life of her unborn child. Please don't judge her so harshly. In her circumstances I would have been hysterical."

He cupped her face in his large palm, his thumb caressing

her soft, satin skin. "You have such compassion in you. Eleanor nearly cost you your life."

"No, Mikhail. Jacob nearly cost me my life. Eleanor tried as hard as she could. There is no blame, or all of us must share in it."

He turned away from her. "I know I should have kept you by my side. I should never have sought the refuge of the earth's healing powers. It took me too far from you. Gregori thinks only of my protection."

In the mirror, Raven could see pain etched clearly on his face. "There was a moment, little one, when I awoke to your cry, and I was encased in the soil and powerless to help you. Only my fury fed the storm. As I clawed my way to the surface, I felt every slice of the blade, and I knew I had failed you. In that moment, Raven, I faced something so terrible, so savage and monstrous in me, I still cannot examine it too closely. If he had slain you, no one would have been safe. No one." He made the admission in a tight, controlled voice, his back rigid. "Not Carpathian, not human. I can only pray that if such a thing should ever happen again, Gregori will slay me immediately."

Raven stepped in front of him and framed his face with her hands. "Sometimes grief brings things out in people better left hidden. No one is perfect. Not me, not Eleanor, and not even you."

A faint, self-mocking smile touched his well-cut mouth. "I have lived centuries and endured vampire hunts, wars, and betrayals. Until you came into my life, I have never lost control. I never had anything I wanted so much; I never had anything to lose."

She pulled his head down to her, pressed little healing kisses to his throat, his strong jaw, to the hard corners of his mouth. "You are a good man, Mikhail." She grinned impishly, her blue eyes teasing. "You just have too much power for your own good. But don't worry; I know this American girl. She's very disrespectful and she'll take all that arrogant starch out of you."

His answering laughter was slow in coming, but with it the terrible tension drained out of him. He wrapped his arms around her and lifted her off her feet, swinging her around, crushing her to him. As always her heart jumped wildly. His mouth fastened on hers as he whirled them across the room to land on the bed.

Raven's laughter was soft and taunting. "We can't possibly again."

His body was settling over hers, his knee nudging her thighs apart so he could press against her soft, welcoming body. "I think you should just stay naked and waiting for me," he growled, stroking her to ensure her readiness.

She lifted her hips invitingly. "I'm not sure we'll know how to do this in a bed." The last word was a gasp of pleasure as he joined their bodies.

His mouth found hers again, laughter mingling with the sweet taste of passion. His hands shaped her breasts possessively, tunneled in her hair. There was so much joy in her heart, in her mind; so much compassion and sweetness. His eternity would be filled with her laughter and her zest for life. He laughed aloud for the sheer joy of it.

Chapter Eleven

Mikhail had been gone for two long hours. Raven wandered around the house, familiarizing herself with the rooms. She liked her solitude and was grateful for the time to try to sort things out logically. As hard as she tried, she could not make what she had become seem real to her. Only Mikhail was sanity. He was on her mind continually, invading her thoughts, pushing out everything insane until there was only him.

His blood was in her veins, his scent on her body, his mark at her throat and breast. The feel of his possession was in every step, every movement of her body. Raven wrapped his shirt closer. She knew he was alive and well; he had touched her mind often, sending warm reassurance. She found she welcomed the brushing touch, craved it, was aware that he shared the same deep need to merge often with her.

With a sigh she enveloped herself in his long, warm cape. All at once the house was too stifling, like a prison instead of a home. The long wraparound porch beckoned to her; the night seemed to call her name. She caught at the doorknob, twisted. At once the night air rushed over her, cooling and filled with intriguing scents. She wandered out onto the porch, leaned against a tall column and inhaled deeply, drawing the night into her lungs. She could feel a drawing, a calling. Without conscious thought she stepped off the porch and began to wander along the path.

The night whispered and sang, beckoning her into deep forest. An owl hissed softly across the sky; a trio of deer stepped warily from cover to dip velvet muzzles in the cold stream. Raven felt their joy in living, their acceptance of their daily life-and-death struggle. She could hear the sap in the trees thrumming like the ebb and flow of the tide. Her bare feet seemed to find soft ground, avoiding twigs and thorns and sharp rocks. The rush of the water, the sound of the wind, the very heartbeat of the earth called to her.

Entranced, Raven wandered aimlessly, enfolded in Mikhail's long black cape, her hair falling past her hips in a thick cascade of blue-black silk. She looked ethereal, her pale skin almost translucent in the moonlight, her large eyes so dark blue that they were purple. The cape parted occasionally to reveal an intriguing glimpse of bare, shapely leg.

Something rippled in her mind, disturbing the tranquil beauty of the night. *Grief. Tears.* Raven halted, blinked rapidly, tried to determine her surroundings. She had wandered as if she was in a beautiful dream. She turned in the direction of the intense emotion. Without conscious thought, her feet began to move forward. Her mind automatically processed information.

A human male. Early twenties. His genuine grief ran deep. There was anger toward his father, confusion, and guilt that he had arrived too late. Something deep in Raven responded to his overwhelming need. He was huddled against a broad tree trunk, down low near the timberline. His knees were drawn up, his face buried in his hands.

Raven deliberately made a sound as she approached. The man lifted a tear-streaked face, his eyes wide with shock as he spotted her. He began to scramble to his feet.

"Please don't get up," Raven said quietly, her voice as soft as the night itself. "I didn't mean to disturb you. I couldn't sleep and came out walking. Would you prefer me to leave?"

Rudy Romanov found himself staring in awe at a dream

figure that seemed to materialize out of the mist. She was like nothing he had ever seen before, as shrouded in mystery as the dark forest itself. Words caught in his throat. Had his grief conjured her up? He could almost believe the ridiculous, superstitious tales his father had told him. Tales of vampires and women of the darkness, sirens luring men to their doom.

The man was staring at her as if she were a ghost. "I'm so sorry," she murmured gently and turned to leave him.

"No! Don't go." His English was heavily accented. "For a minute, coming out of the mist like that, you hardly looked real."

Aware that she had little on beneath the long cape, Raven drew it closer around her. "Are you all right? Can I call someone for you? The priest, perhaps? Your family?"

"There is no one, not anymore. I'm Rudy Romanov. You must have heard the news about my parents."

An unholy vision burst in her head. She saw wolves boiling from the forest, red eyes gleaming fiercely, a huge black wolf leading the pack and bearing straight down on Hans Romanov. From the young man's head, she picked up the memory of his mother, Heidi, lying on her bed, her husband's fingers around her throat. For one awful moment she couldn't breathe. What this man had suffered! Both parents taken from him in a matter of hours. His fanatical father had murdered his mother.

"I've been ill; this is my first time out in days." She moved closer to him beneath the outstretched limbs of the trees. She couldn't very well tell him the truth—that she had been involved in the entire horrendous affair.

To Rudy, she seemed a beautiful angel sent to console him. Rudy longed to touch her skin to see if it was really as soft as it appeared in the moonlight. Her voice was a gentle whisper, sexy, soothing, reaching into his mind to calm and heal. He cleared his throat. "My father murdered my mother a couple of nights ago. If only I had come home sooner. My mother called me, telling me some nonsense about him murdering a woman. He had delusions of vampires preying on people in the village. My father had always been superstitious, but I never thought he would go completely crazy. Mother said he and a group of fanatics were hunting vampires and marking prominent members of the community for murder. I thought he was just talking big, like he always did." He glanced down at his hands. "I should have listened to her, but she admitted that no one else seemed to know of the murder. I assumed he'd lied about killing a woman, that it wasn't the truth. Hell, maybe it wasn't, but he was nuts. He strangled my mother. She died with her rosary in her hands."

Rudy wiped his eyes with trembling fingers. Somehow, he had no idea how, his mystery lady was in his mind, providing warmth and understanding. The illusion was so real his body stirred to life, and he became acutely aware that they were very much alone. Unbidden, the thought came to him that no one knew she was with him. The thought was disturbingly exciting in the midst of his grief. "I stayed one more day at the university to take a test I thought was really important. I didn't really believe my father would kill someone, least of all a woman. My mother was a midwife. She brought so many lives into the world, helped so many people. I told her I was on my way home and I'd take care of things. She wanted to go to the priest, but I talked her out of it."

"I wish I had known her," Raven said sincerely.

"You would have liked her; everyone liked her. She must have tried to stop my father. The night of the storm, he went out with a group of outsiders. That's when he must have killed my mother, right before he left the house. He probably was making certain she didn't tell anyone or try to stop him. He was caught under a tree that was hit by lightning. He and the others were burned beyond recognition."

"How terrible for you." Raven swept a hand through her hair, a slow tunneling of her fingers through the heavy fall of silk, pushing it away from her face. Sexy. Innocent. A potent combination.

Mist streamed through the forest toward the house set back against the cliffs. It filtered through the iron gates and poured into the courtyard. The mist stacked into a tall, thick column, shimmered, connected, until Mikhail, in his solid form, stood in front of his door. Lifting a hand, murmuring a soft command, he released the safeguard and entered. Immediately he knew she was gone.

Eyes darkened to black ice. White teeth bared, gleamed. A low growl rumbled, was suppressed. His first thought was that someone had taken her, that she was in danger. He sent out a call to his sentries, the wolves, to aid him in his search for her. Taking a deep, calming breath, he allowed his mind to find hers, to zero in on her location. It wasn't difficult to track her. She was not alone. *A human. Male.*

His breath caught in his throat. His heart nearly ceased beating. His fingers curled into two tight fists. Beside Mikhail the lamp exploded, burst into fragments. Outside the wind rose, whirled in tiny tornadoes through the trees. Mikhail stepped outside and leaped into the air, spread giant wings and hurtled through the sky. Far below him the wolves howled to one another and began to run in tight pack formation.

Mikhail glided silently to the heavy branches above Raven's head. She was pushing her hair away from her face in her curiously sexy, very feminine way. He could feel her compassion, her need to comfort. He could also feel how cold and exhausted she was. The human was grief-stricken, no doubt about it. But Mikhail could smell his excitement, could hear the pounding heart, the flow of blood surging and pooling. He could easily read the man's thoughts, and they were not all innocent.

Furious, more than a little afraid for her, Mikhail launched himself into the air, then settled on the ground a yard away, out of sight. And then he was striding toward them, a tall, powerful figure appearing out of the night, out of the trees. He loomed over them, menacing, formidable, the hard angles and planes of his face harsh and merciless. Black eyes gleamed with something dark and deadly. The moonlight reflected there gave an eerie red glow, even a feral quality, to his unblinking gaze.

Threatened, Rudy scrambled to his feet, making a grab for his mystery lady with a vague idea of protecting her. Although Mikhail was several feet farther away from Raven than Rudy, he put on a burst of blurring speed and his hand was there first, shackling her fragile wrist and yanking Raven behind him, locking her to him.

"Good evening, Mr. Romanov," Mikhail said pleasantly, his tone so low and silky both Rudy and Raven shivered. "Perhaps you would be so kind as to tell me what you are doing at this time of night meeting in these woods alone with my woman." As he uttered the last word, from somewhere close, a wolf howled ominously, the long, drawn-out note echoing a warning on the night breeze.

Raven stirred, but Mikhail's grip on her threatened to crush her bones. *Be silent, little one. If you wish this human to see the dawn, you will obey me. He is Hans Romanov's son. What is in his mind is what his father planted long ago.*

She paled visibly. *Mikhail, his parents . . .*

I am holding on to control by a thread. Do not snap it!

"Mr. Dubrinsky." Rudy recognized him now, a powerful figure in his home village, an unrelenting enemy or a valuable friend. Mikhail's voice appeared calm, serene even, yet he looked capable of murder. "We didn't plan this. I came here because . . . " His voice trailed off. He could have sworn he caught sight of wolves lurking in the trees, their eyes glowing with that same feral quality as the hunter in front of him. One look at that merciless face and Rudy let go of his pride. "I was grieving. She was out walking and she heard me."

The wolves were silent shadows slipping closer. Mikhail sensed their eagerness, the cry of bloodlust. It washed over him and mixed with black jealousy. The pack whispered and called to him as their brother. The beast in him lifted its head, roared for release. The human male claimed innocence, but it was easy to read lust in his body, smell the scent of sexual arousal. It was easy for Mikhail to read the taint of sickness in the son, placed there by the father.

Mikhail's dark gaze swept Raven's small figure. She could stop his heart, take his breath away. She never looked beyond the surface; she had trained herself not to. Mikhail read compassion, sadness, exhaustion, and something else. He had hurt her. It was there in the depths of her enormous eyes. And there was genuine fear. She knew the wolves were out there;

she heard their voices urging him to protect his mate. It was a terrible blow for her to realize just how susceptible he was to their primitive logic, to realize how much animal was really in him. Instantly his arm swept around her, dragged her beneath his shoulder, close to his warmth. He sent out a silent command to the wolves, feeling their resistance, their reluctance to obey. They could sense his antagonism to the human, his own lust for blood, the need to vanquish an enemy that might threaten his mate's safety.

"I heard of your loss," Mikhail made himself say, his arm curving around Raven protectively. "Your mother was a great woman. Her death was a tremendous loss to our community. Your father and I had our differences, but I would have wished his death on no man."

Raven was shivering with cold and reaction to the knowledge that Mikhail could feel such intense animosity toward anyone. She was the light to his darkness, incapable of understanding that he was first and foremost a predator. His hand moved up and down her arm gently, seeking to reassure her. Mikhail reinforced his command to the wolves. "You had better go home, Mr. Romanov. You need sleep, and these woods are not always safe. The storm has left the animals edgy."

"Thank you for being so kind," Rudy said to Raven, reluctant to leave her with a man who looked so capable of great violence.

Mikhail watched the man retreat to the safety of the edge of town, beyond the clearing. "You are cold, little one," he said very gently.

Raven blinked back tears, forcing her trembling legs to begin walking, one slow step at a time. She couldn't look at him, didn't dare. She had simply been enjoying the beauty of the night. Then she had heard Romanov. It was in her nature to help if she was able. Now she had triggered something dark and deadly in Mikhail, something that troubled her deeply.

Mikhail paced beside her, studied her averted face. "You are going in the wrong direction, Raven." He put his hand at the small of her back to guide her.

Raven stiffened, then twisted away from him. "Maybe I don't want to go back, Mikhail. Maybe I don't really know who you are at all."

There was more hurt than anger in her voice. Mikhail sighed heavily and reached for her, his grip unbreakable iron. "We will talk in the warmth and comfort of our home, not here where your body is like ice." Without waiting for her consent, he lifted her easily and moved with a burst of speed. Raven clung to him, her face buried against his shoulder, her slender body shaking with cold and more than a little fear of him, of her future, of what she herself had become.

Mikhail took her directly to the bedchamber, lit the fire with a lift of his hand, and placed her on the bed. "You could at least have worn shoes."

Raven drew her cloak around her protectively, looking up at him from under long lashes. "Why? And I'm not asking about shoes."

He lit candles and crushed a variety of herbs to fill their chamber with soothing, healing sweetness. "I am a Carpathian male. I have the blood of the earth flowing in my veins. I have waited centuries for my life mate. Carpathian men do not like other men near their women. I am struggling with unfamiliar emotions, Raven. They are not easy to control. You do not behave as a Carpathian woman would." A small smile tugged at the corner of his mouth. Mikhail leaned lazily against the wall. "I did not expect to come home to find you gone. You put yourself in danger, Raven, something the males of our race cannot allow. And then I find you with a human. A male."

"He was in pain," she said quietly.

Mikhail made a sound of annoyance. "He wanted you."

Her eyelashes fluttered, blue eyes meeting his, startled and unsure. "But . . . no, Mikhail, you're mistaken; you must be. I was only trying to comfort him. He lost both of his parents." She looked close to tears.

He held up his hand to silence her. "And you wanted to be in his company. Not sexually, but still, his human company; do not deny it. I could feel the need in you."

Her tongue touched her lips nervously. She couldn't deny

it. It had been entirely subconscious on her part, but now that he had spoken the words aloud, she knew it was true. She had felt the need for human companionship. Mikhail was so intense, everything in his world so unfamiliar. Raven hated that she hurt him, hated that she had been the one to push him to the edge of his control. "I'm sorry. I didn't intend to do anything but go for a short walk. When I heard him, I felt the need to make certain he was all right. I didn't know, Mikhail, that I was seeking human company."

"I do not blame you, little one, never that." His voice was so gentle, it turned her heart over. "I can easily read your memories. I know of your intent. And I would never blame you for your compassionate nature."

"I guess we both have difficulties to contend with," she said softly. "I can't be what you want me to be, Mikhail. You use the word 'human' like a curse, something less than what you are. Did it ever occur to you that you're prejudiced against my race? Carpathian blood may flow in my veins, but in my heart and my mind I'm human. I didn't set out to betray you. I went for a walk. That's all I did. I'm sorry, Mikhail, but all my life I've known freedom. Changing my blood is not going to change who I am."

He paced across the floor with quick, fluid energy, all power and coordination. "I am not prejudiced," he denied.

"Of course you are. You view my race with a measure of contempt. Would you have been happy if I had fed, using Romanov's blood? Is that acceptable? To use him for food, but not for a few friendly words?"

"I do not like this picture you paint of me, Raven." Mikhail crossed the room to hold out his hand for the cape. The bedchamber was warm and smelled of nature—wood and meadow.

Reluctantly Raven slipped the cape from her shoulders. Mikhail frowned when he saw she was clad only in his crisp white shirt. Although the tails reached her knees and covered her bottom, a generous portion of her thighs was exposed, right up to her hips. The effect was incredibly sexy, with her long, wild mane of hair cascading in waves down to the bed, framing her slender form. Mikhail swore softly, a few choice words in his own language, thankful he hadn't realized she was wearing nothing but his shirt beneath his cape. He probably would have torn out Romanov's throat. The thought of Raven approaching the young man, smiling at him, mesmerizing him with her siren's eyes, bending her head to his throat, touching him with her mouth, her tongue, her teeth . . . His gut clenched in total rebellion at the picture.

He raked a hand through his hair, hung the cape in his closet, and filled the old-fashioned pitcher and basin with warm water. Once he had his imagination under firm control he could answer her with his usual gentleness. "No, little one, after giving it thought, I cannot say I would have been happy had you been feeding."

"Isn't that what I'm supposed to do? A Carpathian woman preys on unsuspecting humans." There was an edge of unshed tears in her voice.

Mikhail carried the water over to the side of the bed, knelt down in front of her. "I am trying to understand my feelings, Raven, and they do not make sense." Very gently he began to bathe her feet. "More than anything I want your happiness. But I feel the need to protect you." His hands were gentle, his touch tender as he removed every speck of earth.

Raven ducked her head, rubbing her temples. "I know you do, Mikhail, and I even understand to a point your need to do it; it's just that I am always going to be me. I'm impulsive, I do things. I decide I want to fly a kite and the next thing I'm doing it."

"Why did you not stay inside? I asked for time to come to grips with my terrible fear for your safety." His voice was so incredibly gentle, it brought tears to her eyes.

She touched his coffee-colored hair with her fingertips, felt an ache in her throat. "I wanted to go outside on the porch for fresh air. I had no other thought, but the night just called to me."

Mikhail glanced up at her, his dark eyes warm with his feelings for her. "It was my mistake, I should have set safeguards to protect you."

"Mikhail, I am capable of looking after myself." Her blue eyes were very earnest, impressing on him the truth of her words. He really didn't need to worry.

Mikhail did his best to keep from smiling. She was too good, always believing the best of everyone. His fingers circled her small calves. "You are the most beautiful woman in the world, Raven. You do not have a mean bone in your body, do you?"

Raven looked indignant. "Of course I do. Don't smile like that, Mikhail; I really do. I can be just as mean as necessary. In any case, what has that to do with what we're talking about?"

His hand moved upward to her rib cage beneath the thin silk of his shirt. "We are talking about me needing to protect the one person who matters to me, the one who can only see good in everyone."

"I do not," she denied, shocked that he would think so. "I knew Margaret Summers was fanatical."

His hand moved upward to caress the soft underside of her breast, to cup the weight of it in his palm. His eyes had gone black and deep with emotion. "You defended her, as I recall."

He was taking her breath away with his absent, leisurely exploration of her body. It was more than physical; she felt him inside her, admiring her, even as he wanted to force her compliance to his will. She felt him in her body, stroking her mind, caressing her heart. She sensed his feelings for her growing and growing until they consumed him.

Mikhail sighed softly. "I am never going to get anywhere with you, am I? You have a way of disarming me. I am the leader of my people, Raven. I cannot have this. I have no choice but to resort to orders."

Her eyebrows flew up. "Orders?" she echoed. "You think you'll give me orders?"

"Absolutely. It is the only recourse open to me that prevents me from being a laughingstock among my people. Unless, of course, you have a better idea." There was laughter in the depths of his eyes.

"How do I divorce you?"

"I am sorry, little one," he answered blandly. "I do not understand this word. In my language, please."

"You know very well you speak English far better than I speak your language," she said. "How does one life mate split from the other? Separate. Break apart. No longer together."

The glint of humor in the depths of his eyes deepened to total amusement. "There is no such thing, and if there was, Raven"—he bent very close, his breath fanning her cheek—"I would never allow you to go."

Raven looked innocent and wide-eyed. The hand on her breast, his thumb stroking her nipple, was making it hard to breathe. "I was only trying to help you. Royalty has so few options these days. You have to worry about what the public thinks. You can rely on me, Mikhail, to help you ponder such issues."

He laughed softly, tauntingly male. "I guess I must be thankful to have such a clever life mate." His fingers slipped a button of the white shirt free. Just one, widening the gap across her breasts to give him more room for his lazy exploration.

Raven's breath caught in her throat. He was doing nothing really, simply touching her, his touch so gentle and loving she was melting inside. "I really am trying to understand your way of life, Mikhail, but I don't think my heart can take it yet." She tried to be truthful. "I know nothing of your laws or your customs. I don't even know exactly what you are, what I am. I think of myself as human. We're not even married in the eyes of God or man."

This time Mikhail threw back his head and laughed loudly, heartily. "You think the pale ceremony of humans is a deeper binding than that of a true Carpathian ritual? You do have much to learn of our ways."

Her small white teeth scraped at her lower lip. "Has it occurred to you that I might not feel bound by Carpathian laws and rituals? You have so little regard for things I consider sacred."

"Raven!" He was shocked, and it showed. "Is that what you think? I have no regard for your beliefs? That is not so."

215

She ducked her head so that her silky hair fell around her face, hiding her expression. "We know so little about one another. I know nothing about who I've become. How can I fulfill your needs, or you mine, if I don't even know what or who I am?"

He was silent, his dark, fathomless eyes studying her sad face, the sorrow in her eyes. "Perhaps there is some truth in your words, little one." His hands followed the contours of her body, shaped her narrow rib cage, her small waist, moved up to frame her face. "I look at you and know what a miracle you are. The feel of your skin, soft and inviting, the way you move, like water flowing, the brush of your hair like silk, the feel of your body surrounding mine, completing me, giving me the strength I need to continue a task that seems so hopeless, but so necessary. I look at the way you are made, so beautiful, your body so perfect, made for mine."

Raven stirred restlessly, but his hands held her captive, tilting her chin so that she had no choice but to meet his black eyes. "But it is not your body that holds me, Raven, not your flawless skin or the perfection of the combination of our bodies when we come together. It is when I merge with you and see who you really are that I realize what a miracle really is. I can tell you who you are. You are compassion. You are gentleness. You are a woman who is so courageous, you are willing to risk your life for complete strangers. You are a woman willing to use a gift that causes you great pain for the benefit of others. There is no hesitation in your giving; it is who you are. There is such a light in you, it shines through your eyes and radiates through your skin, so that anyone seeing you can easily see your goodness."

Raven could only stare at him helplessly, lost in his mesmerizing eyes. Mikhail took her hand, pressed a kiss in the exact center of her palm, slipped her hand beneath his shirt, and held it over his steadily beating heart. "Look beyond my skin, Raven. Look into my heart and soul. Merge your mind with mine; see me for what I am. Know me for who I am."

Mikhail waited silently. A heartbeat. Two. He saw her sudden determination to know what she had bound herself to, to know just whom it was she had formed an alliance with. Her mind merge was tentative at first, her touch so light and delicate it felt like the brush of butterfly wings. She was cautious, moving through his memories as if she might discover something that would hurt him. He felt the breath leave her body as she saw the gathering darkness. The monster that lived within. The stain on his soul. The deaths and battles he was responsible for. The stark ugliness of his existence before she had come into his life. The loneliness that ate away at him, at all the males of their species, the barren emptiness they endured century after century. She saw his determination never to lose her. His possessiveness, his animal instincts. Everything he was, it was all there laid out for her to see. He hid nothing from her—not the kills he had made, not the ones he had ordered, not his absolute conviction that no one would ever take her from him and live.

Raven pulled out of his mind, her blue eyes steady on his. Mikhail felt the sudden pounding of his heart. There was no condemnation there, only serene calm. "So you see the beast you are tied to for all eternity. We are predators, after all, little one, and the darkness in us is only balanced by the light in our women."

Her hands crept around his neck, gentle, loving. "How terrible a struggle all of you must have, and you more than most. To have to make so many life-and-death decisions, to sentence friends and even family to be destroyed must be a burden beyond belief. You are strong, Mikhail, and your people are right to believe in you. The monster you battle daily is part of you, maybe the part that makes you so strong and determined. You see that side of you as evil when in fact it is what gives you your power, the ability and strength to do what you must do for your people."

Mikhail ducked his head, not wanting her to see the expression in his eyes, what her words meant to him. There was an obstruction in his throat that threatened to choke him. He did not deserve her, would never deserve her. She was unselfish, while he had all but taken her captive and forced her to find a way to live with him.

"Mikhail." Her voice was soft; she brushed his chin with the softness of her mouth. "I was alone until you came into my life." Her lips found the corner of his. "No one knew me—not who I was—and people feared me because I knew things about them they could never know of me." She wrapped her arms around him, comforting him as if he were a child. "Was it really so wrong to want me for yourself, knowing I would end such a terrible existence for you? Do you really believe you must condemn yourself? I love you. I know that I love you totally and without reservation. I accept who you are."

He raked a hand through his hair. "I cannot control my emotions at this time, Raven. I cannot lose you. You have no conception of what it was like—no daylight, no laughter, centuries of complete loneliness. I know a monster lives in me. The longer one lives, the more powerful he becomes. I fear for Gregori. He is but a mere twenty-five years younger than I am, but he has had the weight of hunting the undead for centuries. He isolates himself from his own kind. Sometimes we do not see or hear from him for half a century. His power is immense and the darkness in him grows. It is a cold, bleak existence, harsh and unrelenting, and always the monster inside fights for release. You are my salvation. At this time it is all so new to me, and the fear of losing you far too fresh. I don't know what I would do to any who would try to take you from me."

Her hand found his, fingers linking them together.

"Noelle gave birth to a son. Eleanor did the same. There are no women to relieve the terrible black void for the men. Gregori suffers the most. He roams the earth, learning its secrets and conducting experiments none of us dare inquire too deeply into. I have never told anyone this, but he has more knowledge and more strength than I do. We have never had reason for conflict—he always comes through in an emergency—but I feel his withdrawal." Mikhail rubbed his eyes tiredly. "What am I to do? Sooner or later he will make his choice. Either way we will lose him."

"I don't understand."

"There is ultimate power in the taking of life while we feed, and it is so easy, drawing our victims to us. No one can survive darkness and despair for a thousand years. Gregori has lived from the Crusades to men walking on the moon, always fighting the monster inside. The one hope we have for salvation is our life mate. And if Gregori does not find his life mate soon, he will seek the dawn or turn. I fear the worst."

"What is turning?"

"Killing for the pleasure of it, the power, becoming the vampire humans recognize. Using women before feeding, forcing them to become slaves," Mikhail answered grimly. He and Gregori had often hunted their own kind and discovered just how depraved a Carpathian turned vampire could be.

"You would have to stop Gregori?" Fear shot through her like a flaming arrow. She was beginning to understand the complexity of Mikhail's life. "You say he is more powerful."

"Without a doubt. He has had freedom of movement, and far more experience in hunting and tracking the undead. He has learned so much, participated in life across the earth. His tremendous power is only exceeded by his utter isolation. Gregori is more like a brother than a friend. We have been together since the beginning. I would not wish to fail him or hunt him, nor attempt to pit my strength against his. He has fought numerous battles for me, with me. We have shared blood, healed one another, guarded each other when there was need."

"What of Jacques?" She already felt affection for the man who was so much like Mikhail.

Mikhail stood up, dumping the water wearily. "My brother is two hundred years younger than I. He is strong and wise and very dangerous given the right circumstances. The blood of the ancients runs strong in him. He travels, studies, is willing to take the responsibility of our people should it become necessary."

"You carry the burdens of your people on your shoulders." Her voice was very soft. She caressed his coffee-colored hair with gentle fingers.

Mikhail sat up carefully, regarding her with old, weary eyes. "We are a dying race, little one. I fear I merely slow the inevitable. Two of the known assassins escaped. Two other suspects, Anton Fabrezo and Dieter Hodkins, also left on the train. I sent word throughout the mountains, but they have disappeared. I have heard rumors of an organized group of hunters that has emerged recently in this time period. If these men ever hook up with true scientists, they will become even more dangerous."

"I know Carpathians are of the earth, and their healing comes from the earth and all its natural powers. But, Mikhail, perhaps your prejudice and contempt for the human race has made you overlook some of its advantages."

"You persist in thinking me prejudiced. I like many humans." Mikhail found he couldn't resist sliding the buttons open on the white silk shirt that covered her bare body. There was something deep within him, a primitive need that made him want to look at her, to know he could do so whenever he wanted.

She smiled at him, sweeping her hair back in her curiously sexy gesture. The action created a gap in the shirt so that her bare skin beckoned, her full breasts thrust toward him invitingly, then disappeared under a cloud of ebony silk. The sight took his breath away. "Listen to me, my love. Having a few friends and feeling affection for certain individuals of a race does not remove prejudice. You have lived with your abilities for so long you take them for granted. Because you can control the human mind and you use them as cattle . . ."

He gasped, shocked that she could think such a thing. His hand circled her ankle where it was tucked up on the bed. "I have never treated humans like cattle. Many of them are counted among my friends, although Gregori and some of the others think I am crazy. I watch humans grow and wish I could feel the things they feel. No, little one, I do not believe I treat them as cattle."

She tilted her chin, regarding him steadily with her large sapphire eyes. "Perhaps not like cattle, but I feel what you feel, Mikhail. You can hide this from yourself, but I can see it clearly." She smiled to soften her words. "I know you don't want to feel superior, but it is so easy to control us."

He snorted his disagreement. "I have failed to control you at every turn. You have no idea how often I wanted to force your obedience when you placed yourself in danger. I should have gone with my instincts . . . but no, I allowed you to go back to the inn."

"Your love for me caused you to pull back." She reached out to touch his hair. "Isn't that how it should be between two people? If you really love who I am, and you want me to be happy, then you know I have to do what comes naturally to me, what I feel is right."

His finger traced down her throat, through the deep valley between her breasts, making her shiver with sudden heat. "That is true, little one, but that is also true of my needs. You can do no other than to make me happy. My happiness is completely dependent on whether or not you are safe."

Raven couldn't help smiling. "Somehow I think your devious nature is showing. Perhaps you need to examine human ingenuity. You rely heavily on your gifts, Mikhail, but humans must find other ways. We are uniting two worlds. If we decide to have a child . . . "

He stirred restlessly, his dark eyes glittering.

She caught the imperious Carpathian decree before he could censor his thoughts. *You must.*

"If we decide someday to have a child," she persisted, ignoring his authority, "if it is male, he will be raised in both worlds. And if it is a girl, she will be raised with free will and a mind of her own. I mean it, Mikhail. I will never, ever, consent to bringing a child into this world to be a brood mare for one of these men. She will know her own power and choose her own life."

"Our women make their choices," he said quietly.

"I'm sure there's some ritual that ensures that she wants to choose the right man," Raven guessed. "You will give me your word you will agree to my terms or I will not bear a child."

His fingertips brushed her face with exquisite tenderness. "More than anything I want your happiness. I would also want my children to be happy. We have years to decide these things, lifetimes, but yes, when we have learned to balance the two worlds and we know the time is right, I agree absolutely to your terms."

221

"You know I'll hold you to it," she warned.

He laughed softly, cupping the side of her face in his palm. "As the years go by, your strength and power will grow. You already terrify me, Raven. I do not know if my heart will be able to stand the coming years."

She laughed, the sound like music. His hands shaped her breasts, cupped the soft weight in his palms, bent his head to her offering. His mouth was hot and moist and needy, his teeth scraping back and forth on sensitive skin. His hair brushed against her like tongues licking at her ribs. At once her arms circled him as she relaxed back against the headboard.

Mikhail stretched out on the bed, his head in her lap. "You are going to turn my well-ordered world upside down, are you not?"

She tunneled her fingers in his hair, enjoying the feel of its silky thickness against the bare skin of her hips and thighs. "I certainly intend to do my best. You people are in a rut. You need to move into this century."

He could feel his body relaxing and peace stole into him, edging out the terrible tension. The beauty of her inner soul washed over him. How could he fault her need to reach out to someone in pain, when it was her very compassion that had drawn him out of the dark shadows and into a world of joy and light? He might feel pain and anger, but at least he was capable of feeling. Intense emotion. Joy. Lust. Sexual hunger. Love.

"You are my life, little one. We will ask Father Hummer to marry us in the way of your people." His white teeth gleamed at her; his dark eyes were warm with contentment. "I will accept the marriage as binding, and you will erase the word *divorce* and all of its meanings from your memory. That will please me." He grinned at her, male amusement taunting her.

Her fingertips traced the hard line of his jaw tenderly. "How do you manage to turn everything to your advantage?"

His hand found the bare skin of her satin-smooth thigh. "I do not know the answer to that, little one. Perhaps it is sheer talent." He turned his head and nuzzled aside the tails of his shirt to burrow against her.

A low sound escaped from deep in Raven's throat as his

tongue stroked her. Obligingly she moved her legs to accommodate him, to give him room. She tangled her fingers in his thick, coffee-colored hair.

Mikhail delved deeper, drew a shudder of pleasure from her. He could feel the spreading flames in his blood, swift, savage excitement, joy singing in his veins. His arms circled her hips, dragged her closer to him so that he could burrow deeper. He intended to take his time, to give her pleasure. She was his woman, his life mate, and no one could give her the kind of ecstasy he could.

Chapter Twelve

The bedchamber, situated below the earth, was as silent and as dark as a tomb. Mikhail and Raven lay together on the huge bed, their bodies entwined. Mikhail's leg was over her thigh, his large frame curved protectively around hers, his arms sheltering her close to his heart. There was utter silence in the chamber, not even the sound of breathing. To all appearances they were devoid of life.

The house itself seemed to be in slumber, silent, as if it were holding its breath and waiting for night to fall. Sunshine burst through the windows and spotlighted the centuries-old artwork and leather-bound books. Mosaic tiles gleamed on the floor at the entrance, the sun on the hardwood floors bringing out a blondish hue in the wood.

Without warning Mikhail's breath began in a long, slow, continuous hiss, like a coiled, venomous snake prepared to strike. His dark eyes snapped open, malevolent, glowing with a predator's hunger, with the fury of a trapped wolf. His body was sluggish, his tremendous strength sapped by the need for deep sleep. Tuned to the cycle of day and night, he knew it was midday and the harsh, unrelenting sun was at its highest and most lethal peak.

Something was wrong. Something had penetrated the deep layers of sleep to wake him from his needed slumber. His fingers curled, nails like claws raking the mattress beneath him. Too many hours to sunset. He scanned his surroundings, meticulous in his search. The house vibrated with sudden tension, the air stirring with unease. The very foundation seemed to flinch in terror at some unseen menace.

Outside the wrought-iron fence, Rudy Romanov paced back and forth, black anger in his heart, in his mind. Every fourth step he pounded at the fence in a fury of frustration, a baseball bat cracking hard against the thick twisted poles of iron. "Evil! Undead!" The words were hurled into the air toward the house.

Mikhail growled low, his body trapped in the layers of fog, his instincts fully aroused. His lips drew back in a silent snarl, exposing fangs. A long slow hiss escaped again.

Accusations beat in his head with the force of Rudy's anger. "I found my father's proof. He's gathered it for years. Everything! It's all there. The list of your servants. You are evil, the head of the monster. Murderer! Unclean! You turned that beautiful woman into your perverted slave! She would have used me to add to your ranks."

The madness of grief and rage blended with a fanatical desire for revenge. Rudy Romanov believed his father's records and had come to kill the head vampire. Mikhail understood the danger; the very air was thick with it. He called to Raven, brushed her mind with his, a loving, gentle caress. *Wake, my love. We are in danger.*

Raven's breath began, slow and even. With his warning filling her mind, she automatically scanned the chamber. Her body felt limp and lifeless, the need for sleep intensely strong. Her brain felt sluggish, uncomprehending.

Romanov is outside the walls.

She blinked, tried to clear the fog. *Hans Romanov is dead. His son lives. He is outside, and I can feel his rage and ha-*

tred. He is dangerous to us. The sun is up; we are weak. He cannot enter, but we cannot go out.

It took great concentration and a supreme effort to rub her face against the tangle of hair on his chest. She cleared her throat experimentally. "I can answer the door, see what he wants. I'll tell him you're at work. He'll feel silly and leave us alone."

He cradled her head against him. She was still thinking in human terms, unaware of the terrible price of immortality. *You are still so groggy, you are not hearing him. He is in a dangerous state of mind.* She had no idea of the price she had paid for loving him. The sun would destroy her should she ever find the strength to rise.

Raven curled against him like a cat, her need for sleep overwhelming.

Listen to me, little one. You must stay awake! The command was imperious. Mikhail's arms surrounded her with the intensity of his love, his need to protect her.

Raven roused herself enough to scan her surroundings. The blackness of Rudy Romanov's rage was like a living entity, demanding death. The force of it beat in her head. *He's crazy, Mikhail.* She lifted a hand, a slow, difficult movement, tried to push at the heavy fall of hair. The air was so thick or she was so weak; the simple movement took intense concentration. *Last night he was so sweet, grieving for his mother. Now he's convinced we are his enemy. He's an educated man, Mikhail. Did I put us in danger? Maybe I did or said something to make him suspicious.* Raven's mind was clouded with guilt.

His chin rubbed the top of her head. *No, he found something among his father's papers. He was not suspicious last night; he grieved. Something convinced him that his father's accusations were well founded. He believes us to be vampire.*

I don't think anyone will believe him, even if he shows them the evidence he supposedly has. They'll think he's in shock. She feared for Rudy's safety as much as for their own.

Mikhail's fingers brushed her cheek tenderly. It was so like her to have compassion for a man whose entire being was bent on murdering them. Suddenly his body jerked hard against hers. The house flinched, screamed silently a split second before the first explosion reverberated in their ears. Above them, on the first floor, windows shattered; antique furniture splintered. A heartbeat, two heartbeats. Another explosion rocked the house, fragmenting the wall on the north side.

Mikhail's fangs gleamed in the darkness; the hiss of his breath was a promise of merciless retaliation. The smell of smoke, acrid and rank, seeped through the ceiling into their bedchamber, where it swirled and gathered into a pungent, eye-burning cloud. Over their heads flames began to crackle and lick greedily at the books and paintings, at Mikhail's past, at his present. Orange and red tongues eagerly consumed possessions that Mikhail had acquired in the long centuries of his existence. Rudy wanted to destroy it all, little knowing that Mikhail had many houses, many treasures.

Mikhail! She felt his anguish at the death of his favorite home burning above them. The putrid smell of hatred, fear, and smoke mixed.

We must go below. The house will eventually fall. In her mind the grimness he felt echoed sharply.

Raven attempted to drag herself into a sitting position, her movements painfully sluggish. *We have to get out of the house. Going below will only trap us between the ground and the flames.*

The sun is too high. We must go underground. His arms tightened perceptibly, as if he could give her the courage to face what had to be done. *We have no choice.*

You go, Mikhail, she said. Fear clawed at her. She was helpless in her present state. Even if she managed to move herself below to the cellar, she could never burrow into the soil, bury herself alive. She would be insane when the time came to return to the surface. She absolutely could not commit herself to such an act, but it was necessary to encourage Mikhail to do so. He was the important one, the one his people needed.

We go together, my love. He interjected strength into his voice, a strength his muscular body did not echo. His limbs were like lead. It took tremendous effort to drag himself off

the bed, and his body landed heavily on the floor. *Come on;
we can do this.*

The smoke was thicker now, the room beginning to heat
like an oven. Overhead, the ceiling began to blacken ominously. The smoke hurt her eyes, stung enough to burn.

Raven! It was an imperious command.

She rolled off the bed, landing heavily enough to knock the
wind out of her. *It's going up so fast.* Alarm bells were shrieking in her head. There was so much smoke; the house was
groaning above them.

Raven dragged herself, inch by slow inch, following
Mikhail's painfully sluggish movements across the floor.
They could not even crawl; they were so weak, it was impossible to get on their hands and knees. They slid full length on
their stomachs, using their arms to propel themselves forward
until they were at the hidden entrance to the cellar. Raven
would have done anything to get Mikhail to a safe sanctuary.

Heat sucked the air from the room so that their bodies
were bathed in perspiration; their lungs labored and burned.
Even with their combined strength, it seemed impossible to
lift the trap door. *Concentrate,* Mikhail instructed. *Do it with
your will.*

She blocked out everything: her fear, the smoke, the fire,
Mikhail's agony and rage at his burning home, the predatory
beast rising in him. She narrowed her thoughts to the heavy
door, focused, aimed. With infinite slowness it began to
move, a groaning creak of wood and metal protesting movement but obeying reluctantly. Mikhail fed her power with his
own. When the door lay open to them, revealing the yawning
chasm below, they slumped exhausted against each other,
clinging for a moment, their hearts laboring, their lungs burning with the clouds of smoke whirling around them.

Debris rained down from the roof to the ceiling above their
heads. The fire roared like a giant monster, a stormy conflagration, loud and fearsome. Raven slipped her hand into
Mikhail's. He locked his fingers around hers. *The roof went;
the ceiling above us is going to go up fast.*

You go, Mikhail; I'll wait here as long as I can. The hole
below was as terrifying as the fire itself.

We go together. Mikhail's orders were law. Raven could sense the change in him. No longer man, but full Carpathian, a beast gathering its strength, waiting. An enemy was destroying his home, his belongings, threatening the life of his mate. A slow, deadly hiss escaped from Mikhail. The sound made her heart pound. Always with Raven, he was gentle and kind, tender and loving. This was the predator unleashed.

Raven swallowed her fear, closed her eyes, and cleared her mind. For Mikhail, she had to find a way to go down into that dark earth beneath the cellar below them. Mikhail swirled in her as strong as ever. *You can do this, my love. You are light, like a feather, so light you float.* He built the feeling for her. Her body seemed insubstantial, as light as the air itself. Raven kept her eyes closed even when she felt the air stirring gently around her, felt it fanning her skin. She could feel Mikhail in her mind, yet her body was no more than a fleeting wisp, tangled with his.

Darkness enveloped them, caressed them, carried them down to the fertile soil. Raven opened her eyes, astonished and pleased to find herself in the cellar. She had floated like a feather through the air. It was exhilarating. For a moment her pleasure drove out the fear and horror of the fire. She had moved a heavy object using only her mind, and now she had gone through the air, floating like the breeze itself. Almost like flying. Raven leaned against Mikhail, wearily. *I can't believe we did that. We really just floated.* For the blink of an eye, she put aside the destruction happening all around them and reveled in the wonder of what she had become.

Mikhail's answer was to pull her closer, his arms surrounding her, her slender body enclosed and protected by his large frame. Exhilaration faded. She was as much inside him as he was in her, and she felt the ice cold of his bitter, merciless resolve. It was nothing like the white heat of his black rage; this was far, far worse. This Mikhail was all Carpathian, as dangerously lethal as any mythical vampire. The utter lack of emotion, the entire strength of his iron will and total determination was frightening. He would retaliate swiftly and mercilessly. There was no middle ground. Romanov had become his enemy and he would be destroyed.

Mikhail. Compassion and a gentle calm filled his mind. *Losing your home this way—the things that have surrounded and comforted you for so long—it must be like losing a part of yourself.* She rubbed her face against his chest, a small consoling gesture. *I love you, Mikhail. We'll build another home together. The two of us. This is a terrible moment in our lives, but we can rebuild stronger than ever.*

His chin rested on the top of her head, his mind sending hers waves of love, of warmth. But inside that utter coldness remained, unmoved by her words. Only with Raven did he feel tenderness; with the rest of the world it was equal force, kill or be killed.

Raven tried again. *Grief does strange things to people. Rudy Romanov lost both his parents. His mother was brutally murdered by his own father. Whatever he found has made him blame you. He probably feels guilty for thinking his father was crazy. What he's doing is a terrible thing, but no worse than what you did to those who murdered your sister.*

I had no thought for my sister when I struck at the assassins. There was a grimness in Mikhail's thoughts. *The two cases cannot be compared. The assassins attacked us first. I would have left them alone had they not come after my people. I failed you once, little one. I will not fail to protect you this day.*

We're safe here. The people from the village will come and put out the fire. They'll probably take Rudy to a hospital or jail. They'll think he's crazy. And don't worry about people thinking we died in the fire. They won't find our bodies. We can say we were visiting Celeste and Eric, planning our wedding.

She didn't understand and he didn't have the heart to tell her. They weren't safe. The fire was roaring above their heads, consuming the basement floor just as quickly as the upper story. In a short time they would be forced to seek the sanctuary of the earth. He wasn't altogether certain their combined strength would be enough to open the earth. And if it was, he knew he could not send her into deep sleep. His powers were drained, all but gone this time of day.

They would live or die together. They would be forced to lie in the ground. Raven would have to endure burial alive for the remaining hours to sunset, and there were many hours left. Rudy Romanov would inflict an unbearable torture on Raven. Mikhail knew her greatest fear—suffocation. His lips drew back in another silent snarl. The death of his home, beloved though it was, he could forgive, but to lie helpless while Raven suffered the agony of burial—that went beyond forgiveness.

Raven's thoughts were all for Mikhail, for his loss. She felt compassion for Romanov; she worried that his evidence might endanger the others. If Mikhail could have summoned the energy, he would have kissed her. Instead, he did it with his mind. All of his love, his appreciation of her compassion, of her unconditional love, of her selflessness, he put it all into his mind's kiss.

Her eyes widened, went dark violet, then sweetly slumberous, as if he drugged her with his kisses. His hand tangled in her hair. So much silk, so much love. For a moment he closed his eyes, savoring the moment, the way she could make him feel so loved, so cared for. He had never felt that in all his centuries of existence, and he was grateful that he had hung on long enough to experience a true life mate.

Overhead, the sound of the fire grew loud again. A beam fell, crashed on the ceiling above them, sparks raining through the open cellar door, bringing with them smoke and the fetid odor of death. The death of his home. *We have no choice, my love.* Mikhail was as gentle as he knew how to be. *We must go to ground.*

Raven closed her eyes; panic welled up. *Mikhail, I love you.* Her words were wrapped in sorrow, in acceptance. Not of the sanctuary of the earth, but of inevitable death. She wanted to do anything he needed, but this was the one thing beyond her capabilities. The earth could not swallow her alive.

Mikhail could not waste time on arguments. *Feed my command with your remaining strength. Let it flow from you into me, or I will be unable to open the earth.*

Raven would do anything to save him. If that meant giving him her last ounce of strength, then so be it. Without reservation, with complete love and generosity, Raven fed his command.

Beside him, the very earth opened, parted, as if a large cube had been neatly removed from the earth. The grave lay open, fresh and cool, its healing soil beckoning Mikhail, its damp darkness sending horror and sheer terror spiraling through Raven.

She tried valiantly to keep her mind calm. *You go first.* She knew she could not follow him. She also knew it was imperative that he believe she would; otherwise there was no way to save Mikhail.

In the space of a heartbeat Mikhail rolled, with Raven locked in his arms, taking both of them over the edge into the waiting arms of the earth. He felt her silent scream echoing in his own mind. He steeled his heart against the violent fear in her and with his last ounce of strength concentrated on closing the earth over them. Being a shadow in her mind made it easy to read her intentions. She would never have gone with him.

She screamed and screamed; the sound in his head was wild and out of control. Sheer, primitive terror. She begged him, pleaded. Mikhail could only hold her, absorb wave after wave of terror. Her mind was a maze of panic and chaos. He was exhausted, having used his last ounce of strength to get them to safety.

In his life, centuries of living, he had never known what it felt like to hate. Lying there, helpless to send her into oblivion, with his home burning above him and Raven walking the edge of madness beside him, he learned. Once again he had chosen life for them, and in doing so had committed her to terrible suffering. If he was to help her, he had to gather strength again. The only way he could regain what was lost was to cut himself off from her, to rejuvenate himself in the immortal sleep of his kind and allow the soil to replenish him. A fresh wave of hatred ate at him.

Raven. Even their strong mental bond was becoming difficult. *Little one, slow your heart to match mine. There is no need for air. Do not try to breathe.*

She couldn't hear him, fighting desperately for air where there was none. Along with her panic and hysterical fear, she felt a sense of betrayal that he would force his will, his decision on her.

Mikhail refused to commit himself to sleep; instead he stayed alert, his hands in her hair, his body relaxed, absorbing the healing richness of the soil. He would not leave her alone to face what she considered a burial. While she suffered, he was determined to share that terrible burden. The chaos in her mind continued for what seemed an eternity. As her body wore out completely, as exhaustion penetrated the mindless screaming, she began to strangle, the sound a horrible gurgle in her throat.

Raven! His tone was sharp, an imperious command. Her fear was far too great and his powers no more than a mere shadow, insubstantial. Mikhail could feel her throat closing as if it was his own, heard the terrible death rattle.

He closed off his mind for a moment to allow the soil to cradle him, the soothing, healing balm of the earth. It sang to him with soft whisperings, a crooning lullaby. It seeped into his body, revitalizing, energizing. The earth gave him the necessary calm to face her torment. *Feel me, little one, feel me.*

Her mind remained chaotic; the strangling continued.

Feel me, Raven, reach for me. He was patient, quiet, calm in the eye of the storm. *Raven, you are not alone. Feel me, in your mind. Be calm and reach out, just for a moment. Block out everything except me.*

He felt the first stirring, her first try. The earth sang through him, filling his cells until they were like sails billowing in the wind. *Feel me, Raven. In you, around you, beside you. Feel me.*

Mikhail. She was ragged, torn, fragmented. *I can't stand this; help me. I really can't do this, not even for you.*

Give yourself to me. He meant to the healing richness of the soil, but he could make no references to where they were. He allowed her to feel the strength moving into him, a promise of rest and aid. In his mind he kept only warmth and love and the impression of power. She needed to believe in him, needed to merge with him so that she could feel the powers of the soil as he did.

Christine Feehan

Raven knew she was going insane. She had always been terrified of closed-in places. It didn't matter that Mikhail said she didn't need air; she knew she did. It took several tries and every ounce of discipline she possessed to block out the fear, the terror, the truth that she lay buried deep within the earth. She crawled into Mikhail's mind with her last exhaustive effort and retreated from the reality of what she had become, and what she had to do to survive.

Mikhail's hold on her was precarious. She was light, insubstantial in his mind. So quiet, never moving, not accepting the earth's healing powers, not fighting their situation. Raven made no response to his gentle inquiries. He was aware of her only as a small, huddled flicker in a corner of his mind.

It took some time before he became aware of a faint shifting in power, a ripple of awareness, like a searching crystal, an eye opening in the earth beside them. They were not alone. The presence touched him, stirred in his mind. Male. Powerful. Gregori. *You are well, my friend.* There was that cool menace in his mind. They knew one another so well after all the centuries of standing together against all odds.

Gregori had not voiced it as a question and Mikhail was shocked, truly shocked that he could make contact. Raven and he were deep in the bowels of the earth. The sun was at its greatest peak and all Carpathians were weak. How could Gregori accomplish such a feat? It was unheard of, even in the legends and myths of the past.

Your woman needs to sleep, Mikhail. Allow me to assist you.

Gregori was far away—Mikhail could detect that—yet the bond between them was strong. Sending Raven to sleep gave Gregori a semblance of power over her. Indecision. Did he trust Gregori? The power that Gregori wielded was phenomenal.

Low, humorless laughter. *She will not survive this day, Mikhail. Even locked with you, her human limitations will overcome her desire to aid you.*

And you can do this? Even at this distance? You can safely send her to sleep? Take away her torment? There will be no mistakes? Mikhail found himself wanting to believe it. Gre-

234

gori was their healer. If he said Raven would be unable to last buried within the earth, that only confirmed his own belief.

Yes, through you. You are the only person on this planet I have given my allegiance to. You have always had my loyalty. I count you as my family and my friend. Until your woman or some other gives me my life mate, you are the only person standing between the darkness and me.

Gregori would never have admitted such a thing unless he considered the situation a dire emergency. He was giving Mikhail the only reason he could to reassure Mikhail that he could be trusted.

Affection and regret welled up, mingled. *Thank you, Gregori, I am in your debt.*

I intend you to be the father of my life mate. There was a faint note in his voice, something Mikhail could not name, as though Gregori had already insured that he would get his wish.

I have the feeling Raven's daughter would be more than a handful. Mikhail tested his intuition.

I have no doubt I am up to the challenge. Gregori's reply was purposely vague. *I will send your life mate to the sleep of our people that she will no longer be tormented by her human limits.*

Gregori's soft command was clear, imperious, impossible to ignore. Raven's breath left her body in a soft sigh. Her heart slowed, missed a beat, ceased. Her mind was closed to the yawning terror, her body open to the healing power of the rich soil.

Sleep now, Mikhail. I will know if you are disturbed.

You do not have to guard me, Gregori. You have done much for our people, things they will never know. I can never repay my debt to you.

I can do no other, Mikhail, nor would I want to. Gregori withdrew.

Mikhail allowed himself the luxury of sleep to give the earth the chance to bring him to his full, immense power. He would need the strength the soil gave him for retribution. He wrapped Raven tighter in his arms as he took his last breath, certain the immediate danger to them had passed.

The sun seemed to take a long while to sink from the sky. The colors of the heavens were blood red, surrounded by shades of orange and pink. As the moon appeared, the clouds covered it like a thin veil. A ring appeared around the moon like some terrible omen. The forest was dark, eerily silent. Tendrils of fog wound low to the ground around tree trunks and bushes. A gentle wind lazily pushed the clouds, brushed at heavy branches and tried vainly to disperse the smell of smoke that lingered persistently in the forest. The wind fingered the black ashes and burned beams, the blackened stones, all that remained of what had once been Mikhail Dubrinsky's home.

Two wolves nosed at the blackened remains, lifted their muzzles skyward, and howled mournfully. Throughout the forest other wolves answered, sang out their grief. Within a few minutes, the echoes of their tribute died away. The two wolves circled the charred ruins and sniffed at the two shadowy sentinels they found standing sharply alert near the wrought-iron gate.

The wolves swung quickly away, finding something menacing in the two lethal figures. They trotted briskly back into the darkened interior of the forest. Silence once more blanketed the mountains like a shroud. The forest creatures huddled in their dens and holes, rather than face the smell of the ashes and the death of the home of one who was so much a part of them.

Below the earth two bodies lay motionless, lifeless. Into the silence, a single heart began to beat. Strong, steady. Blood rushed, receded. A long, low hiss of air heralded the working of lungs. Dark eyes snapped open, and Mikhail searched the grounds above him. It was well after midnight. The fire was long out; firefighters, investigators, and curiosity seekers had long returned home.

He sensed Jacques and Gregori above the earth. No others, human or Carpathian, were in the vicinity. Mikhail turned his attention to Raven. It was a huge temptation to command Gregori to awaken her, but that was selfish and certainly not in her best interests. Until she was completely out of the ground, Raven was best left asleep. She needed no reminder of her terrible ordeal. He tightened his arms around her motionless, cold body, held her for a long moment close to his heart.

Mikhail burst through the earth's crust, experiencing an odd disorientation as he emerged into the night air. The moment he was able, he launched himself skyward, the better to protect Raven if necessary. Air rushed into his lungs, fanned his body. Feathers shimmered in the sliver of light from the moon; huge wings spread, spanning a good six feet, and beat heavily, lifting the enormous owl into the sky, where it circled above the dark forest, seeking any enemy that might be foolish enough to threaten.

Mikhail needed the freedom of the sky to dull the sounds of Raven's terror, which still echoed strongly in his head. He dived toward the earth, plummeting as close as he dared before dissolving into mist. The stream of drops poured through the trees and collected together until they formed a huge wolf. Mikhail ran effortlessly, sustaining great speed as he swerved through the underbrush, the trees, loped across a meadow and took off again as if shot from a bow.

When his mind was once more clear and calm, Mikhail trotted to the blackened ruins, changing back into his own muscular form, complete with clothes, as he strode toward his brother. He was well aware that all of nature, everything he was so much a part of, could feel his ice-cold rage. It was buried deep, seething below the surface, disturbing the harmony in the air, in the forest. His enemies would not escape.

Jacques straightened slowly, as if he had been waiting for hours. His hand went to the nape of his neck, rubbing at a kink. Mikhail and Jacques stared at one another, dark sorrow in their eyes. Jacques stepped forward and reached for Mikhail in an uncharacteristic show of affection. It was brief and hard, two stiff oak trees exchanging a hug. Mikhail knew Raven would have laughed at the two of them.

Gregori remained hunkered down, low to the ground, his solid bulk rivaling the broad tree trunks. He was totally motionless, his shadowed face expressionless. His eyes were a slash of silver, of mercury forever moving restlessly in the granite mask. Gregori rose slowly, fluid power and raw danger.

"Thank you for coming," Mikhail said simply. Gregori. His oldest friend. His right hand. Their greatest healer, the relentless hunter of the undead.

"Romanov was taken to the hospital and sedated," Jacques said softly. "I told the townspeople that you and Raven were away for a few days. You are popular with the villagers and all of them are outraged by what happened."

"Can we neutralize the damage done to our people?" Mikhail asked.

"We can minimize it," Gregori said truthfully. "But Romanov has already sent out whatever damning evidence he found to several others. We must prepare ourselves for a siege. Our entire way of life will be changed for all time." Gregori shrugged powerful shoulders carelessly.

"His evidence?"

"Fingerprints, photos. He was already drugged, Mikhail. The doctors believe he is completely insane and dangerous to himself and to others. The images I picked out of his mind were confused. His parents; mainly his mother. He evidently discovered her body. Your house. Guilt. The fire." Gregori surveyed the sky above him with a slow, careful sweep of his pale, silver eyes. His craggy features remained utterly still, harsh.

Danger emanated from Gregori. His entire body, his very demeanor spoke of power, of menace. Although Gregori's expression was empty, Mikhail felt the monster in him, wild and untamed, lurking just below the surface, struggling to break free. Their eyes met in a kind of hopeless understanding. Another war. More killings. The more often a male had to kill, the more dangerous the whisper of power, the call to vampire became. Violence was the one thing that allowed a centuries-old male to feel briefly. That in itself was a terrible inducement for one in a dark, hopeless world.

Gregori looked away, not wanting to see the compassion on Mikhail's face. "We have no choice but to discredit him."

"Before anything else, Raven must be safe and guarded while we take care of this problem," Mikhail said abruptly.

"Your woman is very fragile," Gregori warned softly. "Bring her to the surface and clothe her before I awake her."

Mikhail nodded. Gregori clearly read his intentions. There was no way he would have her awaken in what seemed to her a cold grave. Jacques and Gregori moved into the forest to give Mikhail privacy. Only after Raven was safe in his arms did Mikhail think to add her human American garb. Made of natural fibers, easy for a Carpathian to manipulate, he fashioned blue jeans and a long-sleeved shirt. *Gregori.*

Raven woke strangling, clutching her throat, desperate to drag air into her burning lungs. She was confused, panic-stricken, struggling desperately. "Feel the air on your skin," Mikhail ordered softly, his mouth against her ear. "Feel the night, the wind. You are safe in my arms. The night is beautiful; the colors and scents speak to us."

Raven's blue-violet eyes were all over the place, seeing nothing, taking in nothing. She inhaled deeply, and made herself as small as possible. The cool night air was working a slow magic, easing the terrible strangling in her throat. Tears glittered like gems in her eyes, tangled in her long lashes.

Mikhail tightened his hold on her so that she could feel the enormous strength in his powerful frame. Slowly, inch by inch, her body became less rigid, so that she relaxed into him. He touched her mind with a gentle, warm stroke, finding her struggling for control.

"I am here with you, Raven." Deliberately he spoke the words out loud, so he would sound as human as possible. "The night is calling to us, welcoming us; can you hear it? There is such beauty in the song of insects, the night creatures. Let yourself hear it." He used a rhythmic, compelling tone, almost hypnotic.

Raven drew her knees up, lay her forehead on them, hunching into herself. She was rocking back and forth, her hold on reality a tenuous thread. She simply breathed in and out, appreciating the ability to do so, concentrating on the mechanics of it.

"I want to take you to a safer place, somewhere away from here." His sweeping gesture took in the charred remains of his once beautiful home.

Raven's head remained down. She simply breathed in and out. Mikhail touched her mind again. There was no thought of blame or betrayal. Her mind was fragmented, bruised and broken, trying desperately to survive. Her familiar clothes and his presence gave her a measure of comfort. His ice-cold fury, his need for violent retaliation stirred to life.

"Little sister." Jacques emerged from the edge of the timberline, flanked by Gregori. When Raven didn't look up, Jacques sat beside her, his hand brushing her shoulder. "The wolves are quiet tonight. Did you hear them before? They were mourning the loss of Mikhail's home. Now they are silent."

She blinked, her lost gaze focusing on Jacques's face. She didn't speak; his identity didn't seem to register. She was trembling, her small frame shaking, locked between the three powerful men.

You could remove her memories. Gregori suggested, clearly not understanding why Mikhail did not do the obvious.

She would not like such a thing.

She would not know. Gregori put a small edge in his tone. He sighed when Mikhail did not respond. *Allow me to heal her, then. She is important to all of us, Mikhail. She suffers needlessly.*

She would want to do this on her own. Mikhail was well aware that Gregori thought he had lost his mind, but he knew Raven. She had her own courage, and her own ideas of right and wrong. She would not thank him when she learned he had removed her memories. There could be no untruths between life mates, and Mikhail was determined to give her time to come to terms with what they had endured together.

Mikhail found the rose-petal-soft skin of her face, traced her delicate cheekbones with gentle fingers. "You were right, little one. We will build our home together, stronger than ever. We will pick a place, deep within the forest, and fill it with so much love, it will spill over to our wolves."

Her blue-violet gaze flickered with sudden awareness,

jumping to Mikhail's face. The tip of her tongue touched her full lower lip. She managed a tentative smile. "I don't think I'm cut out to be a Carpathian." Her voice was a mere thread of sound.

"You are everything a Carpathian woman should be," Gregori said gallantly, his tone low and melodious, a soothing, healing cadence. Both Mikhail and Jacques found themselves listening intently to the compelling pitch. "You are fit to be the life mate of our prince, and I give you freely my allegiance and my protection, as I have given it to Mikhail." His voice deliberately was pitched low, so that it seeped into her fragmented mind like a soothing balm.

Raven's shattered gaze swung to Gregori. Her long lashes fluttered, her eyes so dark they were nearly purple. "You helped us." Her fingers sought and found Mikhail's, entwined with his, yet her gaze never left Gregori's face. "You were so far away. The sun was out, yet you knew, and you were able to help us. It was difficult for you; I felt it even as you reached for me to take away what I could not endure."

The silver eyes, pale in Gregori's dark face, narrowed to a slash of quicksilver. Mesmerizing. Hypnotic. The voice lowered an octave. "Mikhail and I are bound together; we have shared long, dark years of emptiness without hope. Perhaps you represent hope for both of us."

Raven regarded him steadily, seriously. "That would please me."

Mikhail felt a surge of love for her wash over him, a surge of pride. Raven had so much compassion in her. Although she was mentally bruised and battered, although Gregori's mind was firmly closed to them, his harsh features impossible to read, she realized that Gregori was fighting to survive, that he needed to be drawn into the circle of light, of hope. Mikhail could have told her that Gregori was like water flowing through fingers—impossible to hold or control. He was a law unto himself, a dark, dangerous man on the edge of a yawning abyss of madness.

Mikhail slipped his arm around her shoulders. "We are going to take you somewhere safe." He spoke softly, as if to a child.

Raven's gaze clung to Mikhail's for a long, slow moment. Her smile was genuine this time, reaching her eyes and lighting them for the first time. "If only the three of you could see yourselves. It's very sweet of you to treat me like I'm a fragile porcelain doll, especially when I feel a bit like one, but Mikhail is in me, as I am in him. I feel what he feels and know his thoughts, although he tries to keep them from me." She leaned over to kiss his blue-shadowed jaw. "I love you for trying to protect me, but I'm not weak. I simply have to come to terms with the human bonds my mind puts on me. None of you can do it for me. I have to do it myself."

Jacques extended his hand to Raven with old-world gallantry. She took it and allowed herself to be pulled to her feet. Mikhail rose beside her, his arm sweeping her into the shelter of his body. She needed the contact, the closeness, the solid reality of his hard frame. Gregori was the bodyguard, scanning the air, the ground, moving so that his body continually blocked the prince of their people and his life mate.

The three imposing figures surrounded the smaller one, moving as a unit, an honor guard, their paces slow and leisurely, their minds serene, with no hint of impatience or sign of their desire to get on to the night's work. Hunger gnawed at Mikhail, but that, too, was kept at bay. When her mind touched his, she felt only love and concern, the desire to please her.

Raven enjoyed the feel of the soft leaves under her feet as they moved through the forest. She lifted her face to embrace the wind, inhaled deeply to take in every secret the breeze could carry and would divulge. Every insect, every rustle in the underbrush, every separate sway of a branch lightened the terrible dread in her heart, pushed the fearful memories a little farther away.

"I can take them away completely," Mikhail offered gently.

Raven flashed him a small smile, meant to reassure. Her body moved briefly against his. She was well aware of what a temptation that had been for him, how the other two males thought him insane for not taking the choice from her. "You know I prefer to keep my memories. All of them."

They walked for an hour, Mikhail subtly guiding her up a

winding narrow track deeper into the forest and higher up the mountain. The cabin was hidden back against a cliff. The trees grew thick, nearly to the very walls. It looked small from the outside, dark and abandoned.

It was Jacques and Gregori who transformed the dark interior of the cabin. The layer of dust disappeared with a hand wave. The logs in the fireplace burst into flame. Candles flickered, and the scent of the woods permeated the interior.

Raven entered the cabin without protest. Gregori and Jacques moved quickly through the small building, supplying as many comforts as they were able in a brief period of time. Then they retreated to the sanctuary of the forest to give Mikhail and Raven some time alone.

Raven paced across the wooden floor, putting distance between herself and Mikhail. She was still very fragile, and she wanted to spare Mikhail as much as possible. She touched the back of a chair, curling her fingers around the solid wood. The familiar feel of wood helped to lessen her trembling.

"Thank you, Mikhail, for my blue jeans." She gave him a faint smile over her shoulder. Mysterious, sexy, innocent, and so very fragile. In the depths of her blue eyes he could find no anger, no blame, only love for him shining there.

"I am happy you like them, although I still say they are garb for men, not a beautiful woman. I was hoping they would make you smile."

"Only because you get that pained look on your face." She stood at the window, her eyes easily piercing the darkness. "I never want to do that again." She said it starkly, meaning it. Wanting him to know she meant it.

Mikhail inhaled sharply, cutting off his first response. He chose his words carefully. "Our blood and, ultimately, our bodies, welcome the soil. Overnight the wound on my leg was gone. Your wounds, so deep, all mortal, were healed in six days."

Raven watched the wind tug at leaves on the ground. "I'm very intelligent, Mikhail. I can see for myself that what you're telling me is true. Intellectually, I may even accept it, marvel at it. But I never want to do that again. I cannot. I will not, and I ask that you accept this failing in me."

He crossed the distance separating them. His hand curled around the nape of her neck to drag her into his arms. He held her, there in the old cabin, deep within his mountains and forest. He grieved for the loss of his home, his books, grieved for his past, but most of all, he grieved over his inability to spare Raven. He could command the earth, the animals, the sky, yet he could not bring himself to remove her memories because she had asked him not to do so. Such an innocent, small request.

Raven lifted her head, studying his shadowed features with serious eyes. Very gently she smoothed the deep lines of worry from his forehead. "Don't be sad for me, Mikhail, and stop taking so much on yourself. Memories are useful things. When I am stronger, I can take this out and examine it, look at it from all angles and perhaps grow more comfortable with the things we have to do to protect ourselves." There was a trace of humor and a good amount of skepticism at the thought.

Raven took his hand. "You know, my love, you are not responsible for my happiness, or even for my health. I've had a choice every step of the way, from our very first meeting. I chose you. Clearly, in my heart, and in my head, I chose you. If I had it to do over again, even knowing what I would have to go through, I would choose you without hesitation."

His smile could melt her heart. Mikhail cupped her face in his hands, lowered his head to capture her mouth with his. Instantly electricity crackled between them. She could taste his love in the moist darkness of his mouth. Hunger rose, sharp and gnawing. The sound of blood surging hotly, the beating of hearts, the instant explosive chemistry was nearly overwhelming for both of them. Although his arms slipped around her, dragged her close against his hard frame, his tender mouth carried the unmistakable flavor of intense love. Mikhail's fingers tangled in her silky hair as if he would hold her for all eternity.

Raven melted into him; for a heartbeat of time she was boneless, pliant, honeyed heat warming him. She pulled away first. It was easy to read the clawing hunger in him; it was growing in her. Her body needed nourishment after its grueling ordeal. She lifted long lashes to his beloved, masculine features, took in the sensual stamp of his mouth, the slumbering, sensual invitation in his black gaze.

Raven kissed his throat, her hands going to the buttons of his shirt. Her body clenched, pulsing with heat and hunger. Her mouth moved over his skin. She inhaled his scent, the wild mystery of the night. Inside, the terrible craving grew and spread like wildfire. Her tongue tasted the texture of his skin, traced the line of his muscle, moved back to stroke across the pulse beating so strongly in his throat. "I love you, Mikhail." The words were whispered against his throat. A siren's whisper. Silk and candlelight. Satin and hot, steamy sex.

Every muscle in his body tightened. Need swept through him, anticipation. She was a miracle of beauty, a mix of human frailties, courage, and compassion. Mikhail's fist, bunched in her hair, held her head to him. Her mouth was a silken flame moving over his chest, building heat and fire until his mind was a red haze of hunger.

"This is dangerous, little one." Black velvet seduction was in the molten huskiness of his voice.

"I need you." She whispered the truth, and her breath warmed his flat nipples, doing intriguing things to his chest. She did need him. His hard body, hot and wild, stamped out the feel of the cold earth closing over her head. Her body moved restlessly, suggestively against his. Her hands slid downward, parting the edges of his shirt and lower still to find the zipper where his sex strained to break free. His gasp was audible, a harsh groan of raw need answering the enticing brush of her fingers. "I need to feel your body in mine, Mikhail, real and alive. I need this more than I've ever needed anything. Touch me. Touch me everywhere. I want you deep inside me."

Mikhail tugged her shirt over her head and dropped it to one side. His hands spanned her narrow rib cage, arching her body backwards so he could rub his shadowed jaw across the soft creamy swell of her breasts. The abrasive brush sent flames licking along every nerve ending. His mouth moved up to trace the softness of her lips. His tongue stroked the fragile line of her neck where her pulse beat so frantically, the vulnerable line of her throat, slowly, with great care, before lowering with deliberately tormenting laziness to her nipple. She felt a rush of damp heat, a fiery ache. When his lips closed over her breast, hot and erotic, she cried out and threw her head back, arching into him, offering herself up to the strong pull of his hot mouth.

Without warning, the monster in him broke free, growling possessively and clawing away her offensive blue jeans. Teeth scraped her flat stomach as he dropped to his knees. Through the thin cotton panties she felt the hot moist probing of his tongue, wild, wet, stealing her breath. He ripped away the thin material to attack, stroking and caressing.

Raven cried out, welcoming the untamed beast in him, rising to meet his erotic assault. When he ripped the panties aside she pressed herself to the hot hunger of his mouth. Mikhail growled low in his throat, the sound a rumble of stark possession. He reveled in her wild response to his assault. He needed the uninhibited, abandoned grip of her clenched fists in his hair pulling him in closer to her, the husky, inarticulate cries issuing from her vulnerable throat. Her body clenched, white hot heat raging for release. Her cries became a plea.

Growling with pleasure, his own body burning, scorched, and unbearably sensitive, he held her relentlessly on the edge. The power, the velvet heat, their mingled scents washed over him, became part of his insatiable desire. He wanted her to know that she was his, to burn and need mindlessly as he did.

His own name echoed in his head with her soft, inarticulate pleas, the sound hardening his body to an unbearable ache. The power sharpened his hunger, put such an edge on his appetite, both sexual and physical, that he could barely find enough control to stop from devouring her. And his body demanded her touch, the silken heat of her mouth, the graze of her teeth over sensitized skin. His skin was so hot, aching for her.

With a growl, he took her over the edge, her body rippling powerfully, clenching and unclenching, needing more, needing his invasion, needing his body filling hers. She dropped to her knees, pushed at his pants, tugged until they were at his thighs, until he was free and straining toward her. Raven's nails raked his buttocks; her tongue found his heavy chest muscles.

Her taunting laughter, low, seductive, echoed in his mind. The brush of her silky hair over his thighs was nearly unbearable. It was his turn and he let her know with a growling plea, an imperious demand. When she complied, the hot satin of her mouth, moist and erotic, nearly drove him crazy. If he had been in control, if he had been the one with power, it was now Raven's, and she exulted in it, in what she could do to him.

The growls rumbling in his throat became more animal, almost threatening. His hips moved in a frantic rhythm. Suddenly he could stand it no longer. Mikhail yanked her away from him, down to the floor, thrusting her knees apart to expose her for his possession. He pinned her down, took her with a single hard, powerful stroke of stark possession, filling her tight velvet feminine channel as deeply as was possible.

Raven cried out as he buried himself harder, every thrust stormy and aggressive, each more wild and frantic than the one before. Her tongue stroked his throat. "Feed me, Mikhail. Feed me now while you take me, and then I'll give you everything you need." She whispered it like an enchantress, her very voice a drug adding to the excitement. She had never asked for his blood, his life's fluid, and the idea was as sexy as her mouth on him. His body tightened, impossibly hard, yet her request enabled him to slow down so that he could feel the anticipation as her tongue stroked over his pulse. As he surged deeply into her fiery hot sheath, her teeth sank deep into him. White heat and blue lightning slammed through his body. He threw his head back at the exquisite pleasure-pain of it.

The hot, sweet odor of his ancient blood mingled with their musk scents, the strong pull of her mouth coinciding with the strong grip of her body surrounding his. He matched her movements deliberately, felt her take his blood, his seed, the essence of life into her body. Her body dragged at his, insistent, a sweet torment, a velvet clutching, a milking, with the same dark fire as her silken mouth.

The stroke of her tongue sent an aftershock rippling

through both of them and they lay locked together, his body covering hers, his arms holding her in place, his every muscle rock hard and still in desperate need, as if he had never touched her. His hunger was a terrible thing far beyond craving, far beyond anything he had ever experienced.

Raven's hands smoothed his hair, then her palms rubbed over his jaw. She smiled, pure seduction, her hips arching deliberately into his, her muscles tight and gripping. She brought his head down to hers so that she could fasten her mouth to his, sharing the sweet taste of his blood, taunting, teasing, prolonging his need, bringing him to wild abandonment.

He took control back, drinking deeply of her silken mouth, his tongue stroking down the line of her throat, lingering over her pulse, his teeth scraping, tantalizing, while his body took aggressive possession, plunging deep and hard.

Raven murmured his name, dragged his head to her breast, lifting herself in pleading invitation. His chin rubbed over the creamy swell, delved into the valley between, his blue-shadowed jaw rasping sensitive skin. He cupped her breasts as his mouth closed over her, hot and moist, pulling strongly. She clutched him to her, her body exploding with pleasure, following the rhythm and pace he set.

Mikhail lifted his head, his eyes slumberous, sexy, hypnotic, drawing her deeper into his very mind, his very soul. He nuzzled her breast, his tongue stroking, caressing. Openmouthed, he pressed wet, hot kisses over sensitive skin. His hips surged forward. Once more his eyes met hers, a clear demand.

"Yes, please, yes," she whispered urgently, dragging his head back to the heat of her body. "I want this, Mikhail."

His teeth grazed, pierced above her breast, the pain white hot, even as her body rippled, fragmented with searing ecstasy. Fangs sank deep, the hunger in him insatiable. He plunged into her wanting more, needing the consummate friction of fire and velvet sheathing him. He drank her in, taking her very life into his body, his mind merging with hers, his body claiming hers in pure male dominance.

Dangerous. Sweetly dangerous. Hot pure sex laced with pure love and a complete merging of souls. He wanted it to last forever, this moment while they shared the same body, same skin, same mind. Fast and hard, slow and deep, each stroke exquisite torment, her blood filling every cell, swelling his strength, draining her as her body drained him. He felt himself hardening impossibly, swelling, stretching, relentlessly pushing his invasion to the maximum, taking both of them soaring, careening over the edge without control, exploding into fiery fragments, dissolving, falling to earth.

Raven lay beneath him, listening to their combined heartbeats, her fingers threaded in his dark espresso-colored hair. Her body belonged to him; she belonged to him. His tongue caressed her skin, traced a single drop of blood over the swell of her breast. He rained kisses over her breasts, up her throat to find her mouth, gently, tenderly. His hand spanned her throat, stroked with the pad of his thumb, reveling in the soft satin texture.

It amazed him that she had chosen this moment to commit herself to their life as Carpathians. He had no doubt that she loved him and was committed to him, but he had known she was repulsed by the idea of how she would be forced to live. After a horrifying, traumatic experience, she had committed herself to her new life without reservation. As long as they were together, Mikhail was certain she would never be predictable.

"Do you have any idea how much I love you?" he asked softly.

Her long lashes fluttered, lifted, so that her violet eyes locked with his. A slow, fascinating smile curved her mouth. "Maybe, just a little." She smoothed a line from his forehead. "I'll be fine tonight. Do what you have to do and don't worry about me."

"I would prefer that you slept for a while." He shifted, eased his weight off her, surprised to find that he was still partially dressed.

"That's only because you have so much anger toward Romanov you don't want me to know what you're doing." She propped herself up on one elbow so that her thick mane of silky hair spilled across her body, a thin veil over her breasts.

His gut clenched hotly at the sight, his dark eyes going

black with a sudden flare of desire. She laughed softly, tauntingly. He bent down to taste temptation, his tongue bringing her nipple to a hard peak.

Her fingers stroked through his thick hair tenderly. "You think to protect Jacques by leaving him here with me as my bodyguard." Her eyes softened, warmed. "You think you are going to do something I will be unable to accept, but I believe in you, Mikhail. I think you are a great and fair man. You have every right to despise Romanov, but I know you can put that aside and do what is right. He is a young man, confused and angry, shaken and traumatized by his parents' brutal deaths. Whatever he found that linked you to those deaths has driven him into a breakdown. It's a terrible tragedy."

Mikhail closed his eyes and breathed out slowly. She was effectively tying his hands. How could he go out and kill a man for torturing Raven when she was compassionate enough to forgive him?

"Go feed before you see him. You made me weak, and if you'll forgive a little crude Carpathian humor, I'll expect you to bring me home dinner."

Startled, he stared at her. For a long moment there was silence; then they burst out laughing. "Get dressed," Mikhail ordered with mock sternness. "I cannot have poor Jacques tormented by you."

"I fully intend to torment him. He needs to learn not to be so serious."

"Jacques is the least serious of all Carpathian males. He has retained his emotions far longer than most. It has only been a few centuries since he has lost them."

"He is serious when it comes to ordering females about. He has definite ideas on how we should behave. I intend to take that up with him."

His eyebrow shot up. "I am certain you will keep him occupied while we are gone. Do me a favor, little one; do not be too hard on him."

They were both laughing as they dressed.

Chapter Thirteen

Rudy Romanov was heavily drugged. The scent was a stench in Mikhail's nostrils. The idea of taking contaminated blood into his body was repulsive to him, but it was necessary. He would be able to read Romanov's thoughts at will. Raven had sent him off with complete trust and faith in his love for her. Though every cell in his body demanded Romanov's death, Mikhail could not betray her confidence in him.

"Allow me," Gregori said softly, easily reading Mikhail's desire.

"There is great risk to your soul," Mikhail pointed out.

"The risk is well worth the continuation of our race. Romanov is a danger we cannot afford. We should be concentrating our efforts on finding women to continue our race, not fighting off vampire hunters. I believe it is only a handful of human women, women with great psychic ability who can mate with our males."

"On what do you base this theory?" Mikhail asked softly, a thread of menace creeping into his tone. Experimenting with women was an unforgivable crime.

Gregori's silver eyes narrowed, glittered. The black emptiness was growing in Gregori, a dark stain spreading over his soul. He made no effort to hide it from Mikhail. It was as if he wanted to show Mikhail just how desperate the situation was becoming. "I have done many dark, ugly, unforgivable things, but I would never use a female for experimental purposes. I must be the one to take Romanov's blood if you insist on the continuation of his life." Gregori was not asking.

The two Carpathians moved easily through the narrow halls of the psychiatric ward of the hospital. The humans experienced a cold sensation, nothing more, as the two passed unseen through the building. They streamed through a lock hole, a flow of vapor like a heavy tinted fog, swirling through the room to wrap around Romanov's body like a shroud. Romanov cried out, fear gripping him as the mist wound around him like a snake, slithering over his ribs, his wrist, curling around his neck and beginning to wind tighter and tighter. He could feel it on his skin, a vice that continued to twist his body like a corkscrew, but as Romanov clawed at the vapor, his hands passed right through it. Voices hissed hideously, whispered, threatened, so quiet as to be mere threads of sound in his head. He clapped his palms over his ears in an attempt to stop the insidious murmuring. Saliva dribbled from his slack mouth; his throat worked convulsively.

The mist separated, one part trailing to a corner and hovering just above the floor. The other slowly thickened, shimmered, began to take shape, until it formed a muscular, broad-shouldered man with pale eyes of death. Rudy began to shake uncontrollably, backing into a corner, making himself as small as possible. The apparition was too vivid, too menacing to be anything but real.

"Romanov." Gregori's fangs gleamed white in the darkened room.

"What are you?" The words came out a hoarse croak.

The pale eyes glittered, narrowed to unblinking slits. "You know." The pale eyes stared into Rudy's, stared deeply. Gregori's voice dropped to a low black velvet assault. Hypnotic. Mesmerizing. Compelling. "Come to me; feed me. Become my servant until I see fit to give you the curse of darkness."

There was dawning comprehension in Romanov's eyes,

horror, and what amounted to terror. But he inched closer, moving his shirt away from his jugular. Gregori whispered again, his voice so seductive, so compelling, a tool of power. "You will serve me now, come at my bidding, inform me when it is necessary." He bent his dark head slowly.

Romanov knew his soul was lost. He could feel such power in the stranger, immense strength, and the ability to do things no human could imagine. Immortality. The seduction beckoned him. He went willingly, turning his head to expose his throat. Hot breath, piercing pain as the fangs sunk deep. Romanov could actually feel his life's blood flowing like a river from his body. The pain was intense, a burning hell he was helpless to stop. Nor did he wish to. A curious languor swept over him; his eyelids were far too heavy to lift.

The mist thickened in the room, wrapped around Gregori, streamed between the Carpathian and his prey. Reluctantly, with a growl of protest, Gregori lifted his head from his feeding and contemptuously allowed the limp body to slump to the floor.

You nearly killed him, Mikhail snapped.

He deserves death. He is rotten and empty inside, already corrupt. He wants endless nights, helpless women, the power of life and death over mankind. There is much in him like his grandfather and father. He is a hollow shell with worms eating what good is left in him. His mind is a maze of deviant desires.

He cannot die this way, Gregori. It was a hiss in Gregori's mind, a sign of Mikhail's displeasure. *As it is, we have enough attention directed at our people. If Romanov dies from severe blood loss . . .*

I am not so careless. Gregori shoved the body aside with his foot. *He will live. It was his grandfather that began this . . .*

His name was Raul; do you remember him? He was demented as an old man, vicious as a young one. He beat his wife and went after young girls. I stopped him once. Mikhail was suddenly thoughtful.

And earned not only his hatred, but also his suspicion. He watched you after that. Spied on you every chance he got, hoping to find something to condemn you. Something gave you away—a gesture, the way you spoke; who knows? He passed his suspicions on to Hans. Gregori gave the body another push with his foot. *Romanov used a fax machine to send copies of the evidence to several individuals. The originals are in his house, under the floorboards in his parents' bedroom.* Gregori watched as Rudy Romanov attempted to crawl away from him. *Sooner or later they will come.*

Gregori's body shimmered, dissolved, so that mist swirled in the room, long snakelike ribbons of fog where the Carpathian had been. The vapor approached Romanov where he cowered close to the floor, streamed close to his head, his throat; then the mist poured from the room, leaving Romanov sobbing helplessly.

Mikhail and Gregori glided through the corridor, swiftly, silently, hurrying into the night's freshness. After the depravity of Rudy's mind, they needed the connection with the earth again. Once outside, Gregori forced the drugs through his pores to rid himself of the poison. Mikhail watched him do it, marveling at his ease. Gregori was quiet on the journey to Romanov's cottage. Mikhail respected his need to breathe in the night's scents, to feel the ground beneath his feet, hear the music of the wolves, the night creatures calling with their soothing rhythms.

In the safety of the Romanov home, Gregori made his way unerringly to the papers crudely hidden beneath the floorboards. Mikhail took the old photographs and the bundle of papers without even glancing at them. "Tell me everything in his mind."

Gregori's silver eyes glittered dangerously. "A man named Slovensky, Eugene Slovensky, is a member of a secret society dedicated to wiping out vampires. Von Halen, Anton Fabrezo, and Dieter Hodkins are the so-called experts who investigate and mark victims for kills. Slovensky recruits, and confirms and records kills."

Mikhail swore softly, eloquently. "Another vampire hunt will destroy our people."

Gregori shrugged his massive shoulders. "I will hunt and destroy these men. You take Raven and go far from this place.

I feel your protest, Mikhail, but it is the only way, and we both know it."

"I cannot trade my happiness for your soul."

The silver eyes moved over Mikhail, then sought the night. "There are no other choices left to us. My only hope of salvation is a life mate. I no longer feel, Mikhail; I fulfill my needs. There are no longer desires of the body, only of the mind. I cannot remember what it is to feel the things you feel. There is no joy in my life. I simply exist and do my duty toward our people. I must have a life mate soon. I can only hold out a few more years; then I will seek eternal rest."

"You will not seek the sun, Gregori, not without coming to me first." Mikhail held up his hand when Gregori would have protested. "I have been where you are, alone, the monster in me struggling for dominance, the stain on my soul dark. Our people need you. You must remain strong and fight the monster crouching so close."

Gregori's silver eyes glittered dangerously in the darkened room, pale and menacing. "Do not overestimate my affection or loyalty. I must have a mate. If I feel something, anything— lust, possession, *anything*—I will take what is mine and dare anyone to take her from me." Abruptly Gregori's large frame shimmered, dissolving into water crystals, and streamed from the house out into the welcoming arms of the night. *Let us leave this house of madness and death. Perhaps it is the tainted blood I took into my body speaking.*

With a sigh, Mikhail followed Gregori into the night. The twin ribbons of vapor glinted in the moonlight, joined the tendrils of fog rippling several feet above the forest floor. Anxious to return to Raven, Mikhail streamed through the trees toward the clearing that separated the houses from the deep forest. As he flowed past the priest's cabin and into the meadow, his mind rippled with uneasiness. The warning jarred enough that he retreated back to Father Hummer's home and, in the shelter of the trees, took back his human form. His mind touched Raven's. Nothing threatened her.

"What is it?" Gregori materialized beside Mikhail.

They scanned the immediate area for danger. It was the soil that told of violence—trampling boots, droplets of blood.

Mikhail raised stricken eyes to Gregori's pale ones, and they both turned simultaneously to look at the cabin of his old friend.

"I will go first," Gregori said, with as much compassion as he was capable of interjecting into his voice. He stepped smoothly between Mikhail and the entrance to the priest's home.

The neat little cabin, so comfortable and homey, had been destroyed, ransacked. The simple furniture was broken, the curtains askew, old pottery dishes smashed. The priest's precious books had been torn, his pictures slashed to ribbons. Father Hummer's herbs, so carefully kept in tins, lay in a heap on the floor of the kitchen. His thin mattress was in scraps, his blankets shredded.

"What were they looking for?" Mikhail mused aloud, wandering around the room. He stooped to pick up a rook, curling his fingers around the familiar chess piece. There were bloodstains on the floor, on the old carved rocking chair.

"There is no body," Gregori pointed out unnecessarily. He reached down and picked up a very old leather-bound Bible. The book was well worn, the leather shiny where the priest's fingers had so often held it. "But where there is stench, there is a trail." Gregori handed Mikhail the Bible, watching as their prince wordlessly slipped the book under his shirt, against his skin.

Gregori's broad, muscular frame bent, crackled. Glossy fur rippled along his arms, claws burst from his fingernails, and fangs exploded into a lengthening muzzle. The huge black wolf was already springing for the window, changing on the run. Mikhail followed, leaping through the trees, circling back, nose to the ground. The scent led away from town toward the deep forest. The trail climbed higher and higher into the mountains. The direction took them away from Raven and Jacques. Whoever had taken Father Hummer wanted to be alone with him to do his dirty work.

Mikhail and Gregori raced at a ground-eating run, shoulder to shoulder, dark deadly purpose in their hearts. They ran noses to the wind, lowering their muzzles occasionally to the trail to assure themselves that they were following the priest's scent. Their powerful muscles rippled along their backs, their hearts and lungs working like well-oiled machines. Animals scurried out of their path, hunkered down in terror at their passing.

A pungent, unfamiliar odor marked a tree on their present course. Mikhail broke stride. They had crossed the boundaries of Mikhail's wolf pack and entered another's territory. Wolves frequently attacked intruders. Mikhail sent out a call, allowing the wind to carry their message in an attempt to locate the dominant pair.

With the smell of the priest's blood, it was fairly easy to follow the trail. But a strange uneasiness began to grow in Mikhail. Something was eluding him. They had covered miles at a dead run, yet the trail never changed. The scent was not fresher, not fading, simply the same. A slight noise above them was their only warning, a curious grinding like rock against rock. They were in a narrow ravine, with steep walls rising on either side. Both wolves immediately dissolved, became tiny droplets of fog. The shower of rocks and boulders from overhead pelted uselessly through the insubstantial mist.

Simultaneously, Mikhail and Gregori launched themselves skyward, bodies forming as they landed with catlike grace on the cliff above them. There was no priest and certainly no attacker. Mikhail glanced uneasily at Gregori. "No human could have done this."

"The priest did not walk this distance, and no mortal carried him," Gregori said thoughtfully. "His blood was used as a trap then, to draw us here." Both were scanning, using every natural weapon they possessed. "This is the work of a vampire."

"He is clever enough not to leave his own scent for us," Mikhail observed.

A pack of wolves boiled from the trees, red eyes fixed on Mikhail. Snarling and snapping, the animals sprang for the tall, elegant figure standing with casual grace so close to the edge of the cliff. Gregori was a whirling demon, flinging animals down the ravine, snapping bones as if they were matchsticks. He never made a sound, and his speed was supernatural—so fast he seemed to blur.

Mikhail never moved from his spot, sadness filling his soul. Such a waste of life. A tragedy. Gregori was able to destroy life so easily, with no feeling, no regret. That told Mikhail, more than anything, just how desperate his people's plight really was.

"You take too many chances," Gregori growled in reprimand, materializing beside Mikhail. "They were programmed to destroy you. You should have made certain you removed yourself from harm's way."

Mikhail surveyed the destruction and death surrounding him. Not one body had gotten within ten feet of him. "I knew you would never allow such a thing. He will never rest now until he destroys you, Gregori."

A faint, wolfish grin touched Gregori's mouth. "That is the idea, Mikhail. This is my invitation to him. He has the right to challenge you openly if he so desires, but he is betraying you to mortals. Such treachery will never be tolerated."

"We need to find Father Hummer," Mikhail said softly. "He is too old to survive such a brutal attack. The vampire will not keep him alive once the sun begins to rise."

"But why this elaborate plot?" Gregori mused aloud. "He must have known you would not be caught in the ravine or by the wolves."

"He delays me." A flicker of fear touched Mikhail's black eyes. Once more his mind sought Raven's. She was teasing Jacques.

Suddenly Mikhail inhaled sharply. "Byron. It is well known in the village that he is Eleanor's brother. If Eleanor, her child, and Vlad were targets, it stands to reason that Byron is also." Even as his body bent, contorted, and feathers sprouted, shimmering iridescent in the faint light beginning to streak across the sky, he was already sending a sharp warning to the young Carpathian male. The powerful wings beat strongly as he raced the sun to go to the aid of his brother's best friend.

Gregori surveyed the mountains, his pale eyes moving along the shadowed cliffs above the forest. He stepped off the edge of the cliff, his body shape-shifting as he plummeted toward earth. Wings beat strongly, lifting him into the sky, straight for the jutting rock surface rising above the treetops. The entrance to the cave was a mere slit in the rock wall. It was easy enough to unravel the safeguards. In order to squeeze through the narrow opening, Gregori dissolved into mist and streamed through the crack.

The passage began to widen almost at once, twisting and turning through rock. Water trickled from the walls on either side. And then he was in a large chamber: the vampire's lair. He had the scent now. A glint of satisfaction appeared in Gregori's silver eyes. The vampire would find no resting place here. The undead would find that no one made a threat against the prince without merciless retaliation from Gregori.

Raven paced restlessly across the floor of the cabin, sending Jacques a little self-mocking smile. "I'm very good at waiting."

"I can see that," Jacques agreed dryly.

"Come on, Jacques"—Raven made the length of the room again, turned to face him—"don't you find this even a little bit nerve-wracking?"

He leaned lazily back in his chair, flashing a cocky grin. "Being caged up with a beautiful lunatic, you mean?"

"Ha, ha, ha. Do all Carpathian males think they're stand-up comedians?"

"Just those of us with sisters-in-law who bounce off walls. I feel like I am watching a Ping-Pong ball. Settle down."

"Well, how long does something like this take? Mikhail was very upset."

Leaning back with studied casualness, Jacques tipped his chair to a precarious angle and raised an eyebrow. "Women have vivid imaginations."

"Intellect, Jacques, not imagination," she corrected sweetly.

He grinned at her. "Carpathian males understand the fragile nature of women's nerves. They just cannot take the adversity that we men can."

Raven hooked her foot around his chair and sent him crashing to the floor. Hands on hips, she regarded him with a superior glint. "Carpathian men are vain, dear brother-in-law," she proclaimed, "but not too bright."

Jacques glared up at her with mock ferocity. "You have a mean streak in you." He suddenly came to his feet; his dark eyes were instantly sober, restless. "Put this on." Out of nothing he fashioned a heavy cardigan.

"How do you do that?" It seemed like magic to her.

"A Carpathian can make anything natural of the earth," he informed her in a slightly distracted tone. "Put it on, Raven. I am beginning to feel trapped in this cabin. We need to get out into the night where I can smell trouble coming."

Raven pulled the warmth of the cardigan close around her and followed Jacques out onto the porch. "The night is almost over," she observed.

Jacques inhaled sharply. "I smell blood. Two humans; one is familiar to me."

"Father Hummer," Raven said anxiously. "It's his blood." She started down the stairs, but Jacques, more cautious, caught her arm.

"I do not like this, Raven."

"He's hurt, Jacques. I feel his pain. He is not a young man."

"Perhaps. But how is it he is up here? This cabin is very remote; few know of its existence. How does the priest come to us nearing our weakest hour?"

"He could be dying. Mikhail trusts him," Raven said staunchly, her heart already going out to the priest. "We have to help him."

"You will stay behind me and do as I say," Jacques commanded, forcing her resisting body behind him. "I gave Mikhail my word that I would guard you with my life, and this I intend to do."

"But . . . " Raven swallowed the rest of her protest, easily reading his resolve.

"Scent the wind, Raven. You are Carpathian. Do not always believe the obvious. See with more than your eyes and your heart. I have called Mikhail. He is far from us but will return with all speed. And the dawn approaches." Jacques had moved off the small porch to the grove of trees, turning slowly in a full circle. "There is another."

Raven tried, inhaling the night air, scanning in every direction to find hidden danger. She felt uneasy, but she could only detect the slow approach of the priest and his human companion. "What am I missing, Jacques?" Then she felt it, too, a feeling of disturbance in the natural harmony of things, a power that was out of balance with the earth.

She saw Jacques catch his breath sharply; his black eyes, so like Mikhail's, glittered with sudden menace. "Get out of here, Raven. Run. Get out fast. Do not look back. Find shelter from the sun and wait for Mikhail."

"I can help you." Terror was rising. Something terrible threatened them, something Jacques feared. Raven could not find it in herself to run away and leave her brother-in-law to face danger alone. "I can't go, Jacques."

You do not understand. You are more important than I am, than the priest, than any of us. You are our only hope for the future. Leave this place. Do not make me fail my brother.

Indecision warred with her conscience. Father Hummer limped into view, far more frail than she remembered him. His face was battered and swollen almost beyond recognition. For the first time he looked every one of his eighty-three years.

"Go, Raven!" Jacques hissed, again making a slow circle, never once looking at the advancing priest. His eyes were restless, moving constantly, searching, always searching. *You must leave now.*

Another man came into view. He looked remarkably like Eugene Slovensky, but his hair was blonder and he was obviously younger. He moved up behind the priest and with the flat of his palm on Edgar Hummer's back, shoved viciously.

The priest stumbled forward, fell on one knee, tried to rise and fell full length, his face in the dirt and vegetation. The blond viciously kicked him. "Get up, damn you, old man. Get up or I'll kill you where you lie."

"Stop it!" Raven cried, tears glistening in her eyes. "Father Hummer!" Impetuously she rushed down the stairs.

Jacques sprang forward and cut her off, intercepting her so fast that he was merely a blur. He shoved her roughly back toward the porch. *It is a trap, Raven. Get out of here.*

But Father Hummer! she cried to Jacques in protest.

"Come here, lady," growled Slovensky's look-alike. He bent, grabbed the priest by the collar, and dragged him to his knees. A wicked-looking knife gleamed at the priest's throat. "I'll kill him right now if you don't do what I say."

Jacques turned then, red lights beginning to glow in the depths of his dark eyes. He growled a low rumble of warning that sent shivers along Raven's spine and drained the color from the priest's assailant.

Around them the wind picked up, hurtling leaves and twigs against Jacques's legs. A creature seemed to materialize from nowhere, hit him hard in the chest, picked him up and drove his body into a tree trunk.

Raven screamed. *Mikhail! Where are you?*

I am coming. Get away from there.

Jacques and his undead attacker crashed from tree to tree. Claws slashed; fangs ripped and tore. Branches cracked under the weight of their bodies. The two locked in mortal combat were shape-shifting continually. The vampire, strong and high from a fresh kill, flung himself at Jacques, beating him down, inflicting draining cuts all over his body.

Run, Raven. It is you he wants, Jacques warned. *Go while you can.*

She could hear Jacques breathing heavily, see his growing weakness. Raven had never actually attacked another human being in her life, but it was clear Jacques was in trouble. *Hurry, Mikhail.* There was desperation in her message. Dawn was streaking across the sky when she leapt on the vampire's back, trying to drag him from Jacques.

No, get back! Jacques's cry was sharp, imperious, and laced with terror.

No, Raven! Mikhail echoed the command from a distance.

No, woman, do not! Gregori's voice whispered fiercely in her head.

Not understanding, but certain she was in deadly peril, Raven tried to jump off. The vampire clamped one hand around her wrist in a viselike grip and turned his head, triumph in his glowing eyes. Sharp teeth bit into her wrist, and he was gulping dark, rich blood. It burned and hurt like a red-hot brand. Her flesh was ragged and gaping, his fangs tearing at her.

Mikhail and Gregori mentally struck together at the vampire's throat. Although such an attack was not very successful against one of Carpathian blood and they were still some distance away, their combined assault closed off the undead's air momentarily. Jacques struck the vampire with renewed ferocity, driving him backward, dislodging Raven so that she fell free. Blood sprayed in a shower of crimson droplets across the forest floor, and for one moment both fighters froze, distracted by the red shower, turning almost in unison toward her.

"Close that wound!" The vampire snarled, his voice gruff.

Raven, you will bleed to death. Jacques struggled for calm, wanting her to understand the seriousness of the situation.

The vampire struck, claws ripping at Jacques's stomach so that he was forced to bring his hands down to protect himself. The vampire's head contorted, lengthened to a long muzzle, and lunged like a wolf at Jacques's exposed throat, ripping and tearing.

Raven screamed and threw her body at the vampire, beating wildly at his head and shoulders. Contemptuously he dropped Jacques's body so it lay broken like a rag doll in the rotting vegetation. He dragged Raven's wrist to his mouth, his eyes smiling into hers, and deliberately ran his tongue across the wound to close it. Her body and mind rebelled at the hideous contact, her stomach heaving and protesting the unclean touch.

"Remember, mortal, she is mine," he commanded Slovensky. "I will come for her this night. Get her out of the sun." The vampire released her and launched himself skyward.

Raven spit into her hands and stumbled forward toward Jacques's motionless body. "That vampire killed him," she screamed hysterically. As her hands touched the forest floor she scooped up handfuls of dirt. "Oh, God, he's dead. You let that thing kill him!" Using her slender body as a shield so no one could see what she was doing, Raven packed the wounds in Jacques's throat with the soil and her healing saliva. *Drink,*

Jacques, now, so that you can last until Mikhail and Gregori arrive. Her wrist over his mouth, Raven continued to sob dramatically, thankful for once that men often thought women hysterical in a crisis.

Mikhail! Jacques is mortally wounded. He is in the sun. She sensed the approach of the human male and twisted her wrist gently in warning. Jacques was so weak; feeding blindly, he nearly missed the signal. His loss of blood was enormous.

With great dignity Raven covered his head and her handiwork with her cardigan and bent as if kissing him good-bye. *Don't let me down, Jacques. You must live. For me, for Mikhail, for all of us. Don't let them win.* Even as she sent the words to him she could detect no pulse, no hint of his heart beating.

Slovensky gripped her shoulder and yanked her to her feet. She was deathly pale, dizzy, very weak. "Enough crying. You give me any trouble and I'll kill the priest. If you harm me, the vampire will kill the priest." He shoved her down the trail.

Raven lifted her chin, regarded him coolly with red-rimmed eyes. "Then I guess, for your sake, it's imperative you keep Father Hummer in excellent health, isn't it?" Raven knew from touching the man that he didn't believe for one moment that the priest was an advocate of the devil or one of Mikhail's servants. He had seen the vampire's power and craved it, believed he would soon be rewarded.

James Slovensky could easily see the contempt and the knowledge in her large blue eyes. He didn't like the picture reflected there and gave her a shove toward the trail.

It took every ounce of her control and determination to make her way over the uneven ground. She had never known such weakness. She couldn't even help Father Hummer. It took total concentration to put one foot in front of the other. Once she sat down hard, shocked to realize she hadn't tripped over anything. Her legs had simply given out. Not looking at her captor, Raven pushed herself up again. She didn't want him touching her. She was cold, inside and out, afraid she might never be warm again.

Feed on the priest, the vampire ordered, rage smoldering in his tone.

Raven blinked, finding herself looking around even though the voice was in her head. The vampire had established a blood bond with her, could monitor her at will. *Go to hell.* She contended herself with the childish retort.

His laughter taunted her. *You gave your blood to Jacques. I should have guessed. He will not live; I made certain his was a mortal wound.*

Raven summoned up contempt, flooding her mind with it. It was becoming difficult to think clearly, and she had fallen too many times to count. Her captor thrust her into the back seat of a vehicle beside the priest and began to drive at breakneck speed down the mountains. Raven rolled over, grateful that the windows had been blackened and the interior was dark. Lethargy was taking over; her body felt like lead.

Feed! The vampire was sharply imperious.

Raven was thankful that she could defy him. She couldn't sleep, didn't dare until she knew Jacques was safe. Mikhail and Gregori were racing the sun, powerful wings beating strongly as they flew toward the old cabin. They would burrow deep into the soil the moment they were able, taking Jacques with them.

Raven. The call was closer, filling her mind with love. *You are so weak.*

Save Jacques. Come to me tonight, Mikhail. The vampire knows my thoughts. He thinks he is safe, that I can be used to trap you. Don't let him be right. She tried desperately to send the words clearly to him, but her brain was sluggish.

"Raven?" Edgar Hummer touched her forehead, finding her ice cold. Her skin was so pale, she seemed nearly translucent, her blue eyes sunken, like two bruised flowers pressed into her face. "Can you talk? Is Mikhail alive?"

She nodded, surveying his swollen face with dismay. "What have they done to you? Why would they beat you this way?"

"They say they're certain I know where Mikhail keeps all of his spare coffins. According to Andre . . . "

265

"Who is Andre?"

"The treacherous vampire in league with these killers. He is a true undead, feeding on children, destroying all that is holy. His soul is lost for all eternity. As far as I can tell, Andre appears to be deliberately perpetuating the vampire myths. He claims that Mikhail is the head vampire and if they succeed in killing him, those under his influence will be returned to mortal existence. He must have established a blood bond without their knowledge and he uses it to give them orders."

Raven closed her eyes weakly. Her heart was struggling to pump without necessary blood; her lungs cried out for oxygen. "How many of them are there?"

"Three that I've seen. This one is James Slovensky. His brother Eugene is their supposed leader, and their muscle man is Anton Fabrezo."

"Two of them stayed at the inn with the American couple. We thought they had left the country. This Andre must be a lot more powerful than anyone suspects."

Her voice was fading, her speech slurring. Father Hummer watched as she tried to lift her arm to push her hair away from her face. Her arm seemed too heavy; her face seemed too great a distance away. He did it for her with gentle fingers.

Raven! There was anguish in Mikhail's voice.

It was too difficult to answer him; it required far too much strength. The priest shifted so that her head could fall against his arm. Raven was shivering with cold. "I need a blanket back here for her."

"Shut up, old man," Slovensky snapped. His eyes continually searched the sky through his windshield. The sun was up, but heavy clouds dimmed the sky, hiding the light.

"If she dies, Andre will make you wish you had died too," Edgar Hummer persisted.

"I need sleep," Raven said softly without opening her eyes. She didn't even wince when Slovensky's jacket landed on her unprotected face.

Mikhail had to get out of the sun. Without dark glasses or any substantial protection from the rays, his skin and eyes were burning. He landed on the low branch of a tree and changed to human form as he jumped the remaining seven feet to earth. Jacques's body lay in the sun, a cardigan covering his neck and face. Without looking to see the extent of his brother's injuries, Mikhail lifted him and glided above ground toward the network of caves a mile away.

A huge black wolf burst from the clearing to join him, loping easily beside him, pale silver eyes gleaming with menace. Together they raced through the narrow passages until they found a large, steaming chamber. The black wolf contorted, fur rippling along muscular arms as Gregori shape-shifted to his true form.

Mikhail laid Jacques's body gently on the rich soil and lifted away the covering. He swore softly, unshed tears burning in his throat and eyes. "Can you save him?"

Gregori's hands moved over the body, the vicious wounds. "He stopped his heart and lungs so that he could conserve his blood. Raven is weak because she fed him. She mixed her saliva and the soil and packed it in tight. It is already beginning to heal the wounds. I will need your herbs, Mikhail."

"Save him, Gregori." Mikhail's body rippled with thick, glossy fur, bent, stretched, took shape as he ran along the maze of passages upward out of the bowels of the earth. He dared not think of Raven and how weak she was. The heaviness was invading his body already, demanding he go to ground, that he sleep.

Summoning his immense strength and a will honed to iron over hundreds of years, Mikhail burst into the open at a flat run. The wolf's body was built for speed and he used it, running flat out, eyes narrowed to tiny slits. Paws hit the ground; back feet dug into soil to leap rotting logs. He never slowed, racing through ravines and over rocks.

The overcast sky helped to ease the effects of the sun, but his eyes were streaming as he approached the cabin. The wind shifted, bringing the foul stench of sweat and fear. *Man.* The beast snarled silently, all the pent-up rage in him exploding into white-hot fury. The wolf skidded to a halt, body low to the ground, once more the predator.

The wolf kept downwind, gliding through thick brush to creep up on the two men waiting in ambush. A trap for him. Of course the betrayer would know Mikhail would rush to aid his brother. The vampire was cunning and willing to take chances. The betrayer had lain in wait, feeding Hans Romanov's fanaticism. It was probably the undead who had commanded Hans to murder his wife. The wolf slunk low on its belly, crawled forward until it was within feet of the larger of the two men.

"We're too late," Anton Fabrezo whispered, half rising to stare down the trail in front of the cabin. "Something sure happened here."

"Damn truck, it would have to overheat," Dieter Hodkins complained. "There's blood everywhere and smashed branches. There was a fight, all right."

"Do you think Andre killed Dubrinsky?" Anton asked.

"That's our job. But the sun's up. If Dubrinsky's alive, he's somewhere sleeping in his coffin. We can check the cabin, but I don't think we're going to find anything," Dieter said with irritation.

"Andre isn't going to be happy with us," Anton worried aloud. "He wants Dubrinsky dead in a big way."

"Well, he should have provided us with a decent truck. I told him mine was breaking down," Dieter snapped impatiently. He believed in vampires, and that it was his holy duty to exterminate them.

Dieter stood up cautiously, surveying the landscape carefully. "Come on, Fabrezo. Maybe we'll get lucky and Dubrinsky will be in the cabin already laid out in his coffin."

Anton laughed nervously. "I'll drive in the stake; you cut off the head. This vampire-killing stuff is messy."

"Cover me while I scout it out," Dieter ordered. He took a step through the thick foliage, his rifle cradled in his arms. The bushes directly in front of him parted and he was face to face with a huge, heavily muscled wolf. His heart nearly stopped, and he froze, unable for a moment to move.

Black eyes glittered malevolently, streaming and red-rimmed. Sharp white fangs glinted, glistened with saliva. The wolf held him with those black eyes for a full thirty seconds, striking terror in Dieter's heart. Without warning it lunged, jaws wide, head low, caught one booted ankle and crushed down with incredible power, breaking through leather and bones with a loud, sickening snap. Dieter screamed and fell. The wolf instantly released him and sprang back, regarding him with impersonal eyes.

From his position in the bushes, Fabrezo had seen Dieter Hodkins go down screaming, but he couldn't see why. The terror in Hodkin's tone sent fear spiraling through him. It took a minute for Anton to find his voice. "What is it? I can't see." He didn't try to see either, sliding further down in the bushes, holding his gun up and ready, finger on the trigger ready to spray anything that moved. He wanted to yell at Dieter to shut up, but he remained quiet, his heart pounding in alarm.

Dieter tried to bring his rifle into firing position. Between the pain and the terror those black, venomous eyes were inducing, he couldn't quite get the barrel around fast enough. Those eyes were far too intelligent, held rage and fury. That death stare was very personal. And it was the eyes of death that mesmerized him. He couldn't look away, not even when the wolf lunged for his exposed throat. At the last he didn't feel a thing, suddenly welcoming the end. The deadly eyes staring into his changed at the last moment, suddenly saddened as the wolf made the kill.

The wolf shook its shaggy head and eased into the bushes behind Anton Fabrezo. He could hear the heart thudding with terror, bursting with life. He could hear the blood rushing hotly through the body, smelled fear and sweat. Joy washed over the wolf, the need for blood, for the kill. Mikhail pushed it down, thought of Raven, her compassion and courage and the need to kill vanished. The sun broke through a small hole in the heavy cloud cover and a thousand needles pierced his eyes.

I need those herbs, Mikhail. The sun is climbing and time is running out for Jacques. Finish it now.

The wolf waited for the clouds to move back in place and then it walked boldly into the open, deliberately keeping his back to Fabrezo. Anton's eyes narrowed, and an evil smile twisted his mouth. His hand raised the gun, his finger finding the trigger. Before he could pull the trigger the wolf whirled in midair and smashed into Anton's chest, driving through bone, ripping straight for the heart.

The wolf leaped over the body, his manner contemptuous as he loped to the cabin. His eyes were tearing continually, streaming water no matter how narrow the slits. The heaviness spreading through his body was far more difficult to ignore. Aware of time passing, the wolf sprinted up the stairs to the door. One claw contorted, lengthened to fingers so that he was able to grasp the doorknob and push the heavy door open. The need for sleep was almost overpowering and Jacques was waiting for the herbs.

Distorted, clawed hands hung the bag of precious herbs around the thick, muscular neck, and then the wolf was in a dead run, racing the climbing sun as it burned away the thick cloud covering.

Thunder cracked unexpectedly. Thick black clouds, heavy with rain, blew across the sky, providing Mikhail with dense cover from the sun. The storm rolled in over the forest fast, with wild winds kicking up leaves and swaying branches. A bolt of lightning sizzled across the sky in a fiery whip of dancing light. The sky darkened to an ominous cauldron of boiling clouds. Mikhail bounded into the caves and raced along the narrow maze of passages toward the main chamber, shape-shifting as he ran.

Gregori's cool silver gaze slid over him as Mikhail relinquished the herbs. "It is a wonder you have been able to tie your shoes without me all of these centuries."

Mikhail sank down beside his brother, one hand over his burning eyes. "It is more of a wonder you have stayed alive with your ostentatious displays."

Ancient language, as old as time, flooded the chamber. Gregori's voice was beautiful yet commanding. No one had a voice like Gregori's. Beautiful, hypnotic, mesmerizing. The ritual chant provided an anchor in the uncertain sea in which Jacques was floating. Rich soil mixed with Gregori's saliva was a collar around the wounded Carpathian's neck. Gregori's blood, old and powerful beyond measure, flowed in Jacques's starved veins. Gregori crushed and mixed herbs, adding them to the mixture around Jacques's neck.

"I repaired the damage from the inside out. He is weak, Mikhail, but his will is strong. If we put him deep within the earth and give him time, he will heal." Gregori pushed a poultice into Mikhail's hand. "Put that on your eyes. It will help until we get you in the ground."

Gregori was right. The poultice was soothing, a cool ice melting the fire. But somewhere deep inside another nightmare was starting. A yawning, black, empty hole that began to stretch, to crawl through him, whispering dark, insane thoughts. No matter how many times his mind reached for Raven's, he found emptiness. Intellect told him she was in a deep sleep, but his Carpathian blood cried out for her touch.

"You need to go to ground now," Gregori pointed out. "I will fix the safeguards and ensure we are not disturbed."

"With a big sign saying 'Gregori lies here, do not disturb'?" Mikhail asked softly, his voice a low warning.

Gregori lowered Jacques's body deep within the healing earth, in no way disturbed by Mikhail's sarcasm.

"You may as well have written your name in the sky with that display, Gregori."

"I want the vampire to be very clear about who I am, whom he has chosen for his enemy." Gregori's shoulders shrugged in a lazy ripple of power.

Need crawled along Mikhail's skin like a thousand biting ants, stinging his organs and gnawing at his sinews. He raised red, swollen eyes to Gregori's harsh, yet curiously sensual features. There was such power in Gregori; it blazed in the silver of his eyes. "You think with Raven that I am complete and no longer have need of you. You deliberately draw the danger to yourself, away from me and mine, because in your heart you believe you can no longer hold out. You welcome the danger of the hunt; you are seeking a way to end this life. Now, more than ever, our people need you, Gregori. We have hope. There is a future for us if we can survive the coming years."

Gregori sighed heavily, looked away from the steel in Mikhail's eyes, the censure blazing there. "There is purpose in saving your life, but for me, not much else."

Mikhail pushed a hand through his thick mane of hair. "Our people cannot do without you, Gregori, and quite simply, neither can I."

"You are so certain that I will not turn?" Gregori's smile was humorless, self-mocking. "Your faith in me exceeds my own. This vampire is ruthless, drunk on his own power. He craves the killing, the destruction. I walk the line of that madness every day. His power is nothing, a feather in the wind compared to mine. I have no heart and my soul is dark. I do not want to wait until I cannot make my own choice. The one thing I do not want is to force you to seek me out to destroy me. My life has been my belief in you, in protecting you. I will not wait until I must be hunted."

Mikhail waved a tired hand to open the earth above his brother. "You are our greatest healer, the greatest asset to our people."

"That is why they whisper my name in fear and dread."

Beneath their feet the ground suddenly shook, heaved and bucked, rolled perilously. The center of the earthquake was obviously a great distance away, but there was no mistaking the howl of rage produced by a powerful vampire at the destruction of his lair.

The undead had entered his lair confidently, until he found the body of the first wolf. Each turn or passage entrance was marked with one of his minions, until his entire pack lay dead at his feet. Fear had turned to terror. Not Mikhail, whose sense of justice and fair play would be his downfall, but the dark one. *Gregori*.

It had not occurred to the vampire that the dark one might take a hand in this game. Andre hurtled himself from the safety of his favorite lair just as the mountain heaved and the chamber walls collapsed. Cracks widened in the narrow passageway and the rock faces inched closer and closer together. The clap of granite grinding against granite nearly burst his eardrums. A true vampire making numerous kills was far more susceptible to the sun, and to the terrible lethargy that claimed Carpathian bodies in the day. Andre had little time to find a safe hole. As he burst from the collapsing mountain, the sun hit his body so that he screamed with the agony of it. Dust and rock spewed from his home, and the echo of Gregori's taunting laughter drifted down with the debris from the earthquake.

"No, Gregori." There was amusement in Mikhail's soft voice. He floated into the soothing arms of the earth. "That is a good example of why they whisper your name in fear and dread. No one understands your dark humor the way I do."

"Mikhail?"

Mikhail stayed the hand closing the blanket of soil over him.

"I would not endanger you or Jacques with my challenge. The vampire cannot get by my safeguards."

"I have never feared Andre. And I know your spells are strong. I think our friend has his own problems finding somewhere to rest out of the sun. He will not be disturbing us this day."

Chapter Fourteen

Father Hummer walked the circuit of the rock walls surrounding them. There were no windows, and their prison seemed heavily constructed, the walls so thick, he was certain they were soundproof. No light penetrated the walls, and the complete darkness was oppressive. The priest had piled every blanket available over Raven's ice-cold body, but he was certain she had died from loss of blood. He could not detect a pulse or breath since they had been shoved into the room. After first baptizing Raven and administering the last rites to her, Father Hummer had begun to carefully feel his way around the room in hopes of finding a way to escape.

The vampire, Andre, was using Raven to draw Mikhail to this place. Edgar, knowing Mikhail as well as he did, knew the plan could not fail. Mikhail would come, and God have mercy on Slovensky's soul.

A small sound, a shuddering wheeze of lungs laboring, drew his attention. Father Hummer felt his way back to Raven. Her body was shivering uncontrollably beneath the pile of blankets. She was as cold as ever. The priest put his arms around her, seeking comfort for both of them. "What can I do to help you?"

Raven opened her eyes. She could see clearly in the darkness, examining the tightly constructed cell and then Father Hummer's worried face. "I need blood."

"I'll be happy to donate, my child," he responded instantly.

She sensed his weakness. In any case, Raven could never take blood in the Carpathian manner. Her mind reached for Mikhail's, an automatic reaction. Pain exploded in her head. She moaned softly, clutching her temples.

Do not try, little one. Mikhail sounded strong, reassuring. *Conserve your strength. I will be there soon.*

Is Jacques alive? Sending the message put shards of glass in her skull.

Thanks to you. Rest. It was an order—a clear, imperious demand.

A smile tugged at the corner of Raven's soft mouth. "Talk to me, Father; distract me." She was very weak but did not want to draw the priest's attention to it.

"I'll keep my voice low just to be safe," Edgar said, close to her ear. "Mikhail will come, you know. He would never leave us here." He rubbed his hands up and down her arms to try to bring heat to her laboring body.

Raven nodded her head, a difficult task when it felt like lead. "I know what he is like. He would give up his life for us in a heartbeat."

"You are his life mate. Without you, he would become the vampire of legends, a monster without equal in the human race."

Raven fought for each separate breath. "Don't believe that, Father. We have our own evil monsters. I have seen them, followed them. They are every bit as bad." She clutched the blanket closer to her. "Have you ever met Mikhail's friend, Gregori?"

"He's the one they call the dark one. I've seen him, of course, but only once. Mikhail has voiced his fears for him often."

Raven's breath wheezed in and out, a harsh sound in the

quiet of the cell. "He's a great healer, Father." She took another shuddering breath. "And he is loyal to Mikhail. Do you believe there is hope for their race?"

The priest made the sign of the cross on her forehead, on the insides of each of her wrists. "You are their hope, Raven. Don't you know that?"

Mikhail touched her mind with his. He was closer, the bond between them powerful. He flooded her with love, enfolded her in strong, protective arms. *Hold on, my love.* His voice was a black-velvet seduction of tenderness in her mind.

Do not come to this evil place, Mikhail. Wait for Gregori, she pleaded.

I cannot, little one.

Lights flickered in the cell, on, off, back on again, as if a generator was being powered up. Raven's hand found Father Hummer's. "I tried to stop him, to warn him, but he will come."

"Of course he will." Edgar's eyes were blinking in the sudden light. Father Hummer was worried about Raven. Her breath sounded strangled, labored.

The heavy door clanged and creaked as it swung open. James Slovensky peered at them. His eyes fastened on Raven's face as if drawn irresistibly. Her blue eyes met his across the room. "What's wrong with you?" he demanded.

A faint, taunting smile curved her soft mouth. "I'm dying. I think that's plain enough even for you to see." Her voice was low, a mere thread of sound, but so musical that it was impossible not to be entranced by it.

Slovensky advanced farther into the room. Raven could feel Mikhail in her, building his strength, his power, crouching, waiting to strike. She also felt a sudden uneasiness. *Wait. The vampire comes.* She dragged a shuddering breath into her laboring lungs, the sound loud and distressed in the room.

Slovensky was shoved carelessly across the room with one powerful swat from Andre's hand. He stood framed in the doorway, flushed from a fresh kill. His eyes were flat and held a kind of contempt, a merciless promise of savagery. "Good morning, my dear. I am Andre, come to take you to your new home."

He glided across the room, clearly enjoying his power over them all. As he approached her, his eyes darkened with rage. "You were told to feed on the priest."

"You were told to go to hell." She said it in her soft, musical voice, deliberately baiting him.

"You will learn it is better to obey me," he snapped. Angry at her defiance, he caught the priest by the front of his shirt and hurled him against the stone wall. It was done coldly, callously, without thought of the consequences. "If you are not going to use him for food, we have no need of him, do we?" The vampire's smile was wholly evil.

Father Hummer's body had fallen to the floor heavily, his skull cracking audibly on impact. There was a gasping sound as his lungs fought for air, then a soft sigh as they gave up the fight.

Raven bit back a scream, struggled for air, her grief so overwhelming, that for a moment her mind couldn't function. *Mikhail, I'm sorry. I angered him. This is my fault.*

She felt the warmth of his love surround her, the brush of his fingers so tender on her face. *Never that, my love.* She felt his sorrow mingle with hers. Raven lifted her blue-violet eyes to the face of the vampire. "Now, how do you expect to control me?"

The vampire bent down, his smile evil, his breath foul. "You will learn. Now you will feed." He snapped his fingers, and Slovensky nearly tripped over his own feet to run out of the cell and return with a glass of dark, murky liquid. His hand trembled as he passed it to the vampire, careful to avoid the razor-sharp long nails. "For you, my dear; breakfast." The vampire held the glass close enough for her to smell the contents. Fresh blood tainted with something else, some herb she didn't recognize.

"Drugs, Andre? Isn't that stooping a little low even for one such as you?" She had to fight every moment just to breathe, to keep from breaking down and sobbing out her grief for the priest. If only she hadn't angered the vampire.

Andre's face darkened when she uttered his name with such contempt, but he simply stared into her eyes, flooding her with compulsion, the need to obey him.

Loathing him as she did, fearful for Mikhail and grief-stricken over the priest and Jacques, Raven summoned every ounce of strength she possessed and fought a mental battle with him. Her head nearly exploded with pain and only when little beads of blood appeared on her forehead did he relent.

The vampire pushed down his fury at her rebellion. She was close to death and if she died all his scheming would be for nothing. "You will die if you do not feed. I know Mikhail knows this. Do you hear me, prince? She dies. Force her to accept what I offer."

You must do this, little one. Mikhail's voice was gently coaxing. *You will be dead before I can reach you, and above all else, you must survive.*

The blood is drugged.

Drugs do not effect Carpathians.

Raven sighed, looked once more at the vampire. "What else is in it?"

"Only herbs, my dear, herbs that will confuse you a bit, but will ensure that my friends have plenty of time to study Mikhail. They can keep him alive, a prisoner here. Is that not what you want? That he remain alive? The alternative is to kill him immediately." He pushed the glass at her.

Her stomach knotted in rebellion. It would just be so much easier to close her eyes and stop struggling for every breath. She could barely stand the pain in her head. She was responsible for Jacques's grave wound, for Father Hummer's death. Worst of all, her beloved Mikhail was racing straight into the arms of the enemy because of her. If she just stopped . . .

No! Mikhail's voice was sharp and imperious.

Do not! Gregori added his strength to Mikhail's protest.

The vampire wrapped his hand around her throat in his fury that she might choose death and defeat him. His touch made her skin crawl; her stomach roiled in protest. Suddenly the vampire screamed and leaped back away from her, his face contorted in fury and pain. Raven could see his charred and blackened palm, still smoking as he held it to his chest. Mikhail had sent his own warning and challenge.

"You think he win," the vampire snarled at her, "but he

will not. Now drink!" His hands closed around her wrist, steadying her hand.

Raven's mind splintered and screamed at the close proximity of such evil. The crumpled body of Edgar Hummer lay in plain sight, no more than a heap of refuse to the vampire. Touching Andre, she could read his mind easily. He was the most depraved being she had ever encountered.

The drug would confuse her enough that he could make her believe she belonged to him. Mikhail would be kept alive, living in pain and torment, too weak to attack his captors. Slovensky enjoyed inflicting pain. His brother was eager to dissect a vampire, experiment on one. The vampire was certain the Slovensky brothers would die at the hands of the avenging Carpathians. She read it all, the betrayal and the hideousness of the undead's plans.

Mikhail! Do not come to this place! She resisted the compulsion to drink the tainted blood, struggling feebly in the vampire's foul hold. *I will not allow you to fall into their hands. I will choose death.*

"Drink!" The vampire was becoming alarmed. Her heart was stuttering with effort. There was a smear of crimson across her forehead, indicating agony.

"Never," she said between clenched teeth.

"She dies, Mikhail. Is this what you want for her? She dies in my arms, with me, and I have won anyway." Andre shook her in his fury. "He will commit suicide the moment you relinquish life. Are you so stupid that you do not realize that? He will die."

Her blue-violet eyes searched the gaunt face. "He will destroy you first." She said it with complete conviction.

My love. Mikhail's voice was black velvet, soothing in her pain-filled mind. *You must allow me to decide this matter. You give me no choice but to force your compliance. This should be our decision together, but you cannot see beyond the threat to me. He cannot defeat me. Believe that; hold on to that. He cannot separate us. We live in each other. He does not understand our bond. Together we are too strong for him. I will allow him to capture me. I allow it; that is all.*

The vampire knew the moment Mikhail's will dominated. Raven allowed the glass to be brought to her lips. Even under compulsion, her body tried to reject the nourishment. The vampire could feel her stomach heave and fight. Her bond with Mikhail allowed her life mate to calm her enough to accept what the vampire offered.

Her heart and lungs responded almost immediately to the liquid. Her breathing became less labored; her body grew warm. The moment Mikhail relinquished her will, Raven attempted to squirm away from the vampire. He tightened his arms around her, deliberately rubbing his face against hers. His laughter was cruel, gloating even. "You thought him strong, did you not? But, you see, he jumps to do my bidding."

"Why are you doing this? Why do you betray him?"

"He betrays all of our people." Mikhail strode through the door, tall and strong, looking invincible.

Slovensky flattened himself against the wall, trying to appear inconspicuous. Andre pressed a razor-sharp claw into Raven's jugular. "Be very, very careful, Mikhail. You could kill me, there is no question, but she will die first." Andre dragged her even closer, locking her in front of him as he lifted her body completely off the ground. Blankets scattered as Raven was dangled helplessly, her eyes fastened on Mikhail.

Mikhail's smile was tender, loving, as he focused on her face. *I love you, little one. Be brave.* "What do you wish, Andre?" His voice was gentle and low.

"I want your blood."

"I will give it to Raven to replenish her."

Raven's heart slammed against her ribs. Deliberately she leaned into Andre's claw. A dot of blood beaded, trickled down her neck. The vampire tightened his arm around her ribs, nearly cracking them. "Do not do such a stupid thing again," he reprimanded her, then turned his attention back to Mikhail. "You cannot come close enough to her to give blood. Drain it into a container."

Mikhail shook his head slowly. *He wants my blood for himself, love, to become more powerful, to aid the drug in confusing your mind.* Already he could feel the effects of the drugs in her. She was struggling to stay with him. *I cannot allow him my blood.* The words echoed sadly.

Raven reached for Gregori. *You must come.*

The drug he has given you is an ancient one, Gregori explained, the words brushing softly in her mind, *made from the pressed petals of a flower found only in the northern regions of our lands. It will disorient you, but that is all. The vampire will attempt to plant his own memories of you with him and then will use pain to control your thoughts. He has established a blood bond, so he can monitor you. When you think of Mikhail, he can cause you pain. It is not the drug, it is the vampire. Censor your thoughts as much as possible to conserve your strength. When you reach for Mikhail as your mind and body must, Andre must not know. You focus better than any Carpathian I have known. He knows nothing of our bond. I can find you anywhere. The moment I am finished attending Jacques, I will go to Mikhail. You have my word Mikhail will survive. We will find you. Stay alive for the sake of all our people.*

The vampire and Mikhail stared across the room at one another. Power emanated from Mikhail's every pore. He looked coolly amused by the vampire's dilemma.

A ripple of malevolence distorted the tense vibrations in the room, striking at Raven's temple. *Mikhail!*

She screamed the warning in her mind as Slovensky shot him three times. In the small cell, the noise was a loud clap of thunder reverberating off the rock walls. The bullets drove Mikhail backward and he fell beside Father Hummer, his precious blood staining his white silk shirt a vivid crimson.

"No!" Raven fought the vampire in earnest, fear lending her strength that the loss of her blood had taken. For a moment she wrenched herself nearly free but was jerked back, the vampire's hands around her throat, squeezing hard. Raven fought down panic. She didn't dare pass out. *Gregori, Mikhail's down. They shot him.*

I feel it. All Carpathians feel it. Do not worry. He will not die. Gregori was clearly moving closer. *They were very care-*

ful to inflict flesh wounds that bleed heavily, not mortal wounds such as they gave Jacques. He is conveying to me the extent of his injuries.

The vampire dragged Raven with him to the door. "The others will come, but it will be too late. Do not think he will get out of this," he hissed in her ear. "Slovensky and the others will die for this deed, and with them all records of what occurred in this place. You will be mine, far away where they cannot find you."

Raven kept her eyes and mind focused on Mikhail, broadcasting to Gregori everything she saw: Slovensky manacling Mikhail's wrists and ankles, chaining him to a wall, laughing, taunting, kicking at him. Mikhail remained silent, his dark eyes very black, glinting like ice.

The vampire lifted her slender body, ran with blurring speed from the place of death and destruction, launched himself skyward, his talons gripping Raven as he sped into the night.

Gregori merged his mind with Mikhail's easily. Over the centuries of battles, wars, and vampire hunters, they had exchanged blood many times to preserve one another's life. Mikhail was in pain, his blood loss great. The shooting had been a deliberate attempt to weaken his immense power. Slovensky was busy taunting Mikhail with graphic details of torture.

Mikhail's black eyes smoldered an eerie red, a burning flame he turned on Slovensky as the man approached him. The power in those chilling eyes stopped Slovensky for a moment. "You'll learn to hate me, vampire," James Slovensky snarled. "And you'll learn to fear me. You'll learn who really holds the power."

A slight, mocking smile touched Mikhail's mouth. "I do not hate you, mortal. And I could never fear you. You are but a pawn in a game of power. And you have been sacrificed." The voice was very low, a musical thread of sound that Slovensky found himself wanting to hear again.

The man knelt beside his victim, smiling his pleasure at the other's pain. "Andre will give us the rest of you bloodsuckers."

"And why would he do that?" Mikhail closed his eyes, his face lined and strained, but the hint of a smile remained.

"You turned him, forced him into such an unholy life, the same way you turned the woman. He is going to try to save her." Slovensky leaned closer, drew his knife. "I think I should dig that slug out of you. We wouldn't want you getting an infection now, would we?" His giggle was high-pitched with anticipation.

Mikhail didn't flinch away from the blade. His black eyes snapped open, blazing with power. Slovensky fell backwards, scrambling away on all fours to crouch against the far wall. Fumbling in his coat, he jerked out the gun and held it pointed at Mikhail.

The ground rolled almost gently, seemed to swell so that the concrete floor bulged, then cracked. Slovensky grabbed for the wall behind him to steady himself and lost the gun in the process. Above his head a rock fell from the wall, bounced dangerously close, and rolled to a halt beside him. A second rock, and a third fell, so that Slovensky had to cover his head as the rocks rained down in a roaring shower.

Slovensky's cry of fear was high and thin. He made himself even smaller, peering through his fingers at the Carpathian. Mikhail had not moved to protect himself. He lay exactly as Slovensky had positioned him, those dark eyes staring at him. Swearing, Slovensky tried to lunge for the gun.

The floor bucked and heaved under him, sending the gun skittering out of reach. A second wall swayed precariously and rocks cascaded down, striking the man about the head and shoulders, driving him to the floor. He watched a curious, frightening pattern form. Not one rock touched the priest's body. Not one came close to Mikhail. The Carpathian simply watched him with those damn eyes and that faint mocking smile as the rocks buried Slovensky's legs, then fell on his back. There was an ominous crack, and Slovensky screamed under the heavy load on his spine.

"Damn you to hell," Slovensky snarled. "My brother will track you down."

Mikhail said nothing, simply watching the havoc Gregori

was creating. Mikhail would have killed James Slovensky outright, without the drama Gregori had such a flare for, but he was tired, his body in a precarious state. He had no wish to drain his energy further. Raven would be in the vampire's hands for the time it took Gregori to heal him. He couldn't allow himself to think of what Andre might do to her. Mikhail stirred, pain shafting through him. More rocks fell on Slovensky in retaliation, covering him like a blanket, beginning to form a macabre grave.

Gregori moved into the room with his familiar silent glide, grace and power clinging to him as he strode through the wreckage of the wall. "This is becoming a bad habit."

"Oh, shut up," Mikhail said without rancor.

Gregori's touch was infinitely gentle as he inspected the wounds. "They knew what they were doing. Placed these precisely to miss vital organs but to bleed you as much as possible." It took seconds to deal with the manacles and free Mikhail from the chains. Gregori pressed soil over the wounds to stop further leakage.

"Check Father Hummer." Mikhail's voice was weak.

"He is dead." Gregori barely glanced at the broken body.

"Be certain." It was an order. Mikhail never ordered Gregori to do anything. That had never been their relationship.

For a moment Gregori's silver eyes glittered as they stared at one another.

"Please, Gregori, if there is a chance . . . " Mikhail closed his eyes.

Shaking his head at the delay, Gregori dutifully went to the priest's crumpled body and felt for a pulse. He knew it was fruitless, knew Mikhail knew it, too, but just the same he checked. Gregori was careful to be gentle with the body. "I am sorry, Mikhail. He is gone."

"I do not want him left in this place."

"Stop talking and allow me to do my job," Gregori growled, easing Mikhail back onto the floor. "Take my blood while I stop up these holes."

"Find Raven."

"Take my blood, Mikhail. The vampire will not harm her. He will have some patience this night. You must be strong for the hunt. Drink what I freely offer. I would not want to find it necessary to compel you."

"You are becoming a nuisance, Gregori," Mikhail complained, but obediently he took hold of the healer's proffered wrist. Gregori's blood was ancient, as was Mikhail's. There was none other that could help as quickly. There was silence as Mikhail fed, replenishing what was lost. Gregori turned his wrist slightly to ease Mikhail away from him, knowing his strength was needed for healing and transporting his prince to safety.

"The priest goes with us," Mikhail reiterated. A wave of heat coursed through the ice of his body, leaving him needy, hungry. His mind reached for his life mate, the need to merge overwhelming.

Pain exploded in her head, in his, so that he gasped and withdrew, his black eyes seeking Gregori's pale ones in agony. *Sleep for now, Mikhail. We will go on the hunt soon enough. We must take care of these wounds first.* Gregori commanded it in a mesmerizing voice. Singsong, a flowing chant of ancient language. *You will hear my words, let Mother Earth welcome you. The soil will heal your wounds and soothe your mind. Sleep, Mikhail. My blood is powerful, mixing with yours. Feel it healing your body.* Gregori closed his eyes, merging completely with Mikhail, flowing in him so that he could find every ragged hole, push out foreign objects, and repair all damage from the inside out with the precision of the most skilled surgeon.

A large horned owl circled the ruined building, then settled on the crumpled wall. Slowly the wings folded and the owl's round eyes surveyed the scene below. The talons flexed, relaxed. Gregori lifted his head, coming back to his own body. He spoke the Carpathian's name softly in acknowledgment. "Aidan."

The owl's shape lengthened, shimmered, formed a tall, tawny-haired man with glittering gold eyes. His blond appearance was unusual for a Carpathian. He carried his body like a soldier, his manner sure and confident. "Who dared to do this?" he demanded. "What of Jacques and Mikhail's woman?"

Gregori growled softly, a slash of pale eyes pinning the male Carpathian. "Bring me fresh soil and prepare the priest's body." Gregori turned back to his work as Byron arrived. Slow, unhurried, the beautiful ancient chant filled the night with hope and promise. No one would believe he was working against time, needing to get Mikhail on his feet this night.

Aidan brought the richest soil he could find, stepping back to admire Gregori as he worked. The poultices were mixed carefully and applied over the external wounds. The wind stirred the dirt and dust from the pile of rocks, carrying warnings to the Carpathians. Two humans were approaching in a truck.

Byron knelt beside Edgar Hummer, reverently running his hands over the priest's face, gathering the small, wasted body up into his arms. "I will take him to sacred ground, Gregori, and then destroy those bodies beside the cabin."

"Who did this?" Aidan repeated.

Gregori simply flooded Aidan's mind with the information rather than bothering with conversation.

"I have known Andre for many centuries," Aidan said. "He is half a century younger than I. We fought together in more than one battle. Our times grow desperate." Aidan glided over the fallen walls, his golden eyes glowing in the darkness. Each leaf on every tree gleamed a vivid silver, bathed in the light of the moon, but Aidan had long ago lost his ability to see in color. His world was dark and gray and would be until he found his life mate, or sought the solace of the dawn. He inhaled, caught the scent of game, the stench of death, the intrusive odor of man. Oil and exhaust issuing from the approaching vehicle fouled the clarity of the air.

He moved through the line of oaks, working to quell the ice-cold predator instinct demanding blood for what one of his kind had done. Their race, so precarious, teetering on the brink of extinction, could not survive another vampire hunt. Every remaining male had pinned his hopes on the survival of Mikhail's woman. If she could adapt to their life, if she could be sealed as a true life mate, if she could produce female children strong enough to live beyond the first year, then all Carpathian males had a chance. It would be a matter of hanging on, searching the world for women such as Raven. For Andre to betray them all was treason as its worst.

Fog began to gather, thicken, an oppressive, nearly impenetrable veil that wound through the trees and closed off the road. The brakes squealed loudly as the driver came to a halt, unable to see in the thick fog. Aidan moved closer, unseen, a dangerous predator hunting prey. "How long before we get there, Uncle Gene?" A boy's voice, eager and excited, drifted on the wind.

"We'll have to wait for the fog to disperse, Donny." The second voice was uneasy. "We get these unusual fog patterns often up here, and it isn't a good idea to be out in them."

"What's my surprise? Can't you tell me? You told Mom I'd have a birthday surprise I would never forget. I heard you talking."

Aidan could see them now. The driver was a man nearing thirty, the boy, no more than fifteen. Aidan watched them, the urge to kill running in his veins, surging through his body. He felt power, in every nerve ending, reminding him he truly was alive.

The man was very nervous, peering into the fog on all sides of the truck, although he couldn't see through the thick veil of white mist. For a moment he thought he saw eyes, hungry and glowing, almost gold. They were animal eyes— the eyes of a wolf—watching them from out of the night. It made his heart pound and his mouth go dry. He pulled the boy closer to him protectively. "Your Uncle James is keeping it for you." He had to clear his throat twice before the words would come out. He knew they were in great danger, knew a predator was waiting to tear out their throats.

"Let's just walk up to the hunting lodge, Uncle Gene. I can't wait to try out my new rifle. Come on, it's not that far," the boy wheedled.

"Not in this fog, Donny. There are wolves in these woods. Other things. It's best to wait until we can see clearly," the man said firmly.

"We have guns," the boy said sulkily. "Isn't that why we brought them?"

"I said no. Guns don't always make you safe, boy."

Aidan crushed down the wild urges. The boy had not yet seen manhood. Whoever these mortals were, he would not kill unless his life or that of one of the others of his kind was threatened. He would not become a vampire, a betrayer of his people. It was becoming too easy to kill. A kind of seduction of power. The wind whipped up around him, swirled in a circle of leaves and twigs. Gregori settled beside him, Mikhail, pale and lifeless, cradled in his arms. "Let us leave this place, Aidan."

"I could not kill them," Aidan said quietly, no apology in his voice.

"If the older one is Eugene Slovensky, he will have much to occupy him this night. His brother lies dead beneath a pile of rocks, an exchange for Mikhail's priest."

"I did not dare kill them," Aidan repeated, making it an admission.

"If it is Slovensky, he deserves to die, but I am grateful that you resisted the urge, knowing the danger to yourself. You have traveled far to hunt the undead for our people. It shows in the darkness of your soul."

"I walk very close to the edge," Aidan said quietly, without apology. "When Mikhail's woman was injured so gravely, Mikhail's fury was felt by every Carpathian in every land. The disturbance was unique, and I felt it was deserving of investigation. I returned to make certain his wisdom continues to benefit our people. It is my belief his woman is the hope for our future."

"It is my belief also. Perhaps a new country would bring you relief. We have need of an experienced hunter in the United States."

With the fog still thick, preventing penetration by the humans, Aidan turned his attention to the carefully constructed prison. With a lift of his hand, the earth shuddered and shook. The building was leveled, leaving only the stones marking the fresh grave.

Into the fog, Gregori rose with his burden, Aidan at his side. They raced across the dark sky to the caves, where the other Carpathian males arrived, one after another to aid in the healing of their prince.

Chapter Fifteen

The night air rushed over her body as Raven was carried through the sky toward some unknown destination. She was dizzy and weak, her mind finding it difficult to concentrate on any one thing. At first she made herself try to focus on whatever might be a landmark, so she could convey it back to Gregori. After a while she couldn't remember why or even what she was doing. On some level, Raven knew it was the drug making her disoriented and sick. It seemed too much trouble to wonder where the vampire was taking her or what he would do to her when they arrived.

The moon was radiant, spilling silver light across the treetops, turning everything into a surreal dream. Things slipped in and out of her mind. Soft whispered words, a constant murmuring she couldn't quite grasp. It seemed important, but Raven was too tired to unravel it all. Had her mind fragmented from chasing the last serial killer? She couldn't remember what had happened to her. The wind felt good blowing over her body, cleansing her. She was cold, yet it didn't seem to matter. Lights danced, colors swirled, the sky sparkled brilliantly above her head. Beneath them a large pool of water shone like crystal. It was all so beautiful, and yet her head ached abominably.

"I'm tired." She found her voice, wanted to hear if she could speak. Perhaps she could wake herself up if she was in the midst of a dream.

The arms tightened fractionally. "I know. You will be home soon."

She didn't recognize the voice. Something in her rose up to rebel at the closeness. Her body didn't like the feel of his against hers. Did she know him? It didn't feel as if she did, yet he held her as if he had a right to her. There was something slipping in and out of her memory that she couldn't quite catch. Every time she thought the pieces of the puzzle began to fit themselves together, pain sliced through her head so violently, she couldn't hold the thought.

They were suddenly walking together, out under the stars, the trees swaying and dipping gently, his arm around her waist. Raven blinked in confusion. Had they always been walking? No one could fly; that was absurd. She was suddenly afraid. Had she lost her mind? She glanced up at the man walking beside her. Physically he was beyond merely handsome, his pale face sensually beautiful. But when he smiled down at her, his eyes were flat and cold, his teeth a flash of menace in his scarlet mouth that struck fear in her heart. Who was he? Why was she with him?

Raven shivered and tried to draw away from the man with a slight, subtle movement. She was weak, and without his support, she might have fallen. "You are cold, my dear. We will be home soon."

His voice sent a ripple of terror through her; distaste was rolling in her stomach. There was a gloating taunt in his voice. For all his seeming solicitousness, Raven felt as if a giant snake was coiled around her, its cold, reptilian body and hypnotic eyes mesmerizing her. Her mind reached out, struggled to connect. *He would come. Mikhail.* She screamed in agony and fell to her knees, pressing her hands to her head, terrified to move, to think.

Cold hands grasped her arms, dragged her to her feet. "What is it, Raven? Come, tell me, so that I may help you."

She despised his voice. It grated on her, sent shivers over her skin. There was power there, and a depraved, secret amusement, as if he knew exactly what was happening to her and enjoyed her suffering, her ignorance. As much as she loathed his touch, she could not stand on her own two feet and had to lean against his strong body.

"You need to feed," he remarked almost casually, but she sensed a hidden excitement in that statement.

Raven pressed a hand to her stomach. "I'm feeling sick."

"That is because you hunger. I have prepared a special surprise for you, my dear. A banquet in your honor. The guests have been waiting impatiently for our return."

Raven stopped walking and stared up at his cold, mocking eyes. "I don't want to go with you."

The eyes flattened, hardened. His smile was a parody, a soulless flash of fangs. She could see his receding gums, the lengthening incisors. He was not beautifully handsome, as she had first imagined, but foul and cruel-looking. "Raven, you have no other place to go." Again he sounded slightly mocking, sickly solicitous.

Raven pulled her arm away from him and sat down abruptly when her legs buckled beneath her. "You are not . . ." The name eluded her with an explosive burst of pain. Blood beaded on her forehead and trickled down her face.

Deliberately, the vampire leaned down and ran his tongue coarsely along her cheek, following the path of her blood. "You are ill, my dear. You have to trust me to know what is best for you."

Raven forced herself to remain calm, to push aside the cobwebs clogging her mind. She had special gifts. She had a brain. Those were two indisputable facts. She was certain she was in grave danger and she had no idea how she had gotten here with him, but she needed to think. She lifted her face to the moon so that it put blue lights in her long, ebony hair. "I'm very confused, I can't even remember your name." She forced herself to look and feel apologetic to appease him if he was capable of reading her mind, and she was afraid he was. "What happened to me? I have a terrible headache."

He offered his hand, his manner suddenly courtly, far more

indulgent now that she was relying on him. "You hurt your head." He drew her up, slipped his arm around her small waist. This time Raven forced herself to accept his touch without flinching.

"I'm sorry; I'm so confused. It makes me feel silly and afraid," she confessed, her large blue eyes enormous, her mind innocent and blank.

"I am Andre, your true life mate. Another stole you away from me. When I rescued you, you fell and hit your head." His voice was singsong, hypnotic.

True life mate. Mikhail. This time when the pain beat at her she accepted it, allowed it to wash over her. It stole her breath and pierced her skull. She was careful not to allow any hint of the agony to show on her face or to spill over in her mind. Calling on every ounce of discipline she possessed, Raven focused her mind. *Mikhail? Where are you? Are you real? I'm afraid.* There was a familiar path and she used it with ease, as if she had always done so.

Little one. The reply was faint, far away, but very real, something to cling to in a world of madness.

Who is with me? What is happening? She made herself lean on the tall man supporting her, kept her mind a jumble of confusion. She found it interesting that her mind allowed her to work on several different levels at once.

Andre is a vampire. He took you from me. I am coming for you.

Something was very wrong. It was all there, if she just reached for it. Raven believed that faraway voice, felt warmth and love enfold her in strong, protective arms. She knew that feeling, that voice. It wasn't quite right. *You're hurt. How?*

Mikhail replayed the recent events in his mind for her. Raven inhaled, feeling as if someone had hit her square in the stomach. *Mikhail.*

Gregori is turning into some kind of tyrant. I would not dare die.

Memory was flooding in and she was terrified. She made herself compartmentalize her thoughts. The vampire touched only the surface, read what she wanted him to read. She was the shivering, confused woman he expected her to be.

Mikhail's wounds looked bad to her. He was in the cave, surrounded by others. Gregori was working on the injuries, and Raven was certain he would put Mikhail to ground and she would be left without a lifeline. Raven lifted her chin. The drug might have confused her momentarily, but she could do whatever she had to do. *I can handle Andre. Do not worry about me.* She used more bravado than she felt.

All at once she had to suppress a surge of relief. Memory, fractured as it had been, came back in full force under Mikhail's soothing mind touch. Mikhail or Gregori or both would come for her, no matter what else was happening. Mikhail would plug up his wounds and crawl if that was what it took to get to her.

"You are very quiet." Andre startled her.

"I'm trying to remember, but it makes my head ache."

They were at the top of a plateau. For a moment she couldn't make out the stone house built into the side of the mountain. It seemed to shimmer in the silver of the moon, one moment a mirage, then a distinct structure, then gone again. Raven blinked her eyes rapidly, taking in every detail, broadcasting to Mikhail. The trick was in not allowing the vampire to know she was thinking of Mikhail. It was Andre who punished her with pain when he knew her thoughts. Confused by the drug, she had been briefly under his power. Now she was simply sick and dizzy. And very, very frightened.

"Is this our home?" she asked innocently, leaning heavily into him.

"We will remain here long enough to dine, my dear." There was that curious gloating she was coming to dislike intensely. "It is not safe to remain longer than that. The other might pursue us. You must feed in order to be strong enough to escape."

Deliberately, trustingly, she curled her fingers around the vampire's arm. "I will try, Andre, but truly I am feeling sick."

Raven took a step toward the threshold, felt Mikhail's instinctive protest. She stumbled unsteadily, fell just outside the door, and lay in a small forlorn heap. With an oath, Andre tried to yank her up, to push her inside, but Raven was limp, unable to move on her own. The vampire lifted her into his arms and carried her inside.

The rock house consisted of a large front room and a hole in the far corner where a ladder led to a lower chamber. The room was cold and dank. Mold grew in the cracks. There was a table and a long church bench. Andre waved his hand to light several candles. Raven's heart stopped, then began to pound in alarm. Chained to the wall nearest the table, eyes dilated with terror, were a man and a woman. The two were dirty and in ragged clothing. Rips in the woman's dress and the man's shirt held the stains of blood. There were bruises on both of them, and the man had several burn marks down his right cheek.

The vampire's smile was cruel and taunting as he surveyed his helpless victims. "Dinner, my dear, just for you." He set Raven carefully on the bench as if she was fragile porcelain. Andre slowly glided gracefully across the stone floor, his red, soulless eyes on the woman. He took his time enjoying her terror, laughing at her husband's impotent raging. As he yanked the woman free of the chain, the man struggled and threatened, cursed Raven. Andre dragged the woman to Raven's side, forced her to her knees and held her still, one hand gripping her hair so that her throat was exposed.

His thumb slid over the pounding pulse. "Feed, my dear. Feel the hot blood pour into your veins, making you strong again. When you take her life you will have such power as you have never known. This is my gift to you. Infinite power."

The woman sobbed and moaned with terror. Her husband pleaded, swore, fought the chains that bound him. Raven sat up slowly and pushed back her heavy fall of hair with a trembling hand. Andre could have seduced his victims, entranced them so that they welcomed death, but he sought thrills at the expense of human terror. The adrenaline-laced blood was addicting, intoxicating. Everyone seemed to be waiting for her reaction. She could feel Mikhail in her, still and motionless, raging that he was not there to protect her from such a terrible decision.

Her large blue-violet eyes lifted to Andre's face, expressive, over-bright, as if she was on the verge of tears. Her hand slid soothingly up the woman's arm. She was extraordinarily gentle, trying to comfort without words. "You doubt me.

Why? What have I done? I honestly can't remember. I would never do such a thing, take a life like this, and neither would you. Why do you test me this way? Have I committed a crime I can't remember? Why would you be so cruel to me?"

Andre's face went dark, the red eyes changing to his normal dark brown. "Do not be so distressed."

"Tell me, Andre. I can't bear not to know. Did the other one force me to do something you can't forgive?" She bowed her head as if ashamed. Her voice dropped even lower. "Take my life, Andre. Take your wrath out on me, not this poor, undeserving woman. I will leave if you do not wish my life bound to yours, although I have nowhere else to go." She met his eyes so that he knew she meant it. "Take my life now, Andre."

"No, Raven."

"Then answer me: why this test? Is it because I'm not wholly like you, because I can't go to ground or shape-shift? You are ashamed of me and wish to punish me."

"Of course not."

Raven put her arm around the woman. "I seem to recall, although I'm not certain, that you said you would hire reliable servants. Is this woman the one you spoke of?" Suddenly her face clouded. "Is she your mistress?" She sounded near hysterics, but her hand was still very gentle on the woman's arm.

"No! No!" the woman protested, but there was confusion and dawning hope in her eyes. "I am not his mistress. That is my husband. We have done nothing wrong."

Andre was clearly at a loss. He had taken Raven in a desperate attempt to save himself. If he forced her to kill, then she would become as dark and as lost as he. Something inside him shifted and turned as he stared down into the innocence in her eyes. "The woman speaks the truth, Raven. She is nothing to me. A servant, if you wish her." His voice was lost and lonely, almost uncertain.

Raven reached out for his hand. His mind was a masterpiece of evil, rotted and twisted. Yet Raven felt sorrow for him. He had once been good, no different from Mikhail or Jacques, but in the dark isolation of his existence he had turned down a wrong path. Andre desperately wanted to feel, to be able to face the morning sun, witness a sunset again. He wanted to look in the mirror and not see his receding gum line and the ravages left by his depraved existence. It was an impossibility; no true vampire could ever face himself in the mirror without experiencing tremendous pain. Raven was his only hope and he clung to it. He wanted a miracle. Because she had been human, he had no idea of what she was capable or incapable of doing.

"Forgive me, Andre, if I have done something to cause you to doubt me," she said gently, compassion welling up so that she wanted to cry. She could not save him, even if she did not belong with Mikhail. No one could. He was far too depraved and bloated with his false sense of power, far too addicted to the adrenaline in a terror-stricken kill. She hated herself for deceiving him, but her life and the lives of the human couple clearly hung in the balance.

His hand stroked her silky hair. "I am not angry with you, my dear, but you are weak and need nourishment."

The woman stiffened, her face a mask of fear. She stayed very still, waiting for Raven's reply. Raven looked confused. "But I can't feed." Deliberately she allowed Mikhail's name to shimmer in her mind, and then she was clutching her head in agony. "I don't know why; I can't think. I think the other did something to make me this way."

Andre dragged the woman up by her hair. "I will return in a few minutes. You see to it Raven comes to no harm." His eyes were flat and cold. "Do not try to leave this place. I will know."

"Andre, stay," Raven whispered, fighting for him in spite of herself.

He swung away from her and sped out, away from the light, back toward the world of death and madness he was familiar with.

The woman clutched at Raven. "Please, let us go. He is evil; he will kill us, make us his slaves until our fear no longer amuses him."

Raven pushed herself upright, desperately fighting dizziness. "He will know. He can see in the dark, smell you, hear your very heart beat." The room was so cold and musty smelling, so depressing. The air itself was stale and told of death. With Raven's sensitivity she could almost hear the screams of the countless victims who had been brought to this place, chained to the stained walls. She was every bit as frightened as the human woman was. "Who are you?"

"Monique Chancellor. That is my husband, Alexander. Why did you help me?"

"Guard your thoughts, Monique. He can read them."

"He is *nosferatu* unclean. The vampire." It was more of a statement than a question. "We must leave this place of death."

Raven rose unsteadily to her feet, hanging on to the back of the chair, the table, to make her way to the door. She stared up at the stars, gazed slowly over the landscape in each direction, taking note of every rock wall, the cliffs rising behind the house. She studied the dwelling itself, the windows, the doors, the structures of the walls, paid particular attention to the wide open spaces leading to the house.

"Please, please." The woman clawed at her. "Help us."

Raven blinked to bring her into focus. "I'm trying to help you. Stay calm; keep out of his way. Draw as little attention to yourselves as possible." She closed the door, having accomplished what she had hoped to do. Mikhail and Gregori would know as much detailed information as she could transmit.

"Who are you?" Alexander demanded suspiciously. He had pulled at his chains so much, she could see his wrists were raw.

Raven rubbed her pounding temple, a growing nausea gripping her stomach. "It isn't a good idea to have open wounds around him." She could smell blood and her body, desperately weak, needed nourishment. Raven ignored the woman sobbing quietly in a corner and went to the man to see if she could find a way to ease his discomfort. As she bent to examine his wrist, his other hand whipped up to clutch a handful of her hair, yanking hard enough to bring tears to her eyes. He dragged her back against his chest so that both hands could grip her throat, fingers digging into soft flesh.

"Alexander, stop, what are you doing?" Monique cried.

"Monique, get the key to these cuffs," Alexander ordered,

his powerful fingers crushing Raven's windpipe so that the room began to spin.

Raven could feel his fear, his frantic attempt to save his wife and himself. He was afraid she was a vampire, cruelly playing with them for some perverse enjoyment. Raven couldn't blame him, but his hands were squeezing the life out of her.

Raven! The cry was close, a ripple of fury moving through her mind.

Alexander's hands were torn from her throat; there was a loud popping noise signaling broken bones. He was slammed into the wall behind them, held so that his feet dangled help-lessly four feet from the floor. Monique screamed as the air rushed from her husband's lungs. He began to strangle, his eyes bulging horribly.

Release him, Mikhail! Oh, God, please. I can't bear to be responsible for another death. I just can't. Raven sank to the floor, drew up her knees, and huddled there, rocking. "Please," she whispered aloud. "Release him."

Mikhail fought his killing rage, managed to suppress it enough to release the human from his mind assault. He hur-tled through the air, tracking Raven easily. He was barely aware of Gregori keeping pace with him to his left, of Aidan and Byron slightly behind him, of Eric and Tienn and a few others struggling to keep up some distance behind. None of them mattered. He had hunted vampires over many centuries and he had always felt a twinge of reluctance, of pity perhaps. There was none now.

Mikhail kept his fury tamped down so that it seethed and boiled like magma in a volcano, so that it sought to escape in any direction it could, needing a violent, explosive release. If he allowed it to seep out, the very earth, the winds, the crea-tures in the mountains would react. It would be a clear warn-ing to the vampire. He felt no pain and he was well fed; Gregori had seen to that personally. The combination of their ancient blood was powerful beyond measure. Even so, a spot of blood soaked through the white feathers on the owl. Instinc-tively, Mikhail shifted and circled to stay downwind so that any passing breeze could not carry that scent to the vampire.

Into the night there came a cry of pure terror, evil laughter, a gloating triumph. Every Carpathian, so tuned to the land, felt the vibration of violence, the disturbance of power, the cycle of life and death. Raven, as psychically sensitive as she was, instantly found her mind drawn to the scene of violence.

Break off, Raven. Mikhail commanded it.

She pressed her hands to her temples. Andre was laughing, flinging himself from the branch of a tree atop a woman attempting to crawl away from him. A smaller body lay crumpled at the foot of the tree, pale and lifeless where he had dropped it. The woman moaned, pleaded for her life. The vampire laughed horribly again, then kicked her away from him, only to force her to crawl back to him, begging to serve him.

"Andre! No, you cannot!" Raven yelled it aloud, dragging herself up to stumble to the door. She ran into the night, spun in a circle to catch the direction. Weakness overcame her and she fell heavily to lie immobile in the grass.

Monique followed her, dropping to her knees beside her. "What is it? I know you are not what my husband thinks. I know you are trying to save us."

Tears were running down Raven's face. "He killed a child; he is taunting the mother. He will kill her also. I can't save her." Raven took what comfort she could as the woman cradled Raven's head in her lap.

Monique touched the dark bruises at Raven's throat. "I am sorry for what Alexander did to you. He is mad with anger and fear for us. You took a terrible risk. That monster might have killed you."

Raven closed her eyes tiredly. "He still might. We can't get away from him."

The night around them carried disturbing vibrations. Somewhere deep inside the forest, an animal missed its prey and screamed its rage. An owl hissed; a wolf snarled.

Raven clutched Monique's hand, was relieved when she could move her legs. "Come on. We have to get inside. Stay quiet and out of sight if you can. When he returns, he will be high as a kite and unpredictable."

Monique helped Raven to her feet, slipping her arm around

the smaller woman's waist. "What did you do to Alexander when he hurt you?"

Raven walked reluctantly back to the stone house. "I did nothing to him." She touched the bruises on her throat. Alexander had complicated things. Andre could not fail to notice the marks on her.

"You feel things we know nothing of," Monique guessed uneasily.

"It is not a comfortable gift. He killed tonight. A woman, a child. I sent him out and traded our lives for theirs."

"No!" Monique denied that. "You have nothing to do with what he chooses to do, any more than my husband is responsible for what that monster did to me. Alexander believes he should have found a way to protect me. He will not forgive himself. Don't be like him, Raven."

Raven stood on the stone steps and faced the moon-bathed land. The wind stirred and the glowing silver light darkened ominously. Monique gasped, clutched at Raven, tried to draw her into the comparative safety of the house. A red stain grew, spread, completely consumed the moon. A low moan rode on the wind, growing louder until it became a howl. A wolf lifted its muzzle to the bloodstained moon and howled in warning. A second joined in. The entire mountain rumbled ominously.

Monique whirled around and ran to her husband. "Pray with me, pray with me."

Raven shut the door and leaned against it. "Don't panic on me, Monique. We have a chance if we can stall him."

Alexander glared at her, his arm protectively around his wife, his hand already swollen and sore-looking. "Don't listen to her, Monique. She almost strangled me; she threw me against the wall with unbelievable strength. She is unclean."

Raven rolled her eyes in exasperation. "I'm beginning to wish I did have all that power you think I have. I'd find a way to keep you from talking."

"He is afraid for us." Monique spoke in a conciliatory tone. "Can't we take off his chains?"

"He would try to attack Andre the moment he returned." Raven made a face at Alexander, completely exasperated with him. "That would get him killed fast." She shivered, turning stricken eyes on Monique. "He comes. Stay very quiet, no matter what happens. Don't draw attention to yourself."

The wind outside howled, an eerie, lonely sound that faded away, leaving in its wake an unnatural silence. Raven heard her own heart beat in the void. She stepped backward just as the door splintered and cracked. The candle flames leapt, threw shadows on the wall, grotesque, macabre; then the lights were snuffed out.

"Come, Raven. We must leave now." Andre snapped his fingers, holding out his hand. The vampire's face was flushed with fresh blood. The glow of evil was in his eyes; his mouth was twisted with cruelty.

Raven regarded Andre with large, accusing eyes. "Why do you come to me like this? Tell me what is going on."

He moved with blurring speed, and at the last moment, Raven remembered she, too, was capable of such feats. She felt his hot, foul breath, smelled death on him. His razor-sharp nails raked her arm as she ducked away. She pressed her small body into the corner. "Don't try to force my compliance when a simple explanation will do."

"You will regret this defiance," he snarled, and hurled the church bench out of his path so hard that it crashed and splintered against the wall only inches from the shivering human couple.

A small moan of terror escaped Monique, and instantly the vampire whirled around, his eyes red and glazed with power. "You will crawl to me like the dog you are." His voice was low, hypnotic, his eyes mesmerizing.

Alexander lunged to the end of his chains, trying to stop Monique, who went to the floor in obedience, her manner sensual and fawning. Raven walked calmly across the room to kneel down in Monique's path. "Hear me, Monique. Don't do this thing." Her blue-violet eyes stared directly into the older woman's. Raven's voice was beautiful, purity itself, low and entrancing. It made the vampire's voice appear foul and disgusting. A look of confusion, bewilderment, and shame crossed Monique's blank face.

The vampire exploded into action, leaping the distance to Raven's side, seizing her by the hair, yanking her backwards, nearly off her feet.

The world erupted around them. The night itself seemed to rage, the wind screaming and howling, gusting across the wide open space to beat at the windows. A dark funnel cloud boiled down from the seething sky and tore the roof from the structure; the whirling mass lifted furniture and scattered treasures collected over the years.

Monique wailed loudly and dragged herself to Alexander, where they clung together. Voices hissed and whispered, low murmurs of fury, of accusation, of condemnation. The mountain rumbled ominously, and the furthermost wall burst outward, spewing rocks and mortar as if dynamited.

Mikhail stood in the center of the ferocious storm, his black eyes as cold as death. He stood tall and elegant despite the scarlet stain spreading across his silk shirt. His body was relaxed, unmoving in the midst of chaos. He lifted a hand, and the roaring of the wind died down. Mikhail regarded Andre for a long moment. "Release her." His voice was very soft, but it struck utter terror in the hearts of all who heard him.

Andre's fingers tightened convulsively in Raven's silky hair.

Mikhail's answering smile was cruel. "Do you wish me to force your compliance, so you come crawling to your death as you forced your victims?"

Andre's fingers spasmed and his arm jerked like a puppet's. He stared in horror at Mikhail, never conceiving of such power. Such mind control did not work easily, on Carpathians.

Come to me, Raven. Mikhail did not take his eyes from the vampire, holding him helpless with his mind alone. So great was his fury, he hardly required Gregori's mind merge to assist him.

One by one the Carpathian males materialized, their faces masks of condemnation. Raven could feel the human couple's terror rising, approaching near madness. She staggered to them, wrapping her arms protectively around Monique. "He will save us," she whispered to them.

"He is like the other," Alexander rasped hoarsely.

"No, he is good. He will save us." Raven stated the truth simply, with great conviction.

Mikhail released the vampire abruptly. Andre looked around him, his mouth twisted sardonically. "Does it take an army for you to go on the hunt?"

"You have been sentenced for your crimes, Andre. Should I fail, the sentence will be carried out by another." Mikhail indicated two Carpathians with his finger and nodded toward Raven. His tall form emanated power and confidence. "You are but a child, Andre." His voice was a pure tone, pitched low and velvet soft. "You cannot hope to match one who has battled so many times, but I offer you the chance you have worked so hard to attain." The black eyes glittered with icy fury.

"Vengeance, Mikhail?" Andre asked sarcastically. "How very common of you." He launched himself, razor-sharp claws extended, fangs dripping.

Mikhail simply disappeared, and the vampire found himself tumbling out of the house on the ground, the savage night closing in on him, the Carpathian males in a huge, loose circle corralling him in. Andre turned in the direction in which the others were looking. Mikhail was standing a few feet from him, a black fury burning in his unblinking gaze.

Aidan advanced on Raven, his glittering eyes golden and piercing as his gaze swept over the mortals huddled behind her. "Come with us," he ordered abruptly. "Mikhail wishes us to see that you are safe."

Raven didn't recognize him, but she did recognize the stamp of confidence he carried, the complete self-possession. His voice was soft and hypnotic, almost mesmerizing. "Did you see where Andre put the key so we can free Alexander?" Raven asked Monique, attempting to move around the other Carpathian male blocking her path.

Without warning, Raven's eyes widened, and she clutched her side, a strangled cry catching in her throat. She went down hard, curling in agony, a crimson smear across her forehead, trickling into her eyes. Monique threw herself to the floor beside the younger woman. Raven was completely unaware of her. She was no longer within the confines of the house, had no knowledge of Aidan or Byron or even Monique and Alexander. She was outside with the blood-red moon spilling down on her, facing a demon of immense power and strength. A demon whose eyes had glowing red flames leaping in them, whose smile was cruelty itself. He was totally without mercy. He was tall, graceful, supremely confident, and she knew he was going to kill her. There was an animal beauty in the fluid way he moved. There was death and damnation in those soulless eyes. He was absolutely invincible. He had struck her body a mortal wound and glided away with blinding speed. There was no pity and no feeling in him. He was without mercy, relentless, ruthless, and without remorse.

See him as he is, a killer, a stalker of mortals and Carpathians alike. Andre hissed in her mind. *Know him for the beast that he is. You see an educated man who controls you with his mind. This is the real Mikhail Dubrinsky. He has hunted hundreds of us, perhaps thousands of his own people, and slain them. He will murder us and feel nothing but the joy of ultimate power.*

Andre's mind was merged fully with hers so that she was looking through his eyes, feeling his hatred and fear, feeling the pain from the blow Mikhail had administered when Andre had attacked him. Raven struggled to break away from the vampire's hold on her mind, but Andre knew he was going to die and hung on to her with total determination. She would be his last revenge. With every blow Andre received, with every burning wound Mikhail inflicted on him, Raven would feel the same pain. The vampire could at least glory in that pain.

Raven could see his plan clearly, knew Mikhail felt the initial rush of agony overwhelming her. She could barely breathe, but, wanting to spare him, she tried to close herself off from him. But Mikhail was far too strong to allow her such a withdrawal from him. She could feel his utter cold fury, his lack of mercy, his desire for battle, the urge to kill the renegade. She could feel his sudden indecision as he realized what the vampire was doing.

Raven. Hear me. Gregori. Calm in the eye of the storm.

His voice beautiful, hypnotic, soothing. *Give yourself to me. You will sleep now.*

Gregori gave Raven little choice in the matter, but even so, she gave herself up willingly, gratefully, to the hypnotic voice and went under immediately, removing Andre's last threat to Mikhail.

A long, slow hiss of air escaped Mikhail's lungs. He moved, a blur too fast to see. Andre's body flew backwards under the blow. The crack was loud in the unnatural silence. Andre struggled to his feet, eyes glazed, wildly seeking his antagonist.

"I have won." He spit a mouthful of blood and pressed a trembling hand to his chest. "She saw you as you are. What you do here cannot change that." He did not take his gaze from Mikhail's body, didn't blink, didn't dare. It seemed an impossibility for even a Carpathian to be that fast. There was something terrible in those black, merciless eyes. Without Raven awake and aware, there was not a shred of pity or compassion.

Andre took a cautious step backwards, focused his mind, and aimed. Fiery light crackled and snapped, then hit the ground where Mikhail had been. The noise was tremendous; the blow shook the earth. The whip of electricity sizzled and retreated, leaving a patch of blackened, scarred earth behind. Andre screamed as something snapped his head back and a huge gash opened around his throat, spewing bright crimson blood in a fountain.

The fourth blow opened Andre's chest, smashing through protective bones and muscle to the heart. Those black, merciless eyes stared into Andre's without pity as Mikhail ripped the heart from his chest. Mikhail contemptuously dropped the still pulsing organ to the ground beside the lifeless body, ensuring that the vampire could not rise again. He stood over his fallen enemy, fighting to control the beast in himself, the wild surge of triumph, the addicting rush of power that shook his body. He felt none of his earlier wounds, only a sheer joy in the night, in his victory.

The wildness in him grew dangerously, spread like molten fire. The wind whipped up and carried a scent. *Raven.*

Mikhail's blood surged hotly; his fangs ached and hunger grew. He scented the humans, the one that had touched his life mate. Bloodlust shook him, and the Carpathians stepped farther back, as the power seemed to radiate from Mikhail's body, as the need to kill nearly overwhelmed him. The wind swirled around him in a constant eddy, and Raven's scent remained elusive and faint. *Raven*. His body clenched, burned. *Raven*. The wind whispered her name and the turbulent storm raging in him began to ease.

Mikhail's mind reached for the light, the path back from the world of violence. "Destroy this thing," he snapped tersely, to no one in particular. He gathered energy from the sky and bathed his hands in it, removing the tainted blood from his body. He moved with blinding speed back inside the ruins of the vampire's lair, materialized out of thin air, and loomed over Monique, who was holding Raven's lifeless body in her arms, rocking her.

Chapter Sixteen

Raven became aware of her surroundings slowly. She was on a bed, her body without clothing. Mikhail was behind her, his hands tangled in her thick, damp hair. She recognized the feel of his sure fingers working to braid her hair, his movements calm and deliberate, very matter-of-fact, putting her at ease despite her shadowy memory. She appeared to be in an old castle that was small and inevitably drafty. The bedchamber was warm, and Mikhail had flooded it with the essence of soothing herbs and the romance of flickering candlelight. He had cleaned them both so that their bodies only smelled of each other and the scent of the herbal soap he used. He took his time braiding the length of hair while she tried to orient herself to her new surroundings. Mikhail touched her mind, found it confused, desperately holding on to sanity. She was afraid of him and even more afraid to trust her own judgment.

Raven studied each corner of the room, each wall, every detail, while her heart pounded frantically, the sound loud in her ears. The room was beautiful. A fire glowed in the fireplace; long, tapered candles emitted a light fragrance that mingled with the soothing scent of herbs. A well-worn Bible lay on the small end table beside the bed. She didn't really recognize anything, yet it was all strangely familiar.

The quilt on the bed was thick and warm, the material soft against her bare skin. She noticed for the first time that she was naked. At once she felt vulnerable and shy; yet again, she felt as if she belonged here with him. Mikhail's hands slipped from her hair to the nape of her neck, his fingers massaging aching muscles. His touch was familiar, stirring alarming sensations in her body.

"What did you do to Monique and her husband?" Her fingers twisted in the quilt. She tried to ignore the heat of his body as he moved close behind her so that their skin touched, so that the hair on his chest rasped against her back and the hard length of him pressed tight against her bottom. He felt right. He felt a part of her.

Mikhail placed a kiss on a bruise near her throat, then moved to stroke her leaping pulse with his velvet tongue. Her body clenched in anticipation. Her mind seemed confused. "They are safe in their home, loving one another as they should. They remember nothing of Andre and the atrocities he committed against them. They know us as good, close friends." He kissed another bruise, a feather-light touch that seemed to send a flame licking through her bloodstream. His hands moved to her small waist, slid up her narrow rib cage to cup her full breasts. His mind touched hers, and Raven mentally shied away from him.

"Why do you fear me, Raven? You have seen me at my worst, as a killer, a dispenser of justice for our people." His thumbs stroked her nipples, a slow, erotic brush that sent liquid heat curling through her. "Do you believe I am evil? Touch my mind, little one. It is impossible for me to hide anything from you. I never concealed my true nature from you. You looked upon me once with the eyes of compassion and love. Of acceptance. Has that all been forgotten?"

Raven closed her eyes, long lashes sweeping down on high cheekbones. "I don't know what to believe anymore."

"Kiss me, Raven. Merge your mind with mine. Share your body so that we are completely one being. You trusted me before; do so now. Look at me with the eyes of love, in forgiveness for the things I have been forced to do, for the beast in my nature. Do not look at me through the eyes of one who would wish to destroy our people and us. Give yourself to me." His voice was seductive, a black magic spell, his hands caressing every beloved inch of her satin skin. He had committed every hollow, every curve to memory. His body burned with need and his hunger was rising. Her hunger, his. Very gently, so as not to alarm her, Mikhail pressed her slender body to the quilt, his muscular frame covering her smaller one like a blanket. She was so petite, so fragile beneath his exploring hands.

"Why have you become my life, Mikhail? I've always been alone and strong and sure of myself. You seem to have taken over my life."

His palms slid up the curve of her body to frame her face. "You are my only life, Raven. I will admit I took you from all you knew, but you were never meant to live in isolation. I know what that does, how desolate life can be. They were using you up; they would have destroyed you. Can you not feel that you are my other half, that I am yours?" His mouth drifted over her eyes, her cheekbones, each corner of her mouth. "Kiss me, Raven. Remember me."

She lifted long lashes and searched his black, hungry gaze with blue eyes that had darkened to deep purple. There was a burning intensity in the heat of his gaze, of his body. "If I kiss you, Mikhail, I won't be able to stop."

His mouth found her throat, the valley between her breasts, lingered for a moment over her heart, his teeth grazing sensitive skin before he returned to her mouth. "I am a Carpathian male, long in the world of darkness. It is true that I feel very little, that my nature revels in the hunt, in the kill. To overcome the wild beast we have to find our one mate, our other half, the light to our darkness. You are my light, Raven, my very life. That does not take away my obligations to my people. I must hunt those who prey on mortals, those who prey on our people. I cannot feel while I do so or madness would be my fate. Kiss me; merge your mind with mine. Love me for who I am."

Raven's body ached and burned. Needed. Hungered. His

heart beat so strongly; his skin was hot, his muscles hard against her softness. Every touch of his lips sent a jolt of electricity sizzling through her.

"I cannot lie to you," he whispered. "You know my thoughts; you know the beast that dwells inside. I try to be gentle with you, to listen to you. Always that wildness breaks free, but you tame me. Raven, please, I need you. And you need me. Your body is weak; I can feel your hunger. Your mind is fragmented; allow me to heal you. Your body cries out for mine as mine does for yours. Kiss me, Raven. Do not give up on us."

Her blue eyes continued to search his face, rested on his sensual mouth. A small sigh escaped. His lips hovered over hers, waited for her answer.

It was in her eyes first, that moment of complete recognition. Tenderness rushed over her and she caught his head in her hands. "I think I'm afraid I made you up, Mikhail. That something so much a part of me, so perfect, can't be real. I don't want you to be what I dreamed of and the nightmare to be real." She brought his face the inch separating them and fastened her mouth to his. Thunder pounded in her ears, in his. White-hot heat streaked and danced, consumed her, consumed him. His mind touched hers gently, tentatively, found no resistance, and he merged them together so that his burning need became hers, so that the wild, unbridled passion in him fed hers. So that she knew he was real and would never leave her alone, could never leave her alone.

He fed on her sweetness, exploring every inch of her soft mouth, building flames until they leaped and roared. He caught her slender hips, so small they fit his hands, dragged her beneath him so that his knee could part her thighs, so that her mouth, so hot and urgent, was roaming over the hard muscles of his chest. Her tongue stroked over his pulse and his body clenched, burned, swelled until he thought he might burst from his skin.

Mikhail caught her thick braid at the nape of her neck, holding her to him, his other hand probing in the silky triangle of curls. She was hot and slick with needing him. He murmured her name softly, pushed urgently against her creamy heat. Her tongue stroked again, a long, lingering caress. Small teeth grazed and his heart jumped; his body nearly exploded. There was piercing sweet pain as she found the spot over his leaping pulse, pleasure hot and wild as he drove into her tight velvet sheath of fire. He cried out with the ecstasy of it, pressed her head to him as he surged forward, driving deeper and deeper, as his blood, rich, hot, powerful, fed her starving body.

He hung on to control by a thread, both hands lifting her hips so he could create a fiery friction that sent her rocketing over the edge, her muscles clamping around him until he gently pushed at her mouth, until she released him and he sank his teeth into the swell of her soft breast. She gasped and cradled his head to her as he fed voraciously, his body hard and demanding as it took possession of hers. The aftermath of his fear of losing her, of his violence this night was poured into her body. The heat built; the flames leapt until their bodies were slick with sweat, until she was clinging to him, her body pliant silk, white-hot heat, until they were one single entity, body, mind, heart, and blood. His cry was hoarse and strangled, mingled with her soft throaty threads of sound as he took them both careening over a cliff, scattering them to the very heavens, to the rolling seas.

I cannot lose you, little one. You are my best half. I love you more than I can ever express. Mikhail rubbed his face over hers and kissed her damp hair.

She touched her tongue to a bead of sweat, smiling up at him tiredly. "I think I would always recognize you, Mikhail, no matter how damaged my mind."

He rolled over, taking her with him so that his weight would not crush her smaller body. "That is how it should be, Raven. You suffered much these past days, and it will stay fresh in my mind for all eternity. Tomorrow night we must leave this region. The vampire is dead, but he has left behind a trail that could destroy our people. We must move to a more isolated area, where perhaps our people can survive the coming persecution." He brought up her arm to examine the long, deep scratches left by Andre.

"You're so certain it is coming?"

Christine Feehan

A faint, bitter smile touched his mouth as he waved to snuff out the candles. "I have too often in my lifetime seen the signs. They will come, the assassins, and humans and Carpathians alike will suffer. We will retreat for a quarter of a century, perhaps a half century, give ourselves time to regroup." His tongue found the angry marks, and bathed them gently with his healing touch. It was comforting and felt right to her.

Her lashes drifted down, their combined scents lingering in the bedchamber, a soothing fragrance. "I love you, Mikhail, all of you, even the beast in you. I don't know why I became so confused. You aren't evil; I can see so clearly inside of you."

Sleep, little one, in my arms where you belong. Mikhail drew up the quilt, wrapped protective arms around her, and sent them both to sleep.

It was a small group that gathered in the darkness of the tiny churchyard on consecrated ground. Jacques was wan and pale, his wound a raw scar still in the stages of healing. He slipped his arm around Raven's slender shoulders, swaying a little unsteadily. She glanced up at him with a quick reassuring smile. Behind Jacques, Byron stood close to make certain his friend didn't fall. Off to one side Aidan stood alone, tall and straight, his head bowed slightly.

The churchyard was on the castle grounds, old, with exquisite ancient architecture, the chapel small but beautiful. Stained-glass windows and a high rising steeple threw a darker shadow across the small graveyard. Scattered tombstones, angels, and crosses were silent witnesses as Mikhail waved a hand to part the welcoming soil.

Out of respect, Gregori had fashioned a wooden box, intricately carved with ancient figures of reverence. He lowered the box slowly into the waiting arms of the earth and stepped back.

Mikhail crossed himself, recited the burial ritual, and sprinkled holy water on Edgar Hummer's coffin. "He was my friend, my guide when I was troubled, and he believed in the need for the continuation of our race. I never met a man, human or Carpathian, with more compassion or light in him. God shone in his heart and through his eyes."

Mikhail waved his hand and the earth filled in until it was as if it had never been disturbed. He bowed his head, fought unexpected grief, felt the blood-red tears that escaped unchecked. It was Gregori who secured the headstone and Gregori, a nonbeliever in Mikhail's faith, who led the final prayer. Their voices, so beautiful and mesmerizing, rose in a Latin chant in the priest's honor.

Mikhail inhaled the night air, sent regret to his wolves. The answer was a chorus of mournful howls echoing through the dark forest.

Gregori's body bent first, feathers shimmering iridescent in the moonlight. A six-foot wingspan spread and he glided to the high branch of a nearby tree, razor-sharp talons digging into a branch. The owl's body went motionless, blended into the night, simply waited. Aidan was next, a peculiar golden color, powerful and lethal, just as silent. Byron's form was shorter, more compact, his feathers a mantle of white. Mikhail's solid form wavered in the shadows and he launched himself into the night sky, the other three following.

As if in perfect understanding they soared higher, shimmering feathers beating strongly as they raced silently toward the clouds high above the forest floor. The wind rushed against their bodies, under their wings, riffling feathers, brushing away every vestige of sadness and violence left behind by the vampire.

In the air they wheeled and banked sharply, four great birds in perfect synchronization. Joy erased dread and the heavy weight of responsibility in Mikhail's heart, lifted guilt and replaced it with rapture. The powerful wings beat strongly as they raced across the sky together, and Mikhail shared his joy with Raven because he couldn't contain it, not even in the owl's powerful body. It spilled out, an invitation, a need to share one more pleasure of Carpathian life.

Think, my love; visualize what I put in your head. Trust me as you have never trusted me before. Allow me to give you this gift.

There was no hesitation on her part. With complete faith in

him, Raven gave herself into his keeping, reached eagerly for the vision. The slight discomfort, the strange disorientation as her physical body dissolved, did not faze her. Feathers shimmered, sprouted.

Beside her, Jacques stepped back, allowing the smaller female owl to hop onto a tall stone angel before his own large frame compressed, reshaped. Together they launched themselves into the night, soared high to join the other four powerful birds circling above them.

One of the males broke formation, circled the female, and dipped close to cover her body with one wide wingspan. Playfully she dropped low to slide away. The other males walled her in, curbing her antics as she learned the joys of free flying. The male owls stayed in close formation, the female in the center, circling above the forest, climbing high into the mist. For a space of time they dipped and swirled, clearly playing, soaring high, plunging toward earth, pulling up to fly through trees and over the heavy blanket of fog.

After some time they settled into a leisurely flight, once more with the males protectively surrounding the female. Mikhail felt the night remove every vestige of tension and dissipate it to the four corners of the earth. He would take Raven far away from the village, give her plenty of time to learn Carpathian ways. She represented the future of their race, his future. She was his life, his joy, his reason for existing; she was his hold on all that was good in the world. He intended to see that her life was filled with nothing but happiness.

Mikhail dropped lower to cover her feathered body with his, touching her mind, feeling her joy. Raven responded by filling his mind with love and warmth and a child's wondrous laughter at the new sights and sounds and smells she was experiencing. She raced him across the sky, her laughter echoing in all their minds. She was their hope for the future.

DARK DESCENT
by Christine Feehan

*To Brooke Borneman and Diane Stacy
in appreciation for all you do.*

Chapter One

Veins of lightning lit the clouds, dancing whips of white-hot energy illuminating the midnight sky. The earth rumbled and rolled, unsettled and flinching as the creature clawed its way through the soil to burst into the air, instantly fouling every living thing it touched. Leaves shriveled and blackened. The air vibrated with alarm. The vampire settled to earth, turning its head this way and that, listening, waiting, its cunning mind racing, its rotten heart beating with a mixture of triumph and fear. He was the bait, and he knew the hunter was not far behind, close on his trail, drawn straight into the heart of the trap.

Traian Trigovise burrowed through the soil, following the stench of the undead. It was too easy, the trail too well marked. No vampire would be so obvious unless he was a rank fledgling, and Traian was certain he was dealing with strength and cunning. He was an ancient Carpathian hunter, a species nearly immortal, blessed and cursed with longevity, with timeless gifts and the need for a lifemate to make him complete. He was first and foremost a predator, capable of becoming the most loathsome and evil of all creatures, the undead. It was his sheer strength of will and duty to his race that kept him from falling prey to the insidious whispers and call of power.

When the tunnel veered upward toward the sky, Traian continued onward, pushing deeper into the dirt, feeling his way, listening to the heartbeat and energy of the earth around him. All was silent, even the insects, creatures often summoned by the evil ones. He scanned the surface, taking in a large area, and discovered three blank spots, evidence that more than one vampire was close.

He found a web of roots, thick and gnarled, humming with life, reaching deep into the earth. He whispered softly, respectfully, touching the longest, deepest artery, feeling its life force. He chanted softly in the ancient language, asking for entrance, felt the response moving through the thick old tree. Leaves shivered as the tree reached toward the moon, embracing the night even as it shrank from the presence of the foul beings. Imparting secrets and conspiring to help, the tree spread its roots to allow Traian into the intricate system protecting and nourishing the wide trunk.

The hunter was careful not to disturb the soil or the root system as he maneuvered his way carefully through the labyrinth, pushing through the surface just far enough to scan his surroundings from inside the cage of safety of the overlapping roots above ground. He shape-shifted as he emerged, a shadow hidden amongst the thick branches and leaves.

For one moment he could see only his prey, the tall, thin figure of Gallent. He recognized the vampire as one of the ancients sent out by their prince so many centuries earlier, just as he had been. The undead continually twisted, sniffing the air suspiciously, his gaze darting along the ground. He clicked his long fingernails together in a peculiar repeated rhythm.

The wind rushed through the grove of trees, and the leaves rustled and whispered. Traian allowed his gaze to shift, quartering the area, searching with his mind more than his acute vision. The breeze brought the echo of that strange rhythm to him, coming from his left. Then from his right. Two more of the undead waited to fall upon him and rip him to pieces. He shifted again, drifting with the breeze through the cage of roots, rising as molecules into the night, allowing the friendly wind to take him higher into the cover of leaves.

Dark clouds swirled into a boiling cauldron. Lightning veined the murky, spinning mass. He hovered there with a small, humorless smile in his mind. Discretion really was the better part of valor in some circumstances. He would pick his own battleground. Then he heard the clicking of the fingernails again. The sound was growing louder. With each click, droplets of water fell from the cloud. Tiny droplets that never quite reached the ground. The beads collected in midair, formed a large, shimmering pool. He could see his reflection clearly in the pool. Not the scattered molecules, or an illusion, but the real man amongst the leaves. It was his only warning, and it came just a heartbeat before the attack.

He caught movement from the corner of his eye and instantly reacted, somersaulting through the sky, shifting into his true form, grateful for the leaves that hampered the nearly invisible silvery net meant to entangle him. Spears spiraled through the air, along with tiny darts tipped with poison from the tree frog, and showers of red-hot embers that burrowed into the skin and burned for weeks. Insects clouded the skies, and all the while the clicking of the fingernails went on relentlessly.

Traian launched himself at the shadowy figure orchestrating the fight, ignoring the two lesser vampires. Gallent was directing the action, a leader in evil, as he had been a leader among Carpathians. Traian burst through the sky, his fist already snapping out, driving toward the vampire's chest.

Gallent shimmered transparently. The fist passed through his body harmlessly even as the undead struck back with razor-sharp talons. The hand came from Traian's left, the swift, sure movement of a full-fledged master. The knifelike nails drove deep through flesh and muscle, all the way to the bone. One of the lesser vampires hurled himself onto Traian's back, sinking his teeth into his target's exposed neck.

Traian simply evaporated, leaving the smear of blood on the shivering leaves and the scent of the ancient gift driving the vampires into a frenzy of rage and hunger. He traveled quickly through the night. The Carpathian Mountains were riddled with networks of caves, where rich soil deep beneath the earth waited to welcome him. He was close to home. He had been steadily traveling back to his homeland to see his prince but had become sidetracked when he came across the vampires.

His shoulder throbbed and burned. His neck was a fierce torment. There were a hundred places on his body that ached from the embers and darts. He found an opening into the cool interior of the mountain, went deeper still, through a labyrinth of tunnels into the earth. He floated down into the bed of rich soil and just lay there, feeling a sense of peace and solace in the wealth of welcoming minerals.

Austria

The theater doors opened to allow the smartly dressed crowd out. They emerged laughing and talking, a crush of happy people pleased with the performance they had witnessed. Lightning forked across the sky, a brilliant, dazzling display of elemental nature. For a moment the long, sequined gowns, furs, and suits of varying color were lit up as if caught in a spotlight. Thunder crashed directly overhead, and the ground and buildings shook under the assault. The light faded, leaving the night nearly black and the crowd almost blind. The throng broke into couples or groups, hurrying to their limousines and cars, while valets tried to work fast before the rain began to fall.

Senator Thomas Goodvine stayed beneath the entrance archway, bending his head toward his wife to hear her over the buzz of the crowd, laughing at her softly spoken words, nodding in agreement. He pulled her beneath his shoulder to prevent her from being jostled by the steady stream of people hurrying to avoid the weather.

Two trees formed the unique archway to the theater, the branches interlocking overhead to form a small protection against the elements. The leaves rustled and the branches clicked together in the rushing wind. Clouds whirled and spun, weaving dark, ominous threads across the moon.

Another burst of lightning illuminated two large men pushing against the stream of theatergoers, apparently determined to gain shelter in the building. The flash of light faded, leaving only the dim lighting of the archway and the streetlights flickering ominously. Thelma Goodvine tugged at her husband's jacket to bring his attention back to her.

"Down! Get down!" Joie Sanders plowed into the senator and his wife, her arms outspread, sweeping them both to the ground. In one move she rolled up on her knee in front of them, a gun in her outstretched hand. "Gun, gun, everybody down!" she shouted. An orange-red flame burst from two revolvers in a steady stream toward the couple she'd been assigned to protect. Joie returned fire with her usual calm and dead-on accuracy, watching one man begin to topple, almost in slow motion, his gun still firing but up into the air.

People screamed, ran in every direction, fell to the ground, crouched behind flimsy cover. The second gunman grabbed a woman in a long fur and dragged her in front of him as a shield. Joie was already pushing at the senator and his wife in an effort to get them to crawl back inside the relative safety of the theater. The second gunman propelled the sobbing woman forward as he fired at Joie, who rolled again to cover her charges' line of retreat.

A bullet sliced through the flesh of her shoulder, burning a path of pain and spraying blood over the senator's trousers. Joie cried out, but steadied her aim, ignoring the churning in her stomach. Her world narrowed to one man, one target. She squeezed the trigger slowly, precisely, watched the ugly little hole blossom in the middle of the man's forehead. He went down like a rock, taking his hostage with him, falling in a tangle of arms and legs.

There was a small silence. Only the clicking of the branches could be heard, a strange, disquieting rhythm. Joie blinked, trying to clear her vision. She seemed to be looking into a large, shimmering pool, staring at a man with flat, cold eyes and something metal glinting in his hand. He rose up out of the crowd, slamming into Joie before she could scramble out of the way. She twisted just enough to escape the lethal blade, driving the butt of her gun upward into his jaw, then slamming it back down on his knife hand. He screamed, dropping the blade so that it went skittering along the sidewalk. His fist found her face, driving her backward. The man followed her down, his face a mask of hatred.

Something hit the back of his head hard, and Joie found herself staring up at one of her men. "Thanks, John. I think he smashed every bone in my body when he fell on me." She took his hand, allowed him to help her out from under the large body. Joie kicked the gun from the limp hand of the first man she'd shot, even as weakness overwhelmed her. She sat down abruptly as her legs turned to rubber. "Get the senator and Mrs. Goodvine to safety, John." The wailing sirens were fading in and out. "Someone help that poor woman up."

"We've got it, Joie," one of the agents assured her. "We have the driver. How bad are you hurt? How many hits did you take? Give me your gun."

Joie looked down at the gun in her hand and noted with surprise she was aiming it at the motionless attacker. "Thanks, Robert. I think I'll just let you and John handle things for a while."

"Is she all right?" She could hear the senator's anxious voice. "Sanders? Are you hurt? I don't want to just leave her there; where are you taking us?"

Joie tried to lift her arm to indicate she was fine, but her arm seemed heavy and uncooperative. She closed her eyes and breathed deeply. She just needed to be somewhere else, just for a short time while the medics fixed her up. It wasn't the first time she'd taken a hit and she doubted it would be the last. She had certain instincts that had taken her to the top of her profession. It was very dangerous at the top.

Joie could blend in. Some of the men liked to call her the chameleon. She could look strikingly beautiful, plain, or just average. She could blend in with the tough crowd, the homeless, or the rich and glamorous. It was a valuable gift, and she used it willingly. She was called in for the difficult assignments, the ones where action was inevitable. Few others had her skill with knives or guns, and no one could disappear into a crowd the way she could.

She took herself out of her body, watched the frantic scene around her with interest for a few minutes. The others assigned to the senator and the Austrian agents had everything under control. She was being put into an ambulance and hustled away from the scene. More than anything, she detested hospitals. She simply took herself away, soaring free. She wanted to be outdoors, under the sky or beneath the earth in a world of subterranean beauty—it didn't matter, as long as it wasn't within the walls of a hospital.

Joie felt weightless, free, skimming through the mountains she had studied so carefully. As she soared free, she planned a trip caving with her brother and sister as soon as the senator and his wife were safely back home. She crossed space. Smelled the rain. Felt cool and moist in the mist of the mountains. Far below her, she saw the entrance to a cave, spotlighted by the small sliver of moon that managed to peek around the thick cloud cover. Smiling, she dropped down to enter a world of crystal and ice. Whether she was dreaming or hallucinating didn't matter; all she cared about was escaping from the pain of her wounds and the smell of the hospital.

Traian lay in the cool earth, gazing up at the high, cathedral-like ceiling. His body hurt in so many places, he just wanted to rest. The beauty of the cave was breathtaking and took his mind off his physical pain. Then he turned his head and saw her. She was hovering just overhead to his left. A woman with a cap of dark hair and large eyes. She was staring down at him in complete astonishment.

"You're hurt," she said. "If you were real, I'd send the paramedics."

"What makes you think I am not real?"

"Because I'm not really here; I'm in a hospital many miles away. I don't even know where here is."

"You look real enough to me."

"What in the world are you doing lying in the mud in the middle of a cave?" Her soft laughter rippled through him. "You didn't mistake this for a beauty spa, did you?"

His heart nearly ceased beating. Those simple questions turned his world upside down. He was aware of everything—the coolness of the interior, the blue of the ice, the dramatic sweep of architecture formed thousands of years earlier. He was mostly aware that her hair was a rich brown and her eyes were a cool gray. Her mouth was wide and curved at the corners, and she had laugh lines.

He was seeing in color. After hundreds of years of a bleak, gray existence, living in a world without color or emotion, there she was. The other half of his soul. Staring down at him with curious eyes and an amused grin. There was blood on her shoulder and bruises on her face, a tear in the gown she wore.

"You seem a bit overdressed for a cave," he pointed out.

She shrugged, her laughter soft and inviting. "Yes, well, a lady likes to know she looks her best when the cave crickets come calling."

"You are hurt, too."

"A small bit of trouble with some unpleasant fellows. What about you? And do you often go swimming in the mud with a gaping hole in your shoulder? You have heard of infection and gangrene, haven't you?"

"How good of you to notice. A small run-in with a

group of unsavory ruffians. I was uncharacteristically slow."

"You have an incredibly sexy accent. Do women fall all over you just at the sound of your voice?" She was very good at placing people by their accents, but his was different; there was a rich turn to his words. As dreams went, this was a fun one.

"I have not noticed such a phenomenon, but I will watch for it in the future."

"Nice cave. I love caves. This one looks like a wonderful place to explore."

"I do not believe it has been discovered yet," he replied pleasantly. Peace seeped into his body. His soul. Genuine laughter found its way into his heart.

"Really? You just sort of stumbled in blindfolded, did you? An interesting way to explore caves. Where am I? I'd like to come back here."

It was his turn to arch his eyebrow. "You floated through the air blindfolded?"

She grinned at him. "I do that sometimes when I don't want to be wherever I am. A bad habit."

Her form shimmered and her smile faded. "They're doing something nasty to me, I can't hold the projection."

He sat up, bit back a groan as the embers beneath his skin burned fiercely. "Do not go yet."

"I'm sorry." She looked down at her arm, looked back at him, tears swimming in her eyes. "They're cleaning my wound. It hurts like a bear."

And then she was gone. Just that fast. Vanishing without a trace. He sat there alone in the dark of the cave, astonished at how life could change in the blink of an eye. She was real. Her psychic abilities were strong. He had shared her space, shared her mind, and the path was imprinted on his brain. She would not escape him.

Traian lay back and waved his hand to close the soil over him, stilling his heart, his breath, allowing the song of the earth to send him into a deep, healing sleep.

Chapter Two

"You're losing it, Joie, there's nothing here." Gabrielle Sanders sank gracefully to the ground and drew up her knees as she regarded her sister with cool gray eyes. "Stop making yourself crazy and enjoy the view. It's breathtaking up here. You've been in a frenzy for hours now." Tipping her head back, she stared up at the sky. "We've been climbing forever. If you were going to find anything, you would have done so by now."

"I'm not losing my mind, Gabrielle," Joie insisted. "I've already lost it."

There was a sudden silence. The wind paused. A hawk screamed as it missed its prey. Gabrielle exchanged a long look with her brother, Jubal. They both stared at their younger sister. She seemed focused entirely on the rock surface she was studying. "Well, that's a relief," Gabrielle replied, laughing. "All this time I thought I was the abnormal one."

Joie let her breath out slowly. She knew she was acting crazy, almost out of control. What was she going to tell Gabrielle and Jubal? That she really had lost her mind some weeks ago and this was a last-ditch effort to hold on to her sanity? That she wasn't joking, and she belonged locked up somewhere on heavy medication?

What are you doing? The voice came out of nowhere, unexpectedly as it always did, catching her by surprise. Masculine. Sometimes amused. Sometimes teasing. Always alluring. She tried not to hear it. Tried not to respond. But she could never help herself. She always talked to him. Laughed with him. Wanted him. In spite of the beauty of his voice, this time he sounded infinitely weary, strained, as if he were in pain.

"Come on, I'm so close to the entrance I should be able to see it. Jubal," Joie appealed to her brother, "you know I'm right. I'm always right. There's a network of caves, most of them unexplored, and we're right on top of it." Joie was certain she'd already begun her descent into madness. She'd rather be with that voice in her head than with any real person in the world. She lived to hear that voice. She thought about him day and night, was consumed by him. Joie lifted her chin. *I'm proving you don't exist so I can get over you. I have a list of would-be lovers a mile long, and I'd like to have a little fun for a change.*

Now is not the time. Get out of here. It is dangerous.

Of course you would say that. You don't want me to know you aren't real. Look, honey, it's been fun, but we have to break up. I can't have a mythical lover, even if you're an awesome lover in my dreams. A girl wants to have the real thing once in a while. It isn't like I can introduce you to my family. Hey, guys, this is my invisible pal, Traian. He has a name like a locomotive, but that's my fantastic imagination.

Traian is a very old and respected name. Go away from here, Joie. I will not comment on your name, as it would be considered extremely rude.

Comment away, Traian. You're not real and neither is this conversation, so insult me all you want.

"You're always looking down when you should be looking up, Joie," Gabrielle said with a sigh. "If you reach straight up, you might be able to catch a cloud. Have you even noticed the flowers? They're gorgeous. I wish I knew what they were called. For once in your life, think of something besides caves." She waved her arms to encompass the countryside. "This is Dracula country. If you'd forget your obsession with caves, we might be able to explore the old castles for a change."

The flowers that are pink with a yellow middle are called Tratina. The white daisies are Marguarete. I cannot remember offhand what the blue ones are called, but it will come to me.

Are you eavesdropping on our conversation?

You are thinking loudly. And denying my existence, which seems to be a habit of yours lately.

Joie gave a little sniff. He was a figment of her imagination and he knew the names of the flowers. "Gabrielle, the pink ones are Tratina, and the white daisies are Marguarete. I have no idea what the blue ones are called."

"You're a walking encyclopedia," Gabrielle said, impressed.

Jubal stared at the wild countryside surrounding them, on either side and below. There were many deep gorges and several caves. Green valleys and plateaus made the view breathtaking. Below them, in the heavier depressions, water had soaked the ground, causing peat bogs. There were vivid green beds of moss and numerous shallow ponds winding their way around stands of birch and pine. It was magical, and yet Jubal was uneasy. The air was crisp and cold and the sky seemed clear, yet a strange mist covered the surfaces above them. At times he thought something moved in the mist, something alive and terrifying.

"Joie, give it up and let's get out of here," he said. "This place feels haunted to me. I don't like the vibes."

Gabrielle turned her head. "Really?" She arched a winged brow at him. "That's strange, Jubal, I feel the same way. Like we shouldn't be here, or that we're intruding in some way. Do you suppose it's all the vampire stories we were listening to at the inn last night? Normally, creepy stories are amusing, but I definitely feel apprehensive." She raised her voice. "What about you, Joie? Does this place give you the creeps?"

"We came here to explore the caves," Joie said firmly. "We're always very respectful when we go spelunking, so there's no reason to be nervous. I know the opening is here; I'm so close to it." She walked carefully around an outcropping of the mountain, stepping over her brother's outstretched legs without even glancing at him. "The entrance is here, I know it is," she muttered.

The others feel the threat of the vampires. You must go, Joie.

Oh, now you're going to tell me you believe in vampires. I just picked up that thought from Gabrielle. You aren't real, so be quiet and stop trying to frighten me away. I'm not leaving until I know for certain.

You already know; you just cannot admit the truth. I am trapped and will not be able to rescue you should you come upon them.

"Rescue me?" Joie nearly shouted the words, her dark eyes flashing with indignation. She turned her head to smile in reassurance at her brother and sister.

Gabrielle and Jubal exchanged a long, amused glance, used to Joie and her ramblings when she was on the scent of a new cave. Few people were as adept as their sister at discovering magical worlds below the surface.

Rescue me? She hissed it into his mind. *You can just bite me, Traian. Do you have any idea how annoying it is for someone like me to be treated like a ditzy little woman who can't fend for herself?*

I would not mind biting you. This time his voice purred with sexual innuendo. *But another time would be better.*

Joie shivered in spite of herself, yet heat curled deep inside her. *If you keep this up, my brother and sister are going to figure out I'm crazy and have me committed. Then where will you be?* Strands of dark hair blew across her face, hiding her expression from her siblings. *And just for your information, Sir Galahad, I am not the 'in need of rescue' type, so get over that one fast. Sheesh. First it's vampires and now it's rescuing. Will you just be quiet and let me figure this out? I don't suppose you want to tell me, give me a hint or two, if you're really down there and know where the opening is.*

Jubal leaned back in the tall grass with his hands behind his head, studying the cloud formations. He didn't want to look at the unusual tendrils of mist that seemed to wind around Joie's legs as she walked carefully around the outcropping. "You're like a hound dog on the scent of a criminal, Joie," he said. "You would have made a great detective."

"She would have," Gabrielle agreed with a little grin. She concentrated on the bright blue flowers with their symmetric petals. The beautiful masses of flowers were unusual, yet something sinister seemed to lie beneath the ground, just inches from the soft petals, an obscene, malicious presence. Staring at the flowers, Gabrielle swore the ground rose up an inch or so as if something were tunneling beneath it. The wind rushed over the mountainside. She sat up quickly, blinking rapidly.

"What is it?" Jubal asked.

"I don't know. For a moment I thought I saw something moving beneath the soil. This place gives me the creeps."

"Joie, come on. We're getting out of here," Jubal decided, reaching a long arm to gather their gear. "The sun will be down in a couple of hours anyway."

Joie examined every inch of the outcropping and the niche on either side. The rock was grown over with scrub and grasses. Wildflowers lifted their bright heads toward the sun. Joie narrowed her gaze and stepped up as close as possible, focusing completely on the jutting surface and every crack and shadow. "I've never felt so driven in my life. I don't think I can leave without finding it," she admitted honestly. "I'm sorry—if you two want to take off, go ahead. I'll come along as soon as I can."

Jubal and Gabrielle exchanged a long, knowing look. "Sure thing, sis, we'll just leave you up here all by yourself. Knowing you, you'd disappear into a cave and mate with a troll," Gabrielle said.

"Ha ha," Joie answered.

"What's the name of this mountain range?" Jubal asked idly, but his gaze was on Joie as she scanned the rock surface. "The bogs are even beautiful. If it wasn't so freaky up here, I could live in this area." When Gabrielle arched a black eyebrow at him, he laughed. "I could. I don't need to live in a city. I've got the same genes as the two of you. I just like to have money, you know. I need it for the two of you, to bail you out of all the trouble you get into."

"You idiot," Joie said affectionately, although she didn't look at him. "You have enough money to retire from that silly job of yours and do something useful with your life. Something *humanitarian*. There's a small crack running the length of the rock here. There's something funny about this, Jubal, Come look at it. It just isn't right the way it is."

"My *humanitarian* contribution to the world is looking after you two thrill seekers," Jubal pointed out as he got lazily to his feet. "Without me to curb your antics, the world would be a frightening place." He looked up at the strange, moving mist. "Rather like this place." He sauntered slowly over to examine the surface of the outcrop.

"We're in the Apuseni Mountains, part of the Carpathians, you heathen," Gabrielle informed her brother. "If you paid even the slightest attention to anything we said, you'd know that. And you could no more give up your luxury condo and live in the mountains than you could swim the English Channel. And, I might add, *we* take care of *you*."

"Hey! I can swim," Jubal objected. He ran his hand over the rocks, frowning as he did so. "Just because I don't like to swim doesn't mean I can't. I wasn't born with gills like the two of you. She's found something, Gabrielle. This is a pattern, but it needs to be . . ." He trailed off, dug his fingers around several of the smaller rocks, and began to rearrange them.

"There's a surprise," Gabrielle said and rose to her feet also. The cool mountain air fairly vibrated with excitement. "You could always come and research hot viruses with me," she invited, slinging her arm around her brother.

"Yeah, I'll get right on that, Gabrielle, because I'm a crazy man and want to die a miserable, but noble, death," Jubal said, ruffling his sister's dark hair. "I think I'll stick to my stocks and bonds and let you do your wacko research all by yourself. There it goes. Wow, look at that." The crack widened when he placed the last rock in the sequence. "This is man-made, not natural. Damn it, Joie, don't go in." He snagged his backpack and pulled out a logbook, carefully entering the time. "We're just doing a cursory exploration, and it's nearly sunset. No one knows where we are." Muttering, he hastily anchored the logbook near the crack where his sister had slipped inside.

Gabrielle shouldered her gear and followed. "It's extremely tight, Jubal," she cautioned. "Pass me your gear; it's the only way you're going to get through."

Jubal took one last look at the sky, noting that the clouds that had been floating so lazily overhead were now spinning ominously, a gathering of a great force. His chest scraped as he maneuvered through the jagged crack and into the narrow hall. Behind him the wind rose in a sudden shriek, lashing at the mountain, while strange, haunting cries echoed off the peaks. Mist swirled around the mountaintop, a mini tornado that snatched the logbook and sent it skittering down the hillside to land in one of the many bogs, where it slowly sank beneath the dark waters.

Joie moved quickly through the narrow hall, well ahead of her brother and sister. The ceiling dropped with every foot, so she was forced to bend over, eventually crawling on all fours and then sliding on her stomach. She could feel the cool air coming from a subterranean chamber. Everything inside her demanded she keep going, even when she had to maneuver her body at odd angles to slither through the tunnel.

"Slow down, Joie," Jubal cautioned. "Stay within sight of us."

"I don't like the way she's acting," Gabrielle whispered. "I've never seen her like this. She always obeys the safety rules, you know that, Jubal. Something is really wrong." She felt sick, her stomach churning, her mind filled with dread. "Something terrible is going to happen if we don't stop her."

Jubal waited, but Gabrielle didn't move; she remained wedged in the narrow hall, blocking him from continuing. "Keep going, Gabrielle," he said. "We'll catch up to her and talk sense to her. She's been caving for years. She's not going to forget everything she's ever learned."

"Ever since she was hurt in Austria, she's been different," Gabrielle pointed out. "Distracted. Driven."

"She's always very focused when she's going into a cave. And this is a big discovery, an unexplored cave. We have no idea what we're going to find. Of course she's excited."

"You know it isn't just that; she's been different this entire trip. Even before that. She's quieter. Joie isn't quiet. Now she seems to be somewhere else half the time. I feel like we're losing her, Jubal—as if something is pulling her into another world where we can't follow."

Jubal sighed loudly. "I wish I could say I don't know what you mean, but that's why I came on this trip. I've been worried about her too." He reached out and pushed at his sister. "Move it. I can't even hear her now."

"I can't move, Jubal." Gabrielle sounded scared. "I really can't."

"Are you stuck?" Jubal was very calm, but inside a dark dread was stealing over him.

"No," Gabrielle whispered. "I just can't move. Have you ever heard the term 'paralyzed with fear'? I think I really am."

Joie pushed forward as the ceiling lifted, allowing her to walk once again. Eventually the hall opened into a large chamber. "Hey, you two, it's much better in here. There's a large gallery." She shone her light around the area, noting the fingerlike formations surrounding a large abyss that yawned in the middle of the chamber. She climbed into her rigging as she struggled to hold on to reality. "Gabrielle! Jubal! I'm going to begin my descent." Joie tested her harness and glanced back toward the hall. "Gabrielle! Jubal! Are you two okay?"

"Wait for us, Joie," Jubal ordered. "Gabrielle has a bad feeling about this and so do I. I'm thinking we should regroup for a few minutes and talk this over. This could be more trouble than we want."

Joie fought back laughter that bubbled up out of nowhere. "Talk it over? Nobody's in more trouble than I am right now, Jubal. I can't turn back. I have to make this descent or go live in a padded cell for the rest of my life. I am not kidding you."

Jubal caught at Gabrielle's leg. "She isn't joking; she sounds on the verge of hysteria. Move it, Gabrielle. Right now."

Jubal rarely used that tone with either of his independent sisters, but it had the desired effect. Gabrielle scooted forward, driven by the fact that her brother obviously shared her growing fears for Joie.

Joie sat on the edge of the precipice, staring down into the black abyss. She didn't look up when her brother and sister joined her. Jubal rested his hands on her shoulders. Gabrielle sat cautiously beside her and took her hand. "So tell us. What's going on, Joie? We always stick together. There's no need to hide anything from us."

"Does insanity run in the family?" Joie continued to stare down into the well of darkness. "Because if it does, someone should have warned us."

"You think you're insane?" Jubal struggled to understand. Joie was the one who laughed all the time, who found humor in everything. She lit up the world with her smile, and she certainly never seemed to suffer from depression.

"I hear voices. Well . . ." she hedged, "*a* voice. One voice. All the time. We have conversations. Long conversations. Sometimes very intense and sometimes humorous." She felt the color rise beneath her skin and was grateful it was dark in the gallery. "Sometimes sexy. I find myself staying up all night just to be able to hear his voice and spend time with him." She shrugged her shoulders. "He even has a name. Traian Trigovise. How could I think up a name like that? He has an accent. A European, very sexy accent."

Gabrielle tightened her fingers around Joie's hand. "When did this start? When did you first hear this voice?"

Joie shrugged, remaining silent. Neither Jubal nor Gabrielle spoke, waiting her out. Finally she sighed. "When I was shot in Austria. You know how much I hate hospitals. When they took me there, I did my little disappearing act." She looked at her brother and sister. "I thought I was dreaming when I first saw him, but I'd been experimenting for some time with astral projection. I guess I succeeded, I don't know. I think we connected because we'd both been in a storm, in a battle and wounded." She shrugged helplessly. "It's the only reasonable explanation to me. He didn't go away. I could hear him talking to me in my mind. He found something important in the caves. I was already planning a trip here with you two, so I figured I could see if he was real."

"Joie," Jubal reprimanded gently. "Telepathic communication? With someone else? I know we can use telepathy, but we've never met anyone else who can."

"Is it really that far-fetched? I can take myself somewhere else. I know when I'm in danger. You're weird with patterns, and Gabrielle can do all sorts of strange things. We're all able to use telepathy with each other. Is it such a stretch to believe others can use it, too? I have to go down there. I have to know if he's real, if he's here, in this place. I feel him. I can't explain it, but it's like he's crawled inside of me somehow and I *need* him. I need to prove this to myself."

"Why didn't you tell us right away, Joie?" Jubal asked.

"Because I don't want the voice to go away," Joie admitted with stark truth. "I saw a counselor. He said I was having a break with reality, schizophrenia, probably brought on by the trauma of being shot. I didn't want to point out it wasn't the first time I've taken a bullet; it wasn't the worst injury and it won't be the last. I didn't take the medication the counselor prescribed. I thought maybe it wasn't so bad to live in a fantasy world part of the time. I still function and do my job." She managed a faint smile, her sense of humor rising even in the middle of such a serious conversation. "Do you think many people want a schizophrenic bodyguard? They get two for the price of one."

"Come on, Joie, you can't believe you're going crazy. You're . . ." Gabrielle paused in search of the right words. "You're *you*. You can do anything. You excel at everything. You *can't* hear voices."

Joie smiled up at her sister. "I'm definitely hearing a voice. Right now he's telling me to get out of here. He's saying it's dangerous and that we're all in mortal danger. He actually used the word *mortal*. I don't use that word. Do you think I have a split personality? I've always preferred male activities. I've always been such a tomboy. Maybe this is just my male side coming out. And just so you know how really screwed up my mind is, he's sexier than I am."

"Maybe your intuition is telling you not to make the descent, Joie," Jubal cautioned. "We haven't planned this out adequately."

"I don't have a choice," Joie said sadly. "Not this time. We have the rigging. We have the supplies. We're all dressed warmly enough. I can go down and look around. If I'm not back in a couple of hours, you can go for help."

Gabrielle shook her head. "We all go. We stick together, Joie. If you have to do this, then we do it together like we always have."

"Then we should stop talking and get moving," Jubal said decisively. Joie wasn't going to change her mind. Whatever was compelling her into that black abyss was too strong to fight. Worse, the dread was still growing inside him. He glanced down into the dark hole. Evil lurked close by, and he had the feeling they were going to come face to face with it.

Chapter Three

"Joie, this is out of this world," Jubal said softly, in awe. He turned in a full circle, shining his light on the walls of the gallery. The descent had been a long one, well over two hundred feet. "I've never seen anything like it. What a find. The ice formations are incredible. I swear I actually saw a vein of gold in more than one place. There are so many halls and galleries to explore."

Gabrielle cautiously moved around an ice sculpture that rose like a living flame from the floor. "Look at this. When I shine my light on it from this angle, I'd swear the thing had gems in it. It's as brilliant as a polished diamond but reflects the light as if it were red like a ruby." Movement caught her attention, and she turned her head to watch Joie as she examined the glacial ice that formed the gallery. "Be careful, I suspect that a good number of viruses previously unknown to us come from insects and even perhaps the fungi in caves such as this one. These microorganisms exist with no light and few nutrients, locked inside the ice, yet still capable of living. There's such a wealth of information down here."

Joie ignored both of her siblings. She was so close now, she could almost feel him breathing. Somewhere in this labyrinth of halls he was waiting for her. Smoldering. Angry that she had disobeyed him. He was real, not a voice in her head, not a part of a split personality. He was real and alive and in pain. She could feel his pain, throbbing through her body, beating at her head.

Tell me. She demanded it. Forced him to deal with who she really was, not who he thought she should be.

Tell the others to be quiet. They are in danger. I have battled the same enemy three times since you found me in the cave. I am a prisoner and wounded and extremely weak. I cannot aid you much in the battle, and the enemy has powers you cannot possibly comprehend.

Joie gave him a mental image of rolling her eyes in exasperation. *Sorry for the fluff in my head, but I'm usually found wrapped in cotton or bubblewrap to protect me from all the evil people in the world.* She signaled her brother and sister to silence, switching easily into hunting mode. She moved through the halls with confidence, recognizing the feel of him now. Knowing she was moving toward him. *I doubt very much if I'll need your aid, Mr. Brawny, but I'll keep it in mind. How many?*

There is one with me now. The others will return well fed and high with a lust for killing. You do not want to meet them.

Then I guess I'd best pull your butt out of trouble and get the heck out of Dodge.

You do not act like any of the women I know act.

Thank you. I appreciate your saying so.

Joie dropped to her knees and crawled through a narrow, tubelike passage. Jubal and Gabrielle followed close behind. The steady drip of water reminded Joie of the clicking of the branches at the theater the night she was shot. There was a peculiar rhythm to the drops, almost as if some unseen hand, not nature, guided the water's descent. The tube began to widen until she could once again stand.

A strange, growling noise assaulted her ears. It sounded like a cross between a hyena laughing and a dog growling viciously. Immediately she held up her hand behind her, signaling Jubal and Gabrielle to stop while she scooted closer. She used the tall columns of rock and ice formations as cover.

Traian was literally pinned against a wall of ice. Blood ran down from each shoulder and leg where sharp, twisted stakes had been thrust through his body to pin him like an insect on a board. Joie held her breath to keep from crying out in dismay. It was no wonder she could feel the pain radiating from him. She knew Traian was aware of her presence, but he didn't make the mistake of giving away her position. He watched the creature hovering over him with cool eyes.

"You seem nervous, Lamont," Traian observed.

The creature hissed and without preamble bent his head to Traian's neck and sank his teeth into the pulse beating there.

Joie could easily see the long incisors stabbing into flesh, something she'd only seen before in films. She dropped to the ground, crawling on her stomach, using her elbows to propel herself across the floor between two columns of ice to get into a better position for attack. She came up on her knees behind a large ice formation, her gaze fixed on her target.

He is very dangerous, especially now when he is filled with the blood of an ancient. Traian's voice was calm in spite of the ghastly creature tormenting him.

Joie stared at the hideous thing. It was tall and emaciated, the skin shrunken around its skull, almost as if it were dead. Tufts of hair stood straight out, a curious gray-white color, while the rest of the hair hung in oily, twisted ropes. He gulped down the blood, smearing it on his lips and stained teeth, all the while making growling noises in his throat. He seemed more animal than man.

My family always warned me if I hung out underground too long I could end up with a troll. At the risk of seeming shallow, I have to say he isn't very handsome and doesn't appeal at all to me. Her hand went up to the back of her neck, sliding down between her shoulder blades in a well-practiced move, came out with the knife she always carried.

The creature lifted his head alertly and looked around the large gallery with suspicious eyes. Joie remained motionless, hardly daring to breathe. The cold air rushed through the chamber and touched Traian and the creature with icy fingers. Immediately Lamont caught at one of the stakes pinning his victim to the ice flow.

"None of your tricks, ancient one. Your blood belongs to us now. The others will be back soon with a victim to force you to our bidding. You are far too weak to resist."

What is he?

He is vampire. The undead. And there are others. You must get your family out before the others return.

Traian watched his tormentor intently. The vampire leaned close to the gaping wound in Traian's throat, his breath a sickly green vapor as he licked at the blood with a thick, dark tongue. "I just might kill you instead. A stake through the heart." He lifted a lethal-looking stake over his head and gave a maniacal laugh.

Vampires are difficult to kill. You will only get one chance. Go for his heart.

Joie threw the knife with deadly accuracy. It hummed as it rocketed across the chamber and buried itself deep in the vampire's chest. The creature screamed, the sound cracking the ice so that sharp daggers broke from the high ceiling and rained down like deadly missiles. Joie flung her body over Traian's, protecting him from the falling ice. The vampire went down hard, thrashing wildly, the sounds echoing through the cavern, and then there was sudden silence.

Joie moved back slowly, slipping a second knife from the scabbard on her calf. "That didn't look so difficult to me. If you want, I'll give you a lesson or two."

"What took you so long?" Traian asked.

She made her way cautiously around him, kicking aside the bigger chunks of ice. "Bad directions. You know how traffic in these places can be." She leaned close to study one of the pins slicing through his shoulder to hold him to the wall. "I hate to point this out to you, but you're in a bit of a mess. What was all that he-man macho crap telling me to stay away? If you ask me, you're in serious need of rescuing."

Traian arched an eyebrow. His skin appeared pale, and he was clearly weak from loss of blood. Unattended wounds from a recent battle seeped more of his precious life fluid. He shook uncontrollably, unable to maintain his body's temperature. His hair was black and matted with blood. "I am certain I would have thought of something. He has friends. They will be returning soon, and when they see him, they are not going to be happy. And if I do not incinerate his body, he will rise again."

"Lovely thought," Joie said and turned to keep a wary eye on the repulsive corpse. "Lucky for you I travel with a doctor. My sister Gabrielle is quite mad, always peering into microscopes and lecturing us about how we're parasites on earth, but she does have certain skills." She whistled softly to signal to her brother and sister to enter the ice chamber.

Gabrielle avoided looking at the vampire as she studied the daggers of ice pinning Traian to the wall. "You do know the strangest people, Joie," she said. "I don't even want to ask where you met him."

"If I pull out the stake, is he going to bleed to death?" Jubal inquired.

"Just do it before the others come back," Traian advised, "or we are all going to die. Vampires are very dangerous. You were lucky."

Joie sniffed indignantly. "I was fast and accurate and very good. There's no need to feel inferior." She signaled to Jubal even as she flashed a smug smile at Traian. "I have a gift."

Jubal took hold of the stake in Traian's left shoulder with both hands and yanked with all his strength. Blood spurted, but Gabrielle pressed her palms over the wound hard. "The first-aid kit is in my pack, Joie, but I don't know how we're going to get him to the surface. He needs blood as quickly as possible."

"Just take them all out," Traian instructed. "We really have to hurry."

"Do what he says, Jubal." Joie caught the sense of urgency emanating from Traian. Little white lines were etched around his perfectly sculpted mouth. "Vampire babe is twitching." To her horror, the knife was vibrating, wiggling back and forth as if slowly emerging from the rotted flesh. "Hurry—we may have a little problem with handsome. He seems to be coming back to life."

"Pack the wounds with mud. Hurry," Traian said.

Joie didn't want to take her eyes off the ghoulish creature, but the dark compulsion in Traian's voice alarmed her. Gabrielle obeyed him. Always meticulously careful of germs and microorganisms, she scooped up handfuls of gooey soil and, before Jubal could stop her, smeared it over Traian's shoulder and the rest of the gaping holes in his flesh.

Without warning, Traian reached out and dragged Jubal close to him, murmuring something Joie couldn't quite catch. He bent his head toward Jubal's exposed throat. Neither Jubal nor Gabrielle protested; rather, they stood quietly, as if enthralled.

Fury burned through Joie. "You blood-sucking fiend! Touch him and you die! I'm not kidding you. Let him go or I'll tear your heart out. And don't try using your voice on me, because it won't work." As she hissed the words out in a low, smoldering voice, she moved to aim the knife she had drawn from the sheath strapped to her calf. At the same time, she tried to keep the vampire in sight.

"If I do not get blood, we are all going to die," Traian said calmly. He looked at her, his gaze steady and honest.

She let her breath escape between her teeth as she reached out and jerked Gabrielle away from him, thrusting her sister behind her. "Release them now."

"We have only minutes."

"Then don't waste time." Her hand didn't waver. Neither did her stare.

Traian spoke softly to Gabrielle and Jubal, and both reacted immediately, Jubal hurrying to safety.

"Tell us what's going on," Joie said. "It isn't as if we didn't witness the zombie man on the ground here, doing his sorry imitation of Dracula."

"I am Carpathian, of the Earth. All the stories I told you were true, not made up to entertain you. I lived the battles; they were not fiction. I need blood to survive, but we do not kill for sustenance. I have fought the vampire for hundreds of years." His voice was every bit as steady as his gaze. "This one will rise again, and he has friends. You cannot stop them, nor can I without blood to build my strength."

Jubal caught at Joie and tried to drag her backward, away from the wounded man. She held up her hand. "He's telling the truth, Jubal. I can feel them coming—can't you?" She handed her knife to her brother, ignoring her trembling hand. "If I'm making the biggest mistake of my life, I expect you to avenge me."

She made her way to where Traian remained slumped against the blue ice, pulling off her helmet as she did so. "Go for it, but remember, my brother can hit a bull's-eye every time."

Traian touched her then, circling her wrist with his long fingers and drawing her slowly, inexorably to him. Joie's heart skipped a beat, then began to pound, whether in fear or excitement, she didn't know. She knew only that her mouth went dry and her insides were melting at an alarming rate. His eyes went dark, focused on her completely, shutting out everything else. Everyone else. He pulled her into the shelter of his large frame.

Joie felt his every muscle, hard, defined, rippling with power. He should have smelled of sweat and blood, but his scent was masculine, clean, inviting. Sexy. The world seemed to drop away. Danger didn't matter. His arms swept around her, held her close so that her heart beat with the same rhythm as his. She placed her hand over his chest, felt his heart beat strongly against her palm. She lifted her gaze to his and was instantly lost in the burning intensity she saw there.

There was a storm of emotion between them, a dark cauldron every bit as roiling and wild as the gale raging above ground. Mesmerized, she could only stare up at him. His fingertips brushed the hair from her neck. Sent fire racing through her bloodstream. Where he had been businesslike and abrupt with Jubal, he was gentle, even tender as he enfolded Joie closer. He bent his head to hers.

Gabrielle made a small cry of protest, stepped toward them with every intention of stopping him. Traian lifted his head, his eyes glowing with a strange fiery red, halting her in her tracks. His eyelids drifted down, his arm curling around Joie possessively so that she nearly disappeared from sight, completely engulfed in his embrace. There was something very protective, yet predatory in his posture.

His lips barely skimmed over Joie's skin. She felt it. A brush of butterfly wings, no more, yet that slight touch sent heat spreading through her body. He kissed her eyes until she closed them. Sensations increased. He whispered to her, in her mind an intimate, soft litany of words in an ancient tongue. His voice wrapped her in velvet, an erotic spell of enchantment she willingly embraced.

Joie felt his breath warm on her neck. His tongue swirled over her pulse. Once. Twice. Her entire body clenched, every muscle contracting breathlessly. Waiting. Wanting. His lips feathering over her neck sent heat pooling low, and her legs went weak. One arm, of its own accord, slid upward to curl around his head, to draw him closer, cradle him to her. White-hot lightning pierced her skin. Sent whips of lightning dancing in her bloodstream, a pleasure bordering on pain. Nothing had prepared her for the sheer erotic fire coursing through her body. A soft moan escaped her. She moved restlessly against him.

Traian pulled her closer, imprinting his body against hers, feeling every lush curve and soft, rounded line. Lifemate. He had waited so long. Endured so much. There was no shield providing her with a protective barrier. She knew exactly what he was doing and yet she accepted him, accepted his need for her blood. It rushed through his body with the force of a freight train; his shrunken, starving cells soaked it up; tissue and muscle and damaged organs demanded sustenance. He wanted to savor the moment, savor his first taste of her, his first touch on her skin.

Even as Traian struggled for sufficient control to blur the horrified gazes of her siblings, he was aware of the undead struggling to rise again the two vampires rushing through the maze of halls to reach him before he could escape. He took from Joie only what he needed to have strength when the battle came. He couldn't risk her being too weak to defend herself. They would have more than one skirmish with the undead before they were out of the labyrinth of caves.

Very gently, almost reverently, he swept his tongue across the pinpricks to close them. "Thank you, Joie." His arms held her up, his body taking her weight.

She shivered as she lifted her lashes to study his face. At once she was caught and held in the dark depths of his eyes. "You're welcome."

"I hate to break up the love fest the two of you are having," Jubal snapped, "but we've got a little problem. The knife just fell out of the dead thing's chest, and he's beginning to thrash around. It isn't a pretty sight."

Jubal's voice broke the spell Traian seemed to have woven around Joie. She pulled her gaze away with an effort and looked over at the creature clawing the floor of the cave. "He looks angry," she observed.

Chapter Four

"He is not the only one," Traian agreed. "His friends are coming this way fast, and they have murder on their minds."

The vampire struggled to a half-sitting position on the floor, blood and spittle running down his chin. His red-rimmed eyes fixed on Joie with a mixture of hate and fear.

She glared at him. "What the hell did you do to my knife, you fiend? Do you have any idea what a knife like that costs?" She held out her hand to Jubal for the knife she had given him. "Give that to me. I think I'm going to need it."

Traian put her firmly behind him and signaled to Jubal and Gabrielle to move away from the vampire. They did so carefully. He was making hideous noises, his talons cutting deep gouges into the ice.

Jubal handed his sister the knife. "Let's get out of

here while we can. I don't think I want to meet any more of these things."

"I'm going to pretend I never met this one," Gabrielle said firmly.

Joie watched Traian closely. He seemed to be gathering something unseen into his hands. She could feel the buildup of energy in the chamber. The gallery was actually warming, increasing the dripping of the water dramatically. Between Traian's palms, light glowed, a bright orange-red, emitting heat. It appeared just smaller than a basketball, the energy coiling and spinning.

The vampire screamed in rage and attempted to rise, stabbing at the air with his claws and clicking his twisted nails rapidly in a summons. The ball left Traian's hands, hurtling through the chamber to pass cleanly through the vampire's chest, leaving behind a gaping hole where the heart had been. The creature slumped to the floor, limp and unmoving, a foul stench filled the cavern.

"Handy little trick," Joie observed. "You'll have to teach it to me."

Traian managed a boyish grin. "Finally, something impressed you."

A terrible howling, like that of a demon pack, echoed through the subterranean caverns, sending chills down Joie's spine. "I think that's our cue to leave."

"Can we climb? How do we know where they are?" Gabrielle asked anxiously.

"What the hell are they?" Jubal demanded.

"Vampires," Traian answered. "And they are coming for us. We have to get out of here now." He indicated a small break in the wall of ice. "That way. I will seal it up behind us. It will not stop them, but it will slow them down."

Gabrielle didn't wait for a second invitation. Clutching her pack, she ducked into the crevice and scooted down the ice chute. Jubal started to say something, thought better of it, and followed her into the ice tunnel.

"In all of our conversations, it didn't occur to you to mention a few pertinent facts such as how you're a peculiar sort of man who likes blood and has vampires and other mythical creatures stalking you? You might have mentioned, just once, that you weren't telling me cheery bedtime stories but that you lived this sort of life. Didn't you think that might be important in the grand scheme of things?" Joie arched an eyebrow at Traian.

"I took into consideration your fear that you had lost your mind. It occurred to me that if I started talking about vampires being real and not fictional, you would have yourself committed." His smile was slow and incredibly sexy as he stepped back to allow her to precede him. "You will need your pack. We may be trapped in here most of the night."

The ice chute was cold after the unexpected heat Traian had generated in the chamber. Before she could disappear down the slide, he wrapped his arms around her, drawing her back against his chest. He climbed into the chute, sat down with her on his lap, and pushed off into the spiraling tube.

Joie slid down into the freezing world of blue ice and crystal, knowing he was right. She would have had herself committed at the mere mention of vampires. "I still might," she muttered aloud. "I don't think having a boyfriend who has a neck-biting fetish is too sane."

"Boyfriend?" She heard the genuine amusement in his voice. "I have never been anyone's boyfriend before." He buried his face in the warmth of her neck. "I told you not to come here. I am not certain I can get your family out alive. There is something in this cave the vampires are determined to find. Or protect."

His arms held her snugly to him, his body protecting hers from the biting cold, the ice slivers and hard, jagged edges that could tear through fabric and skin. She reached out, caught at a thick crystalline handhold, and jolted their downward slide to a stop. "This formation isn't entirely natural, is it, Traian?"

With a startling rasping sound, crickets poured down the tube around them. Traian shifted, turned. Joie felt the gathering of energy, of heat, of power. She opened her mind instantly to him, flooding him with her strength and energy, generously sharing everything she had, everything she was. The impulse to do so should have frightened her. It didn't. She belonged with him. Shoulder to shoulder. Mind to mind. They were connected in some way she didn't understand, but it felt right. She didn't trust people, other than Gabrielle and Jubal. She was naturally private and always very careful in close relationships, yet the moment she heard Traian's voice, the moment she laid eyes on him, even when she'd thought he was a fantasy, she had known he was somehow a part of her.

Below her, she heard Gabrielle cry out as the insects reached her. Jubal murmured softly in reassurance. Above her, a scream of rage and hatred announced that the undead's companions had found his lifeless body. Traian began to chant in a soft voice, his hands moving quickly in a pattern Joie couldn't quite follow, the movements blurring with his incredible speed.

"Let go," he ordered, and dragged her hands from the hold so that they plunged down the slide toward the bottom.

She could hear the ominous cracking of ice. The tube above their head was veined in a starburst pattern that spread rapidly outward. At the entrance, the ice began to fall in large chunks, some sliding down the tube toward them. Traian hit the ground running, with Joie in his arms. "Hurry!" he called to Jubal and Gabrielle.

A sound was building behind them, a great roar and a thunderous clap as the tube collapsed in on itself. The earth shook beneath their feet, and an ominous rumble emanated from the walls and ceiling surrounding them. Jubal caught Gabrielle's hand and followed Traian at a dead run through the narrow hall.

Joie clung to Traian, feeling somewhat silly being carried when he was so hideously injured, but the man wasn't even breathing hard. Sharp daggers of ice fell from the ceiling as they rushed through the tunnel. Several times, Traian redirected a lethal missile as they raced along the well-worn path. Traian stopped so abruptly, Jubal ran into him. Very slowly Traian allowed Joie to stand on her own feet. His arm remained around her. They were on the edge of a precipice. A very narrow bridge, constructed of ice and stone, was the only way across. It appeared dangerously thin in places and had an obvious hole in one section.

"Where the hell did that come from?" Jubal demanded. "That's no natural bridge. Who could have carved such a thing? Can we cross it?"

Traian studied it warily. He shook his head. "I am beginning to be very afraid we have stumbled into a cave we do not want to be in. I fear that bridge is an invitation to death. A trap."

Jubal glared at him. "If you know something, tell us." He caught Joie's hand and pulled her away from Traian. She was already looking upward, searching for another way out of the hall. "Joie, slow down for a minute," Jubal ordered. "I don't understand what's going on here, but I can tell you, this man is dangerous. We don't know him and we don't need to be associated with him." He actually shoved her behind him, the look in his ice-cold eyes making it clear he was prepared to protect his sisters against an obvious predator. "Why are we taking his word for anything?"

Traian swung his head around, his eyes glittering with menace. There was instant silence. Joie wrapped her fingers around her brother's wrist. "I think we can talk about this at a more opportune time. Maybe when the fiends from hell aren't chasing after us."

"Has it occurred to you, he's one of them?" Jubal demanded, glaring at Traian. "He drank your blood, Joie. That ought to tell you something right there."

"It tells her I am different. Not quite human. The fact that I did not kill her—or you, for that matter—tells you I am not vampire." Traian spoke very quietly. "I will not allow any harm to come to her."

Joie made a move to slide past her brother, but he sidestepped, staying between her and Traian. She glared at him. "What is wrong with you? You aren't going all macho and stupid on me, are you, Jubal? I love you dearly, but you can't be serious. Did you see that thing? We've got to get out of here, and Traian knows the way." She tilted her chin to look up at him. "You do know the way, don't you?"

Gabrielle slipped her hand into her sister's. "I'm afraid, Joie. I've got a terrible feeling we're all going to die."

"The vampires are broadcasting terror and images of death to feed your natural fear," Traian explained. "They are hunting something in these caves. The network is very large and, as you can see, not all naturally formed. I stayed to try to find what they are looking for. Vampires do not normally put so much energy into a project. Whatever it is they want, their finding it will not benefit either the Carpathian or the human race."

Jubal nodded toward the raw wounds on Traian's chest. "You've been in a few battles with them."

He nodded. "Yes, and I have noticed changes in their

behavior. Now vampires are running in packs. They used to be out for themselves, or occasionally a master vampire would use the newer ones as fodder for his battles, but lately they seem to be organized."

Jubal shoved a hand through his hair in agitation. "I feel like I'm losing my mind. Vampires are Hollywood creations, creatures in movies. They aren't real." He stared hard at Traian's mouth, trying to see his teeth. "I saw you bite my sister's neck, and I'm sorry, but that puts you into the vampire category as far as I'm concerned. You just go your way and we'll go ours, and we'll pretend we never saw you."

Traian's gaze swept over Jubal, his glittering eyes taking on a peculiar reddish glow in the light from the helmets. He noted Jubal's aggressive posture, his clenched fists. "Do you think to fight me? There is no way to win. I am powerful beyond your imagination, just as the vampires are. You still do not understand the danger you are in."

"You didn't look so powerful lying there while that thing was having you for dinner," Jubal snapped.

"He does have a point, Traian," Joie said. "But we don't have time for this." She could hear a sound accompanying the drip of the water. A soft clicking, like branches banging together in the wind. It made her edgy.

There was no warning. One moment Traian stood in the glare of their lights, the next a huge, shaggy black wolf with a mouthful of lethal teeth sat in his place, eyes focused menacingly on Jubal. Gabrielle screamed and stumbled backward. Jubal reached out to catch her, dragging her away from the abyss to comparative safety beside the snarling animal.

Joie circled the wolf's neck with a restraining arm. "Totally impressive, but not something I want to take home to Mom." Her heart was pounding so loudly, it sounded like a drum in her ears. Even her mouth was dry.

There is no need to fear me. I would never harm you.

"Why would you think I was afraid of you?" Joie demanded. "I'm not in the least afraid. I'm keeping you under control."

It may have something to do with the knife you are holding to my throat. Traian said it casually, a soft amusement in his voice, as if the blade pressed so tightly against him didn't matter in the least.

And that scared her more than the fact he had just shape-shifted into a predator. She looked down at her arm curved around his neck. The fur was thick and luxurious, and her arm was nearly buried in it. But she could feel the handle of the knife in her hand. She let out her breath and slowly eased the blade away from his throat. "I was just making certain you were paying attention," she said as she slipped the blade back into the scabbard.

Traian calmly shifted back into his true form. "Just how many weapons do you carry on you? You seem to be a walking arsenal."

"*You* are a walking arsenal," Jubal accused. "Joie, how did you get mixed up with him? And it's obvious you're talking with him telepathically."

Joie burst out laughing. "You sound so accusing, Jubal. I told you I was talking to him telepathically. We all do it. Don't pretend it's all that unusual for us."

"We have to work at it," Jubal complained. "You seem to communicate with him effortlessly."

"Jubal, we can discuss all this later when we're far away from here," Joie said. "That clicking noise is driving me crazy. I don't like the rhythm; it's not natural."

"I want to get out of here," Gabrielle said. "Joie, find us a way out." Her voice trembled, and she sounded very forlorn.

"We'll get out, hon," Joie said with confidence. "If the two macho boys can stop beating their chests long enough"—she blew her brother a kiss—"we'll figure this out." The dripping of the water was more insistent. She looked anxiously toward Traian. Something was wrong. He knew it. She knew it.

"I will take them across and come back for you," Traian said to Joie. There was no sense in attempting to take his lifemate first. It was clear she would never go without the others, and he didn't want to waste time arguing. He held out his hand toward Gabrielle. "Come with me."

She didn't look at him, but rather at her sister. "Do you trust him, Joie?"

Joie looked up at Traian, noting the lines etched in his strong, timeless face. The dark depths of his eyes. Old eyes. Eyes that had seen too much. He was a man who had been alone too long. She was a looking at a warrior. A man of honor. Joie reached out to brush a caress along his jaw with her fingertips. The touch jolted him. Jolted her. Need slammed into him, a driving punch that shook his existence. Heat flooded her body. Electricity arced between them, lightning flashing in their veins. Instant awareness. They smiled at one another in understanding.

"I would trust him with my life, Gabrielle. More importantly, I would trust him with yours. Please go with him now. I've got that bad feeling I always get when we're in danger."

Gabrielle took Traian's hand, allowed him to draw her to him. They all looked at Jubal.

"Damn it, Joie, I'm your older brother and the man here," he muttered, shaking his head, but he went obediently to Traian's side.

Traian leaned over to catch Joie's chin. "I will be back immediately. Do *not* attempt to engage the enemy.

They must not get their hands on you." There was an underlying urgency in his voice. His dark eyes stared into hers. "Be safe, Joie. I need you to be safe."

He was taking her family to safety for her, when everything in him demanded he take her first. Joie understood his look immediately, recognized how difficult it was for him to do what was important to her rather than to himself. There was a storm of emotion churning inside him, yet his features remained tranquil. Only his eyes burned with intensity. With possession. With promise. With passion.

His mouth fastened on hers, a hard kiss that staked his claim on her. That kiss told her he meant to have her and nothing would stand in his way. She felt his body tremble and tasted his passion, tasted his fear for her.

He pulled away abruptly, lifting her brother and sister easily, as if they were no more than children, shifting into a creature with wings, half man, half bird, and flying across the abyss into the dark where she could no longer see him.

Joie was left standing alone on the edge of the precipice with the darkness pressing down on her. With the strange rhythmic clicking and the dripping water. Heart pounding and mouth dry, she turned toward the sound, shining her light to see what was behind her.

In the small confines she could see water trickling from the side of the cavern; it was not clear, but a milky yellow, and gathered into a foul-smelling pool. She moved cautiously, positioning herself to keep an eye on what was gathering there. Something evil. Something alive.

The water rippled in response to a dark disturbance below the surface. The pool darkened into an oily substance, revealing two red orbs glaring with terrible malevolence. A chill crept down her spine. The hair on her arms stood up.

Traian. Automatically, without conscious thought, she reached out for him, showed him the pool with its macabre secrets.

Move! Get out of its line of vision, Joie.

Chapter Five

Joie stared back at the flame-red eyes in horror, unable to look away. The eyes were real, watching her, some terrible apparition set on her destruction. She had never seen so much malice, so much black hatred pouring from any entity. Her body rebelled, sickened by the evil emanating from the thick slime.

At Traian's warning, she tried to wrench her gaze away, but she was trapped, unable to break eye contact with the red flames. Her airway began to close, choked off by an invisible noose. Instinctively her hands flew up to her throat as if she could pry unseen fingers from around her neck, but there was nothing there. As white stars flashed across a black background, Joie realized dizzily she had only precious seconds to break the invisible hold on her throat. She reached for her knife, following through in one smooth motion with a throw directed by sheer desperation.

The blade sank deep into the fiery left eye. Immediately the water bubbled up in a blackish-red ooze and the hold on her throat loosened, allowing her to breathe. A terrible howl filled the cavern, assaulting her ears. She stumbled away from the poisonous pool, dragging air into her lungs, coughing as her raw throat protested.

In the next moment Traian was dragging her into his arms, his body crowding hers, his hands moving over her to assure himself she was unhurt. As he lifted her, she clung to his strength, not bothering to pretend the encounter hadn't shaken her. He moved quickly through the air, so fast the cold air bit at her face, numbed her arms, and tore tears from her eyes. Joie buried her face against his chest, allowing herself a few moments to recover before she faced her siblings.

"You are teaching me the meaning of fear," he said.

"Really? I thought it was the other way around. I don't think your world is the calm environment a woman like me should be in." Her voice shook, embarrassing her.

"Having courage does not mean being unafraid."

"True, but everyone doesn't have to know I was shaking in my boots. Literally."

"I am not everyone. I still cannot believe you are real," he said softly. His lips moved against her cheek, a brush lighter than a butterfly wing, yet she felt it all the way to her toes. That small caress sent blood rushing through her veins, her heart leaping; his touch warmed her as nothing else could.

"I'm having a difficult time believing that any of this is real," Joie admitted. "And what's up with the wolf? Telepathy, okay, I can accept that. Even your strange little blood fetish, but don't you think changing into animals and flying through the air might be going a little too far?"

His arms tightened possessively. "You do not enjoy flying?"

"I don't enjoy anything when I'm not in complete control. And you didn't have to intimidate my brother."

His arm was curved around her, pressed against the underside of her breasts. "You will not be in complete control when I make love to you, Joie," he told her softly.

She closed her eyes at the velvet sound of his voice. Danger surrounded them. Her family was close. It didn't seem to matter. She was so aware of him, her body ached with need. With hunger. With absolute longing. She felt edgy and hot; a terrible pressure was building inside her.

I feel the same way.

She often spoke with her brother and sister using telepathy, a secret they all shared, but this was different. So much more. An intimacy that whispered of erotic nights and appetites that would never be sated. *Why? Why with you?*

I am your other half. We belong together. I have searched the world for you. Waited lifetimes for you.

Joie tightened her grip on his shirt, burrowed closer to his heart. She was a woman who knew herself well. An adrenaline junkie. A feminist. A believer in justice. She loved her life. Traveling from country to country. One assignment after another taking her into danger. Her recreation time was spent caving, white-water rafting, or skydiving. She was not a woman who wanted or needed a man. She was not a woman who clung to a man.

Joie looked up at Traian, the light from her helmet shining on his face. He had changed her very existence for all time. "I'm not altogether certain I approve of you."

Laughter rumbled in his throat. "Fortunately, your

approval is not strictly necessary. Lifemates simply are. We have no choice in the matter. We are like two magnets that cannot be torn apart."

"Great. I don't know a thing about you except I can't exactly bring you home to my mother and father. My family is very close, by the way."

He put her carefully on firm ground. Jubal and Gabrielle rushed to her, flinging their arms around her and hugging her close. "I had not noticed," Traian said with drawling amusement. "We are not safe. We have to keep moving."

"Wait, Traian," Jubal objected. "We found something. Something really important. You said those vampires were hunting something. You have to take a look at this. I've never seen anything like it."

Traian hadn't relinquished Joie's hand, even when her siblings dragged her into their arms. She felt a little silly holding hands—she'd never really done it, not even in high school. But there was something warm and comforting, something extraordinary about being close to Traian.

"You can bring me home to your parents." He said it softly, honestly, as he followed Jubal and Gabrielle through a narrow hall. "I would never embarrass you, or frighten them. I want to meet them. Anyone important to you is important to me."

Joie tried to prevent her heart from going crazy. She was no young girl, but a fully grown woman. A man shouldn't have such an effect on her, yet he did. There was honesty in his voice. A simple sincerity that shook her. She knew nothing about him, not even what he really was, yet she knew everything. She knew what kind of man he was. The knowledge was instinctive, the one thing she was certain of.

"Where is your family?" she asked.

"I have only my people. My prince." His eyes

gleamed a deep black in the soft glow of the helmet lights. "You are my family. Your brother and sister have become my family." He arched an eyebrow at her. "And we have only just met. A very strange concept for you, but completely natural to me. Lifemates are two people who meet and need to be together, two halves of the same whole. Finding a lifemate is what every Carpathian male dreams of and longs for and fights to keep our world together for, yet few of us ever gain such a treasure. I never thought to experience such an earth-shattering event."

"Are you disappointed that I'm not what you thought I'd be?"

Traian looked down at her. "You do not yet understand the concept of lifemates. I am surprised and even shocked by the idea of a human lifemate, but I could never be disappointed with you. We were made for one another. We complete one another. You are fascinating to me. You always will be."

Joie hurried to catch up with her brother and sister, not wanting Traian to see the pleased grin she couldn't quite hide. Jubal turned toward a shallow alcove in the wall, directing his light onto the ice. There was a sudden silence as all of them held their breath. The creature encased in ice was large, an enormous beast with scales covering its body, a wedge-shaped head, a serpentine neck, and a long tail ending in a sharp spike. The wings were folded in close along the body. It had sharp claws for rending and tearing. One eye was wide open and staring at them through the thick wall of ice.

Joie let her breath out slowly. "That's no dinosaur."

"It has to be," Gabrielle said. "It can't be a dragon. Don't tell me it's a dragon." She glared at Traian. "There aren't vampires. You can't change your shape, and there aren't dragons. The air is bad down here and we're all having a mass hallucination. It can't be anything else."

"Is it real, Traian?" Jubal asked. There was awe, even reverence, in his voice.

"Yes. It is real. I had no idea it was down here."

"Do you think this is what the vampires are looking for?" Joie asked.

Traian shook his head. "They have no interest in the remains of a dragon. But this is definitely a cave the wizards used. I suspected as much. It could be a gold mine of information for our people. The wizards had incredible power and knowledge. It would be terrifying to think that the vampires might get hold of any of the power the wizards wielded. Do not touch anything. We must be very careful in here. The wizards used spells and traps to guard what belonged to them."

"That's what you meant when you said the bridge could be a trap. You thought the wizards had made it," Jubal said.

Gabrielle held up her hand. "We're talking about things found in fantasy books. Legends. Myths. There has never been evidence of dragons existing. Not even when dinosaurs roamed the earth." She reached out to touch her sister. "Joie? Are you certain of this? Certain of this man? He flies through the air. He changes into a wolf. He can talk to you telepathically. He takes your blood like a vampire would." There was pleading in her voice.

Traian pulled Joie closer to him. He was well aware of Gabrielle's influence on Joie. He could easily read his lifemate's mind, just as he could pick up the thoughts of her siblings. Joie loved her brother and sister and would willingly sacrifice her own happiness for them if need be.

Joie felt the possession in Traian's touch, felt the brush of his mind in hers. She smiled up at him in reassurance. At the same time, she reached for Gabrielle's hand. "The one thing that matters is family. And more than anything, we want each other to be happy," she explained to Traian. "I know what I'm doing, Gabrielle. You know I've always relied on my instincts. I know this is right. I don't understand any of it, but maybe I've been preparing for it all of my life. I fit with him. You're right, I don't know him yet, but I fit with him." She rubbed her face, smearing mud across it. "A one and only sort of thing. Silly, but true."

Jubal groaned. "Joie, I never thought you'd turn all mushy romantic on us."

Gabrielle exchanged a long look with Jubal and turned to Joie. "Well, I suppose your life with him will always be interesting."

"My sisters have already put gray in my hair. I won't survive Traian hanging around, howling at the moon, biting Joie's neck. And, just for the record, stay the hell away from mine, Traian. Having a woman bite my neck might be a turn-on—kinky, maybe, but I could handle it. Having a man bite my neck is out of the question. Doesn't do a thing for me," Jubal said dryly.

"Ouch. That hurts, Jubal," Traian said. "I was really looking forward to a snack later." He leaned down to brush the top of Joie's head with his chin. He had to touch her, keep reminding himself she was real. Even when they were speaking telepathically while he searched the complex of caves for whatever the vampires were frantic to find, he almost believed he had made her up.

Gabrielle managed a grin. "Well, he fits in with our weird family, Joie. I can't wait to see Mom and Dad's reaction."

"I need to seal this area off, slow the vampires down, and get all of you out of this cave," Traian said.

"I'm not so eager to leave," Joie responded, studying

the huge body of the dragon. "This is a treasure. There must be other fascinating things down here."

"You are being hunted," Traian said severely. "I am getting you out of here now. I will come back later and find whatever the vampires want so badly."

"When you're alone," Joie said.

"When I am alone," Traian confirmed. He urged them through the narrow hall. "You must not touch anything, no matter how inviting it appears," he added as a precaution.

Jubal glanced at Joie. "It isn't like you to agree to stay behind. Are you certain he doesn't have you under a spell?" He groaned. "That sounds so melodramatic and stupid. I can't believe I said it."

"I'm a professional, Jubal, and I don't need to make a point. This is his area of expertise, not mine."

The hall opened into a gallery. Tall columns in a Gothic style were carved into the walls. The high cathedral ceiling was impressive. Pillars of ice and crystal formed two rows down the room, each holding several round globes of varying colors. Joie peered into one of the largest, a milky blue natural sapphire. As she stared at it, the color deepened, darkened, began to swirl with alarming speed. Mesmerized, she moved closer. The ground beneath her tilted, rippled. She felt a pulling, a drawing as if the swirling sphere called to her.

Traian clapped his hand over her eyes and pulled her away from the globe. "Do not look at them. Gabrielle, come away from there." There was urgency in his normally calm tone. "Jubal, just pull her with you. I can feel the aura of power in all of these objects. Until we know what they are, we need to give them a wide berth."

Joie was stunned that she had been so quickly pulled into the globe's influence. "I thought wizards were supposed to be good."

"Absolute power corrupts. It is something one learns when one's life spans hundreds of years." Traian crowded close to Joie, keeping his body between her and the tall pillars.

Joie laughed. "Don't let Jubal or Gabrielle hear you say that. If you tell them you've been alive for a few hundred years, they might change their minds about us."

"I heard it already," Jubal said. He was pacing right behind Gabrielle, pushing her through the long, wide-open room. There were clear crystal sculptures of mythical creatures. Small, blood-red pyramids made of stone were set into chiseled-out archways in the walls. It was difficult not to stare at the gems and strange objects surrounding them, but Traian was obviously fearful of their safety, and they were ever conscious of the deadly creatures following them.

A deep boom shook the network of caverns. They stopped in the last one and stared at a solid wall in front of them. "There has to be a way out," Traian said. "Wizards were not able to shape-shift or fly. They were much as you are. There must be an opening leading to the surface."

"We have our gear," Joie pointed out. "We can use it to climb."

"Not with vampires so close on our heels. They will not need gear to climb. They can take to the air to pursue you. They hit the trap I set for them and were buried under a mudslide, but it will only slow them down. Look for something that does not feel right. There will be a hallway leading up to the entrance."

"Like the rocks outside the cave. The pattern was all wrong," Joie said. "Jubal, you're good at patterns. Find us the opening, and hurry. Jubal's rather infamous in our family for his mathematical mind," she told Traian.

"He can see a pattern in just about anything. That's how he makes all his money."

They could hear scratching, a terrible sound amplified by the acoustics of the cavernous room. Great claws scraping at the earth, digging to get at them. They spread out, walked along the wall, carefully examining every surface. All the while they could hear the vampires tunneling furiously through the mud and ice. The sounds grew louder, closer, and Traian dropped back, facing the wall where the creatures were certain to break through.

"I've got it!" Jubal said triumphantly. "We were expecting up, but it's down. The floor. See the pattern on the floor, Joie?"

"Open it," Traian said tersely, not looking, his attention centered completely on the far wall.

Jubal studied the squares, pyramids, and starburst patterns of stone beneath the layers of muddy ice. In the center of each symbol were hieroglyphics, pictures carved into each stone. He stepped on various ones, taking his time, choosing each stone carefully, following the pattern he could see laid out before him.

At last a large stone slid aside to reveal steps carved into the ice. Jubal hesitated. "Are you certain this is the way?"

"It has to be the way," Traian said. "Take your sisters and go."

Jubal was cautious, shining his light down the narrow staircase. The stairs appeared to be a bridge over a dark, fathomless abyss. "It's another bridge, Traian. Do I trust it?"

"You have to. It must have been their way out."

Jubal took a deep breath and stepped onto the first stair, found it solid, and reached back to aid Gabrielle. "Hurry, Joie."

"Come with us, Traian," Joie pleaded.

Water gushed in a dark, muddy stream from the side of the wall. Insects poured into the gallery. The wall to Traian's left collapsed in an oozing pool of dark sludge.

Two hideous creatures flopped onto the floor of the chamber, abominations in the crystal perfection of the room. Gaunt and cadaverous, they were covered in black muck. Baring their jagged, spiked teeth, they stared at Traian from red-rimmed eyes filled with venomous hatred.

Chapter Six

"Gabrielle, run," Joie urged. Fear clawed at her insides, but she dropped back to protect her sister and brother. "Jubal, go, don't look back." She would always stand between her brother and sister and danger. And she couldn't leave Traian. She wouldn't leave him. Not to face hideous monsters on his own. It didn't matter that he claimed to have hunted vampires all his life, she was incapable of abandoning anyone to face danger alone. And somehow, Traian was connected to her. A part of her blood and bones. Of her heart and soul. She would stand with him.

Jubal caught Gabrielle's hand and jerked her down the stairs in a race for their lives. Behind him, the thick slab of stone slid back into place, locking Joie in the cavern above them. She was grateful and relieved that her brother knew her well enough not to waste precious time arguing and that she could count on him to protect Gabrielle.

Both her knives were gone. Joie always carried two, but she'd used both, one on the vampire feeding on Traian, the other in the eye of the pool. She kept a distance from Traian, giving him room to fight. She could taste fear in her mouth. She had no gun, no knife. *My fourth dan black belt doesn't look too promising considering that those very nasty things have wicked-looking talons and mouths full of shark teeth. We could use a gun or two. Maybe a machine gun.*

Stay close to me. I want you where I can protect you. They can move the earth, rain down missiles from the ceiling. They will not fight in the way you expect. Traian had never really experienced gut-wrenching, bone-deep fear before. He had never had anything to lose. Now there was everything. A woman whose mind he walked in, whose body he didn't yet know intimately.

I gathered that.

For some reason her simple words made him relax, want to smile. Joie didn't panic easily. She didn't lack for courage and she was committed to fighting with him. She wasn't going to faint because vampires were real and had come with vengeance and death in mind.

Don't count on it. Her wry amusement told him she was a shadow in his mind, looking for strategy on how to defeat the enemy. *If they get their hands on me, I'll be trying to faint. Do they have a weakness?*

Ego.

Joie took a deep breath as the creatures slowly pulled themselves up to their impressive heights. Fire burned in their eyes. A foul stench permeated the cavern, choked off all the cool, clean air and replaced it with a thick putrid substance.

Which is the stronger?

Traian noted her calm manner. She accepted that they would have to fight their way clear. Having battled with the same vampires on three occasions, Traian was well aware of their strengths and capabilities. *The one with the incisors over his lower lip—he is extremely powerful. He is called Valenteen and is a master vampire. The other is called Shafe. There might be more, so stay very alert.*

Well, darn, and here I was expecting I'd take a nap.

Traian worked at keeping a straight face. Even in their desperate situation, Joie could let him know her feelings. *I was worried you might be.*

Joie tapped her foot. "If it isn't the troll brothers. How are you? Just dropped in to be neighborly? I'm so glad you didn't bother to dress formally. It's just a small get-together we're having." Deliberately she walked across the stone patterns in the floor, keeping their attention centered on her. "We're in the midst of redecorating. What do you think? Too many crystal balls?" She indicated the largest, nearly a foot tall, resting on a tall pillar of black obsidian. "They're very valuable. You can see your future in them. This one answers questions and finds objects." She reached out as if to pat the smooth sphere.

Joie was fully aware that Traian was keeping his body between her and the vampires. The two creatures stood in a swirl of steam and mist, coated in black ooze. The moment she mentioned the spheres, greedy eyes stared at the globe.

Surprisingly, Joie felt warmth along her palm as she positioned it above the crystal ball. The crystal had leapt to life at the close proximity of her hand. For a timeless moment, she saw her own face swirling in the mists of the globe, she saw Traian standing behind her, reaching for her, love etched into the lines of his face, hunger and desire burning in the depths of his eyes. She couldn't look away from him, from the intensity of his love. He couldn't feel that way about her, could he? He didn't know her. How could two people be so drawn to one another, recognize love so quickly?

Get away from that thing.

Joie blinked, looked up. The white swirls of mist were filling the cavern, consuming Traian. Consuming her. In the tendrils of fog, something moved. Something dark and menacing. She caught a glimpse of another shape in the shadows curled protectively around an object, but she couldn't make it out with the white mist and gray shadows merging together. A dark shadow loomed over Traian.

Watch out! She tackled him. Shoved him aside. Her momentum carried them both away from the vampires and close to the outer wall of the cavern. An array of weapons adorned the nearest alcove. Glittering gems decorated wicked-looking knives and long spears and swords. Here was a virtual treasure trove for Joie. She was drawn to the weapons, yet something held her back, some finely tuned warning system that prompted her to put her hands behind her back and ignore them.

Traian calmly regarded the black shadow that was emerging from the fog in the cavern. "Justice has come, Valenteen," he said to the master vampire. "A shadow warrior has been awakened and he is seeking our deaths. Do we fight each other?"

Valenteen growled harshly, shaking his head, backing away from the large, smoky creature emerging from the shadows.

Joie twisted her fingers in the back of Traian's shirt, peeking around him at the thing Traian had identified as a shadow warrior. It was insubstantial, made of ever-moving black and gray smoke. It's eyes glowed an eerie red, not like the bloodshot eyes of the vampires, but fierce flame burning brightly.

I wouldn't mind waking up now.

Traian reached behind him, circling her bare wrist with his fingers. Gently. Barely there. Just a whisper of contact, yet it was enough. They were together. It was all that mattered. He would shield her from the warrior, from the vampires.

Can you get out of here by yourself? It suddenly occurred to her that he could shape-shift, perhaps become as insubstantial as the mist. Maybe even burrow through earth and ice as the vampires had done.

The vampires dissolved, leaving behind a pool of black goo. It bubbled and spat a poisonous brew at the shadow warrior. Joie gasped. There was a strange silence. An icy blast of air cleared the stench from the chamber and pushed the smoky creature away from Traian and Joie.

It matters little if I could. I would never leave you behind.

His voice was reassuring. Calm. Steady. Confident.

Jubal and Gabrielle are still in the caves. Jubal will be hurrying to find his way up toward an entrance. He's a good caver, but if they go after him . . . My brother and sister can't protect themselves from the vampires.

Both vampires have remained in this room. They will not leave or move to give away their presence to the warrior. I do not sense any others close by. The shadow warrior has not attacked because we haven't touched anything. If we draw his attention to us, or take something the wizards left behind, he will strike.

Voices whispered. Filled the chamber with temptation. Before she knew what she was doing, Joie's fingers were nearly curled around a knife with a wicked-looking curved blade. It called to her. Her palm itched to feel the weapon in her hand. She clenched her fist, resisting the temptation. The voices increased in strength. She glanced toward the spheres, saw them all active, the clear colors swirling with life, with deeper hues and sparkling gems.

Traian caught both of her hands in his. *Talk to me. Tell me about yourself. Everything you can think of. Look only at me. Look into my eyes. See me. Only me.*

His hands were much larger than hers, enveloping them. When she obediently tore her gaze from the jeweled daggers and knives, she was caught in the black depths of Traian's gaze. The world narrowed for her.

Around them, smoke and mist drifted upward from the floor, creating a world in the clouds where voices muttered, the words in an ancient tongue, harsh, yet not foul, insistent, yet not commanding. Colors pulsed in the room, bright banners from the spheres, which were alive with heat and energy.

Look only at me, Traian reiterated when she would have turned her head toward the pulsing lights. *This is a trap. Think of me. Let me tell you who I am, what I am. What I need and want. I want to know everything about you and your family. Talk to me. Tell me who you really are, what you stand for. Tell me what you need and want.*

His voice was mesmerizing, tugging at her heart when she thought there should be only physical attraction. He was easily the sexiest man she'd ever encountered. They were in mortal danger. Vampires huddled somewhere in the room, awaiting their moment to strike. A warrior come to life out of the shadows guarded centuries-old treasures in a world of sorcery, yet Joie was fascinated by the man in front of her. *You don't make sense.*

I make perfect sense.

He smiled, a flash of dazzling white teeth. She nearly stopped breathing. *You know I work as a bodyguard.*

Silly profession, placing your precious body between someone else and danger.

She laughed softly in her mind. Traian felt the vibration pulse through his body, touch him in places he had long ago forgotten.

You spent several lifetimes chasing vampires. I'm catching very interesting memories in your mind, unless you spent all of your life watching Dracula movies. I think you've placed your precious and very sexy body between danger and people many times. And don't say you're a man and that it makes a difference. That would seriously annoy me.

Growls of hatred mixed with the insidious whispers. The smaller vampire, the one Traian had identified as Shafe, emerged from the black goo, hissing and spitting, dragging himself across the floor on his belly. His claws scored the stones as he tried to stop himself from answering the summons. His eyes were on the largest crystal ball.

Even with Traian's mesmerizing eyes and hypnotic voice, it was nearly impossible for Joie to ignore the drama being played out in the swirling mists of the cave. The voices were insistent, chanting a steady rhythm, drawing the vampire toward the glowing crystal. Greed and fear were on the face of the creature as it edged closer and closer. All the while, the dark shadow of the warrior, guardian of the wizard's treasures, watched dispassionately.

Joie shivered. Fear was a living, breathing entity nearly choking her. At times, through the rising mist coming off the stone floor, she could make out a suit of armor on the warrior; at other times it was as insubstantial as the clouds.

Traian pulled Joie into his arms, drawing her tightly against his chest. His movements were deliberately slow, careful, wary of drawing the warrior's attention to them. *We are going to float upward, Joie, just drift toward the ceiling above us.*

She was afraid. Battling human adversaries was one

thing; facing down vampires and warriors made up of smoke and shadow was something altogether different. She slid her palm up Traian's chest, the solid wall of flesh and blood reassuring her. Her arm curved around his neck. She locked her fingers there, fitting her body tightly against his. His much more masculine frame was hard like an oak tree. There was little give to the defined muscles beneath his skin. She felt her feet leave the ground and she closed her eyes, sending up a quick prayer.

Traian watched the warrior. Colored lights pulsed through the cavern, lit the mist so that wraithlike creatures appeared to be moving within it. Ghosts of the wizards, lost so long ago. He tightened his arms around Joie. She fit perfectly to him, her mind comfortable in his, drawing knowledge and studying tactics. He could feel her there inside him, sharing his memories and gathering information on his battles with vampires, fully prepared to join him should there be need.

More than anything else, he wanted her to know him as a man. He wanted time with her. He wanted to hear her laugh, to see warmth and acceptance in her eyes the way he had imagined during their long-distance chats. And he wanted her out of danger. Things were going to happen fast and ferociously. He focused on one thing. Getting Joie to safety.

They drifted higher in the cavern, and Traian clouded their image with more mist, more smoke, so that they seemed part of the haze. He took care that their movements were slow and lazy and as natural as possible, so that nothing would trigger the instincts of the warrior.

The shadow creature was motionless, even while the smoke that made up its body whirled and spun in dark threads. The fierce eyes remained fixed on the vampire crawling toward the temptation of the pulsing crystal orb. Shafe drew closer, closer, reaching out to the visions and promises of wealth and power swirling inside the globe.

Triumphantly the vampire placed his palms around the beckoning crystal. The moment he touched the globe, the shadow warrior threw back its head and roared. For a brief moment the smoke around it cleared. It stood tall and straight, dressed in glittering multihued scaled armor. And then it was smoke again, rushing across the wide expanse of floor, not quite touching the ground.

Valenteen, the older vampire, oozed from the black pool, shifting into the form of a snake. It slithered to the nearest wall and began to burrow through the earth. Joie strained to see below her, to see the shadow warrior as he reached the undead cupping the crystal ball.

Your light. Turn it off.

Her heart jumped. *We need the light.*

I see fine in the dark. We want to escape this chamber. I can take us through the air shaft and do not want to chance drawing the warrior's attention.

As she doused the light, Shafe screamed hideously. Colors glowed in the rising mist. A dark blood-red stain slowly began to invade the smoky fog. It spread like a virus. A violent clash of light and sound conjoined as the vampire's voice shrieked and wailed until Joie buried her face in Traian's neck.

She was trembling. His gut knotted. *We are almost out. Do not look. This is a trap and we will seal it up so no others can find it.*

You're thinking you'll come back tomorrow night and find out what the vampires were searching for.

I have to find out. I have been in these caves several weeks, fighting the vampires on and off. I destroyed more than one, yet they remained. That is highly unusual and it worries me. Worse still is the fact that Valenteen was not the only master. There was another in

*the group, Gallent. I was able, after several battles, to
destroy him, but he was clearly with this group. And I
sense another . . .*

Joie sighed and hugged him tighter. *This is not happy
news. Sounds like our gang problems. We'd better start
looking on the Internet for a site called vampires of the
world, unite.*

Above her head, he smiled. *It had not occurred to me
to check there, but if we find such a thing, are you
volunteering for undercover work?*

She made a small growling noise of dissent and bit
his shoulder hard.

The air shaft was narrow, but he angled their bodies
until they slipped through, taking them to the upper
levels. As soon as she felt the ground beneath her feet,
she turned on her light, caught his hand, and sprinted
through the tunnel toward the entrance.

"Valenteen is not following us. Although he is a master vampire, he will not attempt to fight me alone."

His words stopped her. Joie wanted to make sure that
Jubal and Gabrielle had made it to safety, but the idea
that a creature as hideous and lethal as a vampire
wouldn't fight Traian alone was frightening. What did
she know of him, after all? He was a voice speaking to
her in the night. A man who drank blood and shifted
shapes.

"I am a man of honor. A man who has found the
one woman. The only woman." He put a gentle hand
on her shoulder. "I know this happened too fast and
you do not altogether trust it."

"If I don't think about it, I trust it, and that scares
me, Traian. I'm not particularly a trusting person. All
this time I thought I was still in control after all, I did
rescue you. But now you're saying those creatures won't
attack you while they're alone."

"I am an ancient hunter. I have been tried in battle

for more years than I care to remember. I know the ways of the vampire and I am much skilled in what I do." There was no arrogance or bravado in his voice, only acceptance and truth.

"And these vampires?"

"Should not have been together. They should not be here, in the Carpathian Mountains, so close to our prince and many of our males. I was returning to my homeland when I first came across them. I knew they were desperate to find something in that cave. Although it was risky to pit myself against so many, it was my duty to my people to stay and discover what they were looking for. Even after you found me and I recognized who you were, I stayed because the vampires were so frantic to find something. I had no idea this was a cave of wizards."

"And what is the significance of wizards to a vampire? I know what it would be to humans. Most of us don't actually believe the fairy tales about wizards and crystal balls. And dragons. That was very cool, by the way."

"You saw the spheres in that room. Ancient spells and power remain in them. We don't want vampires, or anyone, for that matter, to get their hands on things best left alone. Carpathians are of the Earth. We have gifts, but we do not wield power in the same way as the wizards did."

"Is it possible some are still alive?"

"I would think it likely. At least I would think some of their descendants remain and have retained their knowledge, or at least a portion of it."

Joie sighed. "Lovely thought. Anyone who created that shadow warrior is not going to be counted among my best friends."

"Nor mine."

Joie followed him through the long hall, not looking

at the beauty and magnificence of her surroundings as she normally would. She turned the information over in her mind. "You grew up a long time ago."

He grinned at her, his teeth flashing in the light of her lantern. "Well, yes. I have lived for centuries. I barely remember my parents anymore." His smile slipped away. "The memory of my childhood days has faded. I catch glimpses at times. I do recall the years just before leaving my homeland. The way the prince looked at us all. I saw it in his eyes. His own death, the decline of our people, his dread for all of the warriors he was sending away from home. Our women were so few, even then the numbers were declining. Back then we had alliances with humans. Now we keep to ourselves and just do our best to blend in."

She listened to the sound of his voice and heard the sorrow that ran deep. In his mind she saw the battles, sometimes with childhood friends. Saw his inner demons, the insidious whispers of power, the dark stain that slowly spread over him, calling to him. And he was always alone. In every memory, he was always alone. Joie wanted to comfort him. She caught his hand, tangled her fingers with his. She meant it to be a brief gesture, but he tightened his grip.

"I grew up very differently," she said, ducking her head to avoid a large crystal formation. "My family is very close and very loving. We all talk at the same time and give each other all sorts of unwanted advice. My dad tells outrageous stories. He used to sneak into our bedroom at night with a flashlight shining on his face and tell scary stories until we screamed and laughed and Mom came running in to chastise him. We all knew she knew he was doing it, and she was really laughing, too. Once, after he read us Stephen King's *Cujo*, he put whipped cream on the muzzle of our huge mutt and shoved him into the bedroom. It's a wonder we all survived his sense of humor."

She laughed at the memory, deliberately sharing with Traian the warmth of her childhood, the love in her family. "We're all a little bit crazy, but it's okay with us."

"Do you think I will fit in?" He brought her hand to his chest and held it against his heart. "I would not mind having a family after all this time."

He was a tall man with wide shoulders and eyes that had seen far too much, yet the lost note in his voice turned her heart over. Joie smiled at him. "I can't wait for you to meet my mother."

Chapter Seven

The night air was crisp and clean and so fresh, Joie gratefully dragged it deep into her lungs. Fear was dissipating now that she was out in the open. She pulled her helmet from her head to allow the wind to comb through her hair. Stretching her arms toward the moon, she laughed softly. "I love the night. I love everything about it. It doesn't matter if its stormy or not."

She turned her head to look at Traian. His face was beautiful in the moonlight. "Worthy of a Greek god," she murmured, astonished that she *felt* so much for him, that her emotions were so strong and connected with his. His hair fell like black silk around his face to his shoulders. There wasn't so much as a smear of mud on his face. All traces of blood were gone from his chest, leaving only the raw gashes on his flesh.

Joie shook her head, stepping away from him, putting distance between them. She needed space, needed to find balance. "Thanks a lot for leaving me standing filthy and wet all by myself while you're all shined up and looking good. I'm not even going to ask how you did that."

His teeth gleamed at her, more the smile of a wolf than a man. "I have my little secrets. You are shivering. Hand me your pack and take this jacket." He enfolded her in the warmth of a suit jacket.

Joie decided not to ask him where he found the jacket either. "How did you find the way out? I couldn't see a thing." She sank down because all at once she was tired and she wanted to feel the ground under her. Traian had changed her entire life in the blink of an eye, and she didn't want to think too much about the bizarre world he lived in.

"There were signs if you knew what to look for. In the old times, Carpathians and Wizards were not enemies. We lived side by side and enjoyed the benefits of both races. We often used the same glyphs. I saw them as we moved through the halls." He crouched down beside her, touched her chin with gentle fingers. "Let me take you back to the inn where you are staying. You are tired and hungry and want a shower. You are also very worried about your brother and sister. You needn't be. I planted the symbols in your brother's mind to assure that they would find their way out quickly."

"Thank you, that was thoughtful of you. I was concerned, although both are experienced cavers. I just wanted them safe and away from vampires and traps. They'll be worried about me. I know Jubal hated leaving me behind, but he'll want to get Gabrielle back to safety as soon as possible. He'll take her straight to the inn." Joie swept a hand through her hair, pushing it back from her face. "I am tired, Traian. I feel as if I could sleep for a month."

He drew her to her feet, then simply lifted her, cradling her against his chest. Joie burst out laughing. "This is so medieval. Male carries little woman over mountain. Oh, the utter humiliation of it all." She wrapped her arms more tightly around his neck in case he thought to put her down. Joie allowed her head to drop back as she scanned the heavens. "If you ever tell a single soul I let you do this, I'll have to hurt you. I just want to be very clear on this."

Traian wanted to kiss her. More than anything, it seemed necessary to bend his head and find her mouth with his. Just taste her. Put in his claim. "What is your position on kissing?"

Joie stared up his mouth. The wicked, sinful temptation of it. "I'm thinking it over," she conceded. "If I let you kiss me, I'll melt on the spot. That's a given. I already know that, and it's so very humiliating. Worse than being carried around like I'm a fainting, weak bundle of femininity."

"True, but it would be worth it," he pointed out seriously.

She sighed and lifted her hand to his face, her fingertips tracing his sinful mouth. "Yes. But there's another consideration, Traian. You're going to be addicting. And then I won't be able to get you out of my system and I'll get all weepy when we have to part, and that's just more than I can bear, crying over some idiot man. Do you see the complications here?"

"Hmmm. I do see that might be a problem if we were ever to part, but since we are truly lifemates and have no choice but to be together, I do not really think it is of much importance. In fact, under the circumstances, being addicted to my kisses would be an asset." His strong teeth nipped her finger.

"The lifemate thing—see? That's part of the problem. I have this overwhelming need to be mistress of my own fate. I don't think I'm cut out to be a lifemate if it entails a *have to* sort of relationship. I'm a *want to* sort of woman. There is a difference."

"That is good, Joie. I do not foresee any problems whatsoever, because as we think so much alike. I am definitely a *want to* sort of man. And I want to kiss you."

There was a devilish smirk on his face, one she couldn't possibly resist. And who wanted to anyway? His mouth was descending toward hers, and Joie lifted her face to meet him halfway. Because this kiss was her choice, and he needed to know it.

Her lips were soft, yielding, welcoming even. After all the long centuries, Traian felt like he had come home. It didn't matter where they were, whose world they were in, she would always be home to him. The Earth stopped spinning, just as he knew it would. Bursts of starfire rained down around them. The embers smoldering deep in his belly burst into flame and raged through his bloodstream. His body knew her almost as intimately as his soul, though he hadn't even really touched her yet.

Joie couldn't think, couldn't breathe, forgot whether it was night or day. It was impossible to get her brain to function. She could only feel. Nothing had prepared her for the unrelenting pressure building so swiftly in her body, the heat rising, flames dancing along her skin, creating an inferno deep inside. Passion coiled tighter and tighter, a spring threatening to explode. Her breasts ached. Her fingers found the silk of his hair, crushed the thick mass in her palm. "You shouldn't be able to do this to me," she whispered into his mouth. Into his heart. "I don't let anyone inside."

"I am already inside you." His lips took hers again, over and over, long, drugging kisses that shook them both.

"It has to be the danger factor," she said. "It's the only logical explanation."

"Is there logic? I cannot remember." He couldn't get enough of her. Mud from her face smeared his. Her clothes were wet, soaking his. His wounds burned, but he couldn't feel the discomfort when his body was so heavy and hard with need.

His voice shook her. It was possessive. Husky. Perfect. A seduction in itself. It was Joie who pulled away, framing his face with her hands. She rested her forehead against his. "I need a minute here. I can't breathe, or think, or want anything but you."

His mouth curved into a smile. "Is that supposed to stop me?"

Her gray eyes studied every inch of his face. He could see her confusion. "Why do I feel like this? Does this make sense to you, Traian? I don't jump into relationships. All I can think about is having sex with you. Not just sex—wild, uninhibited sex."

His smile widened. "I think kissing you is the best idea I have ever had."

She couldn't help smiling back. He made her happy in a way she never had been. Complete when she hadn't known a part of her was missing. "Why you? You aren't even human."

"Your entire family has telepathic abilities. Are you certain *you* are human?"

Laughter spilled over. "Please don't ever ask my father that. He's outrageous, and he'll tell you some absolutely horrible and untrue tall tale, and we'll all be mortified."

The raw affection in her voice told him her father's outrageous stories never really mortified her and she loved the man very much. "That gives me hope. At least I know you plan on introducing me to your parents, but the list of dos and don'ts is growing." He bent his head to steal another kiss. "Hang on. I am about to take you flying."

She made a noise somewhere between laughter and strangling. "Has it occurred to you I might be afraid of flying?"

"You were engaged in astral projection the first time I laid eyes on you," he pointed out.

"I thought it was drug-induced," she admitted. "I'd been experimenting, but I didn't really believe I was actually accomplishing it. I thought I just sort of hypnotized myself. I would never have been so open with you had I thought you were real." Joie turned her face up to the sky, her head cradled on his shoulder.

"Then I am glad you thought you made me up. I think I will like your family very much. I have not had a family in so many years, the idea of one did not occur to me. Yet now, when I watch you with your brother and sister and feel the love you have for them, it makes me envious."

Her heart turned over at the longing in his voice. Joie had never thought she would feel so intensely about a man. The mere tone he used could make her shiver like the caress of fingers, or wrap around her heart like a fist. "I've never wanted to give myself to anyone, not wholly," she admitted, looking up at him. "Not all of me. I didn't want anyone to see inside me. But you already do, don't you?"

"Yes." Holding her close, protectively, he took to the air.

They soared across a night sky so dark it was nearly purple. A blanket of stars sparkled overhead. The few remaining storm clouds drifted rather than spun. Far below them the ground dropped away—mountains and valleys, forests and lakes hiding secrets best kept hidden for all time. A mixture of old and new.

Joie's breath caught in her throat. She was half terrified and half fascinated at the shape Traian had assumed. He had the enormous wings of a huge owl, yet human arms held her against the soft, feathered breast. The feathers tickled her skin, sent a shiver down her spine when she realized it was all too real.

Is this not better than thinking you are crazy?

The masculine amusement would have earned him a punch had they been on the ground. Sheer exhilaration was taking the place of fear. *I'm not certain I want you running around in my brain. It was perfectly natural to think I was hearing voices.*

Even when you are able to speak to your brother and sister telepathically?

That's entirely different. We've always been able to speak to one another, but not anyone else. We just thought it was a Sanders sort of thing. My mom and dad can do it too.

It could be considered arrogance to think that only your family was capable of telepathic communication.

Lights from the inn lit the ground below them. Traian dropped to earth some distance from the building, where the shadows were deep. Music spilled out of the two-story building, floating out in all directions. People mingled on the wraparound verandah and on most of the balconies, some dancing, some talking, and others pressed close to one another.

"The festival," Joie said. "I forgot about it. Look at me—I'm a mess."

"You look beautiful to me," Traian objected. "Which room is yours?"

"Second story, third balcony on the left." She grinned at him. "Are we floating?"

"Is the window locked?"

"That wouldn't stop me. I have second-story skills."

His eyebrow shot up. "I am very impressed. I am a

hunter and I am certain those skills could come in handy."

She narrowed her gaze, locking her fingers behind his neck. "They come in handy for a bodyguard. I do have a business, and I'm known to be one of the best."

"I'm sure you are." He took her into the sky fast, enjoying the way she clung to him, tightening her arms and gasping as he shot up.

Don't you laugh at me.

I'm not laughing.

I can feel you laughing. You know, it isn't normal to fly through the sky.

It is normal for me.

The balcony floor felt solid beneath her feet. She let go of his neck immediately. "Great, I *would* have to do this with a hundred people around."

"They cannot see you. I have shielded us from their eyes."

She glanced at him over her shoulder. "We're invisible? Sheesh. Is your life easy or what? I wouldn't mind being invisible in my line of work. No wonder those things are afraid of you."

"They fly, and they can cloak their presence as well."

Joie pushed open the door to her room. "How perfectly charming of them. Where do they come from?"

Traian followed her into the room. She heard his heavy sigh and turned around to face him. "I'm not going to like your answer."

"Vampires are Carpathians who have chosen to give up their souls for a brief moment of power, the thrill of the kill. Our males lose their emotions and the ability to see in color after the first two hundred years of existence. Some earlier, some later, but all of us eventually lose everything we hold sacred if we do not find a lifemate. Our race has few women and fewer children. We are on the verge of extinction. There is little hope, and more and more of our males are turning."

There was compassion in her eyes. "How terribly sad for all of you. So you and the other hunters are forced to police the vampires. Even if they were once boyhood friends . . . or family."

He nodded, astonished at the wealth of understanding he read in her expression. She clearly saw what others did not: deep below the surface, every destruction of a childhood friend or cousin had cut pieces out of his soul until he feared there was little left. Yet her understanding, the compassion washing over him, changed something. He felt it, felt the first healing touch and the power a lifemate wielded. She stood there in her filthy clothes with mud smeared all over her face, and she was beautiful to him. A lump the size of his fist rose in his throat, and he turned away from her, afraid of allowing her to see the emotion threatening to choke him. How could she possibly understand what she meant to him?

"I'm sorry, Traian. I know I can't begin to understand what it must have been like, but I feel the weight of it in your mind." More than that, she felt how alone he had been. The intensity of his pain shook her. His life had been stark. Ugly. Bleak. She caught frightening glimpses of scenes in his past. Terrible battles that lasted for hours. Severe injuries. Death all around him. No one to comfort him. No one to care.

Joie closed her eyes briefly, overwhelmed by longing, by the need to wrap her arms around him and just hold him. "I have to contact Jubal and Gabrielle. I can feel that they're close, so I'm certain they made it." When she picked up the phone to dial their rooms, her hand was trembling.

Traian waited while she talked to her siblings, assuring them she was fine and that she would meet them downstairs after she showered. She was instantly relaxed, laughing, her voice soft with love, firm with reassurance. He had forgotten so much. Just the tone of her voice brought back memories of his life before he left his homeland to answer the call of his prince.

Joie was uncomfortably aware of her appearance now that Traian was staring at her. "I need to take a shower."

"Is that an invitation?"

She stared at him, at the hard angles and planes of his face. At his dark, fathomless eyes. If the attraction between them was merely physical, Joie would have thrown him on the bed and ripped his clothes off right there. But he stirred unfamiliar feelings in her. Deep and frightening feelings for a woman in charge of her own destiny.

With indecision written so clearly on her face, Traian felt as if his world was balanced on the point of a needle. He was afraid to move. Afraid to speak. He knew their joining was inevitable. He would have her. She was his. She belonged to him. But he still wanted it to be her decision. He wanted her to want him in the same way he wanted her.

"It's a small shower stall," she said.

She put both hands behind her back and knew that she was afraid of the next step. But she took it because she was nothing if not courageous. She lifted her chin and smiled at him in invitation.

He didn't wait for her to come to him; he took the few steps separating them and swept her up into his arms.

Joie smiled at him. "This is becoming a habit."

Chapter Eight

Steam fogged the clear glass of the shower door, rose up to curl around the two bodies standing beneath the spray of hot water. Joie allowed the water to pour over her, drenching her hair and skin, washing the grime from her body. The shower stall was small, forcing her into close contact with Traian. She thought she was completely prepared for the sight of his very masculine body, but found she could barely breathe. He was all defined muscle, his chest wide, his hips narrow. She dared not look below his waist. The man had no modesty when it came to his desires. And he desired her.

"Are you going to keep scooting back every time I get close to you?"

There was a hint of amusement in his voice. His tone was like velvet, sliding over her exposed skin, setting every nerve ending on alert. Her mouth went dry. "It's the only safe thing to do. Before I actually met you, I thought about having you all to myself, alone and naked and . . ." She trailed off a little desperately. The erotic fantasies were wonderful when he wasn't standing in front of her, larger than life and still nearly a stranger. "Now I have absolutely no idea what I'm going to do with you."

"I distinctly remember you telling me you had lovers lined up," he said, his hands framing her face, his thumb tilting her chin so that her gaze met his. "What were you planning to do with all of *them?*"

There was a little bite to his voice and his white teeth came together with a definite snap. Joie tried not to let the sudden smile blossoming inside her show on her face. "You weren't real. I could say anything." It was impossible to look away from the dark intensity of his eyes, the hunger there. His emotions were as naked as his body. "I keep thinking this is happening too fast. I don't really know you. How did I end up bringing you to my room? Standing naked in the shower with you? I'm a private person, and not very trusting, yet here you are."

It was all he could do not to kiss her. Traian knew he could easily sweep aside her every objection. The attraction between them was mutual. Electric. All-consuming. She would respond to him with the same fierce need he had for her. "Joie." He whispered her name, an ache in his voice. "If you want to talk about this, I suggest we get out of the shower and put the width of the room between us. We have been in each other's minds for weeks. You know me. You know more about me than most people could learn in a lifetime. You know my character and what I stand for. And you know this is no passing fling. This is forever."

"Forever." She tasted the word. "That's a long time, Traian." The water poured over her body and steam encircled them as she leaned into him so that the tips of her breasts pressed against his chest. She felt him hard and thick and heavy with a man's need, a temptation and a pleading. "You're asking me to make a decision, the enormity of which I can't possibly comprehend. I love my family, Traian. I really love them and would never be happy without them."

He bent his head to hers. Close. His mouth was inches from hers. "I know what I am asking of you, and I know you have reservations about your family. I do not want to go back to an existence without you. Spend your life with me, Joie," Traian tempted softly. He feathered kisses down her face, over the corners of her mouth. His teeth tugged at her bottom lip. "Spend several lifetimes with me, an eternity. Be with me. Say you want me that much. Let me be part of your family."

She looked up at him, at the intensity burning in his eyes. It was so hot it branded her, seared her all the way to her heart. Joie felt the pull of his need, of his loneliness. He was a dangerous predator, not quite human. Powerful beyond anything she had ever dreamed of. And sexy. Heart-stoppingly sexy. Her arms were already sliding around his neck, her body molding itself to his. "Can we be together, Traian? How? Tell me how." Because she had been alone in the midst of a family she loved. Always surrounded by people, friends, family, she was always apart. She never knew why until she heard his voice. Something had been missing from deep inside her, some essential part of her.

"You can become as I am. Still Joie, still part of your family, but with the gifts and vulnerabilities of my race. Or I can age as you age. My strength will weaken and I will be more vulnerable to our enemies. It is your happiness that counts, Joie. I want to be in your life always."

Butterfly wings fluttered in the pit of her stomach. She felt she was on the edge of a great precipice. Joie tried to pull back before it was too late. The enormity of what he was offering was both frightening and exhilarating. He swamped her with his loneliness, with the intensity of her own feelings, so completely foreign to her. She tried to take refuge in humor. "I don't even know if you're good in bed."

"I want you to acknowledge to me that you know what I am offering you." His mouth skimmed over her face, tracing her high cheekbones, her chin, moved lower to find the pulse beating frantically in her neck. His warm breath bathed her in heat, a seductive temptation every bit as powerful as the feel of his body heavy with need.

She was in his mind, saw the choices clearly. His teeth sinking deep, making her his, bringing her into his world. Or Traian staying with her as if he were human, aging along with her, his great strength slowly fading, always vulnerable to enemies. Two choices. Two worlds. Only a heartbeat of time to choose.

She knew she needed to answer him, not because he demanded it, but because the intensity of her feeling for him was so strong, *she* needed to settle her future in her own mind. His teeth nipped her skin, his tongue swirled over the tiny ache. She felt the throb in her deepest core, the clenching of muscles aching for relief.

"Joie." He breathed her name again. "I will love you to the end of your days."

The water poured over her, heightening her sensitivity to pleasure. She heard the honesty in his voice. The purity. Joie tilted her head to the side to give him better access, closed her eyes in anticipation. She was certain. She might not understand why it was right, but she had never been surer.

His teeth sank deep. White-hot pain pierced her body, giving way instantly to sheer ecstasy. Lightning flashed in her bloodstream, hot whips of pleasure tormenting her. Heat welled up, threatened to consume her. She held him to her, closer, moving her body enticingly. It should have frightened her, the way he fed on her, devoured her with a hungry, craving lust more sexual than anything else.

Traian traced every line and curve, every hollow, etching her body in his memory, wanting the moment to last several lifetimes. The rush hit him hard, a sexual hunger mixed with a dark craving nearly uncontrollable. For centuries his appetite had been insatiable, a terrible hunger that could never be assuaged, but now her blood satisfied his inhuman need. But his sexuality remained unappeased. Hard and hot and heavy with desire. His tongue swept across the pinpricks on her skin. His lips traveled down to her breast. Ancient words beat in his head, words of a ritual imprinted on him before his birth. Once said, there was no going back. Traian and Joie would be bound for eternity.

The small sound escaping from her throat only urged him on. His tongue teased and danced over her taut nipple, caught the droplets of water as they beaded on her skin. "I claim you as my lifemate. I belong to you. I offer my life for you." His hands shaped her body, slid up to cup her breasts.

His face was dark, his gaze intent as he looked into her eyes. Joie felt a strange wrenching in the vicinity of her heart. A part of her tasted fear, wanted to cry out for him to stop, but another part embraced his words, understood the importance of each promise uttered. Her hands slipped over his chest, and she leaned forward to taste his skin, her teeth nipping his chest directly over his heart. She had never been a biter, but something urged her to sink her teeth deep, to connect them together. She swirled her tongue over his heavy muscles.

She was killing him. His body hurt, a hard, painful

ache; he was desperate for relief. "I give to you my protection, my allegiance, my heart, my soul, and my body. I take into my keeping the same that is yours. Your life, happiness and welfare will be cherished and placed above my own for all time. You are my lifemate, bound to me for all eternity and always in my care." The words spilled out of him, the Carpathian ritual marriage, as old as time. He felt thousands of tiny threads binding them together as they were meant to be joined.

He caught her chin in his hand, lifted her face to his, finding her lips almost blindly, wanting to devour her. She opened her mouth to him, melted into him. Traian caught her up in his arms, kissing her wildly, and carried her to the bed, cradling her in his lap so that his heavy erection pressed tightly against her buttocks. He whispered softly in his language, a strong command, even as his fingernail lengthened and he drew a line over his chest.

Joie kissed his throat, her lips drifting down his neck, unerringly finding his chest and the gash there. A hot flame burst inside him, a firestorm of emotion and sensation. The back of her head fit into his palm as he held her to him, encouraging her to make the exchange. Heat poured through his body. He burned for her, his body hard and painful with need, even as pleasure swept through him. Traian shifted, lowering Joie to the comforter, following her down so as not to break the connection between them. When he was certain she had taken enough for a true exchange, he whispered the command to halt and closed the wound himself. At once his mouth was on hers, stealing her breath, giving her his own.

Joie couldn't remember how she ended up beneath him, his hips wedged between her legs. His hands were everywhere, stroking, caressing, inciting. There wasn't an inch of her skin that he didn't explore. She heard her own strangled cry as his fingers sank deep inside her, felt her muscles clench tightly around him. Ready. Waiting. Desperate for his invasion. Her fingers caught at his hips, pulling him to her in a frantic attempt to find relief. She had never wanted or needed anything more than to feel his body deep inside hers.

Traian, certain she was ready for him, pinned her hips and thrust into her in one long, deep stroke. She gasped with pleasure, arched upward toward him, meeting him thrust for thrust. He cried out, unable to stay silent as he surged into her. She was a silken glide of fire and velvet as her feminine sheath gripped him tightly.

Joie clung to him, unable to do much more than hold on, lifting her body eagerly to meet his as he drove harder and deeper, merging them together in a fiery tango that she wanted to go on forever. They were skin to skin. Their hearts beat with the same wild rhythm. The air crackled with electricity, and sparks leapt from nerve ending to nerve ending. The pressure built and built until she thought she might have to scream with the joy exploding through her.

Then she felt him in her mind. Felt the sensations in his body, the gathering of a great force, much like a volcano. Hot. Thick. An inferno of desire and hunger mixed with intense emotion and pure lust. He filled her with flames and heat, an outpouring of pressure building from his toes to the top of his head. At the same time, he felt her every reaction, the waves of pleasure swamping her, racing to overtake them both, consume them completely.

Joie cried his name, clutched his body tightly as they went over the cliff together, free-falling through space in wild exhilaration. She couldn't catch her breath; her heart was pounding out of control. "I think I see fireworks," she whispered into his chest.

He laughed softly. "I think we produced the fireworks." He lay over her, his body pinning hers, locked tightly inside her while he kissed her slowly. Thoroughly. Leisurely. Savoring her. "Thank you for finding me, Joie."

"My pleasure, Traian," she answered. He was moving yet not moving, and each small shift sent ripples of aftershocks through her entire body. "I can hear our hearts beating. Really hear them, like pounding drums. And I can hear the blood moving through your veins. Is that normal? Because if it is, eww, ick, and yuck."

He laughed softly, the sound vibrating through her entire body so that her muscles gripped even more tightly around him. "Think about turning the volume down. Our minds are very powerful. You can control the volume with a thought." His teeth tugged at her lower lip. "Think about it and you can hear a pin drop in the next room. But if you want quiet, you simply turn the volume down."

"I don't feel that much different inside. I thought I would notice changes."

"You haven't gone through a conversion, Joie. It takes three blood exchanges. We have only exchanged one time." He caught her firmly in his arms and rolled, taking her with him, so that she was straddling him.

He filled her completely, still hard and thick so that every movement sent pleasure dancing through her body. His hands cupped her breasts. "I want to look at you. I still have a difficult time believing I actually found you. That I am with you."

Deliberately Joie moved, a long, slow glide up and down as if riding a thick pole. She felt him shudder with pleasure and arched back, pushing her breasts into his hands, getting a better angle to take more of him deep inside her. "Why are you waiting?"

He watched himself, slick and wet from her body. "I

want to give your body time to adjust to the changes."
It was difficult to get the words out, difficult to have a
coherent thought when she was gripping him so
strongly with her muscles, riding him harder and faster
with long, deep strokes. Fire licked at his belly, flames
erupted over his skin until the heat rushed to one central
spot, collected there, and raged out of control.

He let the sexual ecstasy wash over him, through him,
take possession of him, all the while watching the glide
of her body, the way her muscles moved beneath her
skin, the way her breasts pushed into his palms and her
nipples teased and tempted him. The sheer enjoyment
on her face. Her thoughts, completely taken up with
giving them both pleasure, were enough to send him
over the edge. He picked up the rhythm, thrusting upward, driving into her as she came down over him. Each
stroke took his breath, took his heart. Her body caressed his. Was wet and hot and tight. Brought him to
the brink and left him wanting more. He felt her muscles contract, grip, squeeze, and grip until they both
went up in flames together.

Joie lay beside him, unable to move, wanting to laugh
with joy. Her fingers found his, tangled, and held on.
She believed in living life to the fullest, but she had
always thought she would do so alone. For the first time
in her life, she felt complete and utter satisfaction. Complete and utter peace.

"I feel exactly the same way," Traian said. "I cannot
help wondering—if you had been the Carpathian and I
the human with a beloved family, would I have been as
trusting as you have been? You cannot know what your
faith and trust mean to me."

Joie turned her head, a mischievous grin on her face.
"I decided I liked flying and the shape-shifting would
be cool. And if you do something so silly as to cheat

on me or run off with someone else, I'm very good with a knife."

He raised an eyebrow. "I thought you would be worried about giving up food. It does smell good. I have even sampled some from time to time."

"No one said anything about giving up food." She eyed him with suspicion. "There are certain things women can't do without, Traian. Chocolate at certain times of the month is essential to health. Not necessarily my health, but the health of all males in the vicinity. I'm not giving up chocolate, not even for great sex."

He propped himself up on one elbow, the pad of his finger tracing a circle around her breast. "Chocolate is that important, is it?"

"Essential. Absolutely essential. That's nonnegotiable."

"What kind of chocolate must you have?"

"Dark chocolate, of course. Is there any other kind?"

He dipped his head to pull her breast into his mouth, suckling strongly just to feel her reaction. His tongue swirled over her nipple before he kissed her. His kiss was long and slow and thorough. When he lifted his head, he laughed softly at her expression. She stared up at him, bemused, one hand touching her lips in wonder where the taste of dark chocolate melting in her mouth was very real.

"How did you do that?"

"You need and I provide—that is how it works. I believe you wanted to see your brother and sister tonight."

She allowed him to pull her up. "Anytime? You can do that anytime? Wow. I think I'm going to like this lifemate business."

Traian laughed, hardly able to believe the happiness blossoming inside him. Hardly daring to believe Joie was real.

Chapter Nine

Joie stood in the doorway of the lounge, her gaze scanning the crowd as she always did, getting a feel for the throng, picking out the ones most likely to cause trouble and the ones who might be interested in more than they should. She noted a tall, dark-haired man in the corner who looked up when she walked in with Traian. He quickly glanced away from them, taking a sudden interest in his drink, but she could tell he was watching them carefully. A second man drew her interest. He sat in one of the high-backed chairs near the fire, a newspaper in his hands. He was short and slender and wore reading glasses. He was looking over the top of the thick rims at Gabrielle.

Jubal turned and waved to Joie. Gabrielle looked up, gave a glad cry, and rushed toward her. Joie prepared herself to be practically bowled over as her sister embraced her, hugging her joyfully. Over Gabrielle's shoulder, she noted the man in the glasses looking past her to Traian. Recognition flickered across his face, and he carefully folded the newspaper and laid it on the small table in front of him before rising.

Traian, Joie warned. She set Gabrielle gently to her side and just a little behind her.

Traian scanned the room, was slightly shocked when he realized the slender man was human yet seemed to recognize who and what Traian was. Moreover, he was expecting Traian, had come to the inn in the hope of finding him. Traian noted with amusement that Joie had tried to position her body between him and the stranger. The rush of joy and affection, a lightening of his heart and soul, made him tremble. He couldn't remember if anyone in his long lifetime had worried about him or tried to protect him. That small gesture meant the world to him.

Behind it was her faith in him. She'd made a leap of faith, committing herself to his life, his world. She believed he wanted her happiness above his own, and she wanted to give him happiness. He had a mad desire to scoop her up and run back to her room, where he could make love to her all over again. He looked at her, allowed the thought to shimmer in his mind, to glow hot in his eyes.

Joie laughed. "Stop that."

Gabrielle looked from her sister to Traian and made a rude noise. "Oh, no. Joie, we leave you alone with him for a few minutes and you seduced him, didn't you?"

Joie shrugged unrepentantly. "You have to admit, he's pretty hot."

"I'm telling Mom."

"Well, you tattletale, if you say one word to Mom, I'm going to tell her you were thinking of taking that job researching the Ebola virus. You know what she'll do when she hears that."

"You wouldn't dare," Gabrielle said. She pushed at Joie's shoulder as the slender stranger approached, trying unsuccessfully to move her sister aside for a better look. "Now that is a hottie, Joie. There's more to a man than muscle." She grinned at Traian. "No offense or anything."

"None taken," he assured her.

"Your tongue is hanging out, Gabrielle," Joie whispered. "Stop ogling him. For you to be falling at his feet, he must have an IQ of two hundred." She glanced up at Traian. "No man she's ever looked at could carry on a normal conversation. I think she can see straight through to their brains." She nudged her sister. "Your eyes are popping out of your head."

"I was just looking," Gabrielle hissed back. "At least I didn't throw myself at him and show off by doing in underfed trolls fresh out of the grave."

"I was happy she did that," Traian pointed out.

"Yes, well, I suppose you would have been, under the circumstances," Gabrielle conceded. "But she has a major hickey on her neck. If Mom saw that, there'd be consequences."

Traian bared his strong white teeth at her. "I think I can handle your mother."

Gabrielle and Joie looked at each other and burst out laughing. "It isn't possible, Traian, even for you," Joie said.

The slender man stopped in front of them and held out his hand to Traian, although Joie noticed that his gaze continually shifted to Gabrielle. "I'm Gary Jansen. Mikhail Dubrinsky sent me. He asked me to convey his apologies, but unforeseen circumstances prevented him from coming himself. Should there be need, he asked that you put out a call to him and he will send Falcon.

Mikhail's brother is in Italy at this time, so I was sent to gather the information and aid you in any way I can."

Traian gripped Gary's hand firmly. "I am Traian Trigovise. This is my lifemate, Joie Sanders, and her sister, Gabrielle. I trust the prince and his lifemate are well?"

"Raven has been ill," Gary said briefly.

Traian caught the echo of Gary's thought. *Miscarriage.* Joie slipped her hand into his, an offer of condolence that betrayed the fact she'd been a silent shadow in his mind. She might not understand the importance of the news, but she could feel his sorrow. "We need to speak somewhere quiet," Traian said. "I have news the prince must hear."

Jubal joined them, slipping an arm around his two sisters and waiting to be introduced. Traian did so as they followed Gary from the lounge to the comparative quiet of his room.

"Nice," Jubal commented. "We're on the second story with small balconies. This is great." He looked out the double doors to the spacious verandah. "Joie, we should have asked for the ground floor."

A dull red swept under Gary's skin, and he glanced at Gabrielle as he hastily cleared clothes from a chair. "Sorry about the mess."

Gabrielle smiled at him. "You should see my room. We were in a cave, and our clothes were filthy. All I could think about was taking a hot shower." She blushed for no reason, turning away from Gary to study the verandah Jubal seemed so interested in.

"Mikhail wanted me to ask you why you did not simply give him the information when you requested that someone join you here," Gary said.

"Had I used the common telepathic link, the undead would have heard what I had to say," Traian said. "I have never exchanged blood with the prince and do not have a private telepathic link. It was better to keep my news confidential."

Gary nodded toward the Sander siblings. "Forgive me for asking, but you are certain everyone in this room can be trusted?"

"I am more certain of them than I am of you," Traian answered.

Gary smiled, relaxing for the first time. "That's good enough for me. I can give Mikhail your news, although he asked me to have you return home as soon as you are able. He has called in the ancients his father sent out. He needs their knowledge to make informed decisions in the ongoing war with the undead."

"Where is his second? I fear the life of our prince is in danger. I do not like the fact that the undead dare to gather so close to our homeland."

"Gregori is in the United States but will be returning soon. Falcon and Jacques stay close to the prince."

"There are many undiscovered caves in these mountains," Traian said. "I went to ground in one of them and came across several vampires. They were hunting something beneath the earth and they were so frantic to find it, they began to hunt me, instead of avoiding me as would be usual. We had several battles. I destroyed two of them, although more than one master vampire travels with them and they are extremely powerful. I was severely wounded after one of the battles, and they found my resting place. Instead of killing me, they decided to use my blood so they could continue searching. Joie and her brother and sister found us. Joie killed one of the vampires."

"Sort of," Joie corrected when Gary looked at her with admiration. "The darn thing fried my favorite knife. Traian had to incinerate it before it was really gone." *He isn't like you, Traian. He's human.*

Few humans are trusted with the knowledge he has

of our people. He must be much respected for Mikhail to send him to me.

"Vampires are very difficult to kill," Gary said, "and with even one master vampire in the vicinity, it is too dangerous to engage in battle." He rubbed the bridge of his nose. "I'm a biochemist, not a hunter, but I've seen the results of what the vampire can do to humans. It's terrifying."

Gabrielle shuddered visibly. "I think Joie was having fun down there in the cave, but all I wanted to do was hide under the bed. And I kept thinking about viruses and touching all those microorganisms down there." She made a face. "I think I'll leave vampire hunting to the experts. If I never see or hear of another one, I'll be happy."

Joie grinned at her. "And here I was planning on making it my new career."

"That's not funny, Joie," Jubal said. "What you do is bad enough. You give us all gray hair. You stay away from those things."

"How did you get involved with all of this?" Gabrielle asked Gary curiously.

He looked sheepish. "I actually developed a compound to paralyze the system of Carpathians, thinking, of course, they were vampires. The compound was twisted into a poison and used to torture and dissect whomever the human society of vampire hunters deemed one of the undead. When I tried to expose them and rescue one of their victims, I met Gregori." He shrugged his shoulders. "I can't describe Gregori or what meeting him was like, but it changed my life. The society would like to see me dead, so as a protection, Gregori brought me here to help with research. I like it here and have developed strong friendships, so I stay."

Who is Gregori? There was so much respect in Gary's voice, Joie was curious.

He is second to the prince. A great hunter and healer. He is lifemate to the daughter of the prince.

Joie looked up at Traian. "I can see the Carpathians have a complex society. Why didn't we know of its existence until now?"

"We take great care to blend in to the human world. It has been our way for centuries and has worked well for us. Unfortunately, our race is on the verge of extinction." Traian gathered Joie to him. "Without lifemates, we will not survive."

"Lifemates?" Jubal echoed.

"We mate for life. Once a male finds the woman who is his other half, he binds her to him, as you do with a marriage ceremony. If she is a human and does not live fully in our world, it can be very difficult. Lifemates cannot be parted for long periods of time. We have a strong telepathic link and must touch each other's minds frequently or one begins to grieve for the other. As Carpathians cannot walk fully in the human world, it is usually best for the human to walk in our world," Traian explained.

Jubal and Gabrielle exchanged a long, apprehensive look. "What exactly does that entail?"

"Jubal—" Joie protested.

"No, Joie, I want to know what he's talking about." Jubal didn't look at his sister but rather at Traian. Man to man. Expecting an answer. Demanding one.

"Joie has consented to come fully into my world, Jubal," Traian said, his voice low and without inflection. "I will protect her and watch over her and see to her happiness at all times. The conversion will not take her from your family. She would never be happy apart from you. I hope you and your sister and your parents will be able to accept me into your world, your family, the way I know my people will accept Joie into mine."

Jubal swore softly and turned away from them to

stare out into the night. "Joie, did you think this through? Do you know what he's asking of you?"

Joie went to her brother, put her arms around him. "I've never felt as if I truly belonged, Jubal. I accepted that I was different, and yes, I've been happy because I like the work I do and I love my family dearly, but I want more than that. Traian offered me more, and I grabbed the opportunity with both hands."

"Do you hear what he's saying to you? This isn't like a human marriage, Joie, where you can walk away if things don't work out."

Traian stood beside Joie, his fingers laced with hers. "Lifemates not only want to be together, Jubal, they need to be. They find a way to work things out. A male Carpathian knows what makes his lifemate happy and does everything within his power to do it for her. And it works both ways. We always have telepathic communication open to us, so, in a sense, we are used to living in each other's heads. I know that is a big adjustment to make, and I am doing my best to give Joie as much space as she needs. But she is already learning quickly."

"It's what I want, Jubal," Joie said. "Be happy for me."

"I know you, Joie. You aren't going to be satisfied sitting on the sidelines while vampires are hanging around. You're going to go save the world."

Joie couldn't lie to her brother. "Probably. On the other hand, I have no intention of giving up my business. I thought Traian might work with me."

"This is where it is necessary for you to have faith in me, Jubal," Traian said. "I cannot allow anything to happen to Joie."

Jubal laughed without humor. "You don't know Joie if you think you're going to be protecting her. More than likely, it will be the other way around."

"Forgive me for butting in, but I've been around the Carpathian race for some time now," Gary said. "Traian is an ancient Carpathian male. He is far more powerful than you can imagine. They do not allow their women to come to any harm."

"But then you haven't met someone like Joie before," Jubal pointed out. "She's the guardian of the world."

"Stop picking on me, Jubal. At least I go after people, not little organisms that you can't see and can't do anything about."

"Hey now," Gabrielle objected, "don't turn the spotlight on me."

A small smile curved Traian's mouth. "I think you are misjudging me because of our first meeting, when I was being held prisoner. I have survived countless battles with the undead, Jubal. A master vampire is every bit as powerful as our greatest hunter." He looked at Gary. "Mikhail should know they are traveling in packs, and I have heard disturbing rumors that they are planning something. I also believe it is important to discover whatever it is they are seeking. Vampires always seek power. They would never waste time working the way they are unless it resulted in more power."

Gary nodded. "I'll tell him."

"I'll be returning to the cave just before sundown tomorrow. I hope to surprise them before they rise. In any case, I will do my best to discover what they seek."

"Why just before sundown?" Jubal asked curiously.

"I am weak and vulnerable while the sun is high," Traian admitted without hesitation. "The vampire is also at his most vulnerable. If I rise before them, I may be able to destroy them before they regain their strength."

"Well, of course I'm going with you," Joie said.

Traian brought her fingertips to his lips, breathed warm air over her hand. "I can travel faster on my own,

Joie. And you have not yet learned to prevent them from reading your mind. I would be at risk because of your unguarded thoughts."

Joie's gaze flickered to Gary. The man nodded. "They are adept at reading our thoughts and even controlling us. Traian can go in without their being aware of his presence, but they would know the moment you were near."

Joie frowned. "I don't like the idea of you going in alone. There are several of them, and you've admitted there's more than one master vampire. I might be able to help. Could you block them from reading my thoughts?"

"Probably, but the more tasks I have to perform, the more energy I expend. I have to go in fast and hard and get out the same way."

Jubal immediately stepped to his sister's side. "What if we were nearby, waiting just in case you run into trouble?" he suggested.

Gabrielle nodded. "I think that would be best, Traian. We might not be able to incinerate the things, but we can slow them down for you."

Traian looked at the three of them. Family. Solidarity. Jubal and Gabrielle might not agree with Joie's choice. They might be afraid for her. But when it counted, they stood with her. He bent his head and kissed Joie right in front of them. It was that or humiliate himself with tears shimmering in his eyes. As it was, a lump threatened to choke him. "Thank you for letting me be a part of your family, Joie. They are wonderful." He looked at Jubal. "I appreciate the offer, but it is safer for me if you are here, a distance away where the undead cannot perceive a threat to them. Should I have need, I will contact Joie immediately." He looked at Gary over their heads, and the prince's messenger nodded carefully. He would watch over Traian's lifemate and family. A matter of honor in the Carpathian world.

Chapter Ten

Joie was dreaming of a hot, moist mouth pulling strongly at her breast, of hands stroking her body. Of lips traveling down her bare skin to her navel, swirling kisses and teasing bites over her stomach. Hands on her thighs tugging her legs apart. She was already damp with invitation.

She opened her eyes as the waves of sensation burst through her like a gift. The wealth of Traian's silky dark hair slid over her skin, the sight more erotic than she had ever imagined. His fingers moved inside her, found secret ways to shimmer fire through her veins. And then his tongue took the place of his hands, stabbing deep, tasting and teasing and stroking her until she was crying with joy and her body no longer belonged to her. Wave after wave, orgasm after orgasm rippled through her body, so that she bucked and jumped as he held her firmly, his mouth devouring her, claiming her, feeding her sheer pleasure.

She clenched her fists in his hair, holding on while she took the wild ride, while the earth moved and her body shattered into fragments. He took possession of her then, kneeling above her, dragging her hips to him, thrusting deep with powerful strokes while she came over and over in a mind-numbing climax that seemed endless. He was everywhere, in her body, in her mind, their hearts beating in the same rhythm. She could feel the intensity of his emotions, a tidal wave of longing and love, of absolute need and hunger, of caring and loyalty, far more than she could understand, but real all the same.

Joie clung to him as his body rode out the storm of roiling emotions, each thrust deeper and harder in a fierce, possessive joining. Thunder roared in his ears, lightning sang in his blood, fire raged in his belly until the conflagration merged together at the core of his body. Her feminine sheath was fiery hot, tight and velvet soft, the friction an unbelievable sensation. He tilted her hips, wanting her to take all of him, wanting to crawl inside her body, his home, his sanctuary after several lifetimes of loneliness. He wanted to give her the world, wanted her body to feel the same flames of passion and pleasure as she ignited in him.

He felt her muscles clench around him, the gathering of a great force. He threw back his head, allowed his body to explode with volcanic intensity, thrusting deep, taking her with him, holding her close as they burst into sunlight, the only time he could ever embrace such a thing. His shifted her in his arms, pressed her body to the length of his. "Never go away," he whispered in her ear. "Never leave me to face the endless years alone."

Joie caught his face between her hands, brushed back

the long silk of her hair, and stared up at him. At the lines etched into his beautiful masculine features, put there by battles and years of knowledge of foul things walking the Earth. Put there by sheer loneliness. "I want you always, Traian. We'll find our way together."

He leaned toward her, kissing her gently, with exquisite tenderness, with the overwhelming love in his heart that he couldn't quite put into words but tried to show by worshiping her with his body. He kissed her over and over, long, drugging kisses, his body locked deep inside hers, his hands tunneling in her hair. His mouth roamed over her throat, down to her breast, found her heart unerringly.

Joie felt the swirl of his tongue, and her heart leapt in anticipation. Her body tightened around his. White-hot pain lanced through her, gave way immediately to pleasure. She cradled his head to her while he fed, while his body moved slowly and erotically deep within her. The sensation was unlike anything she'd ever experienced. She writhed helplessly beneath him, arching her hips up to meet him, her breasts aching and full with need. When his hand cupped the weight of one breast, his thumb sliding over the taut peak of her nipple, she pressed his head closer to her, offering more.

Traian swept his tongue across the pinpricks, tasted the temptation of her breast before finding her mouth to share the taste of their life's essence. He took his time, his tongue thoroughly exploring her mouth, teasing and dancing and mating with hers. "Come into my world, Joie. Another step closer."

This time she was locked in a dreamy haze, aware of his body's sensations as she moved restlessly, wantonly under him. As her mouth moved against his chest, taking his precious gift, his fingers stroked her throat, her breast. His body thickened inside her, moved with greater force and purpose. She felt the flames, hot and white and pure, burning in his veins, pulsing through him.

She should have been horrified, but she wasn't. She was overjoyed to be able to bring him such pleasure, so much happiness. She wanted to be fully in his world and she wanted so much more. She moved more aggressively until he was surging into her with strength and power, until she felt the gathering of every nerve ending, every muscle and the flow of blood, until they soared together higher than ever. *I want more time with you. I want to touch your body and know it the way you know mine. I want to see the things you've seen and make you feel the way you've made me feel.*

"We have time," he said. "All the things you fantasize about, all the things that matter to you—we have time for everything." Very gently he stopped her feeding, closing the wound in his chest. He laid her on the bed, his hands gentle, loving, stroking her bare skin while he brought her fully out of the enthrallment. "I have to go, Joie. We've slept all day, and it's almost sunset. I have to find the master vampire before he rises."

"Do you have an idea where to look?" She traced his face, his mouth with her fingertips.

"I hope he did not leave the cave. They were so reluctant to leave it before, but we had not discovered the wizard's traps. It is a dangerous place to be, even for the undead. Maybe especially for the undead."

"Promise me that you'll contact me if you run into any trouble." She looked him straight in the eye, insisting on the truth.

"You are my lifemate, Joie. If I run into trouble, you will know." He bent his head to kiss her. Slowly. Lingering over it. Pouring his heart and soul into it.

Just that fast, Traian was gone. Joie lay on the sheets, staring up at the ceiling, her heart pounding in fear. He was gone, slipping out through the window, a cloud of vapor streaming into the air. It wasn't yet sunset, but she felt as if the sun had gone down on her world.

It is only the effects of our connection. I am with you. Feel with your mind as a Carpathian must. It takes time to learn our ways, I know, but I cannot have you suffering grief when I am alive and well and able to reach out to you.

Determined to combat her sorrow, Joie sat up. *It is amazing how strong the feeling is. And it is a little frightening to think that emotion is stronger than logic. I know where you are, yet I still have such a need to touch you. It makes no sense.* And it didn't. Joie considered herself a very logical woman. She didn't like this out-of-control feeling, a dark dread that stole her good sense and her ability to reason. She lifted her chin. There were changes taking place in her body and mind, but that didn't mean she would give in to melancholy. *I'll be perfectly fine, Traian. You worry about yourself. I'll hang with Jubal and Gabrielle while you're gone.*

And Gary. He knows both the undead and my people. Stay close to him.

Joie did the mental equivalent of rolling her eyes. *As if. Traian, you're going to have to get over your outdated attitude toward women. It must be your age. That man needs protection. He lives in another world, just like Gabrielle. I can see it in him. He's more at home in a lab than fighting vampires.*

But he knows vampires. Stay close to him.

You might have mentioned your archaic attitude and your stubbornness when you were being so blasted charming this morning.

His soft laughter echoed through her head, and then he slipped out of her mind, leaving her feeling bereft. Determined not to give in to the strange reaction to their separation, Joie took a long, hot shower. It was nearly impossible to stand beneath the cascading water without thinking of Traian, but she concentrated on figuring out how to tell her parents that she was essentially married.

Gabrielle stuck her head in the bathroom. "Hurry up! Jubal and I are getting tired of waiting for you two. And you'd better not be doing anything perverted in that tiny little shower stall." She sounded more hopeful than anything else.

"How did you get into my room, you peeping Tom?" Joie threw a wet washcloth with deadly accuracy. "It was locked."

Gabrielle squealed when the cloth hit her square in the face. "I'm picking up your bad habits. Are you in there alone? Because I don't want to see any naked bodies."

"Traian already went back to the cave."

"If he wasn't so drop-dead gorgeous, I'd be afraid he was a troll, he likes to be underground so much. What are you going to tell Mom and Dad?" This time there was glee in Gabrielle's voice.

"I've been rehearsing," Joie admitted. She emerged from the stall, wrapped in a bath sheet. "It has occurred to me to lie to them. And I thought you preferred skinny men. I saw you ogling Gary last night."

"I don't ogle," Gabrielle sniffed indignantly. "I *never* ogle. I just thought he was rather on the cute side." She sighed heavily. "Oh, to be model-thin and beautiful."

Joie glared at her. "You are beautiful, you idiot. You're just crazy. Is Jubal hanging out in the bedroom, because I need my clothes."

"I'll get you something presentable." Gabrielle disappeared.

Joie heard her giggle. Gabrielle never did anything so undignified as to giggle. Unashamed, Joie found she could hear just by consciously thinking about it. Gary had joined her brother and sister in her bedroom.

Joie stalked to the door. "Hello! I hate to remind you all, but I'm stuck here, naked in the bathroom. Vacate or toss me some clothes."

Jubal groaned. "You are so sick, Joie. I didn't need that visual. Gary, you ought to try having a couple of sisters bent on tormenting you. They gang up on me like you wouldn't believe."

Gabrielle blew him a kiss. "We keep your life from being extraordinarily dull and boring."

Joie caught the bundle of clothes her sister tossed inside the bathroom. "Thanks for remembering me."

"I remembered. It just didn't seem all that important."

Gary stood up when Joie entered the room. "Traian left already, I take it? I figured he'd rise as early as possible. There were clouds blocking the sunlight. They sometimes arrange the weather to protect their sensitive eyes." He smiled at Joie. "He wants me to get you to drink some juice this evening."

Joie pressed a hand to her stomach. "I don't think that's going to happen, but I'm sure Gabrielle and Jubal are hungry."

"Starved," Jubal agreed instantly. "I thought Joie was going to sleep forever."

"You'll get used to the different hours they keep," Gary said. "I work in the lab and forget the time myself. If I'm on to something promising, I don't seem to need sleep."

"I'm the same way," Gabrielle said. "Sometimes I look up and it's two days later." She exchanged a long smile of complete understanding with Gary.

Jubal threw his hands into the air. "It's getting a bit thick in here. I'm for food. Come on, Joie. Whether you're hungry or not, we need to stick together."

They waited while Joie found her calf scabbard and

strapped it to her leg. Gary raised an eyebrow, but Gabrielle just shrugged, her grin sheepish. They were used to Joie, and she was nearly always armed with something lethal.

Joie was aware of the exact moment the sun set. She didn't see the orange and red hues, but in the midst of the laughing conversation going on around her she simply knew. She felt the sudden shuddering of the earth as the vampires rose. Her heart leapt in fear. *Traian!* She reached out to him. Touched him. Felt his immediate reassurance. He had not discovered the resting places of the vampires. They had not gone to ground in the cave of the wizards.

"Joie?" Gabrielle touched her hand. "Are you all right?"

Joie looked across the table at her and managed a smile. "I just wish I was with him." She didn't need to say his name.

A dark shadow passed over the inn, moving fast, so that for a moment silence fell in the dining room and people looked at one another uneasily. Gary reacted instantly. He caught Gabrielle's wrist, rising so fast his chair fell backward. "Come with me, right now." He tugged Gabrielle to her feet and began to weave his way through the tables, dragging her with him.

Jubal looked at his meal with regret as Joie smacked the back of his head. "It might be your last meal if you don't move it," she cautioned.

"It might be my last meal anyway," he groused. But he was on his feet and rushing after Gary and Gabrielle.

"Call him back, Joie," Gary ordered over his shoulder. "Call Traian and get him back here. We don't have much time."

Joie didn't hesitate. There was too much urgency in Gary's voice. *Traian. They are here. The undead are*

*here at the inn. Gary says it's urgent that you return as
quickly as possible.*

*Do as Gary says. He will know what to do until I
am able to return. They cannot get their hands on any
of you. Go for the heart if you have to defend yourself.
They often inject poison into the bloodstream, and they
are great deceivers and shape-shifters.*

But ego is their weakness.

One of their few weaknesses.

Gary shoved open the door to his room. "Quick, get
inside and stuff everything you can find in the cracks
around the doors and windows." He tossed Gabrielle
shirts as he hurried to the door leading to the verandah.
"We'll have to hole up in here. They'll try to call us
out, using compulsion. Jubal, there's a small CD player
on the desk. Pick some obnoxious music from the col-
lection and turn it up loud. Very loud."

Joie locked the doors behind her and shoved the
dresser against it. "The keyhole, Gabrielle—stuff something in that as well." If vampires could do what she
had seen Traian do, stream through tiny spaces as vapor, she didn't see how they were going to keep them
out. "So why are they here?"

"Most likely because you are," Gary answered. "The
surest way to bring a Carpathian male out into the open
is to go after his lifemate. They'll want one of you to
invite them in. If you hear a voice talking sweetly, it is
a deceiver. Put cotton in your ears, put your hands over
your ears. Do anything to keep from listening. If one of
you observes another going to the door or even talking,
inviting someone into the room, stop him, even if it
means knocking him out."

Shadows passed across the window, moving back
and forth as if searching for something. The wind
picked up so that the tree branches scraped against the
inn with a sickening screech. Clouds spun and boiled,

casting hideous apparitions across the moon. A stain
spread across the sky, slowly blotting out the stars,
creeping insidiously until nearly all light was extin-
guished. The wind howled against the windows,
slammed into the verandah door, carried with it voices.
Soft. Cunning. Sweet and enticing. Pleading voices.
Cries for help. A woman called out just beyond the
door, begging for entrance, her voice rising on the wind.

"Joie?" Gabrielle looked to her sister for guidance.

Gary was close to her and he put his arm around her
protectively. "Traian will be here soon. We can hold
out until then."

Jubal cranked up the CD player so that it blared
loudly. Something grabbed the door handle and shook
it so hard, the door rattled and splintered. Joie leapt to
place her body between the door and her brother and
sister.

"Gary, get them out of here," Joie ordered.

"Believe me, we're safer inside this room than anywhere else right now. And there's less danger if we stick
together," Gary said. He took up a position at her side.
"Jubal, watch the windows. If you see anything that
looks like smoke or fog trying to get in through a crack,
you have to stuff in a shirt, the blankets, anything at
all to keep it out."

The door was struck again from outside, hard enough
to shake the frame. Gabrielle clapped her hand over her
mouth to keep from crying out.

"You can't come in," Gary said, not raising his voice.
"You have not been invited and you can't gain entrance
into this room."

Maniacal laughter greeted Gary's calm words. A
great weight thudded against the door and began a
steady pushing. The wood began to bulge inward.

Chapter Eleven

In the shape of an owl, Traian streaked across the darkened sky. Joie had no hope of fighting off a master vampire, even with Gary's vast knowledge of the undead. The most they could hope for was to delay the vampires until he arrived. The wind increased in speed so that gusts hurled branches and twigs into the air like missiles. A funnel cloud whirled and spun ominously, from ground to sky, a dark, turbulent monster leaping with greedy outspread fingers toward him. He flew into an invisible barrier, hit the obstacle hard and plummeted toward the ground below.

The black mass stretched wide, forming a ghastly head with a gaping mouth and long, bony arms, reaching for the body of the owl as it tumbled toward the ground. Traian shifted into dark droplets of vapor, merging with the black mass, spreading thin to avoid detection. The tornado dropped from the heavens as if it had never been, leaving behind an eerie calm and a clear sky.

A tangle of silver fell from the tree branches, a fine solid blanket of woven strands. Traian was already shifting again, landing in a crouch on the ground. The silver hit his arm but slid off, landing inches from his feet. Pain streaked through his body. Angry red welts rose immediately on his skin where his flesh had come into contact with the glittering silver. Thousands of stinging insects flew at his face, a solid wall of them, programmed to find and attack. Traian dissolved to avoid them, sliding back into the forest to cling to a tree branch in the shape of a frog.

He reached out with his senses, trying to locate his opponent. Master vampires rarely revealed themselves, especially in battle. Traian knew the undead had deliberately drawn him back to the inn with the hope of trapping and destroying him. *I am in a fight for all of our lives. If you can avoid a confrontation, do so. If not, always go for the most dangerous vampire and go for the heart. Nothing else will put them down. Delay. Stall. Try to avoid a battle.*

He waited, his heart beating a little too hard, fear eating at his mind until she answered. Her voice was calm and steady, even confident. *Don't think about us little mortal people, Traian. We can handle the dead guys. You just don't get a single scratch on you or I'll be upset. And you've never seen me upset.*

The relief nearly overwhelmed him. She was unhurt. *I have learned the real meaning of fear. Always, I have gone into battle with nothing to lose. I do not much care for the feeling.*

Well, it's mutual, Traian, so don't go feeling sorry for yourself. I've got the ugly guys at the door, so I'm going to have to let you go.

Joie made him want to laugh. She sounded like she

was talking to him on the phone and a neighbor had dropped by to borrow a cup of sugar. *Do not get over-confident.* He couldn't help cautioning her, although he knew it would annoy her.

A walk in the park. You worry about yourself.

He could see the insects scattering, returning, flying through the trees in search of any sign of him. And the bugs always returned to swarm around the same rotted trunk of a fallen tree. *I love you, Joie, and I cannot do without you. Keep that in mind when you decide how best to handle the situation. You are deciding for both of us.*

She hissed at him between her teeth. He could hear it clearly, the irritation and annoyance of a woman beyond her limits of patience. His heart did a curious flip, a strange reaction to her feminine exasperation. For some unexplained reason, he felt joy.

The little frog hopped along the tree branch, taking great care to blend in with the leaves and twigs. He was some distance from the fallen tree, and the ground stretching between was covered with debris. Traian glanced skyward at the black, spinning clouds. At his mental command, lightning shot bright sparks into the massive cauldron overhead. The white-hot energy spun into a large ball, breaking away from the clouds and hurtling toward the ground. The air crackled with electricity.

Traian leapt from the branch, shape-shifting into his true form, his hands directing the spinning threads of energy, launching the ball as he melted back into the trees. The sphere slammed into the center of the rotten trunk, carving a blackened hole as it went all the way through to hit the ground, forming a deep crater. White whips sizzled and crackled inside the depression.

Black vapor rose from the trunk of the tree to mix with the dark, spinning clouds. A terrible piercing howl of rage filled the air high-pitched and obscene, it shredded nerves and pierced eardrums. The trees shuddered and shook. Grass and leaves shriveled. The sound bounced from ground to cloud with the force of a clap of thunder. The blast hit Traian in the back and drove him forward, slamming him into a tree. He just managed to whip his head back before he hit.

He inhaled quickly, took in the noxious, foul smell of burnt flesh, and knew he had scored a hit. Fire rained from the sky, red glowing embers igniting the foliage. Hungry flames licked at the grass and leaves, raced up the trees with glee. Traian spread out his arms, gave a command, and the clouds burst open, pouring sheets of water on the rising flames. The sky overhead was black with smoke and whirling clouds. It was impossible to tell where the vampire was. He was experienced enough not to give away his presence by blank spots in the air. He chose to blend into the chaos of his surroundings, sidestepping further battles now that he was wounded.

Traian tried one last tactic, knowing the vampire would disappear for many years, avoiding all contacts with hunters in order to survive. There was one last chance to call him into the open, and Traian used it, risking revealing his position to send a summons into the night. His call was pure and commanding, his voice that of an ancient in full power ordering the vampire to ground.

For a brief moment the hideous creature was outlined in the sky, a ghoul as evil and sinister as centuries of deviant behavior and killing for the sake of watching others suffer could make him. He stared down at Traian with hate-filled eyes, his jagged teeth snapping together in defiance.

A sound burst in Traian's head, swelling in volume, a counter-command of death and destruction. Every cell in Traian's body reacted. He was a jangle of nerve endings, paralyzed, forced into the open.

I am your master. The echo reverberated through Traian's muscles and tissue, through every organ.

No! Joie's whisper was a soft, sensuous counterpoint to the poisonous command. *He took your blood. He's using that as a weapon against you. Shut out his voice. He has no dominion over you, over us. I don't care how strong he is, Traian, or what he is. We're stronger. He can track you through your blood, but he cannot command you.*

Foolish woman. I am in his mind, I own his mind. He is my puppet, and soon all the others will be too. He cannot touch me, but I can find him anywhere. And through him, I can find you and your pitiful family. Join with me. I will one day rule both Carpathians and humans alike.

Joie deliberately laughed, the sound like a breath of fresh air, ripping the dark dread from Traian's heart and clearing his mind. *You are the foolish one. There is only one for me. We will destroy you because you're nothing but a rotten, empty shell. And you're just nasty, if you ask me.*

Traian felt the monster's rage, bursting in his head, in his veins, as if his blood boiled, but he was free of the terrible paralysis. He clapped his hands together and spread his fingers wide, arms outstretched toward the vampire, which was dissolving into the sky. Lightning forked and sizzled. The vampire screamed once, and a putrid smell polluted the night air.

Kill her. Kill all of them. Thunder splintered the sky. The earth rolled and bucked and the storm raged, a wild hurricane slamming into the forest and village.

They throw tantrums.

This time there was fear in her voice. Traian was already racing to the inn, doing his best to countermand the killing storm. *Valenteen is dangerous beyond belief, Joie. Whoever this master is, he commands Valenteen, and that is both shocking and terrifying. I have never seen two masters run together, nor one command another.*

Hurry, they're breaking through the door. Joie's heart was pounding so hard she was afraid it would burst through her chest. *It might not have been such a good idea to tell him I thought he was nasty.* The entire inn shook, the walls swaying as if from the shock of an earthquake. The door to the verandah sagged, splintered again as something struck it with tremendous force. Whispers filled the room, soft, insidious whispers made with sweet voices.

Gabrielle cried out and put her hands over her ears. She took several steps toward the door, nodding her head, her lips beginning to move. Gary leapt to her side, dragged her back, his hand over her mouth. He put his lips against her ear. "They're trying to command you to invite them in. You must not listen to them."

The door burst in the middle. A black swarm of insects flew into the room with the rain and wind. The dense cloud of stinging bugs attacked exposed flesh, biting viciously. Gary threw a blanket over Gabrielle's head, wrapping her face and arms to protect her from the worst of the bites. Jubal cursed and beat at his face and neck in a frantic attempt to keep the insects off him.

Joie stood stoically facing the monster outside her door. His smile was a terrible parody, as was his bow. He looked smug as he watched the black horde of insects biting the occupants of the room. Joie knew she was staring at something far more foul than the creature she had knifed in the cave. He beckoned to her with his clawlike fingers, and she felt a tremendous pull. It was only the vicious bites of the insects that kept her from stepping out of the room and onto the verandah. She had no doubt that he would kill her. That he would kill all of them. She struggled to keep her mind her own, rather than allow his soft voice to intrude and command.

"Tell me why you do his bidding." The only weapon she had was to flatter the vampire's ego. Stall him in the hope that Traian would come before Valenteen could entice her out to him. "It's clear you're much more powerful. Why would you serve such a creature?" She forced interest and admiration into her voice. "I find it hard to believe that a man like you needs someone like him."

Valenteen's lip curled, exposing blackened gums. "I allow him to think he commands me. It suits me to fall in with his plans. We both seek the same thing. If he finds it, I will take it from him."

Joie was being compelled forward, one slow step at a time. She struggled to stay grounded, flinging her hand out to Jubal. Her brother's fingers tightened over hers instantly, gripping her without hesitation. "Of course you'll take it. He's a fool to think he can treat you with so little respect. I've been all over the world and have never encountered a man as powerful as you." She tried to interject a flirty note in her voice, but her acting skills didn't stretch that far. "You should lead them all. Everyone would benefit from your knowledge."

In spite of Jubal's restraining hand, she was jerked another step forward. Joie felt like a puppet on a string. She couldn't stop her body from going toward the beckoning hand, even with Jubal trying to hold her back.

Valenteen nodded his head. "It is true that I have much experience in leading. Perhaps killing you is not the best answer. Perhaps bringing you to my side would serve us both better."

Jubal let go of her hand and caught her around the

waist, lifting her away from the threshold. At once the vampire closed his hand, staring at Jubal's throat. Joie's brother went down hard, choking, coughing, fighting for air. The insects instantly swarmed over him, clogging his throat, attacking his exposed face. Gary made a grab for Joie, but she shook her head and deliberately stepped onto the verandah.

"Help Jubal," she ordered. She kept her gaze on the vampire, trying to appear fascinated. Traian was close. He was with her, moving in her mind, giving her strength. The vampire believed he was still compelling her to do his bidding, but with Traian's aid, she moved on her own. She didn't look behind her to see if Gary was able to fight off the insects. Intuitively she knew it was better for all of them to keep the vampire's attention centered on her.

Her stomach lurched at the prospect of being close to such an evil creature. She could see him clearly now, without the illusion the undead often used on their victims. Flesh hung from his bones. Tufts of hair clung to his scalp. His long, thick fingernails were in the shape of hooked claws, sharp and twisted and black. His eyes were red and streaked with yellow. There was a malevolence clinging to him that sickened her and fouled the air around him.

Instead of trying to stop herself from moving toward him, Joie had to force her shaking legs to take a step. Impatience crossed his face. "Joining with a man so powerful and knowing he's certain to rule those around him sounds like a good idea. I've always admired strength."

Inches from his outstretched hand, Joie purposely tripped on a piece of the splintered door and stumbled. She protected herself with a palm to the ground, her body slightly turned, giving her precious seconds to slide her other hand along her leg to secure the knife strapped to her calf, the blade hidden flat against her wrist.

Valenteen leaned over her, spittle drooling from his mouth as he caught her by her hair and wrenched her to her feet. He dragged her against his body, jerking her head back to expose her throat, and sank his teeth deep, gulping as he drank.

Joie registered the fiery pain of an acid burn as he tore a gaping wound in her throat. Her vision blurred, and the ground lurched as her legs went rubbery. She could hear the sound of his heart, although she couldn't feel it beating. She made no sound of protest, made no struggle, giving herself up willingly. Some of the tension slipped from the undead's body. With every ounce of strength she possessed, everything she was, Joie plunged the knife deep into his chest, driving straight for his heart.

Lifting his head, Valenteen screamed horribly, the sound shattering glass from windows. Gripping her hair, he dragged her backward as his body fought to stay up in spite of the knife in his heart. With his other hand he grabbed her chin with every intention of breaking her neck.

Blood gushed from the wound in her throat so that his hand slipped off. Joie clamped both hands on the back of the fist clutching her hair to hold his hand to her head. Dropping low, she spun around and stood up fast, snapping bones in his hand. He howled as he let her go, raking at her with poison-tipped talons.

Traian emerged from the darkness, his eyes flaming red, dragging the vampire off of her, wrenching his head around hard. The knife handle dropped uselessly to the floor of the verandah, the blade completely eaten away by acid in the blood of the undead. Traian's fist shot out, plunging deep, following the trail of the knife. Valenteen matched the move, driving his good hand into the wall of Traian's chest, through the muscle and tissue, seeking his heart. Traian got there first.

Staring into the vampire's eyes, he ripped the shriveled, blackened organ out and tossed it aside. Lightning forked in the sky, spun until it was a bright white sphere that engulfed the vampire. Valenteen disappeared into ash and cinder, then was gone completely. The heart was incinerated next. Traian bathed his hands and arms in the energy, removing the acid burning his flesh so he could tend to Joie.

She sat on the ground, watching him with a kind of awe. She couldn't talk because of the wound in her throat. She simply sat there, her hands pressed to the gaping tear to try to stem the flow of blood. Gabrielle screamed and ran to her side. "Help me, Jubal, help me lay her down. I need towels, anything at all. Joie, don't you die on us! Damn it, Jubal, she's lost so much blood. Help me."

Gary took her arm and stepped back, taking Gabrielle with him. "Only Traian can help her now."

Jubal looked at the Carpathian. "Do it. Whatever you have to do. Just don't let her die."

Traian looked at their faces, swollen and red from the bites of the insects. He reached down and gathered Joie into his arms, cradling her against his chest. Joie settled against him, her eyelashes slowly drifting down.

Chapter Twelve

"Traian," Gary said calmly. "You're in almost as bad shape as she is. You need blood fast. Use Jubal while I get the soil to pack the wounds. I'll give you more blood as soon as I return."

"She does not want me to use her family," Traian said. He had automatically slowed Joie's heartbeat to lessen the blood loss. He buried his face in her throat, closing the terrible wound as best he could with healing saliva.

"Who gives a damn what she wants?" Jubal snapped. "She only objected because she thought you were a vampire. If you need our blood to save her, take it. It obviously hasn't done anything to harm her or Gary. Gabrielle, help Gary with whatever he needs."

"The garden has rich soil," Traian instructed. He stood for one moment, the lines on his face deep, his chest ripped open, weariness and fear mixed with a turbulent rage in his eyes. Then he leapt to the second-story balcony above them and hurried along the banisters until he found Joie's room.

Jubal took the stairs, streaking through the halls to burst into his sister's room. Flinging the door closed, he approached the bed where she lay. Joie was pale, almost gray, her breathing so shallow it nearly didn't exist. "Can you save her? Tell me the truth, Traian. Is it possible?"

A fist seemed to be wrapped around his heart. Traian raised midnight-black eyes, as cold as ice, to Jubal. "I will allow no other outcome."

"Gary said you needed blood." Jubal sat down beside his sister and took her hand. "Joie means the world to us. I can see she means the world to you too. I'm not going to pretend to understand your relationship; I'll just be grateful for it."

Traian murmured softly, sparing Jubal the initial fright as he opened a vein in his wrist and fed. *Forgive me, Joie. I know you did not want this.* Strength flowed into his depleted body. *If I am to save us, this is our only choice. Both of us are wounded. If I can get enough blood, we will survive.*

There was a faint stirring in his mind. A touch, no more, like the light caress of fingers on his face. Traian carefully closed the pinpricks on Jubal's wrist and gathered Joie to him before he awakened her brother from his enthrallment.

Jubal slipped from the bed to sit on the floor. "I take it you have my blood."

"Yes, thank you," Traian replied formally. "You have all been more than lucky. Any vampire is difficult to defeat, but master vampires have lived for century upon century, growing in strength and power. They use others as minions and puppets and keep themselves from dangerous battles. They sacrifice lesser pawns and slide away when hunters are in the area. They only fight when they are assured of victory."

Jubal watched every movement as Traian laid his hands on Joie's terrible wounds. He seemed to be gone from his own body, staring emptily in space. Jubal could see the lines deepen in his face, his color paling visibly as if his strength were slowly being drawn from him.

Gary and Gabrielle burst into the room. Gary set a bowl of rich, dark soil on the floor beside the bed, and Gabrielle dumped various herbs into a second bowl. Gary handed candles to Jubal. "Spread these around the room and light them. We don't want any artificial lights on, just the candles. Gabrielle, mix the herbs together in the bowl. We want the scents to blend." He put his hand on Traian's shoulder. "Joie was a surprise to Valenteen. She was wonderful, unbelievable. She didn't even hesitate. It never occurred to a vampire that a woman would stand between others and danger. And he certainly never thought she would be willing to plunge a knife into his heart."

"She used my memories," Traian explained as he mixed healing saliva into the soil and packed the wounds in Joie's throat. "She flattered him and stalled him, hoping I would get there in time. And when I didn't, she did what she always does, she courageously put herself in harm's way in order to get close enough to make certain she destroyed him."

Gary took handfuls of the mixture and packed it into Traian's chest. "Even with all I know, the draw to go to him was so powerful, I doubt that we would have survived."

"He was a master vampire and he ran with another much more powerful master." Traian lifted his head to look at Gary. "I never saw the other one clearly. He took my blood in the cave, yet I did not remember him.

I cannot go near our prince. You will have to relay to him all information. Until the vampire is found, and I very much doubt that he will remain in this country now, I will stay away from Mikhail. We cannot take a chance with his life."

"He won't see it the same way," Gary pointed out.

"You know I am right. He should not chance his life by entering into battles in the way that he does. His purpose is to serve and lead our people, not hunt the vampire. We have many hunters and only one leader. His brother is strong and powerful, but he has been damaged by the torture he endured. He cannot lead. If the vampire or humans managed to kill Mikhail, I fear our race would be mortally wounded." Traian didn't look up at Gary to see if he agreed or not. He gathered Joie into his arms. *You must accept my blood, Joie. This will convert you to my race, and it is not a pleasant experience to go through.*

Again he felt her touch, gentle, tender, on his face, yet she lay motionless in his arms. A faint smile appeared in his mind as if she found his warning amusing. He turned his body slightly, not wanting to drain his strength further by masking their presence from the others. The soothing aroma from the herbs and candles mixed with the sounds of chanting in his mind as other voices far away joined in the age-old healing chant. He took the smallest amount of blood possible from her and quickly opened his own vein. She accepted his blood just the way she did everything else where he was concerned, with complete faith. It humbled him that she did so.

When she had taken enough for an exchange, Traian laid her gently on the comforter. "Perhaps you all should leave the room. She would not want you to see her this way."

"You need blood and care yourself," Gary pointed

out. "You're weaker than you think, Traian. Take my blood and let me help the two of you through this. I know what to expect. Gabrielle and Jubal can wait in their rooms."

"We'll stay," Jubal said decisively. "She's our sister."

Gabrielle watched Traian feeding from Gary. It should have repulsed her, but instead she was fascinated. It seemed such a noble moment to her, one being reaching out to aid another. Gary seemed completely unafraid and matter-of-fact about giving blood, as if it were an everyday occasion. "If it's messy, Traian, Joie would want me here to see to her needs. She's very meticulous about certain things." Gabrielle lifted her chin, prepared to fight for her right to stay.

"Your wound is deep, Traian. You need to go to ground. Even with my blood, you don't have strength enough to heal that gash. He nearly tore out your heart," Gary said. But he was watching Joie. The first ripple of pain crossed her face and sent a shudder through her body.

Traian felt the pain take her, a fire burning with the force of a torch in the center of her body, blossoming outward like an explosion. He merged with her, trying to take the brunt of the pain, determined to make her initiation into his world as easy as possible. Traian was amazed at Joie's siblings, certain they would be horrified and afraid as the convulsions started, when Joie was violently sick and it was impossible to control the waves of unrelenting pain. They worked together as a team, seeming to understand that he couldn't talk or direct them. His full attention was on blocking as much pain as possible and helping Joie through the conversion.

Gary kept the room clean and smelling of the soothing aromas from the herbs and candles. All of them picked up the words to the ancient healing chant. Gabrielle wiped beads of blood from Traian's brow. He managed a faint smile, but his complete attention was clearly on his lifemate.

The moment he was able, Traian sent Joie into a deep sleep. Exhausted, he looked up at them. "I have to take her away for a few days. We will be unable to get in touch with you, but she is alive and she will heal quickly." He avoided all references to the ground. Joie's family had been through enough without knowing the specifics of where he would take her.

Gabrielle leaned over and brushed a kiss on the top of Traian's head. "You take care of her. We're depending on you. I'm not sorry she found you, not after watching the way you've cared for her."

Traian could see she was blinking back tears. "Thank you, Gabrielle. As soon as possible, I'll bring her to you."

"I'll stay here with them," Gary offered.

Traian shook his head. "Warn Mikhail. I don't want to send the information to him on the chance that the one who took my blood could find a way to use me to harm him. Let him know there is something in that cave of value to the vampires and that there are numerous traps. He'll understand when you tell him it is a cave the wizards used."

Gary nodded. "Jubal and Gabrielle may come with me, if they choose."

Traian rose, Joie in his arms. "Go then, go tonight. The rules that have always applied to vampires seem to be changing rapidly. You will be safer under Mikhail's protection." He slipped out onto the balcony, into the night where he belonged. Where he was comfortable. The wind blew into his face, ruffled his hair, brought him messages from creatures around him.

He took to the skies, the sleeping Joie in his arms, and headed for a small cave he remembered from his younger days, a cave of healing with hot springs and glacier-water pools. Far below his homeland stretched out before him, a place he had not seen in many years. The sight brought back memories of his parents and his childhood friends.

He was home and he held his lifemate in his arms.

She will never be safe. You will always be linked to me. I spared your life, but I can take it whenever I choose. And I will take hers.

Traian did not hesitate. He sent a clap of deafening thunder back along the mental path the vampire had initiated, a bolt of lightning streaking through the sky like a spear homing in on prey. Just as quickly, he moved his own position, fully prepared for a war in the sky.

An explosion of pain burst in Traian's head. He rode it out, certain he'd scored a hit.

You will pay for that.

I am an ancient warrior. I do not fear you or any other of your kind. If you wish to pursue me or mine, I welcome the opportunity to carry out your death sentence. Traian moved again, certain of reprisal. He had not displayed fear or awe, or even respect, and the vampire was used to his minions admiring him.

A shower of hot stones poured from the sky. Traian protected Joie, covering her body with his like a blanket. The stones fell harmlessly around them, but the attack was a halfhearted attempt. The vampire was fleeing and simply wanted to instill fear in Traian.

He hugged the sleeping Joie closer to him. "I have been a warrior so long, I barely recall any other existence. Even a master vampire cannot change my chosen path. If he should come to find us, Joie, I will not turn away. He will not take you from me, nor will he take me from you." He made the promise to her aloud beneath the stars. And then he took her deep beneath the surface to the healing caverns.

Chapter Thirteen

Joie awoke quickly. One moment she knew nothing, and the next she was fully conscious. She heard the steady fall of water, the thrum of life beating in the earth. She knew where she was and how she got there. She felt different, completely alive, yet her body ached and her throat felt torn. She turned her head to look at the man holding her. Traian lay beside her, his arms around her, one hand on her bare stomach, his fingers splayed wide. They were lying in a deep hole in the damp soil of a cave. Overhead the ceiling sparkled with crystals, and water shimmered in a pool not far from them. She knew it, saw it, yet it should have been impossible, buried in the soil as they were.

"I'm seeing what you've seen," she guessed. Her voice was different, husky, not at all the way she'd sounded before.

"Yes." His teeth nipped her shoulder. "We're in a cave I used to swim in as a young man."

Joie looked around her, reached out, and touched the damp soil. "It's a darned good thing I don't have a cleanliness fetish. Aren't beds appropriate when you're injured?"

"The soil heals us." He kissed her neck, swirled his tongue over the wounds on her throat. "We can remove all traces of dirt easily. Our wounds were packed earlier with soil but are very clean now. I will repack them before we go to sleep again."

"How lovely for us. Are there worms in this particular little bed of soil? And did I happen to mention worms in any of our talks?"

"I do not believe you did."

"There was a reason for that." Her fingers tangled with his. His hand on her stomach was soothing her in some way she didn't understand. Her insides ached. "Did someone take a baseball bat to me?"

"No. The conversion is difficult."

She didn't want to remember the horror of that seemingly endless pain. The complete loss of control. The helpless feeling she had or the look in his eyes. Especially the look in his eyes. Begging forgiveness. He'd looked guilty, terrified of losing her. She recalled the blood-red tears that had fallen on her face. "Yes, it was. For both of us."

Traian nuzzled the top of her head with his chin.

"What about Jubal and Gabrielle? It must have scared them to see that nasty little vampire ripping out my throat."

He felt the tremor run through her and pressed his body closer. "They were incredible." He still had trouble believing that neither of them looked at him with blame. And Gabrielle had been so generous in her parting words to him. "They are both fine. Gary took them to our prince. They are with Mikhail and his lifemate, under their protection. I like your brother and sister very much.

"I never really thought about it before. We live in the world with humans and protect them, but to keep our race safe, we have always remained apart. This has been my first close contact with humans. Gary is an extraordinary man and obviously trusted by our prince. I feel genuine affection and admiration for Jubal and Gabrielle. I never would have expected to feel this way." Traian rubbed her nose with the pad of his finger, and then traced her mouth.

Joie smiled and nibbled gently at his hand. He touched her continually, as if seeking the reassurance of physical contact. "You'd better have a deep affection for them. It's the only safe thing to do with those two. And with my parents also, I might add. They're going to drive you crazy, so you have to love them, otherwise you'd do them in. I can't wait for you to meet my mom and dad." She burst out laughing at the thought.

"Why do you do that?" Traian asked suspiciously. "You have a wicked way of laughing every time you mention introducing me to your parents."

"Don't worry, I'll protect you from them. Jubal, Gabrielle, and I always go home for visits together. If we team up, we have a chance."

"I am Carpathian," he pointed out.

"Like that's going to matter. But you keep thinking it will." Her hand fluttered to her throat, still raw and sore from the attack. "How come I didn't wake up gorgeous and perfect?" Joie glared at him. "I had visions of a makeover."

"You are gorgeous and perfect." He sounded puzzled. "I woke you early to give you more blood, but you'll be going back to the ground until you are fully healed." He touched his chest. "We both will."

She turned her head to look more fully at him, and her breath caught in her throat. "Oh, Traian, let me see." She rose up onto her knees in spite of his restraining hands. "You're really hurt."

Her eyes held worry, concern. Her hands moved over his chest with anxious, caressing strokes. Traian held his breath, shocked at the tidal wave of emotion sweeping through him. "It is of no consequence, but thank you for worrying."

"It's of great consequence," she contradicted him. "How do you do that healing thing? Can I do it to you? Would it work?" She was already leaning over him, her tongue swirling around the edges of his mangled skin.

Traian closed his eyes. Her tongue was soothing, a gentle caress that took him by surprise. She was attempting the healing chant in her head, the words soft and hesitant, but she got them right. His eyes burned, his throat clogged, and even his chest felt tight. It had not occurred to him that she would try to take care of his wounds.

"Silly man," she whispered. "Of course I'm going to take care of you. I *need to* take care of you."

He didn't open his eyes, afraid she might see tears there. "I thought you were a *want to* kind of woman."

"True, but women get to change their minds all the time. Right now I need to do this." She laughed, and her breath was warm against his bare skin. "You'd be surprised at the things I need to do." Her mouth was moving dangerously lower.

"Oh no, you don't," he objected. "You need to heal first, Joie. I am going to give you blood and put you back to sleep."

She laughed again, blew warm air over the head of his erection. "Really?" Her tongue licked him as if he were an ice cream cone. Swirled and danced and did outrageous things. "I'm back to the 'I'm a *want to* kind of woman.' I want a lot of things right now. And I want you wanting me enough to stop worrying about whether or not I can make love in my delicate condition. And I want your body inside mine. Only you will do, Traian. I've fallen desperately in love with you, so, darn it, you have a few responsibilities." She proceeded to show him exactly what she meant.